A GRAND JOURNEY DOWN-RIVER . . .

Mark Twain lit a cigar. "I've had a wonderful day today, Wentworth. I ask myself why a murderer would be following me, and I don't get any good answers. If somebody was looking to rob me, he's missed a dozen opportunities—not that I carry around enough money to be worth bothering with these days. And while I have my share of enemies, they're more likely to write a scurrilous article about me than hire an assassin. Still, nothing would make me happier than a telegram at the next town telling me that the New York police have found their man, and are calling their detective home."

"Then we should have a grand journey down-river," I said.

"Oh, I'm having a grand journey already," said Mark Twain. "It would be close to perfect if it weren't for this highly improbable notion that somebody on board might want to kill me."

Death on the Mississippi
A MARK TWAIN MYSTERY
by Peter J. Heck

Death on the Mississippi

A Mark Twain Mystery

Peter J. Heck

BERKLEY PRIME CRIME, NEW YORK

DEATH ON THE MISSISSIPPI

A Berkley Prime Crime Book
Published by The Berkley Publishing Group
200 Madison Avenue, New York, New York 10016

Copyright © 1995 by Peter J. Heck

Book design by Rhea Braunstein
Map by Peter J. Heck

First edition: December 1995

Library of Congress Cataloging-in-Publication Data

Heck, Peter J.
    Death on the Mississippi: a Mark Twain mystery / by Peter J.
Heck. — 1st ed.
        p. cm.
    ISBN 0-425-14939-0 (Trade pbk.). — ISBN 0-425-14938-2
(hardcover)
    1. Twain, Mark, 1835–1910—Fiction. 2. Authors, American—
19th century —Fiction. 3. Mississippi River—Fiction. I. Title.
PS3558.E313D4 1995
8'.13 54—dc20   95-18212

PRINTED IN THE UNITED STATES OF AMERICA

10   9   8   7   6   5   4   3   2   1

To my parents,
Preston P. Heck and Ermyn Jewell Heck,
who taught me to love good books,
and who introduced me at an early age
to Mark Twain's writings.

St. Paul

La Crosse

Hannibal

Missouri River

St. Louis

Cincinnati

Ohio River

Cairo

Memphis

Arkansas River

Helena

Napoleon

Mississippi River

with Major Tributaries
and Important Towns

Red River

Natchez

New Orleans

Gulf of Mexico

Historical Note and Acknowledgments

A reader familiar with the writings of Mark Twain will recognize many of the anecdotes and quips herein as being adapted from his work, with due allowance given for Twain's own intention to entertain or instruct the reader. For instance, Twain's story of the treasure in Napoleon, Arkansas, which I have borrowed as the "McGuffin" for my plot, can be found in *Life on the Mississippi*, chapters 30 and 31. I have taken the liberty of assuming that it was, in fact, a true story rather than a tall tale setting up a comic anticlimax.

The novel is set in the early 1890s, when Twain needed money to pay off his debts in the wake of several bad investments, and might plausibly have gone on the riverboat lecture tour described here. But while I have done careful research into the history of the period, and into the biography and personality of my protagonist, the Samuel Clemens/Mark Twain who appears in these pages is a fictional character, and the events of the novel are entirely fictional. And, while Mark Twain wrote more than one detective story of his own, he never, to my knowledge, solved a murder case.

In addition to Mark Twain, a few historical characters are mentioned in passing: Twain's family, especially his wife, Livy; William Dean Howells, Twain's editor and friend; Henry H. Rogers, his benefactor; and George Devol, the most notorious of riverboat gamblers. All other characters who appear in the plot of this novel are entirely fictional creations, and should not be mistaken for any actual person, living or dead.

Special thanks are due to George R. R. Martin, for allowing me to tap his riverboat expertise; to Darwin Ortiz, for nineteenth-century gambling lore; to the staff of the Mark Twain House in Hartford, Connecticut; to my agent, Martha Millard; and to my editor, Laura Ann Gilman, whose insight and judgment have been all a first-time novelist could ask. Any weaknesses that remain despite their efforts are entirely my own doing.

Finally, my wife, Jane Jewell, has been a partner and an inspiration throughout the writing of this book. I might have been able to start the book by myself, but without her I doubt I could have finished it.

1

After I completed my four years at Yale College in 18—, I faced the inevitable decision of what to do for the rest of my life. Conscious as always of our family's standing as one of the oldest and most respectable in New England, my father encouraged me to read for the bar. Alas, my notions were at odds with his. I had learned that the world extended a considerable distance beyond Connecticut, and I was determined to see as much of it as possible. When it became clear that my parents would neither encourage nor support me in this ambition, I determined to find a means to accomplish it without their aid. And so, I found myself applying for the position of traveling secretary to Mr. Samuel L. Clemens, who was represented to me as a travel writer of some reputation. I wonder to this day whether I might not have done better at the law.

Mr. William Dean Howells, an old friend of the family, had heard of the opportunity, and recommended me. Accordingly, I sent off my letter, and was invited to meet my prospective employer, who was giving a series of lectures in New York City prior to departing on a tour of the West. Being no fool, I took the opportunity to glance over the titles of some of his books—written under the curious pen name "Mark Twain." While I had no time to read them, I could see that, as I had been told, they consisted of travel accounts—to the wilds of California and the Sandwich Islands as well as the great cities of France and Italy. Here, for certain, was my ticket to the world. And if my patron could make a living merely by traveling around the world and writing about what he saw, why, surely a Yale man could hope to do as well.

On the day of my appointment, I traveled down to New York on the railroad, determined to make a good impression and secure the position on the spot. I arrived in New York late in the afternoon and took my dinner in Grand Central Station, in the basement restaurant, then made my way downtown to the Cooper Union, where my prospective employer was to lecture.

It was my first visit to this thriving city, and I decided to take a cab downtown, since there was still plenty of light for a look around. Some other time I wanted to ride the subways, which my mother said were dirty and dangerous; but this time I was in no hurry, and eager to see the sights of New York City. There was a line of hansom cabs on the west side of the station, and I climbed aboard the first one, which had a serviceable-looking bay gelding between the poles. The driver (a greasy fellow wearing a dented bowler hat) flicked his reins, rounded the corner, made a right turn onto Park Avenue, and headed south.

I was struck at once by the magnitude of the buildings and the size of the crowds that thronged the streets; the station itself was the largest building I had ever been inside. More than once, I found myself craning my neck out the window of my cab to peer down the side streets or to gaze up at the buildings as we passed. (Surely, I told myself, a travel writer ought to be observant!)

At first, the street we followed was as wide as a football field, with islands of greenery along the middle—hence its name, Park Avenue. We passed the impressive Murray Hill Hotel at Fortieth Street, with a line of elegant rigs in front that made my hired conveyance and its driver look decidedly frugal. The pedestrians in this affluent neighborhood were well-dressed and unhurried, manifestly at home among the handsome buildings lining the street. Even the few children I saw were clean, well-behaved, and firmly attached to their governesses.

At Thirty-fourth Street, where the subway emerged from its caverns, the street changed its name to Fourth Avenue, and the character of the neighborhood altered. Now my cab contended for the right-of-way with heavy-laden delivery wagons, and the crowds along the sidewalk moved along with evident purpose. The shops were now more numerous, and made no pretense to exclusivity. And every corner seemed to have its newsboy, bawling out his singsong inducements to purchase his papers. I saw other young boys, too—usually gathered in conspiratorial groups, planning some sport or mischief. One gang of half a dozen urchins ran full tilt across the trolley tracks in front of an onrushing train—just in time to escape the clutches of a pursuing police officer, who pulled to a halt, puffing and shaking his fist at the laughing boys.

I had heard that New York was at once the grandest and the most wicked city in the United States, and by the end of my ride, I was ready to believe it. It was hard to imagine that so many sights and events could be crammed into a two-mile carriage ride. But at last we reached the lecture hall, in a clean, well-lit area of the city. I arrived about twenty minutes early, and from my vantage point in the middle of the auditorium, I watched the seats filling up with prosperous-looking citizens and their wives, as well as a few less respectable-looking characters. At the appointed hour, the lights dimmed and a little white-haired fellow with a large mustache shuffled out onto the stage. Nothing could have prepared me for the surprise that was about to follow.

In a quiet, almost conversational voice, with a noticeable western drawl, he began to say the most preposterous things. His casual posture was a sharp contrast to his formal attire; but his subject matter, poor diction, and undignified language were an even greater contrast. He began with an

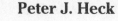

4 incoherent story of some outlandish wager concerning a frog, followed by a tale of being cheated in a horse trade, and continued with long-winded, highly improbable tales of his travels—all interspersed with irreverent observations of the great and powerful. Having grown up in a quiet corner of Connecticut without much straying forth, I found much of his talk frankly incredible.

So, apparently, did the audience; no sooner would he utter some absurdity than they would break into peals of laughter. He kept his composure remarkably well at this ridicule, and indeed kept up his talk, slowly and calmly, as if he didn't care in the least whether they believed him or not. The audience neither hooted nor stormed out, but seemed willing to wait complacently to see what impossible statement he would make next, and howl at it as uproariously as at the previous—with frequent applause, as well. They even clapped after he told a ghost story in Negro dialect and frightened some poor girl in the front row half to death with the shout, "You've got it!"

I was frankly at a loss to understand either the audience's behavior or the lecturer's willingness to tolerate it. I began to wonder whether he might be inviting the audience's laughter on purpose, but dismissed that notion as ludicrous. After all, I had it on the best authority that he was a highly successful and respected literary figure. Still, I was completely amazed when he finished and the audience rose to their feet to applaud him. I had never seen such a singular performance before. Indeed, it gave me some reason to wonder whether I might not better abandon my notions of travel altogether.

Despite my misgivings, I made my way backstage and found Mr. Clemens surrounded by a large group of notables and others who had come to pay their respects—ranging from several gentlemen and ladies in the height of fashion to a swarthy immigrant in worker's clothes and two men dressed in a sort of nautical uniform. I would eventually get used to the fact that in almost every city we visited, half the local people of importance and out-of-town celeb-rities, an appalling number of fortune hunters, gamblers, rivermen, and other characters too disreputable even to list here would apply for free passes on the ground that "Sam and I go back twenty-five years." But I am getting ahead of my story.

The group began at last to thin out, and the lecturer took note of me standing quietly to the side and turned to address me. "You must be young Cabot. Howells says he knows your father, is that right?"

I nodded my assent and shook his hand. "Well," he said to the remaining throng, "this big young fellow has come all the way from New London to see me, so I'll ask your leave. Mike, Mr. Snipes, I'll see you tomorrow." The two men in uniform murmured their assent, and I followed Mr. Clemens along the hallway.

He led me to a dressing room and plopped himself in a comfortable-looking seat. I took his broad gesture as an indication to seat myself in a nearby chair, and declined his offer of a cigar. He took one out for himself, and I waited while he clipped the end and applied the match.

I am not sure how I expected a literary man to look, but I took the opportunity to examine Mr. Clemens carefully. He stood perhaps five feet eight, and still wore the dark evening dress that was his "uniform" for lectures. He wore his white hair long, in the fashion of two decades ago, and he sported a large mustache. His piercing eyes—sur-mounted by bushy brows—bespoke a lively intelligence, while his drawl suggested an origin somewhere in the West. A sly smile and the now briskly burning cigar provided a sense of warmth in the midst of all the snowy-white hair.

"W. W. Cabot," he said, taking an experimental puff. "What would the initials be for?"

"William Wentworth, sir. I'm named after my mother's older brother. At school, there were quite a few other fel-lows named William, so everyone called me Wentworth."

"Wentworth Cabot; well, it has a respectable enough air

Peter J. Heck

6 about it, for whatever that's worth. So, young man, do you
have any notion what I want a traveling secretary to do for
me?''

It seemed a simple enough question. ''Why, travel with
you, and handle your correspondence and papers,'' I responded.

''Just as I thought. Cabot, I suppose you think a travel
writer makes his living by traveling and writing about it.
Is that so?'' The cigar smoke was getting thicker.

I had never thought of any other possibility, and said so.
Clemens nodded, took another puff, fixed his gaze on me,
and began to talk.

''I can't say as how I expected much else. I don't expect
you've read any of my books, either.'' He waved away my
stillborn protest. ''Don't sham, young fellow, you'll never
get the job that way. I'd smoke you out in two minutes if
you tried it.'' I restrained myself from commenting that his
cigar was on the verge of doing exactly that.

''The fact of the matter is, I can't really travel at my own
pleasure any more. Every town I set foot in expects a lecture, if not a solid week of 'em. I can put off the little
towns with halls the size of a tomcat's coffin, but the big
ones will pester me to distraction. I'll end up doing them
anyway, so I might as well schedule them in advance and
let the people know I'm coming through. So my traveling
secretary has to set up my schedule of lectures—deal with
the booking agents and hotel managers in every city I'm
going to, collect the fees, buy the train tickets, and in general run my whole life so I have time to see enough of the
dratted place to write about it.

''If that's not enough, you have to arrange mail for-
warding to my local address in each city, so I don't miss
anything of importance. You have to find out the location
of the hotel and the train station and the lecture hall and
the telegraph office and how to get from one to the other
and a dozen other places before we even set foot in the
town. If I want to tour the local diamond mine, or elephant

farm, or bottomless pit—every little dog kennel of a town I've ever been in has some such firetrap that they drag innocent visitors out to see, and if I don't write about it, nobody will believe I've been there—you're the one who has to find out where it is and how to see it.

"Besides that, you've got to dig up out-of-town newspapers and decent cigars, carry my papers and correspondence, pry me out of conversations with the local bosses and literary ladies, listen to me try out my jokes in fifty different towns, and generally work like a coolie." He gave me another stare. "You really *haven't* read any of my books, have you."

"No, sir, but I—" He cut me off again.

"Just as well. At least I know you aren't doing it for some sort of imaginary glory, like the last silly fellow I hired as secretary. Lord knows what some people will make themselves important over. I knew a man who bragged all up and down the river that he was assistant cook on a second-rate steamboat out of Cincinnati. Managed to make some capital on it, too—those were the days when you could impress some of the local girls just by traveling on a steamboat, let alone working on one. So there are some people who think working for Mark Twain is something to give themselves airs about."

If I had entered the room with any notion of giving myself airs about employment of the sort he had just described, he had quickly cured me of it, but I refrained from saying so. I had declared my intention to see the world, and had no better way to do it while earning my keep than to hire myself out to Mr. Clemens, or someone like him. Since he was the only world traveler in need of a secretary to whom I had a letter of introduction, I knew I must perforce accept the position—provided he saw fit to offer it. So far, I had no way of guessing whether he was in a mood to do so or not. "I don't mind that sort of work, sir," I told him.

"Aha, but can you do it?" said Clemens. "Have you ever dealt with a theater manager?"

8   I stretched my memory, and had to admit that I had not.
"Ever bribed a hotel clerk?"

That was also beyond my range of experience.

"Ever been seasick? Been shot at? Ever ridden in a stagecoach? Gone up in a balloon? Speak Dutch, or Hindu, or Fiji Island pidgin?" I confessed my lack of these qualifications, and my ignorance of the principal hotels in London, currency exchange rates, customs, and nearly everything else he could think of having to do with his vocation. Finally he asked me, "Damnation, boy, have you ever been outside Connecticut before?"

"Yes, sir. I've been to Newport several times, and I've been to Boston to visit family."

"Boston!" He looked at me with a curious gleam in his eye. "Are you one of those Boston Cabots?"

"My grandfather was from Boston. The majority of my family still live there."

"And Howells tells me you went to Yale."

"I completed my studies just this June, sir."

He looked me up and down, like a man inspecting a horse he means to buy. "And still such an innocent," he said at last. "Well, I'm glad of it in a way. Better to have a cub you can train than somebody who knows it all already. Listen here, Wentworth Cabot, I've half a mind to hire you in spite of everything. Could you be ready for a seven-week journey by Friday?" I told him that would be sufficient time; he named a figure for my salary, and I accepted without further ado.

2

I returned to New London on the next morning's train, said my farewells to my friends and family (who gave my enterprise their reluctant blessings), and packed a trunk for the journey. Thursday, I returned on the early train to New York and checked into the Union Square Hotel, where Mr. Clemens was staying. I paid the driver, and soon found myself in a room adjacent to my employer. I opened the window to let in a breath of fresh air—while I have no general brief against smokers, the previous tenant had evidently been frugal in his choice of pipe tobacco, although far from sparing in its use. The summer sun shone brightly over the buildings on the west side of the little park, and the sound of urban industry and hustle-bustle rose from the street below, mixed with the cries of children at play.

When I checked into my hotel room, the clerk had given me a message from Mr. Clemens: he had gone uptown to meet with his financial backers and a clerk from the steamboat company, and gave me my liberty for the rest of the day. I took a cab all the way uptown to the great Metropolitan Art Museum on Central Park, and spent a pleasant afternoon viewing the paintings of Rembrandt, Van Dyck, Rubens, and other European masters. Feeling that I was not entirely unsuited for my chosen profession as world traveler, I returned to the hotel mentally reviewing the stunning canvases I had seen, intending to spend the hour or so until supper jotting impressions of them in my notebook.

When I stopped by the desk to retrieve my key, I asked if Mr. Clemens had returned yet. "Not yet, but there's another man here to see him," said the clerk. To my surprise, he indicated a solidly built, red-faced man in a cheap-looking suit and weather-beaten slouch hat. Upon my approach, he put aside his newspaper—*The Police Gazette*—and looked up at me. "Sure, and you're not Mr. Clemens, are you?"

"No, I'm his traveling secretary, Wentworth Cabot," I said, smiling to myself at being mistaken for a man so much older. "Mr. Clemens had business uptown, but I expect him back shortly. How can I help you?"

"Paul Berrigan, detective, New York City police," he said, showing a badge. "I was pretty sure you weren't him—a bit young, for one thing—but you might be trying to impersonate the fellow. You never know, in this business. Anyhow, that's him yonder, so the question's moot." He gestured toward the desk, where Mr. Clemens had indeed come in and was talking to the clerk, who pointed in our direction.

I caught his eye and waved him over. The plainclothes-man introduced himself again, and asked whether there was someplace private we could speak.

"Come on up to my room," said Mr. Clemens. "I assume you don't mind if my secretary joins us."

Berrigan nodded. "Your room's good as anyplace. I'd ask you to come by the station if you were a suspect," he said to Mr. Clemens, "but I think we can be pretty sure Mr. Mark Twain doesn't go around murdering people."

"Murder!" I said then looked around quickly to see if anyone in the lobby had noticed. If they had, they evidently had the good breeding not to make it obvious. Mr. Clemens gestured toward the elevator, and we rode up in silence to the room.

Once there, Mr. Clemens lit one of his cigars, and Berrigan began his story. "One of our men found a fellow dead in an alleyway, a few blocks east of here; not quite the sort of neighborhood where you'd expect that sort of trouble. He'd been stabbed in the belly. Looked as if there'd been a struggle—there were cuts on his hands. This was just over an hour ago, and the body was still warm. We found this was in his pocket.''

He handed us a smudged slip of paper with *MR MARK TWAIN, Union Square Hotel* written on it in lead pencil in a decidedly ill-bred hand. ''Do you recognize the handwriting?''

My employer looked at it casually; then his brow furrowed and he reached into his side pocket. He handed the detective another, cleaner slip of paper, which appeared to be hotel stationery. ''This was waiting for me at the desk. See what you think of the match.''

''Bejasus, it's a dead ringer,'' he said. I looked over his shoulder; even to my untrained eye, the slip was clearly in the same hand, although this note was in ink. It read: *MR TWAIN: heard you was in town and waited here but you dint come back—Need to talk—come to 103 Mulberry St. tomorrow morning. Yr old buddy: JACK HUBBARD.*

The detective spread the two pieces of paper on the table. ''So, now at least we have a name and address—dead center in the worst part of town. What can you tell me about this Hubbard?''

My new employer thought for a moment. ''I first met him when I was a river pilot—that'd make it over thirty years ago. He started off as a character actor on one of the old showboats, and he was a pretty good one, from what I hear. But he was making more money on the side at billiards, and after a while he left the stage and just played billiards.

''He used to walk into a place wearing a farmer's outfit: straw hat, dungarees and all. Farmer Jack, the boys called him—and he could talk about chicken feed and henhouses and eggs till you expected him to cackle, but it was all an act, to draw the suckers into a game. I'd bet you a nickel he never laid eyes on a chicken in his life, except on his dinner plate. If he'd stayed in the theater, he'd have been a wonder. But he was a wizard at billiards, too—once you put a cue in his hand, he was the best player I ever saw. Took six dollars of my money, before I learned who he was. But it was worth it, just to see him at the table.''

''And what did he look like?''

''Big heavyset fellow about *his* height,'' Mr. Clemens said, pointing to me, ''with squinty blue eyes and a bushy red beard, at least when I used to know him. None too clean a dresser. That was quite some time ago; he may have changed his act since.''

Berrigan reached for a satchel he'd brought with him. ''You've hit the nail on the head. The officer that found him went to shift the body, and this fell off.'' He took out a tangled mass of dirty-looking red hair—a false beard, it became apparent when he held it up. He gave it a shake and handed it over.

''I should have known those whiskers were a sham!'' said Mr. Clemens, holding the disguise up to the light. ''That's just like Farmer Jack Hubbard's beard, all right— ugliest thing I ever saw. Now I know why it never seemed to fit him. I'm tempted to go to the morgue and see what the old rascal looked like without it.''

''We could arrange that,'' said Berrigan. ''We still haven't found anyone to identify the body for sure.''

''To be honest, cadavers never agreed with my digestion. But I doubt I could help you much in any case,'' said Mr. Clemens. ''I don't know for certain that I ever did see Hubbard's real face, and it's been over ten years since I saw him at all.''

''We still may call you if we don't find anybody. What do you think he wanted with you after all that time? Maybe it'll give us a clue.'' The detective had his notebook out again.

''I'm gathering material for a book about my early days working on the riverboats, and plan to talk to as many of the old-timers as I can find. That much has been in the papers; he probably saw my picture and read about the trip. I'd figure he wanted to talk about that, possibly touch me up for a few dollars—can't imagine what else it could be. As I say, I haven't laid eyes on him in years.''

"Any enemies, old-timers who might have a grudge against him?''

"None in particular,'' said Mr. Clemens. "The boys those days were a pretty rough crowd, though. Every gambler in twenty states rode the boats, and some of them didn't think twice at pulling out a razor when the cards went against them. Not that Jack was any good at cards— he lost more at Red Dog than he ever won at billiards. More likely somebody just tried to rob him.''

"We've ruled that out,'' said Berrigan. "There was forty dollars gold in his pocket. I suppose you don't know who his associates might be these days.''

"No idea. He used to run with a fast crowd in the old days, card mechanics and pool sharks, most of them. George Devol was pretty much the ringleader, but he's dead, by all reports.''

"Who were some of the others?'' asked the detective.

Mr. Clemens thought for a moment. "Wes Horton, Richie the Rat—I think his last name was Clark . . . a big German fellow name of Heinie Schussler . . . Ed McPhee, too. Can't forget old Slippery Ed.''

Berrigan laughed. "Ah, Mr. Twain! A fine-sounding bunch! If any of them are in New York, I haven't heard the names—and they're the type I *would* have heard of. But we'll keep an eye open, and if they're here, we'll find 'em. Will you let me know if you think of anything else that might help us?'' Mr. Clemens promised, and the detective bade us a good evening.

"Well, what do you make of that?'' said Clemens, after the door had closed.

"This is an outrage! I had heard that New York was a den of crime and depravity, but I hardly expected to see it demonstrated so clearly!''

"No, no, Cabot. There's something about this that doesn't smell right," said Mr. Clemens. "Jack Hubbard never called me anything but Sam as long as I've known him. If he got formal, maybe he'd have called me Mr. Clemens, but nobody from the river ever called me by my pen name—I didn't even make it up until years later. So whoever wrote that scrap of paper, I doubt it was Jack. I wonder who *did* write it; do you think it could be our friend the detective?"

I was dumbstruck by this suggestion. "But he showed me a badge!" I insisted.

"The badge could be false—don't tell me you've studied the police badges of every city we're likely to visit, because I won't believe you. It could be stolen. Or Mr. Berrigan could be exactly what he appears to be . . . and even then, I'd lay you odds he'll play the game however's most to *his* advantage. Surely they teach you these things at Yale?"

Mr. Clemens looked at his watch, then waved a hand in the direction of a bottle of Scotch whisky and a siphon on the sideboard. "I took the liberty of ordering in some provisions. Make me one and help yourself, Wentworth." I prepared a drink and handed it to him—my first act in my new capacity as his secretary. Mr. Clemens seemed lost in thought, and I had to clear my throat before he noticed the glass in my outstretched hand. He thanked me, then repeated, "Help yourself, Cabot. Go on—it's one of the perquisites of the position." He smiled, but I could see that his mind was elsewhere.

While I poured myself a dose, he walked to the window and stood with a distant expression, looking out at the street below, slowly sipping his whisky. Then, as if he had arrived at a decision, he downed his glass in one gulp, turned, and walked briskly back to me.

"Fill me up again," he said. "We've time before dinner for you to hear a story. Talking's thirsty work, and so's listening, and a dead man's serious business. There are things you need to know." I stared at him, but held my curiosity in check while I followed his instructions and poured him another glass. When we had both taken a sip from our respective glasses, he began to pace the floor, as if collecting his thoughts. Finally he stopped and fixed me with a stare. ''I want you to promise that you'll keep what I'm about to tell you an absolute secret. It may be a question of life and death—hell, I know that men have already died because of it. This murder today may be another in the string.''

''Shouldn't Berrigan know about it?''

''No. I don't trust him—I don't know for sure that he *is* a real policeman; and even if he is, that doesn't make him trustworthy. But you need to know, because you may be putting yourself in danger, and I won't expose a man to danger without his knowing it. Do you promise—on your honor as a Yale man—not to tell anyone what I'm about to say?''

I thought for a moment; it was clearly a serious matter. But I had cast my lot with Mr. Clemens, and I would not back out now. ''Yes,'' I told him. ''On my word as a Yale man—and as a Cabot.''

''Good,'' said Mr. Clemens. ''We can save a good bit of time and strain on the old man's memory if you've read a book I wrote about ten years ago called *Life on the Mississippi,*'' he said. I shook my head, somewhat embarrassed to admit this deficiency. ''No? Worth a try. Let's see if I can still piece it together.

''This happened in Munich, a dozen years ago. I was there on an extended visit, and made friends with a man I called Karl Ritter in my book, although that wasn't his real name. Poor Ritter was on his deathbed, and knew it—consumption. I did my best to give him a cheerful human presence to make his last days easier. As I soon discovered, he spoke perfect English and wanted to speak it with me. I realized, somewhat later, that having someone he could talk to without being understood by his neighbors took a burden off his mind—here was a foreigner who knew nothing about him except what he decided to reveal—and after some time of feeling me out, he told me his life story.

"You can read my book if you want to know everything Ritter told me—although I kept a few key details out, or changed them enough to keep readers from guessing the whole truth. At any rate, Ritter had moved to America around 1855—had a job in St. Louis making shoes, didn't like it, and moved to a little farm in Arkansas, where he married a local girl. A few years later, the Civil War began, but he decided to stick it out on the farm. One night toward the end of the war, he woke from a sound sleep to find his home invaded by two masked men, who bound and gagged him. From the snatches of conversation he overheard, he realized that the pair were soldiers in disguise, and that they had been searching for something in the house. Eventually they were frightened off and he escaped from his bonds, only to find his wife and child murdered."

"How terrible!," I said. "Surely they were rebel soldiers, and not our own boys."

Clemens shook his head. "These men were Union cavalry, from one of the Wisconsin regiments. Putting on a blue coat doesn't reform a man if he's rotten already, and there were plenty of scoundrels on both sides in the war."

"Did Ritter not apply to their superior officers for redress?"

"That was never likely. First of all, he hadn't seen their faces, and second of all, he was dealing with an occupying army in wartime—normal rules and habits don't apply. More to the point, he meant to take his revenge in person, rather than rely on the state."

He saw that I was about to protest my outrage, and held up his hand to stop me. "Poor Ritter is beyond the jurisdiction of any human court, and I'm not about to play judge. He acted as he did, and I don't know if I would have acted any differently in his shoes. But that's not why I am telling you this story. Do you want to spout off some more nonsense, or do you want to hear the rest?" He glared at me for a moment; I bowed my head in acquiescence, and he continued.

"Ritter managed to identify which outfit the killers had come from, but he bided his time while planning his revenge. After a time, the troop was transferred about a hundred miles north, to a town along the river—a town I referred to in my book as Napoleon, Arkansas, although that wasn't its name. Ritter knew that soldiers are superstitious devils, so he followed them there, disguised as a fortune-teller. He was able to attach himself to the troop and get a close look at a lot of them under the pretext of telling their fortunes. It didn't take him long to spot one of the pair—the fellow had lost a thumb, which made him pretty conspicuous—but he wasn't the one Ritter wanted most, the man who'd done the actual killing. And he found out that the men he was after were both Germans—this was a Wisconsin outfit, and about a third of the men were of German ancestry.

"Ritter had stumbled on another clue that, combined with his sham of fortune-telling, he expected to lead him to his man. The killer had left a thumbprint in blood on a piece of paper in Ritter's house. Now, Ritter had a friend who had served as a prison guard, and from that man he'd learned that a thumbprint is unique—infallible identification of the man who made it. I'm working on a book right now that uses that fact. Anyhow, Ritter pretended that he could read a man's fortune by dipping his thumb in ink and marking it on paper. What he really did was take the prints home at night and compare them to the print left by the killer—in his own dear wife's blood. It took a long time, and interviews with dozens of the soldiers, but finally he found his man."

"Surely, that would have been the time to reveal all to the officers in charge," I said, but Clemens waved me into silence.

"Ritter's long dead, Wentworth. None of us can go back and tell him what he ought to have done. What he in fact did required no small amount of courage, since he chose to confront the other, thumbless man, with his knowledge of the crime—although he concealed it behind the pretense of fortune-telling. His original intent was simply to confirm his suspicions with a confession, and that he got in full detail. But here is where the story becomes interesting. To Ritter's surprise, the poor fellow fell on his knees and offered him a vast hidden treasure, if only he would advise him on how to avoid the terrible fate his 'fortune' had predicted.

"Ritter paid no attention to the fellow's offer. All he wanted was revenge on the man who had murdered his loved ones. He sent the thumbless man away without learning the location of the treasure. That very night he lured the man's companion, the one who'd murdered his family, to a lonely place and drove a knife through his heart. Then he fled. He had his revenge, Cabot, but it gave him no satisfaction. Nothing could bring back his wife and child, and now he carried a load of guilt as well. After years of wandering, he finally returned to Munich, his hometown. His health had begun to fail him, and his terrible adventures of a few years earlier had left him in a morbid frame of mind, so he took a small place as the night watchman in a deadhouse.

"His task was simply to watch the bodies for any sign that one of them might have been declared dead prematurely—for there was a great fear at that time of falling into a deep trance and awakening to find oneself buried alive. Such things do occasionally happen, although less often than the folks of Munich believed. Still, it was a great shock one night for him to hear the alarm that told him that one of the supposed corpses under his charge had come to life. When Ritter went to investigate, he discovered that the revived 'corpse' was the same thumbless soldier who had offered him a fortune so many years before!''

I was astonished, and told him so. "It is surely a sign of some greater plan in the universe that he would find the very man who had wronged him under his power at such a moment," I said.

Mr. Clemens raised his eyebrows but made no reply, except to motion for me to replenish his whisky, which I did. My own glass was still half-full, and so I merely added another cube of ice. He took a long sip, said, "That'll do the job," and continued.

"The two soldiers were Germans, so the coincidence wasn't as remarkable as some I've seen," said my employer, now fishing out a fresh cigar and lighting it. I waited a moment as the aromatic billows of smoke replaced the sharp smell of the match. "I can tell you that for this man of all men to show up in the deadhouse that night was in Ritter's eyes the last stroke of justice long delayed. For all the guilt that he had felt after dispatching the murderer, seeing the thumbless man again brought back all his rage and grief. Suffice it to say that in the morning, the thumbless soldier's place was back among the dead."

"What a monstrous tale!" I exclaimed.

"Perhaps; Ritter claimed that he merely let the fellow expire from the cold, although I'm not convinced that he told me the full truth of it. Still, poor old Ritter was looking his own death in the eye, so I trust the story as a whole. But in any event, the thumbless fellow lived long enough to try to ask Ritter a final favor—to tell his son the location of some ten thousand dollars in gold, hidden back in the little river town in Arkansas where Ritter had played fortune-teller. And so Ritter came at last into the secret that he had turned his back on so many years before—too late to get any good of it. He was an old man, already sick, and knew in his heart that he had no chance of surviving the long voyage to Arkansas to recover it. And so he died without ever laying eyes on it."

"Ten thousand dollars! What a story!"

Clemens nodded. "Just before Ritter died, he told me the location, and made a dying man's last request, which I promised to honor. He begged me to retrieve the gold and send it to the thumbless man's boy, if he proved at all deserving, as a final means of assuaging his burden of guilt. I traced the boy to an address in Germany, and (watching him from a distance, and making discreet inquiries) satisfied myself that he deserved the gold; and so, a couple of years afterwards, I took a journey down the Mississippi, on a boat called the *Gold Dust,* under the guise of researching a book. I did in fact end up writing that book, but my real purpose was to visit a certain town in Arkansas and find a fortune I had promised a dying man to send to a young German boy I had never met.''

''And did you find it? This is a truly astonishing chain of events.'' In truth, I had never before heard anything like it. I had dreamt of the romance of travel all my life, and read more than one wild tale of hidden treasure and dark doings, but I had hardly expected to find myself in the midst of such an adventure.

He rubbed his chin meditatively, staring out the window toward the evening sun. Finally he looked at me and resumed his tale. ''No, I didn't. The fact is, I became aware that someone was following me, someone who knew the story somehow—perhaps the thumbless man had told it more than once—and that if I recovered the money my own life would be in danger. So I did not even land in the town where the money was hidden, and cooked up a cock-and-bull tale to relate the experience, with the names and events changed just enough to keep anyone who didn't know the truth from guessing it. If you'd read my book, you'd know that upon my arrival in Arkansas, I found that Napoleon, Arkansas had been washed away, many years ago, by the river. Sometimes it's to your advantage to have a reputation as a humorist: most readers seem to have taken the story as I intended, as a tall tale with a preposterous ending. But the treasure is real, and it was never even in Napoleon—it was in another town altogether.''

''And the money is still there.''

''As far as I know, yes.''

"And you intend to get it this time."

"That I do." Mr. Clemens eyed me critically. "And I fully intend to send it to that young man, who does not even know that it exists. Do you understand, Wentworth?"

"I had no notion that you would do anything else with it."

"Bosh. You don't know me well enough to be certain of that. I tell you nonetheless that it is my intent to fulfill that promise. The soldier's son is alive and well, working hard to support his family. The years have proven him more than worthy of it.

"The stinger is, I figured it was finally safe to go back for the gold when I heard that the larcenous old buzzard I'd suspected of tailing me was dead—he was a gambler and con man named George Devol, and you'd rather find a copperhead in your boot than tangle with him in his prime. But I don't like it that Hubbard's turned up—dead or alive—just as I'm about to go look for it again. Farmer Jack Hubbard and Slippery Ed McPhee were Devol's main sidekicks in the old days—part of his gambling crew on the riverboats. For all I know, he managed to tip them both off to the German soldier's gold before he died. So this little boat ride and lecture tour could turn out to be more dangerous than you had any right to believe—especially if McPhee shows up, with the idea of getting the gold for himself. It wouldn't be fair not to let you know what you're getting into if you go with me. Are you game?"

"Sir, you can rely on me." I meant it as earnestly as I have ever meant anything, and Clemens nodded his approval.

"Good then, we're a team." We raised our glasses to seal the pact, and took a ritual sip. "Drink up now, Wentworth," said Clemens. "We'll see what sort of fare the cook has in store for us tonight, and I'll tell you some of the other stories you've missed by not reading my books. What a pleasure to have a fresh audience for the old yarns!"

3

Early the next morning, Mr. Clemens sent me to buy newspapers, while he went to the telephone office. When I joined him there, he was just finishing an animated phone conversation. He extracted a promise from the other party to keep him informed, promised to feed him the best steak in New York for his trouble, and ended the connection. He took a few moments to chat with the "hello girls," who operated the phones and who were clearly excited to have such a celebrity in their midst. He paid for the call, and we made our way to the breakfast table to fortify ourselves for the first leg of our trip. Our breakfast consisted of a thick, juicy beefsteak and hot coffee. In between bites, he told me what he had learned: mostly nothing. The source—evidently someone high on the police force—knew nothing more about the death of Hubbard, but confirmed that there was a Detective Berrigan assigned to the case. On the other hand, he (whoever he was) had heard nothing of the supposed connection to Mr. Clemens before the telephone call.

"This should put to rest your doubts about Detective Berrigan," I said.

"You assume that the fellow we saw really is Berrigan," said Mr. Clemens. "Easy enough to find the name of a real officer if you mean to impersonate one. Or to bribe one—which is even easier, if you get right down to it."

"But why go to all the trouble? I can't see what anyone's gained by the charade, if such a thing it is."

He frowned, took a sip of coffee, and shrugged. "You're probably right. I suppose I'll never be so old that I don't get a little spooked when somebody I knew on the river is murdered. It's the timing and the fact that he was looking for me that same day that really bother me. If I'd come home early, I'd probably have seen the poor old villain. He really could play billiards."

"Who is this McPhee fellow you mentioned?"

"A no-good son of a rattlesnake. *Has* been, for as long as I can remember. He's another one I met on the river, right after I became a pilot. He tried to swindle me out of the little bit I had, more or less for the principle of the thing, I suppose. Later that same trip, I saw him jump overboard to get away from a fellow who caught him with a couple of extra cards in his hand. He showed up on our next trip upriver, and acted as if nothing funny had happened, but the boys wouldn't let him off that easily. They started calling him Slippery Ed, and the name stuck, although there's few that remember how he got it."

"How does he manage to continue his career if he's a known cheater? Surely the authorities would be aware of him by now."

"You might be surprised how many people will look the other way if you make it worth their while. There were plenty of riverboat captains who took in more in bribes than in salary. The better the gamblers did, the better the captain and crew did by turning a blind eye."

"I'm afraid I've never understood the appeal of games of chance."

"Ah, there's the mistake everyone makes," said Mr. Clemens. "The minute a professional gets involved, there's no such thing as a game of chance. The professional is there to earn a living. I recall a court case in Nevada, where a miner was arrested for playing a game of chance on the Sabbath and defended himself by claiming that he was playing Red Dog, which was not a game of chance but of skill. The judge picked a jury of six chance men and six

24 skill men, and sent 'em off with a deck of cards to determine the verdict. After a respectable interval for their deliberations, the chance men were broke to the wire, and the verdict was *Not guilty*. From that day on, Red Dog was exempted from all laws governing games of chance. Not that it kept the suckers from playing it.'' He finished his coffee and, with a sigh, pushed away from the table.

After breakfast, a cab took us downtown to Desbrosses Street, through traffic so thick I was afraid we would never get through without an accident. The streets were crammed with everything from bicycles and dogcarts to overloaded freight wagons pulled by six or even eight huge Percherons. I was convinced that we had left the hotel too late, but Mr. Clemens merely sat back and smiled. ''These New York cabdrivers would have given old Hank Monk a pretty good run for his money. This fellow's got a good horse, and he knows he's got an extra fifty cents coming if he gets us in on time, and by gum, he'll do it.''

''Who was Hank Monk?'' I inquired innocently.

Mr. Clemens gave me a strange look. ''I can tell you a most laughable thing. . . .'' He shook his head. ''No, it wouldn't be fair. He was a driver on the old Nevada stagecoach lines. There was an old story—not true, but that's beside the point—about how he once carried Horace Greeley, who made the mistake of letting Hank Monk know he was in a hurry. Hank set off at a breakneck pace and like to have killed poor Horace, but he got him there on time—what was left of him.''

This anecdote did nothing to assuage my worries, but we arrived at the ferry slips in plenty of time—and miraculously, without mishap. Thence we took a ferry across the Hudson River to Jersey City, to catch our train: the Pennsylvania Railroad's Limited Vestibule Express to Chicago. For this we arrived barely in time; luckily, Mr. Clemens had instructed me to send most of our luggage ahead the night before, leaving us to carry only one small carpetbag apiece, containing our toilet kits and a couple of changes of clothing. ''Enough to hold us until we're set up on board the boat,'' said Mr. Clemens. ''Never carry so much that it'll slow you down when you're in a rush.'' I was vaguely pleased to think that I was already benefiting from the advice, however mundane, of a world traveler.

The train took us south through New Jersey, flat country with occasional muddy rivers and unattractive towns, then across the Delaware River to Philadelphia, whence it would take us west to Chicago and St. Paul. There we would board our steamer for the journey down the great Mississippi all the way to New Orleans, with numerous stops along the way to allow for sightseeing and lectures. The steamer was, in fact, a veritable floating lecture hall, which would dock at every city of any consequence for as many lectures as the local citizenry could be expected to attend.

I busied myself in reading over the detailed itinerary my predecessor (about whom Mr. Clemens had very little good to say) had prepared for our journey, and rapidly became befuddled by the complexity of our journey. I despaired of remembering all the riverside towns at which we planned to stop, let alone the hotels, restaurants, railroad stations, telegraph offices, post offices, and local people of note. At last, as we neared the outskirts of Philadelphia, I lay the thick portfolio across my lap and stared off into the pungent atmosphere of our smoking car. Surely I had gotten myself in deeper water than I had bargained for.

Mr. Clemens looked up from his newspaper and divined somehow what was on my mind. ''Here, Wentworth, don't fret. There's no need to turn into a walking Baedeker; if that's all I needed, I could get one a lot cheaper than a secretary, and carry it a lot easier, too. The details will come to you soon enough.''

''I'm sure I don't know how. Learning Latin was child's play to this, at least there's some system to it. Here, I've got to remember a different set of facts for every town in twenty-five states.''

"Oh, you're barely started. By the time we get to New Orleans, I'll expect you to know something. If you don't know anything useful by the time we're back to New York, it'll be time to worry. For the present, just look a day or two ahead every morning and make sure you know what's coming up next. Do you know where we're going when we arrive in Chicago?"

My blank expression must have spoken volumes. He pointed to the papers on my lap. With some embarrassment I fumbled through the pages until I found the information. "The Great Northern Hotel, on Dearborn Street."

"Good boy. Never expect more of your memory than it can handle. That's why people write things down. It's better to know where you can find something than to try to remember it and come up empty. Besides, there are new buildings going up, businesses opening and closing, people moving in and out, a thousand changes every day. I can guarantee you there'll be a dozen or more things that have changed since the last time I was in Chicago."

"How am I ever to learn it, then?"

"The trick is to learn the general lay of the land and fill in the specific map in your head as you need to. If you know that the best place to look for a cab, any time of day or night, is in front of a big hotel, that information is as good for London or Vienna as for Boston. There are exceptions to everything, but better to have your eyes open than your memory stuffed with useless baggage." He stared out the window a while, then turned back to me. "The sooner you get good at this job, the sooner I can forget about the details and let you handle them. So any time you have any questions about the arrangements, better to ask than to wonder what to do."

We took our luncheon at the first seating, shortly before the train pulled into the Philadelphia station. The approach to this city is drab, with mills and manufacturing districts, but the center of Philadelphia is quite handsome, with broad parklands and a picturesque river—the Schuylkill, pronounced "skookill," Mr. Clemens told me.

After a brief stop to take on passengers at Broad Street Station, we turned west, through pleasant farm country interspersed with patches of woods: the famous Pennsylvania Dutch country. The landscape became hilly, then (after we crossed the broad Susquehanna River) gradually turned rugged and mountainous. I commented on the grand scenery we were passing through. Mr. Clemens, busy writing letters, glanced out the window. "You should see the Rockies," he said. "These are barely hummocks." He turned back to his writing and scarcely raised his head until it was time for dinner. As for me, I had plenty to occupy my mind as some of the most picturesque scenery I have ever laid eyes on rolled by, a wonderful moving pageant of mountains and rivers and forests. If Mr. Clemens knew of something better than this, I looked forward to seeing it; for now, Pennsylvania was *fine*.

But while my eyes were busy with the view, my thoughts were on our mission to the west and Mr. Clemens's odd story. Between the scenery and my speculations, I gradually lost track of time. It wasn't until Mr. Clemens quietly asked whether I wanted a drink before dinner that I realized that the sun had moved well ahead of us. I glanced at my watch to see that it was nearly six.

The smoking car began to empty out as other passengers went to the diner, and so we found ourselves with enough breathing room to talk without anyone close by to overhear. I took the opportunity to bring up the questions I had been mulling over all afternoon.

"I've been thinking about Jack Hubbard," I began.

Mr. Clemens gave me a calculating look. "And what exactly have you been thinking, Wentworth?"

"I've been wondering why you're so convinced that what happened to Hubbard has anything to do with us. Couldn't it be pure coincidence that he was trying to get in touch with you just before he died?"

''It could be a coincidence. But if it's not, I'm walking into danger. I just don't fancy the risk.''

''Then why not take the police into our trust when we had the opportunity?''

He took a long hard look out the window; the Appalachian Mountains were painted by a golden sunset. He tasted his drink, sighed, and said, ''A hunch. I have a bad feeling about that detective.''

He paused as a tall gentleman with a full head of gray hair, cut short, and wearing a dark suit of semimilitary cut passed by us, nodding and smiling in our direction as he passed. Mr. Clemens nodded back, absently; I was already becoming used to the fact that a large fraction of the population recognized my employer by sight. As he continued on in the direction of the dining car, I heard the door open again, and a sour look came over Mr. Clemens's face as he spotted the person who'd just entered.

Before I could even decide whether or not to look around, a familiar voice behind me solved my problem. ''Sure, and it's Mr. Mark Twain again. And Mr. Wentworth.''

''Wentworth Cabot,'' I corrected him. It was the New York detective, Berrigan.

''And are you traveling on business, Berrigan, or is this a vacation?'' my employer asked him.

''Business, Mr. Twain, and there's a bit of a funny twist to it. Do you mind if I sit with you a moment?'' He took off his hat and plopped himself in the chair adjacent to me without waiting for an answer. Then he fished out a pipe and tobacco pouch, and began loading it.

''I checked with the desk clerk at your hotel, asking who had left the note for you. It was a tall fellow with a red beard, a bit shabbily dressed, which is why the clerk noticed him. He waited around for another fifteen minutes, then left. The clerk was just as glad to see him go—said he was making the quality folks uncomfortable.''

''That sounds like Farmer Jack to me,'' said Mr. Clemens. "He used to act so countrified that most city folks wouldn't believe he had two cents' worth of brains. It made it easier to find suckers to play billiards with him."

The detective nodded. "We went to the address on the note he'd left for you, and it was a shabby little rented room down in Five Points, which isn't a part of town decent folk go into after dark—not and come back out with a whole skin. The landlord said the tenant was there a few months. And it took a little persuasion, but we got him to look at the body," he said. He popped the filled pipe into his mouth and began searching his jacket pockets.

"There's matches on the table," said Mr. Clemens.

"Right you are," said the detective, taking them. "Well, he recognized the dead man, all right. But he swore he'd never seen him with that phony red beard. And he'd never heard of Jack Hubbard—the room was rented under a different name, probably an alias." He dug into his pocket again, and came up with an envelope. "So we're back to you again, Mr. Twain. Take a look at this."

Mr. Clemens opened the envelope and extracted a photograph, which he looked at, then shrugged and passed to me without saying a word. It showed the garishly lit face of a shabbily dressed man whose eyes were closed in death—or so I had to assume. The sepia tints of the glossy photographic print gave no hint as to the color of the man's hair or complexion. But I had the feeling I had seen him before, though I couldn't for the life of me say where. I told the detective so, and he nodded.

"What about you, Mr. Twain?"

"It's not Farmer Jack Hubbard, even allowing for ten years and the false beard. You think Hubbard killed him?"

"That's one possibility. Killed him and planted evidence to make it look as if he were the one that died."

"Why?" I asked.

"If I knew that, I'd have a better idea where to find him, wouldn't I?" Berrigan's pipe was finally lit, and he puffed a couple of times before continuing. "But all the signs point to some connection to you, Mr. Twain. For one thing, he had your name in his pocket; for another, you had a note in the same handwriting at your hotel, signed by this Hubbard. And for a third, the dead man had Hubbard's phony beard. That's a few too many coincidences, says I. That's why we were hoping you could tell us who the victim is.''

Mr. Clemens took the photograph again and stared at it a while longer. ''If I ever knew him, the name's escaped me. He's a bit too young to be one of the old crew I knew along the river,'' he finally said, passing it back to me.

''But Hubbard's from the river, and he wanted to see you,'' said the detective. ''And now you're headed back there. Are you sure there's not more involved in this trip than you've told me?''

Mr. Clemens shook his head. ''A lecture tour and research for a book,'' he said. ''My backer says my last Mississippi book was a great success, and he suggests I do another one. As it happens, I need the money, so I'm willing to listen to suggestions.''

''Aye,'' said Berrigan, ''I brought along a copy of that very book for reading on the train. I was of a mind it might give me an idea what to look out for.''

''I see,'' said Mr. Clemens, raising one eyebrow. ''So you'll be traveling with us down the river?''

''Unless I catch my man first. Maybe Hubbard planted the beard on this fellow to cover his own escape, or maybe the dead man grabbed it from him. Either way, I think he'll come looking for you. That's why I'm on the train with you, and it's why I'll be riding on the steamboat with you. And it's why I'm wondering if there isn't more to this story than you've told me so far, Mr. Twain.'' He paused, then continued in a lower tone. ''This is a murder we're talking about, Mr. Twain. You could be putting yourself in a lot of danger by withholding information from us.''

''I'm well aware of that,'' said my employer. ''I've been around some rough characters in my time, and lived to tell the tale so far, so I know what they're capable of. I didn't get these white hairs by taking foolish chances, and I'm not about to start. Believe me, if I see hide or hair of Farmer Jack Hubbard, you'll be the first to know.''

I had picked up the grisly photograph for another look, racking my memory, and suddenly recalled where I'd seen the dead man. ''This fellow was at your lecture the other night,'' I blurted, and both of them turned to stare at me. ''He sat slightly ahead of me, on the right-side aisle.''

''Now I'm sure I'm on the right trail,'' crowed Berrigan.

For his part, Mr. Clemens just took the picture from my hands, and looked at it, frowning. ''What name did the landlord say this fellow gave him?'' he asked at last.

''Lee Russell,'' said Berrigan.

''Never heard of him,'' said Mr. Clemens, and his frown went even darker. ''But I'm afraid we haven't seen the last of him.''

4

At dinner, Mr. Clemens ordered us a bottle of champagne—"to celebrate the start of the tour," he said. In keeping with the occasion, he maintained a constant stream of amusing, if trifling, patter all through the meal, entertaining not only me but our fellow diners; but it seemed to me that his mind was elsewhere. After dinner, in a quiet corner of the smoking car, he confirmed my suspicions.

"Murder or no murder," he growled, "a man ought to have a right to his privacy, instead of the police dogging his heels halfway across the blasted continent. You'd think we were the suspects, instead of that old swindler Hubbard. Still, I never would have thought Jack had it in him to stab a man."

"Yes, I wonder what he wanted with you. It makes me shiver to think that you and I might have returned to the hotel to find a killer waiting for us."

"Well, not for you, strictly speaking," said Mr. Clemens, with a wry grin. He swirled his whisky glass and took a meditative sip. "And Berrigan's not here for you, either. You could get off at the next stop and go home to Connecticut and never hear another word of this. But if I decided to take a side trip to Timbuktu on my way to that place in Arkansas"—by which I took it that he meant the town where the gold was supposedly still hidden—"that impertinent flat-footed Irishman would follow me—and to the moon, too, if I decided to go *there*."

He prepared still another cigar—I had already given up trying to keep track of how many he smoked in a day. "And if the detective does try to follow us all the way downriver, what's to stop him from trailing along when I go look for Ritter's money? And what's to stop him from deciding it's stolen property and confiscating it? That'd be the last we ever saw of it, I promise you—never mind that the rightful owner's probably long dead, even if we could figure out who he is." He lit up the cigar and breathed the smoke in deeply.

"I myself am far more concerned about the possibility of a killer following us to the treasure," I protested. "You can't deny that having a policeman near at hand makes us both a good bit safer."

"I wouldn't bet a nickel on it. Unless he's going to scrub my back in the bathtub, and sit up watching me every time I take a nap, and make himself even more of a damned nuisance than he is already, there'll always be a chance for somebody to sneak up behind me and do me in. And besides, I don't think anybody here has that kind of grudge against me."

"But what about that fellow coming to your lecture before he was killed?"

Mr. Clemens scowled at his glass. "Plenty of things happen at the same time and in the same place without being related. Enough people get murdered in New York City as it is; it could be sheer chance that one of them was at my lecture a few days before."

"And that he had your name in his pocket? In the same handwriting as on a note in your hotel? Isn't that a few too many coincidences just to ignore?"

"I'm not ignoring them, Wentworth—I just don't believe that having a detective along will magically clear up all those coincidences. Policemen are very clever at finding sinister implications behind perfectly innocent things; they have to, to justify their impertinence. The way I see it, this rascal Berrigan has managed to convince his chief that I'm being stalked by a murderer and have to be watched every second. If he plays his cards right, he gets a paid vacation on a cruise to New Orleans, and the relatively painless duty of keeping an eye on an old man, whom he undoubtedly expects to be eternally grateful. It's a perfect hoax; almost a work of art, if you admire such things. The biggest danger, from Berrigan's point of view, is that his chief will recognize the whole thing for the shameless fraud it is, and assign *himself* to trail me.''

''I wish I could share your belief that there's no danger,'' I said. ''You still haven't explained the notes.''

''There needn't be anything sinister in the notes,'' said Mr. Clemens. ''It's possible Jack Hubbard found out I was in New York and came looking for a handout. He wouldn't be the first to think that knowing me thirty years ago entitled him to an endless string of baksheesh. He goes to the hotel, doesn't find me, and leaves a note—if he wore his farmer outfit, they wouldn't have let him sit around the lobby for very long; I'm surprised they let him in in the first place. He leaves me a note, and because he's uncomfortable about begging, doesn't call me by the name he used in the old days. Then, on the way home, this other fellow tries to rob him in an alley, and Hubbard defends himself with a knife. In the struggle, the other fellow grabs him by the false beard and it comes off. When Hubbard realizes he's killed the other man, he skedaddles.''

''And how did the *other* man come to have your name in his pocket?'' I persisted.

''He picked Hubbard's pocket. Or Hubbard put it there, to lay a false trail. Or—damn it all, Wentworth, you'll give me a headache if you keep this up! Go see if you can get me another whisky; easy on the soda water, this time.'' I took this as a clear signal to end the discussion; I got him his drink, listened to him chat on general subjects for another half hour, and then retired for the evening. It had been a long day, and despite the unfamiliarity of sleeping on a rapidly moving train, I was asleep almost as soon as my head touched the pillow.

In the morning, I awoke to find the landscape had flattened out, with widely spaced farmhouses each in its little grove of trees—Indiana. A night's sleep had done wonders for me, and I was looking forward to the second day of my new adventure.

Mr. Clemens, wearing a fresh white suit, joined me for breakfast—steak again for him, ham and eggs for me, and plenty of biscuits and strong coffee for both of us. Even before his second cup of coffee, he was grumbling about "being followed halfway to Hell and back," complaining that "a man can't take a breath in peace" and expressing other sentiments less printable. I listened without comment, although I myself was rather pleased that the police seemed to be taking the case seriously. Still, I was being paid to handle his business and correspondence, not to contradict him.

After our meal, my employer and I went to the onboard barbershop, in my own case primarily for the novelty—I had grown used to shaving myself while at Yale, and was in fact a bit apprehensive about exposing my neck to a sharp razor wielded by a stranger on a moving train. But the fellow who shaved me was an expert, and I arose from the chair without as much as a single nick, and feeling much refreshed. By then, we could see Lake Michigan (I could have taken it for an arm of the sea, it was so extensive) on the right side of the train. We pulled into the station promptly at 9:45 central time; I saw Berrigan dismount at the same time we did, but the crowd separated us and I dismissed him from my thoughts. Luckily, Mr. Clemens did not notice the detective, or it might have set off a fresh diatribe.

At our hotel, a sixteen-story building near the Customs House, my employer went to the telephone office to make a long-distance call to New York, while I supervised the

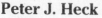

36 delivery of our luggage to the rooms. These were on the top floor, to which I took an elevator with a bellboy carrying the bags. I wondered what business Mr. Clemens might have urgent enough to call New York for on a Saturday morning; I was not long in finding out.

I had barely begun to organize my belongings when I heard him slam the door to his room, and moments later pound on the connecting double door. I opened it, and at his gesture, entered his room. He waved in the general direction of a chair, which I settled myself into while he paced back and forth in an agitated manner, all the while letting loose a stream of invective as hot as anything I'd ever heard in my life.

"Why, what on earth has happened?" I inquired when he finally paused for breath. I had not seen him like this before, and wondered at it.

"I thought Abe Lincoln had done away with slavery, but it was all a barefaced lie, a sham and an imposture. These money-grubbing New York capitalists think they've bought me like a bushel of corn, and now they've gone and hired a scarecrow so the birds can't get at me."

"I'm sure this is all very important, but I don't understand a word of what you're saying," I protested. He stopped his pacing and turned to look at me with an expression that could have ignited one of his cigars from across the room, then shrugged his shoulders and resumed pacing, his hands clasped behind his back.

"Sorry, Wentworth—I keep forgetting that you don't know my affairs yet," he said in a somewhat calmer tone. "The long and short of it is, I've been told I have to put up with Berrigan. It seems my backer, Henry Rogers in New York, specifically asked the police to assign a detective to protect me."

"Surely you can ask Mr. Rogers to recall Berrigan?" I suggested, in as reasonable a tone as I could muster.

"It's not as simple as that," said Mr. Clemens. "I thought I was my own master, and now I've found out otherwise. It's a sad lesson, but I guess I had to learn it.

"My problem is I've never really had much luck with money. I've *made* enough by lecturing and writing—scads of money, enough for a fine house in Hartford, European journeys, the best of everything for my family. I've given away more money to friends in need—some who did little enough to deserve it—than some people save in a lifetime of hard work. But I've never learned how to *keep* money—let alone invest it. You could take all my investments over the years, and not a single one of them has ever been worth spitting at. It would be comical if it weren't so damned painful—a smart man could have made his fortune ten times over by looking at my investments and betting the opposite way.

"Back in '77, I could have bought stock in Bell's telephone company at five hundred dollars a bushel, and I passed it up. Instead, I invested in a steam pulley that pulled thousands of dollars straight out of my pocket. I set up a subscription publishing company that had the greatest, most successful book ever published in America—General Grant's memoirs—and lost every cent because I put a self-important ignoramus who didn't know the first thing about literature in charge of it. But my biggest mistake of all was Paige's typesetting machine—I was convinced that we could sell it to every publisher in the world. It looked like a license to print greenbacks—and it would have been, too, if the damned machine had ever worked right. That was the straw that broke the camel's back—and Sam Clemens's back, as well. I lost close to a quarter-million dollars, a lot of it borrowed, with not a chance in Hell of ever seeing it back."

I murmured some conventional phrase of sympathy, but Mr. Clemens waved his hand as if to dismiss it. "There's nothing to be said, Wentworth. I'm descended from a long line of the improvident and unlucky, and heredity finally caught up with me. I thought I was safe from ever again having to go to work, and here I am back on the road, counting the house as anxiously as in the days when I was an utter unknown. A writer's personal honor is his only stock in trade, and I'm determined to pay off every cent I owe, if I have to go to China, set up the stage myself, and do the Royal Nonesuch.

"But even honor has a price. A man needs money to make money, and I'm lucky to have found a man to back me. I owe a lot to Henry Rogers, whatever people say about him. He's bankrolling this whole lecture tour, keeping my creditors at bay, making sure poor Livy and the girls have enough to live comfortably while I work off my debts. He's even paying your salary, Wentworth. He's been an absolute angel to me, at the very time I need it most—but I just found out the price I have to pay.

"When I called Rogers this morning, I expected that he would pull some strings and get that blasted detective off my back. There's not a man in America, Carnegie and Rockefeller included, who has more real power than Rogers when he decides to apply it. Well, now I find out just where I rank in his scheme of things. This business with the murder and the notes came to his ear, and now he's worried that somebody's looking to kill me. It was at *his* insistence that Berrigan was sent to follow me, to make sure nothing happens to his investment.

"So now I learn that my dear friend Rogers—and he *has* been a friend to me, make no mistake of that—thinks I have to be protected like a champion racehorse. And my opinion of the matter don't signify, no more than the horse's. Detective Berrigan is under orders to stick with me until the murder's solved—or until I die, which seems just as likely."

Having vented his ire, Mr. Clemens spent the rest of the morning dictating letters, on various details of business with which I will not bore the reader. I wrote them up and posted them; then, after we enjoyed a hearty luncheon, he gave me my liberty for the afternoon, and I spent a pleasant few hours investigating the sights of a city new to me. The second city of our nation, Chicago is distinguished by a number of tall buildings, referred to by the locals under the picturesque name of ''sky-scrapers.'' Our hotel, the Great Northern, stands an impressive sixteen stories high, and there are several buildings in the city even taller. Perhaps the most striking is the huge Masonic Temple, a short walk from our hotel, and a remarkable twenty-one stories in height. It being a clear day, I paid twenty-five cents to ascend the elevator to the temple's roof, from which a visitor obtains a stunning panoramic view of the city and the adjoining lake. It was startling to look downward at the backs of soaring birds, or at the antlike creatures scurrying about below them—which my eye at first refused to recognize as full-grown human beings.

After seeing the wonders of human ingenuity, I decided to take a closer look at Lake Michigan. A walk to the waterfront park gave me a close look at a broad harbor, with the open lake beyond a stone breakwater. To the south, I could make out some of the buildings of the Columbian Exposition that were still standing. Much of their grandeur endured despite the fire that had ravaged the site not long before; a large crane hung over them, ready to remove what was left of the ruins. The surface of the lake showed only a light chop (although I was assured that it gets fierce enough in a storm). It is not the ocean, but it is impressive enough.

I returned to the hotel and joined Mr. Clemens for dinner, to find him in a much better mood. ''I've got the answer to all my problems,'' he told me over the customary pre-meal libations. ''If the murder is solved, Berrigan goes back to New York—taking the killer with him. And we can go ahead with our other mission in Arkansas.''

''That seems reasonable to me,'' I said. ''So you're going to tell Mr. Berrigan the whole story, and cooperate with his investigation.''

''Not on your life, Wentworth. I'm going to solve the

damned thing myself. I wouldn't trust Berrigan to figure this thing out even if I thought I could trust him not to *sell* us out. And once we get to Memphis, we're practically next door to the treasure in Arkansas. So I've got to identify the murderer, convince Berrigan's boss I've got the right man, and send them packing before we leave Memphis.''

"How, pray tell, do you intend to do that?'' I asked, intrigued.

"For openers, I'm the only one here who's met Farmer Jack Hubbard in the flesh. So I stand the best chance of spotting him—even after all those years, and without the disguise. Funny I never noticed the phony beard—of course, I was a good bit greener then. But if he shows up, I'll spot him soon enough. I'd lay odds I'll know him the minute he opens his mouth.''

I wasn't entirely persuaded by this plan. "And then what will you do?''

"If I'm convinced he's the man, I'll turn him over to Berrigan.'' He puffed on one of his corncob pipes, then continued: "Or maybe I'll talk to him first.''

I was appalled. "What, talk to a murderer?''

"If he's after the money, he won't find it with me dead,'' said Mr. Clemens, confidently. "I want you to know I take great comfort in that, Wentworth.''

While I found his cheerful determination to take affairs in his own hands preferable to his earlier bitterness, I was dubious of his ability to carry out his intentions. For the moment, though, I had no clear idea what to do about things.

We took a cab to the auditorium, which I had noticed on my walk to the park that afternoon. It was an impressive building, with over four thousand seats, and it had a first-class hotel attached to it. A light shower had begun, so we took along an umbrella. I carried Mr. Clemens's bag with his "lecture suit'' to his dressing room. After stowing the umbrella in a corner, I hung our hats on two pegs, made sure he had everything he needed to prepare for the lecture, and then went out front—I was beginning to pick up a smattering of theater jargon already—to get a seat while he changed for the performance. The large modern auditorium was already nearly full, and there was a decided holiday spirit among the audience.

This was the second time I had seen my employer take the stage, and I was curious to see if I could make any more sense of the performance than the first time. At the appointed hour, the lights in the sumptuous arena dimmed and he strolled out, so casually as to escape notice if one happened not to be paying close attention. But the instant a few members of the assembly laid eyes on him, they began a general round of boisterous cheering, to which he responded with a dignified bow. When they finally fell silent, he rested his chin on his left fist, his left elbow on his right fist, and began his talk.

The first thing I realized was that I could hear his voice quite clearly from the back of the large hall, even though he spoke in an ordinary conversational tone. I also realized that he was employing very few gestures to reinforce his words, in fact hardly moving at all once he reached center stage. I had noticed these things the first time I had seen him, I now realized; but they had not made an impression, probably because my mind had been firmly set on my upcoming interview with my then merely prospective employer.

A few minutes into the "Jumping Frog" story with which he began his talk, I also realized that, while his delivery had all the symptoms of a spur-of-the-moment monologue, with him in jumping from one subject to the next as if at the caprice of a moment, his talk was in fact almost word for word the same as the first time I had seen it. So he had obviously memorized it; and, almost as if by clockwork, this audience laughed at the same moments as the first one had in his retelling of the same absurd incidents. And so it went again: for nearly two hours, he put forward the most absurd fabrications I have ever heard from one man's mouth. I suddenly understood that he was deliberately presenting himself as an object of ridicule, the butt of the audience's laughter. My first reaction was pity—to think that a man of his accomplishments, the author of a dozen books, should be reduced to playing the buffoon for money!

But I remembered that, however an audience that had come to see "Mark Twain" might perceive Mr. Clemens, I had no choice but to see him as my employer—even more, as my benefactor. Painful as it might be to see him pander to the laughter of strangers, that indignity was the price he chose to pay to support his family. It was far more disturbing that he apparently intended to confront a cold-blooded killer, thinking himself immune to danger. Well, I decided, I would just have to make certain that I was present when danger appeared. I had not signed on as his bodyguard, but it would ill become a Cabot to shirk the duty of interposing oneself between one's employer and bodily harm, I thought, should it come to that pass. While I was no trained fighter, the playing fields of Yale had been every bit as capable as those of Eton at teaching a fellow to handle himself in a crisis.

Still, I realized, even a strong six-footer such as I might be of little use against an armed man. Far better than confronting the killer (should he actually be stalking Mr. Clemens) would be letting the proper authorities capture the fellow and question him. A pity that my employer seemed to trust the probable killer more than the detective sent to catch him! Worse yet, the detective's hands were tied by his ignorance of our mission in Arkansas, and the possible motives of the man he was seeking. But unless Mr. Clemens decided to share this information with the detective, I knew, it would be a betrayal on my part to do so behind his back. It was with some trepidation that I realized that the only person with a reasonable chance to solve the case was . . . *I.*

Very well, I would just have to do so—and then turn the

scoundrel over to Detective Berrigan before we reached Memphis in something like three weeks' time. I realized it might be embarrassing to my employer were I to solve the mystery he had determined himself to unravel; but my youth, strength, and superior education were undeniable advantages. Besides, protecting him from a murderer was far more important than salvaging his pride. And perhaps, if I were clever enough, I could manipulate the entire affair so that Mr. Clemens believed that he had solved the mystery himself.

I began mentally reviewing the clues: the two notes, the false beard, the murder victim having been in the audience at Mr. Clemens's New York lecture. At that thought, I resolved to examine the audience carefully for familiar faces once the lecture ended. What would be more likely, if someone were stalking Mr. Clemens, than their being here tonight? So wrapped up was I in chains of evidence and possible explanations of the murder, I hardly heard a word of the lecture from then until the lights came up and the audience rose as one to applaud my employer.

I stood up along with them, scanning the audience as it filed out. The first familiar face I saw was Detective Berrigan, who was standing in the side aisle, also watching the crowd. Then I spotted a man I'd noticed on the train from New York, the gray-haired gentleman with the military air. A tall, fashionably dressed woman with striking blonde hair caught my eye as well, but I was forced to avert my gaze when she caught me staring at her. Of the other faces, two looked familiar, but as they were both respectable-looking women of my parents' generation, I decided that neither made a very good murder suspect.

After the hall was empty, I went backstage to find my employer again surrounded by a small crowd outside his dressing room. Berrigan, who had slipped out ahead of me, watched from a short distance. Offstage, Mr. Clemens was more animated, shaking hands with this person and then another as they greeted and congratulated him. I had joined the fringes of the crowd, trying to catch his eye, when I saw his expression change. I followed his gaze to spot a knavish-looking fellow with a thick mop of curly gray hair pouring out from under a broad-brimmed hat. The fellow grinned, then stepped forward and stuck out his hand and said, "Remember me, Sam?"

Mr. Clemens stared at the hand as if it were a loaded gun. "Slippery Ed McPhee," he said. "I wish I could *forget* you."

5

I instantly pushed my way to the front of the group around Mr. Clemens, prepared to take action. My employer had made it clear that he considered McPhee dangerous, and I needed no prompting to recognize a situation that might turn nasty. Out of the corner of my eye, I noticed that Detective Berrigan had also stepped forward to within an easy arm's length of McPhee. So had someone else—a big, rough-looking man from the back of the crowd.

McPhee broke the tension by laughing. "You always *was* a joker, Sam. Damn me if it ain't been nigh on thirty years. Put 'er there, you ol' dog!" And he reached out to grab Mr. Clemens's hand with both of his, forcing a vigorous handshake on him willy-nilly. I could see from my employer's face that he wanted no part of this artificial camaraderie, but as long as both McPhee's hands were engaged, I saw no immediate threat.

Mr. Clemens pulled his hand free, inspecting it as if to count the fingers. "Well, Ed, I haven't seen you since Nevada," he said, looking the fellow up and down. "You left Virginia City pretty fast, if I remember right."

"You sure do," said McPhee, laughing again. "There was a big Texan took exception to some bad luck at cards, and he didn't want to listen to common sense. The scrapes I used to get into in those days! But you left mighty fast yourself, Sam—or so I heard tell. Some story about a duel, wasn't it?"

"True enough, although I got out without fighting the fellow after all," said Mr. Clemens. His expression had softened, and his voice took on the drawling inflections of his stage presentation. "But you're the last person I ever thought to see come to a lecture. What sort of deviltry brings you to Chicago?"

"Business, Sam, business. A man's got to keep hustling, keep moving all the time, if he's going to keep his head above water. But I couldn't resist coming to see you—we got into town last night, and the first thing I saw was a poster for your show. I told my boys, here's a fellow I knew when we was both no more than tadpoles, and now he's rich and famous, and damn me if I'm going to miss seeing him. Ain't that what I said, Billy?" He turned to the rough-looking man I'd noticed moving forward in the crowd; the fellow responded with a wordless nod, smirking at me around a chaw of tobacco.

I'd seen the same expression more than once on the face of fellows across a scrimmage line—sizing me up as an opponent and deciding they could handle me. Billy was perhaps an inch shorter than I, but stockier and a good bit older—probably at least thirty-five. I didn't think he'd have as easy a time of it as he expected; I had the reach on him, and was almost certainly faster. On the other hand, he was unlikely to restrict himself to Marquis of Queensberry rules. One thing for certain: we'd each seen the other move forward, and recognized what it meant. If there was going to be trouble, he and I would be in the thick of it, and on opposite sides.

All that was communicated in a glance; then Detective Berrigan broke into the conversation. "Mr. McPhee, were you by any chance in New York City recently?"

"What are you, a Pinkerton?" said McPhee, eyeing the detective. "Not that it's any of your business, but I've never set foot in the place in my life. And what makes you think you can step up to a total stranger and interrupt a pleasant bit of talk I'm having with my old pal Sam?"

"Perhaps this crowd isn't the best place for us to talk," said Berrigan. He showed his badge. "But we do need to talk, Mr. McPhee."

"I'd like to be in on that talk," said Mr. Clemens. "Come on down to my dressing room, Ed, and we'll do it over a drink. I'll even give the detective a glass, if he'll take it. This is about somebody we both know from the old days."

"I'll be damned," said McPhee. "You know I don't take to policemen, Sam."

"I'd be lying if I told you I much liked them either, Ed. But this fellow's trying to track down somebody we both know, and he thinks that person might be following me. And the sooner he realizes he's barking up the wrong tree, the sooner he's off my back and on his way home to New York City. Besides, I'm working on a book, and need to find out where some of the old-timers are these days. I reckon you know as much about that as anybody I'm likely to meet in Chicago."

"You've got me curious, Sam—somebody we both know, hey? Well, I've got a clear enough alibi, which is never having set foot in Mr. New York Detective's jurisdiction. But I'm here with a couple of boys who work for me; this is Billy Throckmorton, and his brother Al—that's short for Alligator. If you don't mind them sitting in, just to insure that Mr. Detective doesn't try anything unsportsmanlike, I think I'll take you up on that drink, Sam." The big fellow stepped forward, along with another man who bore a distinct family resemblance, though he was a smaller and smoother-looking model. Billy was still grinning malevolently, but his brother looked worried.

"Plenty of room—my secretary will join us too, so that'll be just six. Come along, Cabot!" He dismissed the rest of the crowd with a wave, and the six of us tramped down the hall to his dressing room.

*   *   *

After a bit of maneuvering for seats and fixing of drinks—somewhat to my surprise, the detective did avail himself of Mr. Clemens's hospitality, to the extent of two fingers of whisky—my employer turned to Berrigan. "Why don't I start, and let you ask your questions after these boys know the lay of the land."

The detective nodded. Mr. Clemens still wore the formal black evening dress that was his stage attire. He had remained standing, one hand on the back of his dressing-table chair, while McPhee and the brothers sat in a defensive line on a wide sofa that dominated the room. I had taken a folding chair near the door, while Detective Berrigan leaned against the edge of Mr. Clemens's dressing table and puffed on a battered-looking briar pipe.

"To put it in a nutshell," said my employer, "there's been a murder in New York, and Farmer Jack Hubbard is right in the thick of it. You remember Farmer Jack, don't you, Ed?"

Slouched on a sofa between his two henchmen, and still wearing his hat, McPhee held a match to a nasty-looking cheroot for a moment before answering. "Yeah, Jack and me go back a long ways. Don't tell me he's gone and killed somebody! That don't seem like his style, Sam."

"It doesn't make sense to me, either," said Mr. Clemens. "Jack was always pretty easygoing, even when somebody else might have gotten hot under the collar. But his name's come up in this murder case, and the police have to follow up their clues. When's the last time you saw him, Ed?"

McPhee scratched behind his left ear, meditatively. "Must have been at Richie Clark's funeral—that was in Cincinnati, four, maybe five years ago. Richie owed me three hundred dollars to the day he died—not that I was ever going to see it as long as there was an unopened bottle in the country. A bunch of the regulars was there: Little Wes Horton, and that Italian fellow that the girls all used to like before he got his teeth knocked out—Vinnie something; Charlie Snipes and Heinie Schussler, too. Been a long time since I saw so many of the boys in one place. But Farmer Jack was there. We stayed up all night, playing cards—him losing, as usual—and shooting the breeze about the old riverboat days. Jack was talking about going east to take one last shot at being an actor, and I heard a few weeks later that he'd gone and done it.''

"So you knew he was in New York,'' said Detective Berrigan, perched on the edge of the dressing table.

"Same as I know the president's in Washington, not that I've ever been there, either.'' retorted McPhee.

"If it came down to it, could you prove your where-abouts for the last few days?''

"Well, the clerk in the Windsor Hotel will tell you when me and the boys got there—about five o'clock yesterday. Took the morning train from Cincinnati, which is where I live these days. I suspect I could find a few people who saw me there, if I needed to. This afternoon, me and the boys went to a baseball game—won ten dollars betting against the Cubs. Cap Anson got three hits. What's all this got to do with me? I thought Farmer Jack was your man.''

"Maybe he is and maybe he isn't,'' said Berrigan. "But we have to follow all our clues, and that means talking to anyone we can find who knew him.''

"Seems to me you've come an awful long way for clues to a killin' in New York City,'' said Al Throckmorton, the shorter of the two brothers, speaking for the first time. He had a high-pitched voice, with a drawling accent halfway between western and southern. He was more respectably dressed than his brother Billy, although not by much. Something about his posture suggested that he might be the more dangerous of the two.

Berrigan opened his mouth again, but Mr. Clemens cut him off with a gesture. "Well, boys, the New York police think that Farmer Jack left town and came west, which is why the detective is here. But if you haven't seen him, there's not much else the man needs to know from you, Ed. Tell me, though, who else is still around that Jack might

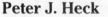
go looking for, if he was on the run? There can't be many of that old crew left.''

McPhee took a sip of his whisky and thought a moment. ''Well, let's see. Little Wes and Heinie settled down. They run a saloon in Cincinnati—nice place if you're ever in town, although neither of them was ever partic'lar friends with Jack. Reds Murphy went west a couple years ago, after he got out of jail—said he was going to open a betting parlor in Frisco, and for all I know, he did. Vinnie the Italian's still playing the game, but he was always mostly a lone hand—never really palled around with the boys. I think he works out of St. Louie nowadays.

''Poor Tom Walker went after a pretty young thing in Louisville, and her old man come looking for him with a Navy revolver. Found him, too. Jury let the old fellow off when it turned out Tom had a derringer in his boot top at the time and somebody swore he made a move for it. Tom was the only man I ever saw give Jack a close run at billiards. I guess that mostly covers it, Sam. If I was making book, I'd figure Jack to head for Cincy. What little's left of the old crowd is mostly down there.''

''Yes, not many of us left,'' said Mr. Clemens. ''I hoped there'd be a few more old river hands I could talk to for my book, and I remember how old Tom played billiards. He managed to get a few dollars out of my pocket before I figured out he was about a couple of thousand miles out of my class. I hear George Devol died, too.''

''So I hear tell, if you can believe the grapevine. About the trickiest man that ever dealt a card. I was sorry to hear about George, if it's the truth. He was a hardheaded old buzzard, but he treated me like I was his own son—taught me all I knew. I try to do the same for these boys—pass on what I've picked up.'' He gestured at the two Throckmorton brothers seated beside him, who seemed not to notice, to judge from their scowls in the direction of Detective Berrigan.

Mr. Clemens rested his chin on his left fist, in much the

pose I'd seen him in on stage, apparently lost in thought for a moment. "I guess that pretty much covers the ground, Ed," he said. McPhee and his cohorts stood up, obviously ready to take their leave. "Oh, one more thing," said Mr. Clemens. "Detective Berrigan has a photograph of the fellow who got killed in New York. Why don't you all take a look at it and see if it's anybody you recognize."

"I don't want to look at no pictures of no dead people," said Billy Throckmorton—he had a deeper voice than his brother, with a more pronounced accent—but by then Detective Berrigan had reached in his pocket and handed the envelope with the photo to Mr. Clemens, who took it out and glanced at it again before passing it over to McPhee.

"Jesus!" McPhee exclaimed, his expression changing. He sat back down, looking almost stunned. "Look here, boys, if this ain't Lee Russell, I'm a goddamn wooden Indian."

"Lee Russell?" said Al and Billy Throckmorton, almost in unison. They joined McPhee on the couch, then Billy took the picture and stared at it. "Yeah, it's him all right," he said, passing it on to his brother. Al took it and nodded, with a grim expression.

"Lee Russell, is it? At last we're making some progress," said Berrigan. "Would you mind telling me anything else you might know about the victim?"

"Can't say as how I know much else about him," said McPhee, regaining his composure somewhat. "He was a cardplayer, a pretty good one. Lee showed up working the trains out of St. Louis a few years ago. Big redheaded fellow, built real solid—and got a good pair of hands on him. He could barely write his own name, but he had a head for the cards. We were on the same circuit, you might say, and we chatted a little about business, mostly names of places to find a game in towns we were going to. He dropped out of sight a couple months ago, now that I think of it—not that I made much of it at the time."

"So you had no idea he'd gone to New York, or what his business there was?" Berrigan had taken out his little notebook and was scribbling in it.

"I can't say we were ever friendly enough for him to tell me where he was going or why," McPhee said. "But I suspect his business was the same in New York as anywhere else—trying to find a card game and make a few bucks."

"Do you have any reason to believe he might have known Jack Hubbard?"

"Well, I did see 'em at the same card table a few times, for what that's worth. It don't mean they were friends or anything. Jack was an old-timer, and Lee was sort of a new man on the scene."

Berrigan looked up from his notebook, scanning the faces of the three men on the sofa. "Either of you other boys remember anything about this Russell character?"

"I seen him a couple of times, is all," said Alligator Throckmorton. "We never talked or nothing." Billy Throckmorton nodded slowly, with a thoughtful expression, then aimed a stream of tobacco juice in the general direction of the spittoon. He missed, then grunted.

"I guess that gives me something to tell the Chief," said Berrigan. "Somebody back in the city may be able to make more of the case, now that we have a confirmed name for the victim. I'm traveling with Mr. Twain, so I won't be in Chicago past tomorrow, but if you think of anything else about Lee Russell or Jack Hubbard, I'm staying at the same hotel as he is—the Great Northern Hotel on Dearborn Street."

Making empty promises to tell the detective anything else they thought of, McPhee and his boys knocked back their drinks and departed, leaving the three of us sitting in the dressing room. Billy Throckmorton favored me with another smirk, as he passed me where I stood by the door.

"Well, well," said Detective Berrigan after they had shuffled out, "as unsavory a bunch of scalawags as ever I saw, and I've seen my share."

"Yes," said Mr. Clemens. "You probably ought to look into their story, on the off chance some of it's true. But don't get your hopes up too high; the name Slippery Ed might be the only thing McPhee's come by honestly since I first met him, and that was before the war.''

Back in the hotel, Mr. Clemens poured himself another drink, while I gazed out the window of his room at the lights of the city below, visible far into the distance despite the soft rain that continued to fall. He settled into an over-stuffed chair and propped his feet up on a hassock. ''Quite a view, isn't it?''

''Remarkable,'' I said. ''To think of the thousands of people out there—and here we are, high above them, look-ing down upon them almost as if they were a colony of insects.''

He laughed. ''Not a bad comparison, Wentworth. I've heard far worse. I once watched an ant climb to the top of a blade of grass, carrying a big dead beetle. I figure it amounted to a man my size taking hold of a railroad car and climbing up a church steeple, then jumping off and climbing up the steeple of the church next door, and think-ing he'd done something to be proud of. Some silly fellow back in Aesop's time decided that ants were a model of industry—and the bulk of the damned human race has been fool enough to believe that ever since.''

''You don't mean to compare all human beings to ants, do you? Even Aesop allowed that some of us might be grasshoppers.''

''Grasshoppers, and crickets, to be sure; they tend to run in my family. I've known the occasional honeybee—my sweet Livy comes to mind. But I've met my share of bed-bugs and termites and boll weevils, and a few bloodsucking mosquitoes, too,'' he said. ''Berrigan might aspire to the dignity of a horsefly. And Slippery Ed McPhee is a one hundred percent pure, guaranteed original, unmitigated humbug.''

''I won't argue with that description. I was surprised that you went so far as to entertain him in your dressing room after all you'd said about him.''

"Oh, that was just the quickest way I could think of to get him to talk. I'd buy the devil himself a glass of whisky if I thought it'd get him to tell me something I needed to know.''

"It certainly was a rare piece of luck that he recognized the murdered man from that picture,'' I said. "It was the last thing I ever expected.''

"I'm not sure I expected it, either—although, looking back on it, I can't say it surprised me. I've seen some damned queer things in my time, queer enough to make me think there's no such thing as a coincidence. You can't believe in coincidences and write novels.''

"Do you think he had anything to do with the murder?''

Mr. Clemens thought a moment. "I doubt he stabbed the fellow himself. Maybe he was capable of it in his younger days, but it stretches credibility a bit too much to think he'd kill a man in New York the day before we leave town, then show up at my lecture in Chicago the day we arrive here. And I don't think he could face down a New York detective quite so smoothly if he'd just run eight hundred miles with blood on his hands. Ed's got a good poker face, but not that good.''

"What do you think he was doing in Chicago, and especially at your lecture, then?''

"Larceny of some kind or another, I'm sure. You don't go in the woods with a gun and a dog unless you're hunting, and you don't walk around with the likes of those Throckmorton boys unless you're planning to get into trouble. Keep your distance from that crew, Wentworth. I saw you move in to protect me, back there in the auditorium, and it made my heart glad to see it—not that I was in much real danger with that many people around, but it's good to know that somebody's looking out for you when things get chancy.

"But you watch out for those Throckmorton brothers. I mean it, Wentworth. There's no such thing as a fair fight with the likes of them. I'll bet you fifty dollars American money to a plugged Mexican peso that Alligator Throckmorton carries a knife. You're likely to find him whittling away at your back while you're trying to stop his big brother from biting your nose off. He'd do it, too—bite it off before you could cry foul. I've seen backwoods boys like that; grew up with them in Missouri, saw them in Nevada and San Francisco, too. They'd like nothing better than to take apart an eastern dandy like you, just for the pure sport of it, and that'd leave me with a secretary I had to carry around in a bushel basket.''

I nodded. ''I'm certainly not looking for any fights, Mr. Clemens. But I don't imagine it's likely we'll see them again. We leave town tomorrow morning, after all.''

He shook his head slowly. ''I hope you're right about that, Wentworth. But Slippery Ed and his like thrive on a big crowd—it's the next thing to heaven for pickpockets, confidence men, cardsharps, and other such two-legged vermin. And the one thing he can be sure of if he follows me is a crowd; a new one in every town, fresh suckers to be robbed. It's like vultures following an army. I thought I had enough trouble with that damned Berrigan. But by jumping Jesus, Wentworth, the time may come when I'm actually glad to have a detective on my tail.''

6

The next morning was Sunday, and I woke to the sound of rain. My watch read 8:20. I put my head under the pillow and dozed a while longer, then roused myself enough to bathe, shave, and dress. A glance out the curtained window revealed a steady drizzle. Hearing no sound through the adjoining door to Mr. Clemens's room, I wandered down to the dining room and breakfasted on coffee and sweet rolls, then (mindful of a promise made to my mother) headed for the hotel desk to determine if there was a church within walking distance.

"I beg your pardon, young man," came an unfamiliar voice at my elbow. I turned to see the tall, gray-haired gentleman I had noticed on the train from New York and again at Mr. Clemens's lecture the previous evening. He gave a little bow and said, "Please forgive the intrusion, but I believe you are traveling with Mr. Mark Twain?" His voice was deep and resonant, in keeping with his exemplary posture and slightly old-fashioned dress, vaguely military in its cut.

"Why, yes," I said, "I am his secretary. And to whom do I have the honor . . . ?"

"Major Roy Demayne, formerly of the Twenty-fifth New Jersey, sir." He gave another little bow. "It is I who will have the honor, in that I am to be one of the passengers on the literary Mississippi river cruise which Mr. Twain will be conducting."

"Ah, I am not surprised. I saw you on the train, and then again at Mr. Clemens's lecture last night. How can I be of service?"

"Well," he said, spreading his hands. "I don't mean to impose, especially on someone as busy as Mr. Twain—and I'm sure his secretary is no less busy. But I myself am an author, a poet to be precise, and I need the advice of an experienced literary man. As I am sure you know all too well, even an intimate familiarity with the muse does not guarantee one's ability to navigate safely through the pitfalls of publication. But I understand that Mr. Twain, in consequence of his stature as one of the foremost literary lights of the age, is familiar with all the publishers on both sides of the Atlantic."

"That may well be," I said. "But I'm afraid I've been with Mr. Clemens—Mr. Twain—only a short while, and I am not yet completely familiar with his affairs. I am sure that he is well acquainted with the leading publishers, but I don't know how *I* can help you."

"Well," he said again, with the same gesture. "I'm not sure this is within your purview, but I believe that a tête à tête with your employer might be of the utmost value in opening doors at the publishers. I have with me samples of my work, including selections from my heroic epic on several sanguinary engagements of the late war, in which it was my honor to lead men into battle in the service of the Union."

"Indeed, sir," I said, my interest piqued. "Which battles were you in?" I had always half regretted being born in peaceful times, when society showered its rewards upon the cautious and the reliable rather than the brave and adventuresome. The ritual combats of the football field were but tame substitutes for what men of the previous generation had seen at first hand.

"Well," said Major Demayne, rubbing his lower lip, "we fought the Secesh all up and down the country, from First Bull Run to the Peninsular campaign. We weren't always in the thick of it, but we were always mighty close to it. Some good men didn't come home to tell about it.''

He shook his head pensively. ''I have taken it upon myself to erect some small memorial in verse to their great patriotic sacrifice. I thought that perhaps Mr. Twain could spare the time to offer some words of advice to a fellow author.''

''Perhaps he could, although I really don't know whether he has any interest in verse.''

''Why, surely he does; he has even included original verse in some of his novels. But perhaps it would be presumptuous for an amateur such as myself to impose on a man of his accomplishment. His free time is undoubtedly precious. That is why I approached you, Mr. . . . your pardon, I don't believe I caught the name.''

I laughed and introduced myself, and we shook hands. ''I'm afraid I can't make promises for Mr. Clemens's free time today or tomorrow; we'll be traveling to St. Paul to board the steamboat. I assume you're on the same timetable, since you're traveling downriver with us. But perhaps once we're on the boat, and things have settled down, he'll have time to talk with you. I suspect there'll be more than one aspiring writer with us—I'm planning to become a travel writer myself.''

Major Demayne's face lit up like a freshly ignited gas lamp. ''Ah, a fellow supplicant to the muse! You know, Mr. Cabot, I have often felt that prose is but a shoddy medium for the depiction of the marvels one sees in traveling. Give me Lord Byron, or someone equally inspired, for mountains or the sea! These modern fellows could learn something about turning a verse from him, or from Sir Walter Scott, you know.''

''Yes, I suppose they could,'' I said. Not entirely certain I could recite a single line of either Byron or Scott, I was in no position to say much more; but the Major paid me no heed and continued with a full head of enthusiasm.

''I call to mind a passage in my canto on the great Battle

of Antietam—which the rebs called Sharpsburg, after the town—that shows what a well-conceived metaphor can do for an ordinary scene. If you can spare a moment, I believe I have it with me.'' He reached into his breast pocket and extracted a thick sheaf of papers, which he tucked under his arm while he fished in the opposite pocket for a pair of spectacles. Then he propped the glasses on the end of his nose and began leafing through his papers.

I had my mouth open to plead other engagements—true enough, if I intended to make my appearance in church this morning—when he glanced over my shoulder and folded his manuscript. ''Well, perhaps this isn't the time or place for a reading. But remind me to show you my verses when we are aboard the *Horace Greeley*, Mr. Cabot—and perhaps then I can impose on you to introduce me to Mr. Twain. A pleasure making your acquaintance.'' He gave one of his little bows, turned on his heel, and walked quickly away.

Before I had time for any thought other than general puzzlement, a familiar voice came from behind me. ''Well, Mr. Cabot, how are we this morning? Any sign of Mr. Twain?''

I turned to see Detective Berrigan, who, from the look of him, had just come in from the rain.

''I haven't seen him yet,'' I replied. ''You seem to have been up and about early this morning.''

''Aye, that I have. I walked up to the cathedral on Superior Street for early mass—a bit farther than I'd wanted to travel in this weather, but that's neither here nor there. On the way back, though, I came past the Windsor Hotel and decided to step out of the rain a moment, and incidentally to ask a few questions of the clerk and the bellboy.''

''And did you discover anything of interest?''

Berrigan smiled. ''Now, would I be telling you all about it if I hadn't? But rather than recount my story twice, why don't we see if Mr. Twain is up and about, especially since it concerns his dear old friends from the river.''

*   *   *

Mr. Clemens answered our knock, dressed in another of his white suits. "Hello, Cabot—and Berrigan. What the blazes are you two up to this early? Have you both been to church?"

"Yes, and another place, too," said Berrigan, saving me from admitting to my employer that I had neglected that duty.

"Well, you'd better come in and tell me the story, whatever it is. There can't be too many other places of interest open on a Sunday morning, at least in this part of town."

After hanging his damp raincoat and derby hat in the hall closet, Detective Berrigan settled into an armchair opposite Mr. Clemens and lit up his pipe. "I took the opportunity, returning from mass this morning, to drop by the Windsor Hotel. You may recall that's where McPhee said he and his boys are staying."

"Yes, he made a point of mentioning it. Do you mean to tell me they aren't there?" Mr. Clemens leaned forward in his chair.

"Oh, they're there all right—I spotted the back of McPhee's head through the dining room door, so there's no disputing that. But the interesting thing is that they didn't all arrive together. First two of them came and reserved a room, and then the next day, the other two joined them."

"Other *two?*" Mr. Clemens and I said it almost together. He looked at me and laughed, then looked at Berrigan. "Slippery Ed, and a pair of Throckmortons, and who else?"

"Well, I shouldn't get too far ahead of myself," said the detective, fiddling with his pipe. "The bellboy is the only one who's seen all four of them; the desk clerk only saw the first two. And he said they were a big fellow and a little one, sort of rough-looking, whom I think we can identify— they checked in before dinnertime on Friday, just as McPhee claimed, and carried their own bags, which were pretty shabby-looking, the boy said, annoyed as he was to miss the tip. Then about noon yesterday, the bellboy saw the Throckmortons come in again, with an older fellow with long hair and a big hat—that's got to be McPhee— and another man. McPhee and the other man both carried their own bags—they looked to be traveling very light, the boy said, one bag apiece. They went out again about an hour later.''

"Any idea who the other man was?"

"The boy described him as older than the Throckmortons, and heavyset, with a country accent and a big beard.''

"Damnation!" said Mr. Clemens. "You don't suppose it's Jack Hubbard. That would be almost too easy.''

"Well, I didn't lay eyes on the rascal myself—McPhee was eating alone—not that it'd do me much good, never having seen this Hubbard fellow.''

"If he's wearing his old disguise again, I'll recognize him in a flash. I wonder if I can manage to get a peek at him." Mr. Clemens stared out the window at the rain. "I can't just sit in a corner of the lobby—they'd spot me ten miles off. There was a time when people didn't know my face, but I'm sorry to admit that's long past.''

"You'd never see hide nor hair of him, if he didn't want you to," the detective agreed. "Of course, it may be someone else entirely. But the interesting thing is that McPhee lied about his having been in the hotel on Friday night. Unless he can prove he was somewhere else in Chicago, his alibi won't wash. And why would he lie to me unless he had something to hide?''

"Slippery Ed would lie just to pass the time of day,'' said Mr. Clemens. "It's a habit with him, like spitting or scratching himself. But you're right about his alibi—it's up in smoke. And if he's with Jack Hubbard, he's smack in the middle of your murder case. Damn it all, Berrigan, I don't like this one bit.''

"Nor do I," said Berrigan. "The best thing I can think of is to settle myself down in the lobby of the Windsor, to see if I can catch a glimpse of this fourth fellow before we leave for St. Paul. Then, at least, I may be able to give you a firsthand description once we're on the train; if you think it's Hubbard, I'll see if the Chicago police will pick him up for questioning. And if I were you, I'd lay low until it's time to board the train—just in case somebody gets funny ideas.''

Mr. Clemens gestured toward the window, where the rain continued to fall. "What choice do I have, with this weather? The only good likely to come of it is that it'll keep McPhee from wandering around looking for mischief. That's the single really admirable thing about him: he's too lazy to go out in the rain, at least as long as there's somebody to be swindled indoors—and there usually is.''

I never did get to church, and the rest of the day passed very much in the manner of a rainy Sunday anywhere. Mr. Clemens spent the afternoon lying in bed smoking, reading, and jotting down notes for his book. Before supper, I arranged for our luggage to be delivered to the station, and we had our meals sent up to his room. He grumbled a bit about being "shut in," but went at his meal with a hearty enough appetite, and seemed content to be spending a comparatively uneventful day before getting down to the tour itself, when he would have to deliver a lecture almost every evening for several weeks—a schedule he admitted to me that he dreaded.

We took a cab to the Canal Street Union Station, where we boarded the Chicago, Milwaukee, and St. Paul overnight mail train at 8:00. After stowing our carpetbags in our sleepers, we retired to the smoking car to await Detective Berrigan's report on his Windsor expedition. Mr. Clemens had barely begun to clip the end of a cigar when the detective entered the car.

"Well, how was the fishing?" said Mr. Clemens as Berrigan sat down across from us.

Berrigan frowned for a moment, scraping at the bowl of

his pipe, then looked up and smiled. "Oho, my little visit to the Windsor, you mean. Well, for a while I thought it was going to be a wasted afternoon. When I arrived, I asked the clerk whether Mr. McPhee was in, and he allowed as how that party had gone out a short while before—hadn't checked out, just left in a group. I figured they'd be back soon enough, with the weather and all, so I settled down where I'd have a good view of the lobby. Good thing I had your book along—it was six o'clock before they got back, and then only two of them."

"Which two?" I asked.

"The Throckmortons, and I could tell as soon as they came in they were in a hurry. They went straight upstairs, and were back again in less than ten minutes, with the luggage. *All* the luggage—the bellboy told me that, after they'd left. He also told me they'd come in a cab, and had it wait while they went upstairs."

"Listen to this story, Wentworth, and remember to tip all bellmen and porters," Mr. Clemens said. "If McPhee had spent fifty cents two days ago, the fellow's lips would've been sealed."

"Well, I can't say I disagree," said Berrigan; having apparently scraped the pipe sufficiently, he pulled out his tobacco pouch. "Of course, the story I told him might've been an influence. Once I'd informed the young lad that the four tightwads were planning to waylay and rob Mr. Mark Twain, he was cooperation personified. He was the one that told me where they'd gone when they left, too— he heard them tell the hack driver to take them to the train station on Harrison Street—the Grand Central, just like New York's. They were in a hurry, too."

"Grand Central—some of the western trains leave from there," I said, recalling my frantic study of Mr. Clemens's lecture route before our departure.

"Good guess, son," said Detective Berrigan. He paused a moment to light his pipe. "I got a cab no more than two minutes after them, and went straight to Grand Central.

Sure enough, I was in time to see them board a train, along with Mr. McPhee—and someone else.''

"And what did he look like?'' Mr. Clemens leaned forward, with an animated expression.

"Well, there's the devil of it,'' said Berrigan. "It was a woman they were with.''

"A woman!'' There was a moment of stunned silence as Mr. Clemens tried to comprehend this revelation—I am certain I had no idea what to make of it. "Are you sure she was with them? What about the bearded man?''

"Well, Billy Throckmorton carried her bag, unless his taste in luggage is fancier than in clothes; and McPhee gave her a hand as she mounted the step. She was with 'em all right. And there was nobody else with 'em that I saw.''

"Damnation,'' said Mr. Clemens. "You can paint me blue if this doesn't blow all my ideas right up the chimney. I wish I'd been there to get a look at them!''

"Well, I don't think you'll have to worry about that,'' said Berrigan. "That was the one other thing I learned. Our friends boarded the six twenty-eight Wisconsin Central, bound for Fond du Lac, Oshkosh, Chippewa Falls, and St. Paul—the same place we're going. I think we'll be seeing them again.''

We had sat absorbing this information for several moments when the car door opened and Major Demayne made his way down the aisle, nodding in our direction as he noticed us and hurrying along in the direction of the coaches. "Who was that old fellow?'' said Berrigan. "I saw you talking with him this morning.''

"Oh, yes, I forgot him entirely,'' I said. "His name is Major Demayne—he's going to be one of the passengers on the riverboat. He told me he's interested in poetry, and he's written a poem about the Civil War. He'd seen me with Mr. Clemens, and he was asking about publishers.''

"The hell you say!'' Mr. Clemens virtually exploded. "I should have known it. The wretched boat will be so full of literary amateurs it's even money to sink before we're out of Minnesota, with every blasted one of them hauling a trunkful of unpublishable manuscripts—novels without a plot, soporific sermons, and improving essays dense enough to make a bishop sick. And *poetry!* I'd rather be locked in a tiger cage than sit through another amateur poet reading me the ungrammatical nonsense that passes for poetry these days!

"Cabot, it'll be worth your neck if that man reads me one single line of poetry. Keep him away from me—I'll eat a skunk for breakfast before I listen to his stuff."

"But sir—" I began to protest. The Major was, after all, one of the paying customers who made the lecture tour possible, and I figured he might even be talented.

Mr. Clemens shook his head vigorously. "No buts about it. I've got enough to worry about with Farmer Jack and Slippery Ed, let alone giving a lecture every night. If that fellow comes within ten feet of me with a piece of paper in his hand, I'll pitch him overboard. And if you're any-where within sight, you'll follow him directly, or my name isn't Samuel L. Clemens."

≈ 7

I rose early the next morning, so as not to miss my first sight of the Mississippi River, which our train was scheduled to reach after stopping at La Crosse, Wisconsin. Mr. Clemens was in much better spirits than the night before, joking and pointing out the passing scenery with an animated expression. Breakfast had been eaten, the waiter had been paid, and a tip had been placed on the table. I was taking my time in finishing my second cup of coffee, while admiring the Wisconsin woodlands, when Mr. Clemens did a quick reconnaissance of the dining car. Satisfied that nobody was paying attention to our conversation, he leaned toward me and said in a low voice, "What do you think of Berrigan's story from yesterday?"

"I must say I'm entirely confounded by it," I replied. "First we hear that McPhee is with a man who resembles Farmer Jack Hubbard, then he boards the train in the company of a woman. He apparently lied about his arrival time at the hotel, then left town—in something of a hurry—on a train that terminates in St. Paul. I think it's a good bet he's following us."

"Well, if you can follow somebody from in front—his train is probably an hour or more ahead of us. But yes, I think our detective's right about that—we'll most likely see McPhee and his boys again in St. Paul, if not all the way down the dratted river."

An intriguing notion came to me. "You say Hubbard is

a talented actor—could it be that he's disguised himself as a woman? That would explain a great deal.''

Mr. Clemens shook his head. "I wish it were that simple. A man the size of Jack Hubbard can't just put a dress on and pass for a woman. He'd stick out like a bobcat in a birdcage. A child could spot him from a mile off—let alone somebody like Berrigan, who's suspicious by profession. No, the woman's probably exactly the sort of person one would expect to be traveling with those scoundrels, nothing more or less.

"As for Farmer Jack, I'd guess that he followed us from New York to Chicago, where Slippery Ed met him and put him up; these old river rats *do* stick together. Then, after Ed talked to us and found out we were hauling along a New York cop, he warned Jack to steer clear. If Jack has any sense, he took the first train leaving Chicago for anyplace *except* St. Paul."

"Cincinnati, perhaps—some of his friends would appear to be there."

"That's what Slippery Ed wants us to think—he mentioned Cincinnati a bit too often and too pointedly for it to be entirely credible. But I wouldn't bet against Jack heading for some river town where he can join up with our boat, if he's so inclined. After what we've learned, I think he's *very* inclined; in fact, I'll be surprised if we don't see Farmer Jack Hubbard in St. Louis, or Cairo—maybe as far down as Memphis. But there's something that worries me even more than that about Berrigan's story."

"What on earth could that be?"

Mr. Clemens glanced around us—the nearby tables were empty, but he lowered his voice even more. "Remember what he told the bellboy? That four men were going to kidnap and rob Mark Twain?"

"Lord, yes," I said, glancing around the dining car in my own turn. "Do you think there's any truth to what he said?"

"I have to consider it a strong likelihood, until

something proves otherwise; if Ed and his boys are in business with Hubbard, they may all know about our Arkansas expedition. But how does Berrigan know that's what they're up to? It's too close to the truth to be just a lucky guess. And if that damned detective has figured out that we're looking for the 'Napoleon' treasure, who the devil else has figured out the same thing?''

The train had begun to slow down as it entered the outskirts of La Crosse, a good-sized, modern city with numerous lumberyards visible from the track. At my employer's suggestion, we quickly got up and moved to the smoking car, before the station stop crowded the aisles with boarding and debarking passengers. We found a pair of seats with a good view out the window on the right side of the car, in anticipation of the river crossing. The previous day's rain having lifted, I anticipated a fine first view of the Mississippi.

Much to my surprise, the mighty river of which I had heard so many stories was barely as wide as the streams with which I was familiar back east. Mr. Clemens must have seen something in my expression, for he asked, ''What do you think, Wentworth?''

''I must say I expected something more impressive, from the stories I'd heard. Why, this can't be more than a couple of hundred yards across. It's certainly nowhere near as broad as the Hudson River where we crossed it in New York. For that matter, the Thames back home in New London, right at the end of our street, puts it to shame.''

Mr. Clemens laughed. ''Yes, and your father's the strongest man in the world, and your mother the prettiest woman. The river's barely started on its way here, even if it is a good five hundred miles from the source already. The one constant about the river is change; that wagon bridge is new since I last came through here in '82, just for one example. And the river changes as much between here and St. Louis as you have from ten years old to now. It'll change as much again before Memphis, and again by New Orleans. You'll get to see that better than most. But don't deprive yourself of the pleasure of really seeing it—not just as a stream of water, but with all the history and legendry that's attached to it. You really ought to borrow my book from Berrigan and read it.''

''But sir, I have you here to tell it all to me,'' I said, smiling. He was right, though—as an aspiring travel writer, I realized, I should keep a sharp eye on everything I saw. And I had let my journal-writing slide—I knew I should be keeping a careful record of my observations, notes for possible articles and books.

''I knew I liked you for some reason, Wentworth,'' said Mr. Clemens, smiling back. ''But there's only so much you can learn secondhand. If you really want to learn the river, you have to keep your eyes on it, and try to see it for what it is—that's what I had to do as a cub pilot. The Mississippi will speak to you in its own good time, and in its own language. You may not always like what it has to say, but at least you won't confuse the reality of it with the sort of nonsense most travel writers try to foist on the public.''

Obediently, I examined the river more carefully. It was still only about a third of a mile wide, picturesque enough between its wooded banks, but considerably less impressive than the Thames or Hudson. Perhaps I had better borrow Mr. Clemens's book from Berrigan after all, I thought.

''Look, Wentworth, here comes a stern-wheeler downstream.'' He pointed to the north, and sure enough, there came an absolutely unmistakable Mississippi riverboat—gleaming white in the sun, with a flag flying between the twin smokestacks up front and a little pilothouse perched between them, high atop the second deck. It looked much like the picture on the flyers I had seen advertising Mr. Clemens's lecture tour. The boat was making a fair turn of speed, running with the current, and I could see a small crowd gathered on her foredeck. Another knot of people

70 was waiting for her at the town dock in La Crosse, now visible from across the river.

"A steamboat landing used to be the biggest thing in town, back when I was a boy," said Mr. Clemens. "That's changed, too. I expect we had more people on the train platform in La Crosse than I see on the boat and dock together. The boats are still running, and I'm glad of it, Wentworth—but I'm afraid their time is almost over. It'll be a sad day when a generation of children grows up along the river without hearing a steamboat whistle blow, and running like blazes down to the dock to watch the boat come in. Even the yeller dogs and the town drunks used to rouse themselves for that—or they would once a day, anyhow."

"Will the *Horace Greeley* be as big as this one?"

"A bit bigger, I'd think—this one's nothing special. I doubt she even has any staterooms for long-distance passengers. And this one has only three decks—usually there's a fourth, smaller deck called the texas just below the pilothouse. I'd think the *Greeley* would be a good bit larger—the flyer I saw said it has eighty-odd cabins."

"Eighty-four," I said, recalling the figure from my file of information on the trip. "Why do they call it a texas deck? Was it invented there?"

"The story I heard was that one of the old passenger boats—can't recall which one, but it was probably back in the forties, when the boats were fairly small—decided to name a cabin for every state in the Union. That's where the name 'stateroom' comes from, by the way. Anyhow, after they'd named all the cabins on the second, or 'hurricane,' deck, they still had one state to go. So they put one more cabin up on the top deck, and named it after the state that was left over—which happened to be Texas.

"But even the *Greeley* won't hold a candle to some of the old side-wheelers on the lower river—the big New Orleans boats used to run three hundred feet long; the *Grand Republic* topped three-fifty. A boat like that could barely turn around up here. Those boats were practically floating palaces—the *Robert E. Lee* cost a quarter-million dollars to build, back when that was real money! So did the *J.M. White,* and they claim the *Thompson Dean* cost more than that. But the *J.M. White* took the prize for luxury. She had a solid silver water cooler, with silver drinking cups, and the food was out of this world—all you could eat, too. Custom-made French furniture, walnut paneling, Irish linen, stained-glass skylights, a cabin so big they needed twelve chandeliers to light it—they didn't stint on a thing, Wentworth.''

That sounded like the sort of life I'd dreamed of when I'd cast my lot as a writer, instead of drudging away at the law. ''What a shame we can't take our journey downriver on the *J.M. White* instead of the *Greeley,*'' I said. ''That would be a trip well worth writing a book about!''

Mr. Clemens gave me a curious look, then slumped back in his seat. ''Ah, but you wouldn't know, would you. The *J.M. White* burned to the waterline six years ago, down in Louisiana. The owners blamed it on passengers smoking on the engine deck, but there were others who said it was no accident. Twenty-eight aboard her died.'' He shook his head with a rueful expression. ''There'll never be another like her. Fine as she was, though, they say she lost money every trip she made.''

''How dreadful! Are accidents common aboard the riverboats?''

''Not as much now as when I was piloting, but still too common. In the old days, the river was wild—snags and sandbars every ten feet, it seemed. The Army Engineers have cleaned most of that up since the war—a blind man could take the wheel from St. Louis to New Orleans and never once scrape anything that'd hurt his boat. But back when I learned the trade, a pilot had to remember the depth of the river every fifty yards, in high and low water, day and night. He had to know exactly where he was: how far along his route, how far from shore, and exactly what he could expect to find in the water ahead. Sometimes pilots made mistakes, and sometimes the river changed its course overnight. A lot of steamboats got killed by an unexpected change in the river. A lot more got killed by damn-fool human error.

"Especially in the old days, the boilers were barely trustworthy under normal running conditions. A boat that lasted ten years on the river was a marvel of longevity, a Methuselah among steamboats. Too damned many of them didn't make it. They weren't designed to take the punishment they got from a captain trying to make up lost time. Or one who'd run the boilers red hot and tie down the safety valve, trying to set some kind of speed record out of sheer cussed pride. Or who'd patch up something that should by rights have been replaced, hoping to get away with it until he got to the end of his run and collected his pay for the cargo. Sooner or later, it would catch up with him, and usually take innocent people with him when it blew up in his face—or to be strictly accurate, in the poor stokers' faces." He stared out the window for a moment, then continued in a lower voice. "My brother Henry was killed in a steamboat explosion."

"Good Lord!" I had never seen him with such a stricken expression, and could think of nothing appropriate to say. After a moment of awkward silence, I blurted out the first question that came to mind. "How did it happen?"

I immediately regretted my bluntness; Mr. Clemens seemed suddenly older and sadder. But he answered me calmly, not seeming annoyed by my breach of propriety. "It was on the *Pennsylvania*—which I'd worked on as a cub pilot, on her trip downriver. This was in 1858. I'd gotten in a fight with the pilot, a vicious man named Brown, to keep him from attacking Henry after an argument. Brown refused to ship with me again. The captain was ready to fire him and put me on as a full pilot in his place, but I was afraid I didn't know the river well enough. So I stayed ashore in New Orleans, waiting for another boat that

would take me on, while Brown piloted the *Pennsylvania*
to St. Louis. But Henry was only a mud clerk, as we called
it—a general errand boy, just beginning to learn the ropes.
If he'd changed boats, he'd have had to start over from the
bottom, and set himself back two or three months—an eter-
nity for a boy of twenty, which is all he was. And so he
decided to stay with the *Pennsylvania,* and do his best to
keep clear of Brown.

"The *Pennsylvania*'s boilers exploded at Ship Island,
just below Memphis. A hundred and fifty lives were lost;
Henry was thrown clear, and landed in the river. The shore
was within an easy swim, but he turned back to the burning
boat and worked to save as many passengers as he could—
exactly as I had advised him to act in the event of an accident aboard ship. By the time he got ashore again, he was
past help; he lived another week in a hospital in Memphis.
I have always believed he would have lived if he hadn't
gone back again."

"Surely you can't blame yourself for his bravery and
altruism," I told him.

"I don't know," he said. "People have always told me
it was none of my doing, and I can't for the life of me
imagine what I could have done differently that would have
saved him. But I can't escape the damnable voice within
my own breast. It's tortured me for over thirty years, and
I'm afraid it will torture me until my dying day." And with
that, he turned his gaze out the train window upon the river,
and we passed the rest of the journey up to St. Paul in
silence. I suppose it is just as well that the scenery along
that stretch of the river was unusually picturesque.

At last we crossed over the river again, and came into
the Union Depot in St. Paul, a thriving city—especially in
conjunction with its "twin," Minneapolis, some ten miles
upstream. Mr. Clemens pointed out several buildings that
had not been there on his previous visit over ten years ago.
He told me that Minneapolis and St. Paul are rapidly ex-

panding toward one another and can be expected to merge into a single large city if the growth continues. What the eventual name of the combined metropolis ought to be is a perennial subject of half-serious rivalry between the two cities, each representing itself as the only true center of civilization and industry in Minnesota.

The railroad station in St. Paul is quite large, and is located a short distance from the banks of the Mississippi, convenient to the steamboat landing. When we alighted from the train, Mr. Clemens decided to see if he could place a long-distance telephone call to New York from the train station, and left me to supervise the transfer of our baggage to the *Horace Greeley,* the riverboat on which we were to continue our journey down to New Orleans. I rounded up a husky colored porter who put our bags on his cart, and followed him down to the docks to look for our boat.

After Mr. Clemens's description, I expected the *Horace Greeley* to be the largest and most elaborate of the half-dozen boats tied up along the landing. Our plan was to stop at a number of towns along the river for lectures, so none of the regular steamboats, which had to keep to a schedule, would have been suitable. Also, different companies provided steamboat service in the various sections of the river, which forced most passengers traveling from St. Paul to New Orleans by boat to change boats in St. Louis. Nor would the usual run of boats be set up for lectures on board ship, as my employer planned for the smaller towns with no lecture hall of their own. So Mr. Clemens's backers had chartered the *Horace Greeley* for the entire length of the river.

As we approached the riverside, I picked out at first one, then another of the vessels tied at the dock as the boat on which we were to take our voyage. My excitement took a decided plunge when the porter finally stopped his cart among a small crowd gathered by the gangplank of the *Horace Greeley.* Granted, it had a fresh-looking coat of white paint, as well as some recently touched up gilt metalwork; and I readily identified the "texas" deck, the lack of which Mr. Clemens had noted on the boat we had seen docking at La Crosse. But the *Greeley* was no larger than the boats on either side of it: the one a regular St. Louis packet of the Diamond Jo Line, the other a freighter being loaded with hardwood lumber for some destination downriver. After Mr. Clemens's glowing portrait of the floating palaces of earlier days, I felt somewhat let down by the rather ordinary vessel we were about to board.

I had barely completed my cursory dockside inspection of our boat when a heavy hand fell on my shoulder and an uncultured voice drawled, "Well, look who's here." I turned around to see Billy Throckmorton's smirking face; his smaller brother Alligator was just behind him.

"Mr. Throckmorton," I said, trying to keep my voice and expression neutral. "What can I do for you?"

"*Mister* Throckmorton, is it?" He laughed, a bit too loudly. "Hell, I ain't never been called 'Mister' Throckmorton before. I must be comin' up in the world, hey, Al? Mr. Fancy City Boy must know quality when he sees it."

"My name is Wentworth Cabot," I said, looking for some way to walk away from the confrontation. The baggage cart blocked me to the left, and the river's edge was behind me; slowly, as if in a bad dream, I saw the smaller Throckmorton brother moving to my right, as if to cut off my escape. "What can I do for you?" I repeated.

"That's a funny name," said Billy Throckmorton. "Ain't Worth Cabbage—that must be a pretty city-boy name, hey, Al?" His brother giggled, but said nothing.

"Excuse me," I said, "but I really have no time for talk. If you have no other business, I must take care of my baggage."

"Ain't Worth Cabbage don't want to talk," Billy Throckmorton said. "I reckon we ain't good enough to talk to the city boy. He's a pretty boy." Then he capped the rhyme with a third variation too coarse to repeat, leering all the while.

"Sir, I advise you to be more civil," I began, but Throckmorton stepped closer and took up a mocking chant: "City boy—pretty boy—****** boy."

It was obvious that the fellow was looking for a fight, and I decided it was wisest to make good my escape before he struck the first blow. I looked to my right again; his brother was no longer in sight, and I was preparing to make a dash in that direction when Billy Throckmorton pushed me hard in the chest with both hands. As I stepped involuntarily back, I tripped over something soft behind my legs and started to topple.

In a flash I realized that Alligator Throckmorton had gone down on all fours directly behind me, to trip me when his brother pushed me—an old schoolyard bully's trick—but it was already too late to do anything about it. It was too late to do anything but watch Billy Throckmorton's apelike grin as I fell helplessly backward into the Mississippi River.

8

I landed flat on my back in the river after a short fall, and went under. Bringing myself to the surface with a quick scissor kick, I spent a few moments spitting out water and shaking my head to clear my eyes. I found myself between two steamboats, facing a sheer embankment—which was perhaps four feet high, just a bit more than I could easily scale. I treaded water looking for the best way to extricate myself without more interference from the Throckmorton brothers.

Before I had time to make more than a quick survey of my situation, I heard a shout of "Here, young feller!" from the bank above, and saw a long arm reach toward me. I swam to it, glancing up to make sure I wasn't setting myself up for another trick, but the face looking down over the edge was that of the colored porter I had engaged to transport the luggage to the steamboat. I took the proffered hand, and at the same time someone else reached a strong arm down to assist me. A moment later I was standing on the bank, between the porter and another man—this one of average height, with a black goatee and a dark blue uniform. He looked familiar, although I couldn't place him at the moment.

I looked around to see what had become of the Throckmortons, and was surprised to see them in full flight, being pursued by a slim figure vigorously brandishing a cane. "You miscreant dogs! Come back and take your medicine,

78   you cowards!'' It was Major Demayne, showing a turn of speed that would have done credit to a man half his age. Either of the Throckmorton brothers might have been a match for him, cane and all, had they stood their ground. But the two bullies clearly wanted nothing to do with the incensed major, and ran from him as if swarms of angry hornets were pursuing them, instead of one aging man with a cane.

"Are you all right, mister?'' The porter looked at me with a concerned expression, and I nodded. "Just wet,'' I said. "I've been overboard before, and never took any hurt from it. Thanks for the hand, though.''

"We'd best get you out of them clothes,'' said the other man who'd helped him pull me out. He handed me my hat, which had miraculously fallen on dry land. "Are you coming on board the *Horace?*'' he asked.

"I've a ticket for the *Horace Greeley;* I'm traveling with Mr. Clemens.'' I groped in my pockets, wondering if my ticket was ruined by the water.

"Oho, you'll be Mr. Cabot, his secretary? I'm Charlie Snipes, chief clerk of the *Horace*. Your cabin is at the aft end of the texas, right next to your boss's. Go on up and dry off—I'll have a boy fetch you an extra towel from the barbershop—and tell me which of those bags will have a dry suit for you. I'll have it brought up to you directly. The porter can load the rest of them, and I'll see that he gets a good tip for his work.''

By this time, Major Demayne had returned, puffing a bit after his pursuit of the Throckmortons. "Dad-burn those rascals,'' he growled. "I wish I had me a good horsewhip—I'd teach them civilized manners! Are you hurt, sir?''

"Not at all, thanks to these two men—and to you, Major. I must say I didn't expect to find so many stout defenders so far from home. But I think I'd better get to my cabin and get into dry clothes.''

"Aye, that you'd better, and when you're changed, I'd

suggest a glass of something to warm up your blood,'' said Snipes. He turned to a young boy on deck, who was leaning over the rail and gawking at the scene on shore. ''Tommy! Show Mr. Cabot here to his cabin, and be quick about it for once!''

I made my way up the gangplank and on board the *Horace Greeley*. It was a long way up from there to the texas deck. I dripped a trail of water at every step, and my wet shoes made a squishing sound. I was never so glad as when my dry clothes arrived.

I had just gotten my dry collar buttoned when a knock came on my cabin door. I opened it to find Mr. Clemens outside. He smiled and said, ''Tarnation, Wentworth, when I told you to study the river, I didn't expect you to immerse yourself so thoroughly in the subject.''

''Given my choice, sir, I should not have chosen the Throckmorton brothers as my tutors. Am I to take this as a typical specimen of western manners?''

''Well, only if you can call the complete absence of the thing a typical example of it. Those Throckmorton boys have about as much to do with manners as a jackrabbit has to do with playing the violin. But if you'll finish dressing and come with me to meet the captain, I think you'll get a notion of hospitality more to your taste. Mike Fowler's an old crony of mine, and he's mighty disturbed to have one of his passengers pitched overboard.''

Mr. Clemens waited while I finished dressing, and I followed him to Captain Fowler's quarters, which were located at the forward end of the texas. As we entered, a blocky fellow with iron-gray muttonchop whiskers jumped to his feet and shook my hand with a firm grip. He stood only about as high as my chin, but his gold-trimmed uniform gave him as much dignity as he could have gotten from a foot of additional height. I recognized him as one of the two nautical-looking men I had seen at Mr. Clemens's lecture in New York. ''Welcome aboard, Mr. Ca-

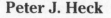

bot,'' he said. ''I hear you was treated pretty rough by those scalawags on shore; I hope you didn't get hurt too bad.''

''Nothing I couldn't cure by changing clothes, Captain. Your boy took them to be cleaned and ironed for me, so I'm sure they'll be as good as new.''

''Good, good. Can I offer you a little something to get the blood flowing again? You'll pardon me if I don't join you, as I've got a full day of work ahead of me. But I can have anything you'd like brought up from the bar.''

''Thank you, sir, a cup of hot tea would go nicely. I think it's a bit early for anything stronger.''

The captain nodded. ''That's easy enough to do—in fact, I *will* join you in that. Sam, what can I get for you?'' Mr. Clemens ordered coffee, and the texas tender—the same servant who had brought me my clean clothes—was dispatched to fetch our drinks.

Captain Fowler motioned us to a pair of comfortable-looking, albeit well broken in, chairs. Mr. Clemens and I had hardly settled ourselves into them when we heard the sound of raised voices, followed by a loud knock on the forward door of the cabin. ''What on earth . . . ,'' the captain began, but before he could finish, the door burst open and Slippery Ed McPhee marched in, followed by a visibly agitated Chief Clerk Snipes.

''I'm sorry, Cap'n—'' said Snipes, but McPhee cut him off.

''Cap'n Mike, I want to know why this damn backstabbing ingrate of a clerk thinks he can throw paying customers off the boat without a chance to say a word for theirself. I paid for my ticket in cash money, and I got as much right to ride as the next man. 'Sides, it wasn't any of my doing that Billy and Al pushed that young feller in the drink. Sam, I'm glad to see you and your boy here—maybe the bunch of us can settle this without no more nonsense from the likes of this dressed-up monkey.''

The captain stood up to his full height and stared McPhee directly in the eye. ''Ed McPhee, I'll ask you to be more respectful of Mr. Snipes, if you want any consideration from *me*. You might think about apologizing to Mr. Cabot here, while you're at it—it was your two roughnecks threw him overboard, and they didn't give *him* no kind of show.''

"Hold on, now, Cap'n Mike, it weren't nothing to get upset about—nothing but high spirits," said McPhee, only a little chastened. "Those boys may horse around sometimes, but it's all in good nature. You used to be a hell-raiser yourself, Sam; you can understand what I mean. I sure hope your Mr. Cabot didn't take it wrong."

"Mr. McPhee, they gave me very little choice what way to take it," I said, not at all satisfied with the fellow's notion of an apology.

"Ed, that won't wash," said Mr. Clemens with a serious expression. "I've been in my share of trouble, and so has Mike Fowler, and I suspect even Cabot here has raised a little hell when he didn't think anybody was looking. But it sounds to me as if your boys came looking for trouble, and went after the first easy target they spotted, a fellow who was minding his own business—which just happened to be my business, too. That doesn't fall under my idea of good fun and good nature."

"That's right, Cap'n," chimed in Chief Snipes. "I was right there, and saw it all. This young gentleman didn't say one cross word; he was looking to walk away, and that big fellow went and pushed him straight overboard. Cap'n, we've got a boatful of high-class folks, some of 'em all the way from New York and Boston. Those Throckmortons would be like boar hogs in a lady's parlor. It'd be just like 'em to go pouring drinks down ladies' dresses, or knocking gentlemen's hats off for a lark. We'd never get another fancy trip like this, once the quality went back east and told what kind of tomfoolery went on."

The captain took his hat off and mopped his bald head with a bright red handkerchief, a troubled look on his face. "Mr. Snipes has a point, Ed," he finally said. "This trip may be my last good chance to keep my boat running. It's too important to let it get ruined by a couple of backwoods rowdies who think it's fun to aggravate their betters. I may not know a whole lot about what the genteel folks from back east like, but I'm pretty sure that throwing innocent folks overboard ain't to their taste—or *mine*, neither, Ed McPhee.''

''I can see I'm outnumbered,'' said McPhee. ''I bought a ticket on this cruise in good faith, thinking I was dealing with honorable men, or old friends at the very least, instead of a reneging chief clerk who takes a man's money and then turns him away. All I wanted was to take one last steamboat ride before my time is up. But I'm not just traveling for pleasure, gentlemen. As it happens, I'm bound for Baton Rouge, to visit my ailing mother—she wrote a letter begging to see her boy one last time, and I could tell from her handwriting that it *would* be the last time.''

''If you're in such a hurry to see her, why not take the train?'' asked the captain.

''Because I love this river, Mike—you know how it gets in your blood. When I heard you was going to be running this trip, and that good old Sam was going to be on board to lecture, I thought it would be a fine chance to travel with some of the old-timers again—share a few laughs, yes, and shed a tear as well, thinking of them what's gone on ahead of us to their reward. It won't be long before we join them, gentlemen.''

''The sooner the better, you rascal,'' growled Mr. Clemens.

McPhee looked at my employer with a hurt expression on his face. ''Why, Sam, what's the matter? I'd almost think you didn't want me on this trip.''

''Slippery Ed McPhee, it'd be a damn sight easier to put up with you if you weren't trying to sell me this sanctimonious hogwash. I'll grant that even you must have had a mother. I'll even grant, for the sake of argument, that she might still be alive and ailing, and—far-fetched as the idea is—that she might want your face to be the last thing she saw before she died. But the notion of you shedding a tear over anything other than lost money gives new meaning to the word 'incredible.' Maybe you could sell that story to some half-wit who didn't know you from thirty years back, but I wouldn't buy it if you printed it on dollar bills and offered them for a nickel a handful.''

Captain Fowler cleared his throat. "Easy now, Sam. Let's try not to let old feelings get in the way of common sense. Mr. Snipes, will you please start from the beginning and tell me what's happened and what you've done about it?''

"Well, like I said, Cap'n, I seen those two Throckmorton boys push young Mr. Cabot off the dock, and so the railroad porter and me went and fished him out. Meanwhile, this other passenger, Major Demayne, waled on those ruffians like a teamster with his stick—it did my heart good to see it, Cap'n.''

"I wish *I'd* been there to see it," said Mr. Clemens, before the captain silenced him with a look and motioned for Mr. Snipes to continue.

"Well, I sent Mr. Cabot on board to his cabin to dry off, and had the porter load his luggage, and tried to get back to my business. Next thing I know, Slippery Ed comes stomping over to me and wants to know how come I let one of my passengers beat up on his boys. Well, that was one too many for me. I told him I'd see him and his boys in the hottest corner of Hell before I ever let 'em set foot on the *Horace Greeley*. And that's when he came storming up here and started with you.''

"Where was McPhee when the ruckus started?" asked the captain.

"Well, I can't rightly say," said Snipes. "I didn't see him until afterwards, when he started ragging me about his boys.''

"Mr. Cabot, did you see Mr. McPhee before the trouble started?''

After a moment's reflection, I said, ''No, sir. I didn't see him until just now, when he came into your cabin.''

''What about you, Sam? Did you see any of this?''

''I was still at the train station, trying to make a tele-phone call. I didn't know anything about it until I got down to the dock and Charlie Snipes told me what had happened. But damn it all, Mike, what difference does it make? If Slippery Ed brought a dog on board, and it bit one of your passengers, would you care whether McPhee was there when it happened?''

''The passenger might not see much difference, Sam, but I would. That's my job. It makes a difference whether the owner sicced it on 'em, or whether they was poking at it and pulling on its tail, or whether it just went hunting for somebody convenient to bite, and took a nip without so much as barking at 'em. What about it, Mr. Snipes? Did those Throckmorton boys start things on their own, or did Mr. Cabot do anything to get 'em mad?''

''It was all their doing, Cap'n. Mr. Cabot would have walked away from it, if they'd given him the chance. I didn't hear him say one word you couldn't say in Sunday school.''

''They told me he sassed them,'' said McPhee vehe-mently. ''I don't have nothing against the boy, but it ain't natural for a man to hold still when somebody makes fun of him—I don't care how pretty he talks and dresses. I'll vouch for Al and Billy; they may be a little rough, but they're not mean. We paid our way, and we've got a right to ride. I'll promise you they won't bother nobody else, Mike. You know me—I wouldn't tell you something and then not do it.''

Captain Fowler looked from McPhee to Snipes and back again, frowning. Finally, he shook his head and gave his verdict. ''Ed, I've got to stick by Mr. Snipes's story. He's my chief clerk, and he's got no axe to grind that I can tell. Those two Throckmorton boys are trouble if I ever saw it, and the last thing I want on this trip is that kind of trouble. I want them off my boat. Mr. Snipes, you'll give them full refunds for their tickets; if they've got any luggage on board, give them twenty minutes to unload it. After that, there'll be the devil to pay if I spot either one of them on board the *Horace Greeley* anywhere between here and New Orleans.

"But nobody's ever going to say Mike Fowler didn't treat them fair and square, Ed, and I don't see how you had any part in this scuffle today. If you want to stay on board, it's all the same with me. I've got no grudges against you, which is saying something, considering how long we've known each other."

"Damn it, Mike, those boys were supposed to help me take care of some important business downriver. How the hell are we going to get things done if I'm on board and they're on shore?"

Captain Fowler looked at McPhee with a disinterested expression. "There's other riverboats, Ed. There's trains the whole way down the river—they're cheaper than this cruise, and faster. There's horses for sale, and rafts, and rowboats, and canoes. For all I care, they can *walk* to New Orleans. But if those no-good Throckmorton boys set foot on the deck of my boat, I'll make them wish they'd been tarred and feathered. And that's the last I want to hear about it."

McPhee opened his mouth, thought better of it, and turned and left the cabin, nearly colliding with the texas tender, who had arrived with our drinks. "Give him back his money, if he wants it," said the captain to Mr. Snipes. "And if those durn Throckmortons are still on the boat in twenty minutes' time, throw 'em off—get the whole crew to do it, if you have to."

Snipes nodded, a thin-lipped smile on his face. "After this nonsense here, it'll be a pure pleasure, Cap'n. I'll see to it directly."

"The river's all changed, Sam," said Captain Fowler. After McPhee and the chief clerk had left, we'd settled back to enjoy our hot drinks, and the conversation had turned to more pleasant subjects—if not without a tinge of melancholy.

"I know it well," said Mr. Clemens. "I saw it happening back in '82. I'd have bet you ten dollars that nobody'd ever make a steamboat man wear a uniform, but look at you, Mike—you could pass for regular navy. And there's not a tenth of the traffic there was in my day. I'm surprised—and more than surprised, I'm really pleased—to see you making a go of it."

The captain smiled. "No more pleased than I am, Sam. I can't say it's been easy. The times when everybody and his brother was riding the boats—and bringing along their dogs and horses, too—those times aren't never coming back. The little fellows got hurt the worst. The railroads took most of their business, and the big steamboat companies took some more, and the towboats took the rest. An independent owner like me can't hardly get enough traffic to pay for firing up the boilers, and I can't see how it's ever going to get any better. I've spent my whole life running a steamboat, and it's made me sick to see the business dying.

"I figured out a while ago that the only way to fight the railroads is to draw a crowd that ain't in a hurry to get someplace, and give 'em something they can't get on the trains. So when that Henry Rogers came along offering me more money than I've seen in ten years to take you downriver on a literary excursion, with loads of history and culture and other such things to cater to the eastern crowd, that was like manna from heaven. If I can make a go of this, I may still have a chance to finish out my days on the river."

"I'd like to see that, Mike. There was a time that was all I ever wanted—until I found out that writing was even better than working. Still, there's a lot to be said for sitting on the deck of a boat and watching the riverbank go by. You've got the old boat looking good, too."

"Thank you, Sam. She never was all that fancy, and it'd been too long since she had a fresh coat of paint. I've hauled some mighty strange cargoes over the years, trying to make ends meet—everything from lumber to livestock— and she got beat up pretty bad. But your Mr. Rogers made sure I had enough money to spruce her up so's the rich folks wouldn't turn up their noses at her. I sure hope this trip pays back all he put into it."

"I'll do my damnedest to make it a success," said Mr. Clemens. "I owe it to Henry Rogers, I owe it to you—and most of all I owe it to my dear Livy and the girls. How I wish I could be with them! But I have a job to do here on the river first, and you can be sure I'll put my whole heart into it."

"I never knew you to do any other way," said Captain Fowler. "Between the two of us, we'll get this old boat down to New Orleans in one piece, and swagger up Canal Street to Monkey Wrench Corner, just like old times."

Mr. Clemens gave a hearty laugh. "That's the grandest plan I've heard all year, Mike. And we'll cap it off with the best meal in the French Quarter, and show them what a pair of old boys off the river can still do."

9

Our meeting with Captain Fowler at an end, Mr.
Clemens decided to take me (with the captain's permission) on an impromptu tour of the *Horace Greeley*. We began by climbing up to the pilothouse, set high
atop the texas.

Somewhat to my surprise, the pilothouse was empty. Mr.
Clemens pushed open the door and looked around. "I
didn't think there'd be anybody here. The pilot's probably
still on shore somewhere; in my day, we didn't use to board
until just before casting off. Nothing really to do until
then."

"That's too bad," I said. "We'll have to come back
when the pilot's on duty."

"Oh, we will," said Mr. Clemens. "I hope to spend as
much time as possible up here once we're under weigh.
But now's a perfect chance for me to size things up without
somebody taking the notion that I'm snooping around on
his territory. Some pilots can get mighty touchy, and that's
even more likely when the person snooping around is an
old-time pilot. So here's my opportunity to poke around
without raising any hackles."

I looked at the unfamiliar array of equipment. There was
a brass-bound wheel, in a blond wood I thought might be
oak; an array of cords with bright brass handles hanging
from the ceiling; an odd-shaped wooden tube, tapered like
the bell of some musical instrument, rising from the floor;

and various other levers and pulleys connected to I knew not what. "Do you know what all these things are?"

"Most of them. The important equipment's pretty much the same as when I was a pilot," he said. "The wheel does what you'd expect it to; this tube lets the pilot talk directly to the engine room—actually, I saw that for the first time on my last trip downriver, when I was finishing that *Mississippi* book. This pull-rope stops the engines, this one calls the captain, and this one blows the whistle"—he pointed in one direction, then the other—"this one tells the crew to set the alligator nets, and this one summons the bartender when the pilot's thirsty."

"Alligator nets? Are we really likely to encounter alligators?"

"Not so much in the upper river these days," he said, with a curious expression. "But we're going all the way to New Orleans, so Captain Fowler had them put on special, right after I told Henry Rogers this was the boat he should charter. Down below Vicksburg, the alligators get so thick that you can hardly get through sometimes. They used to try to dredge them out, but it just didn't work. So when the pilot spots an alligator reef—and it takes a good pilot to spot one from any distance—he signals the crew, and they raise the nets so the alligators can't come on deck. Just as well—a couple of hungry alligators can carry off a passenger before you can say 'boo.' Of course, they don't often get as high up as the texas—they aren't built for climbing. That's why the captain's cabin is always up there."

"My goodness, I never heard of such a thing. Is it very dangerous?" I had seen stuffed alligators and crocodiles in the Yale museum, and did not fancy having those long jaws clamped on my leg.

"Not if you've got an experienced pilot and good strong nets. The most danger is right at dusk, when the pilot might not see the gators in time to set the nets. But I'm sure Mike Fowler has hired somebody who knows that part of the river. It wouldn't do to run with the nets up all night long—

if the gators see they've got you worried, they'll follow you, and jump on board when you least expect it. You've got to put on a brave face to keep the alligators at bay."

"Well, I certainly hope we don't meet with any," I said. The talk of alligators reminded me of my recent run-in with one of their namesakes. "Speaking of dangerous creatures, I was certainly pleased when the captain acted so decisively to eject the Throckmorton brothers. Those two would have made the trip far less pleasurable."

"I wish he'd thrown Ed McPhee off along with them, but Mike's always played fair, and I can't really argue with him. Slippery Ed's probably not as dangerous as he was ten years ago, although I wouldn't trust him to hold my coat if I was saving his drowning sister."

"Perhaps he'll elect to travel with them, since he said he needed them for business."

"Don't get your hopes up, Wentworth. McPhee obviously wants to be on this boat—as Mike pointed out, he could get to New Orleans a lot faster by train, and cheaper, too. No, he's got some monkey business planned, and I'm more and more afraid it has to do with my treasure hunt. We'll have to keep a sharp eye on him, Wentworth—never mind the alligators. Come on, let's take a look at the rest of the boat. We'll pay another visit here when there's a pilot on board."

We spent the next hour visiting various parts of the boat and meeting the crew members in charge of them. Not only did all these people seem to recognize Mr. Clemens, but they greeted him with enormous respect, almost as a hero returning to his home country.

Our first stop after the pilothouse was the engine room, on the main deck; the boilers sat cold, and the well-muscled stokers were amusing themselves with a hand of cards, but they stopped to greet their famous guest when we came through the door. The engineer was a sturdy-looking fellow who introduced himself as Antoine Devereaux—"Frenchy, they call me,'' he said with an accent that bore no trace of the Parisian. Later I learned that he was a Creole from Louisiana.

M. Devereaux was busily inspecting his engines one last time before departure, but he stopped to shake hands with Mr. Clemens. "The captain says fix ever'thing up first-class—spend anything I need to. I guess I got you partly to thank for these new boilers."

"Not me, but Henry Rogers in New York. How do they look?"

"Oh, they don't look like much, but they work just fine. We had 'er out for a test Saturday, and she run sweet as candy. Ain't gonna be a racer, but she never was to begin with."

"Do you remember the old days when they fired the boilers with cordwood?" asked Mr. Clemens.

"Sure do," said the engineer. "Wouldn't go back to 'em if you paid me double. It was tougher on the boilers, and on the boys, too—crew could get mighty tired of takin' on wood if you do it five, maybe six times between St. Louis and St. Paul. Some of the boys, they complain all the time about how dirty the coal is. If they gotta stack cordwood a couple times, they don't worry about the dirt no more, I guarantee you."

On the foredeck, another gang of powerfully built men were wrestling boxes of provisions on board and stowing them for the journey, urged on by a veritable giant of a man: the first mate, Mr. Clemens told me. This individual was apparently of the opinion that no simple order would suffice to convey his wishes; instead he peppered his sentences with such a profusion of oaths, threats, and profanity that I involuntarily glanced aloft to make certain that thunderclouds were not gathering to strike him down.

"Git it up there, ye mud-nosed tadpole. GIT it up there, damn ye! Don't you know how to grab the **** thing, ye **** son of a ******? Get a grip on it—if ye drop the damned thing, I'll fry yer arse and throw it overboard! NO!

You **** ****** ** *** **** bastard! Put yer back into it! Hump it! Jesus H. Christ! HUMP it!'' All this was roared out in a voice that threatened to shatter windows miles away.

Then his eye lit on us, and I cringed involuntarily. But his whole manner changed as he introduced himself. ''Welcome aboard the *Horace*, Mr. Sam. I'm Bob Williams—they calls me Tiny,'' he said in a voice as mild as a Methodist deacon's, all the while peering down at me from what must have been six and a half feet of height. Mr. Clemens introduced me, and the mate's huge right hand swallowed mine in an iron grasp. ''Anybody cause Mr. Sam any trouble, you call for Tiny. They ain't gonna cause *nobody* trouble after I gets done with 'em.'' He grinned broadly. I decided on the spot to do my best to stay on Mr. Williams's good side, and smiled back at him, doing my best not to inspect my hand for damage.

We walked along the deck and stuck our heads into the clerk's office, where Mr. Snipes looked up from a desk, scowling for a moment until he recognized us. Behind him, a pimply youngster transcribed something from loose papers into a thick ledger. I recognized him as Tommy, the boy who'd shown me to my cabin earlier. ''Don't mind us,'' said Mr. Clemens. ''I'm just showing Cabot how the boat's laid out.''

''Oh, Mr. Sam—I've been looking forward to having you on board,'' said Snipes. ''You probably don't remember, but I was a mud clerk on the boat you took downriver back in '82, the *Gold Dust*. Just a boy then, but I got away from work enough to hear you tell some of your stories.''

''Well, glad to hear it. And thanks again for fishing Cabot out this morning.''

''Think nothing of it, Mr. Sam. I'd've done it for anybody. Just hope my work will let me see more of you this time.''

''Well, I expect you'll get the chance. Did you get that little matter of the Throckmortons settled?''

"Not as well as I'd have liked—McPhee's still with us. I'll keep a sharp eye on him, though—if he tries any of his rascally tricks on the *Horace,* I'll take it to the captain again. We stand to make a lot of money this trip, and I don't want him cutting into it."

"Much appreciated," said Mr. Clemens. "We know you'll do what you can."

"Thanks again for pulling me out of the drink," I said. "You look familiar; where have I seen you before?"

"I saw you at Mr. Sam's lecture in New York, when you come for an interview," said Snipes. "Me and the captain were there for a week of meetings with Mr. Twain and Mr. Rogers."

"Yes, exactly—I should have remembered that," I said.

"I never forget a face," said Snipes. "Comes in handy in this line of work."

From Snipes's office, we turned up the stairway (which Mr. Clemens insisted on calling a ladder) into the grand saloon which took up half the second deck of the *Horace Greeley,* the other half being devoted to a lecture hall for Mr. Clemens's talks. This large room served as a lounge and dining room, with a well-furnished bar along one side and comfortable seats along the walls. Small tables occupied the center of the lounge, and a number of the passengers who had already boarded were sitting at them, sipping coffee, tea, or other drinks and chatting among themselves. As Mr. Clemens entered the room, an expectant hush fell.

"Don't mind me," he said, smiling and waving his hand. "If you all stop talking every time I stick my head out of my cabin, you're likely to turn me into a human turtle. We're going to be shipmates for the next few weeks, and we might as well get used to one another."

At that, a group of passengers pressed forward to introduce themselves to Mr. Clemens. I was surprised to notice among them the tall blonde woman I had noticed at his lecture in Chicago; she introduced herself to him as Laura

Cunningham, of Boston. She noticed me at Mr. Clemens's side, and before I could quite gather my wits, she was extending her hand to me and introducing herself. I told her my name, and she smiled. "A Cabot on the Mississippi!" she said. "What, pray tell, are you doing out here, a thousand miles from home? You should be in Boston, acting dull and respectable."

"I'm afraid my branch of the family left Boston long ago," I said. "I'm from Connecticut." At close range, I could see that she was older than I had thought—possibly thirty.

She looked me up and down, a mischievous smile on her face. "Ah, and are your family the black sheep among the Cabots? I never heard of such a thing!"

"Oh, I don't think so," I said. "My father is an attorney in New London, and about as dull and respectable as the Boston branch of the family. I suppose that if traveling with Mr. Clemens as his secretary is being a black sheep, I'm the closest you'll find to that."

She gave a pleasant little laugh, and said, "Then you'll have to be on your best behavior, Mr. Cabot. I know quite a few of your most respectable relatives, and I would be remiss not to report any lapses on your part. I must confess, though, it is a pleasant surprise to find someone with connections to society out here. We will have to speak more." We shook hands again, and I turned to see how Mr. Clemens was faring with the other passengers.

These were a decidedly mixed lot. In a few short minutes, he greeted a pasty-faced clergyman from Boston, Mr. Dutton, traveling with his plump wife and two simpering daughters, Gertrude and Berenice, both of whom cast a speculative eye on me; an overly bejeweled matron from Baltimore with a voice like an army bugle, who introduced herself as the sister of one of his old friends, and an unctuous Chicagoan who tried to tell Mr. Clemens about some gadget he'd invented. Each of them appeared eager to draw Mr. Clemens into an extended conversation, but he simply nodded, offered a few superficialities, and moved on to others in the crowd.

He kept his patience rather well, I thought, especially when a pimply young man with round spectacles and a rumpled suit grasped his hand. "I'm so looking forward to this journey, Mr. Clemens," he said, smiling broadly. "Claude Dexter, of Boston. Ever since I read your *Life on the Mississippi*, I've made a study of the river and dreamed of taking a riverboat cruise. To do so in your company is a special pleasure. It's a pity the boat couldn't have been somewhat more authentic—a side-wheeler would've been much more exciting."

"I'm afraid the *Greeley* is about as authentic as we could afford," said Mr. Clemens. "I suppose we could've done without some of the modern inconveniences." Several of the listeners laughed. "But I'm not quite ready to give up all the comforts just for the sake of nostalgia—and turning her into a side-wheeler would be a real stretch. I'm just glad to be back on the river. If you enjoy the trip half as much as I intend to, it'll be well worth your fare."

"Oh, I expect it will be," said Dexter, beaming. "Still, don't you think electric lights are so much less romantic than oil lamps?"

"Yes, and so much less inclined to start authentic fires," said Mr. Clemens. He nodded and turned toward the bar; as I turned to follow him, I noticed Major Demayne standing there, looking at me and my employer.

"Hello again, Mr. Cabot," the Major said. "I hope you've taken no ill effects from your dunking?"

"No sir, thank you. And I don't think I've thanked you properly for driving away those two bullies; I might have come off much worse had they been waiting for me when I climbed out."

"Aha, I'd heard someone gave those skunks a proper thrashing," said Mr. Clemens. "I guess I ought to thank you as well—secretaries aren't as easy to come to as you'd think these days. Cabot's a bit green, but I think he'll

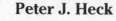
season up pretty well. Can I buy you a drink, Mr. . . . ?''

"Major Roy Demayne, at your service, sir. I confess to being one of your admirers, and a bit of an amateur scribbler, as you might say.''

"I won't let that stop me from buying you a drink,'' said my employer. "What'll it be? I'm having whisky and soda.''

"That would be a most welcome libation, sir. I must say, I've been looking forward to meeting you.''

"I hope it's not a disappointment, Major. I've only the usual number of heads, and I rarely levitate in public. You can probably find half a dozen more interesting characters up any back alley in town.''

The Major laughed. "You have already lived up to my expectations, sir. I have read many of your books, sir, and hope eventually to emulate you in your chosen career, if not precisely in the same genre.''

The drinks came, and Mr. Clemens lifted his glass to Major Demayne. "Again my thanks,'' he said, and I added my sincere appreciation as we all three touched glasses. Mr. Clemens took a sip of his, and then continued. "Writing isn't all that complicated, if you get right down to it. A man has to go into a room with a pile of blank paper and cover it with words—that's the easy part. Any simpleton who's learned his ABCs can do that much. The part nobody can teach you is how to make somebody give you money for the paper once you've got it covered.''

"Surely inspiration counts for something,'' the Major said. "Perhaps everyone has the capacity to tell a simple tale, but the true artist brings something to his subject, some ethereal spark caught from the muse.''

"How true,'' said another passenger—the minister, whose wife and daughters seemed to have left him behind. He looked somewhat askance at the glasses in our hands, but made no overt criticism.

"I've caught more sparks from a cigar than from any muse,'' said Mr. Clemens, ignoring the minister. "My suc-

cess comes mostly from hard work, and keeping my eyes
and ears open—and a touch of luck. There are men out on
the river who can tell as good a story as anything I've ever
put on paper. Any stage driver or hotel clerk could probably
tell you a hundred such. The difference between them and
a successful author is mostly the willingness to spend seven
or eight hours a day putting the stories down and making
them work on paper. I don't claim it's easy, but that's all
there really is to it.''

''Perhaps I can persuade you to examine some of my
own poor efforts,'' said the Major, reaching into his breast
pocket.

A look of panic came over Mr. Clemens's face. ''You
aren't the poet, are you?''

''Only a poor scribbler,'' said the Major, extracting a
thick sheaf of paper from his pocket. ''Would it be more
convenient for you to glance over these efforts of mine on
your own or for us to meet so I can read selections to you?
Verse gains so much when spoken aloud. . . .''

''Verse isn't really my strong suit,'' said Mr. Clemens,
peering around as if to locate an emergency exit. ''Now,
Cabot here might know something about it—he went to
Yale. You'll be glad to read the Major's poems, won't you,
Cabot?'' He fixed me with a stare that left no doubt as to
the answer he expected.

''I suppose I could look at it,'' I began, not certain what
I might be committing myself to, but the Major pressed his
manuscript into my hand before I could continue. I stared
at it, then back at the Major, who had paused, as if in
thought. Then a new expression crossed his face.

''I hope you'll read this carefully, and pass along anything of particular interest to Mr. Clemens,'' he said, more
quickly than before. ''But I fear I've taken up too much of
your time, gentlemen. Thanks again for your hospitality,
sir.'' He bowed and made his departure, leaving his whisky
half-finished on the bar.

''That's about as fast as I ever got rid of a writer who

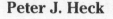
was trying to sell me something," said Mr. Clemens, looking quite relieved. "Most of them are as persistent as chiggers. I suppose he thinks he's paying for my advice, and wants to get his money's worth early, and I suppose he's right, when you get right down to it. Try to read some of it, Wentworth, and tell me if it's worth my time. They do teach you about poetry at Yale, don't they?"

"Not a great deal, sir—" I began, but Mr. Clemens interrupted, a gleam in his eye.

"Are you going to tell me you wouldn't know doggerel if it bit you?"

I was about to reply when a familiar voice from behind me called my name. I turned to see Detective Berrigan, who grinned and said, "I heard about your taking the waters earlier today."

"Not for my health, I assure you," I responded. I began to fear that everyone aboard would know of my dunking, and comment on it endlessly until some other subject for gossip arose.

"Well, I hear the good news of it is that we won't have those two bully boys to worry about. I can't say it pains me to see them go, although professionally I ought to want them where I can keep an eye on them."

"You don't think they had anything to do with that business back in New York, do you?" asked Mr. Clemens.

Before Berrigan could answer, a strident voice called out from across the deck. "Well, Paul Berrigan—what in the devil's name brings you out west?"

"God give me patience," said Berrigan, grimacing. "If that's who I think it is, I'll wire for a transfer back home this instant." We turned to see a lean, lantern-jawed fellow in a loud checked suit striding over to us.

"Mark Twain," the newcomer said. "I'm Andrew Dunbar, with the *New York Herald*. How does it happen that you know Detective Berrigan?"

I thought I heard Mr. Clemens mutter something sulfurous under his breath, but by then the reporter had out a notebook and was firing questions at a distance of about eight inches from Mr. Clemens's face.

"Is it true you've gone bankrupt, Mark? Is that why the police are following you?" He held his pencil pointed toward Mr. Clemens's face, swaying back on his heels and then forward in a most disconcerting manner.

"None of your damned business," growled Mr. Clemens.

"If you won't tell me your side of the story, I'll have to print the rumors, Mark. Do you deny that you're in trouble with the law?" The reporter turned abruptly and faced Berrigan. "Is he involved in a homicide case?"

"Any more of your damned impertinence and I *will* be involved in a homicide case," said Mr. Clemens.

"No you won't," said Detective Berrigan from between clenched teeth. "Exterminating vermin isn't homicide. What in the blazes are you doing on this boat, Dunbar?"

"The *Herald* sent me to cover Mark's lecture tour," said the reporter, not showing the least cognizance of the hostility with which my employer and the detective had greeted him. "He's a public figure, and the public has a right to know what he's up to. Word has it he's flat broke and he's sold his house, his publishing company, everything."

"How sad, if true," said the minister, still lingering on the fringes of the little group around my employer.

"Maybe it's true, and maybe it's not," said Mr. Clemens to the reporter. "But you're not going to find out from Berrigan. And the only thing you're going to hear from me from now on is what I have to say in my lectures. They're included in the price of the tour, so I can't very well keep you out. But I'll warn you—print one word of them, and I'll shut you down for copyright violation."

"You can't do that," said the reporter. "We have freedom of the press in this country!"

"Yes, and a mighty good thing," said the employer, with some heat. "But I have the freedom to keep my mouth shut, and that's what I'm going to do—starting right now.

100   Come along, Cabot.'' And he whisked out the door leading
to the hurricane deck so quickly that I nearly had to run to
catch up with him, clutching the Major's manuscript in my
hand as I followed.

10

I emerged abruptly into the bright sunlight. I must have been dazzled by the light, or perhaps confused by Mr. Clemens's sudden burst of speed—it was the first time I'd ever seen him in anything resembling a hurry. In any case, I was evidently paying too little attention to where I was going, and so collided with a slim young woman standing just outside the door. She gave a little cry of startlement, and I quickly reached out to prevent her from falling. "My apologies, miss," I said. "Are you all right?"

"I seem to be," she said, looking at me with a curious half-smile. "Please don't let me keep you from your business—it must be very important for you to rush about so."

"It was my fault, young lady," said Mr. Clemens, with a courtly little bow. "Please forgive my secretary, Mr. Cabot—he was just following me, and I guess I was too hasty."

"Oh! Mr. Twain!" she said. "Of course I forgive him. My goodness—what a surprise to meet you this way!" The color rising to her cheeks was practically the same hue as her pretty pink dress, a striking contrast to her straight dark hair and brown eyes.

"Not an unpleasant surprise, I hope," said Mr. Clemens, smiling. "But you have the advantage of me—my name and picture must be plastered on every fence in thirty states. At least there's no reward for turning me in to the law. To whom do I have the honor of making my apology, Miss . . . ?''

"Martha Patterson," she said, with a curtsy. "And no, it is hardly an *unpleasant* surprise to meet you—or Mr. Cabot," she added, smiling brightly in my direction.

"My genuine apologies, Miss Patterson," I said, with a bow. She laughed and extended a white-gloved hand, first to Mr. Clemens, who shook it with a fatherly air, then to me. Perhaps it was my imagination, but her eyes seemed to flash as her gaze met mine, and she smiled again.

"Good, now we can all be friends," said Mr. Clemens. "I must say I prefer the company out here to that inside the cabin. Between the poet and that dratted newspaperman, it was getting a bit too thick for me in there. It's almost enough to make me like the detective."

"My goodness, what an interesting lot of people," said Miss Patterson. "Is there really a detective on the boat? I don't think I've ever met such a person."

"I'm afraid so," said Mr. Clemens. "But he's a New York police detective, and not likely to pester respectable folks who haven't done anything."

"I certainly hope not!" said Miss Patterson, folding her hands over her bosom. "Oh, I knew this would be an exciting voyage, but I hardly expected something so dramatic before we even set sail. Meeting you—and Mr. Cabot— and now learning that there's a detective on board, too. Is there a mystery to be solved? I do hope so! Or perhaps I shouldn't ask. . . .''

"No real mystery," said Mr. Clemens. "The detective's got the cockeyed notion that someone wanted by the law back east might be on this boat. Once he gets it through his head that he's on a wild-goose chase, he'll go to New York where he belongs."

"Are you certain that he's on a wild-goose chase?" Miss Patterson lowered her voice and looked around warily, although the three of us were alone on the deck. "Why, there are dozens of people on board already; any one of them might be a—a fugitive from justice! It makes me shiver to think of it.''

''I doubt there's any danger to you, miss,'' I said. ''Even if there were, the detective will know how to handle it.'' I realized that a gently reared young woman would most likely never have had any business with someone of Berrigan's class, and so might find him more interesting than he actually was.

''But the detective can't be everywhere at once,'' she said. ''And if he's come all this way, he must be pursuing someone very dangerous. Perhaps it's a jewel thief—or even a murderer. Do you think someone on board could be a murderer? I wonder who it is. Why, it could even be someone I've met and spoken to!''

''I doubt it,'' said Mr. Clemens. ''Detective Berrigan doesn't make much secret of his identity. If there's a fugitive among us, he'll think twice about staying right under the detective's nose. If the fellow has half the sense of a brick, he's probably already hightailing his way to Mexico. In any case, he's not likely to be looking for young ladies to bother.''

''I suppose you're right,'' said Miss Patterson. ''But why does the detective think the fugitive is on this boat? Oh, my—could it be because of you, Mr. Twain? Are you in any danger?'' Her face took on a concerned expression, and her gaze darted between Mr. Clemens and myself.

''Not as long as *I* can prevent it,'' I said firmly. ''But really, you shouldn't worry, Miss Patterson. We expect this to be a very pleasant cruise, and there's no reason to think there's any danger to Mr. Clemens—and certainly none at all to the passengers. If I were you, I'd put the whole business out of my head and enjoy the voyage.''

''I certainly intend to, Mr. Cabot,'' she said, with another of her bright smiles. ''I am so looking forward to hearing Mr. Twain's lectures. And I'm very pleased to know that Mr. Twain has someone to protect him, just in case there *is* any danger. I'm so glad to have met you both.''

"Our pleasure entirely, Miss Patterson," said Mr. Clemens, bowing, and I did the same. Miss Patterson gave a little curtsy, then went past me into the cabin.

"Well, I'm glad to know that not all the passengers are bores and scoundrels," said Mr. Clemens, smiling. "Be careful, Wentworth—I think she may like you." To my surprise, I found myself feeling quite pleased at the notion.

Standing at the aft rail of the *Horace Greeley,* I had a fine view across the river to the high bank on the far side of the water. Upstream, I could make out at least three bridges and a large island in midstream before the river curved out of sight. The weather had cleared and warmed up considerably since we had left Chicago—only yesterday, although it seemed much longer ago. From our vantage point atop the hurricane deck, the water looked cool and inviting. Well, cool, at any rate—I could testify personally to that.

Mr. Clemens had lit a cigar and was leaning against the rail next to me. We stood there perhaps a quarter of an hour, quietly contemplating the river and nodding to the occasional passenger who strolled past, before he broke the silence. His words startled me out of my musings, and it took me a moment to realize that he was addressing me; after a moment's incomprehension, I asked him to repeat himself.

He chuckled. "Lost in a daydream, are you? I can understand that—I spent half my boyhood staring at the river, dreaming of all the places it would take me when I grew up. Now that I'm grown up, I've been places I never would have dared to dream of back in those days: California, Europe, Egypt, Palestine. . . . There are times I wish I could be just a boy again, back in a little town with nothing on my mind but to play hookey and go fishing. But all I asked you just now, Cabot, was what you saw, looking at the river."

I looked around for a moment before replying. "I see a

high bluff across from us, with a few houses showing through the trees on top; I can make out a hawk's nest up in that tall tree just to the left of the brick house—surprising it'd build this close to a town. There's an island upstream, maybe a couple of them, and some bridges coming down from the high bank to this shore. There are a few little boats tied up along the shore. The water's very clear and calm, and deep enough for big boats.''

''And do you see any magic? Do you see the royal road to romance, fame, and fortune?''

I looked again. ''I'm afraid not. I see the water and the banks, the boats—what I said before. Do you want me to try to see those other things? I'm not sure how to go about it.''

Mr. Clemens shook his head. ''Never mind, Wentworth. It takes a good pair of eyes to look at something and see just what's there. That's always been my problem—I've always looked at things and seen what they ought to be, or what I'd hoped they'd be, or what somebody told me they were. And then gotten mad when it turned out they were no more than I should have expected. But I shouldn't blame myself; it's a common failing.''

''What do you mean, sir?''

He put his elbows on the rail and leaned back. ''Oh, there are plenty of examples right on board this boat. You could start right off with me—an old man who ought to know better, expecting to find thirty-year-old treasure somewhere downriver. You'd think that prospecting for gold, or investing in a dozen harebrained inventions that never worked, would have cured me. Yet here I am, as anxious as a June bridegroom, ready to set off on an expedition that any schoolboy could tell me doesn't have a chance in hell of panning out.

''But I'm far from the only dreamer aboard the boat. Young Miss Patterson obviously expects this trip to bring her romance and excitement, and so she thinks she sees a mystery as soon as she hears there's a detective on board.

She'll be conjuring up dark plots and deep conspiracies, and casting you as the shining knight-errant, Wentworth— you can count on it. I've seen the type a hundred times before.'' Mr. Clemens fixed me with a stern gaze. ''Be careful, young man—there's no way you can live up to her expectations.''

He turned and looked over the river again. ''Berrigan's dreaming, too. He thinks he's on a hot trail—on the slimmest of evidence, as far as I can see. If you want my best guess, that murder back in New York had nothing to do with us. Jack Hubbard probably came to my hotel hoping to talk me into giving him a few dollars to tide him over— actors and gamblers never have any money. He left me a note, then got into a scuffle on his way home, by chance with somebody who'd been at my lecture a few nights earlier. Most likely, the other fellow jumped him—Jack was never the kind to start a fight, although he was big enough to take care of himself when he had to, as he proved in this case. If he'd stuck around, he might have been able to get away with a self-defense plea. Instead, he skedaddled. I doubt that Berrigan will ever lay eyes on him.'' He laughed softly, and leaned against the rail.

''Major Demayne is another sad case. Poets may be the worst dreamers of all; they think that mere words can change the world, and they're right just often enough that there's no persuading them otherwise. I shouldn't condemn his verse without looking at it, but I've seen way too many would-be poets to have much hope for him. The odds are hundreds to one against his verses being readable, let alone publishable. But there's no gentle way to tell him, and no guarantee that even brutal rejection will keep him from scribbling.''

''Then you don't really want me to read his poem?'' I asked, looking at the sheaf of papers the Major had foisted off on me.

''Read it, by all means,'' said Mr. Clemens. ''Just don't expect anything sensible or even competent. Maybe you're better off not knowing too much about poetry—it won't jar you as much to read something really bad. If by some miracle you think his stuff is any good, let me know. Let me know the general tenor of it, anyway. He'll expect some sort of response, and I might as well be in a position to comment semi-intelligently. Since the verse will probably be semi-intelligent at best, the comments needn't be much better.'' He tapped the manuscript and winked at me.

"Yes, sir,'' I said, looking down at the manuscript. "I'll do my best.'' It was as thick as some books I'd had to read at Yale, and (to be honest) I hadn't managed to finish some of those.

"Don't expect it to be Browning,'' he said. "Look at it the same way you were looking at the river, and just tell me what's there. I can handle the rest. I may not like it, but I can handle it.''

We stood for a few minutes watching the water go by. Then I asked, "And what about McPhee? Surely he's far too cynical to be a dreamer.''

" 'Cynical' is too mild a word for Slippery Ed,'' said Mr. Clemens, chuckling. "But he's a dreamer, even so. Every gambler thinks that luck will bring him money, and that money will solve his problems. It never works out. Even when they get money, they turn around and throw it away—like our fugitive Farmer Jack, who'd win hundreds at billiards in an afternoon and lose it all at poker the same night. There's never been a gambler who retired on his winnings. They're all losers, Wentworth—and all because they expect the world to be the way they want it to be, not the way it really is. Sometimes I wish I could have been like Tom Blankenship, a boy I knew in Hannibal—I modeled a character in two of my books after him. He never looked for any more than what he saw in front of him. If I'd been more like him, I think I'd have been a happier man. I might not have become a famous writer, but I think I'd have been more content with life.''

"And what became of this Tom when he grew up?" I asked.

"I got a letter from him just a short while ago. He'd gone west to Montana. He was justice of the peace in some little town there, I forget the name. But I'd pay good money to sneak into his court and hear him decide cases. He'd have put Solomon to shame, I tell you, Wentworth. Perhaps some day I'll look him up." He leaned over the rail again, and puffed on his cigar, his eyes focused on something far away.

The rest of the afternoon of our first day on board the boat went by quietly and lazily. We were scheduled to depart the next morning, on Tuesday, after the last of the passengers had boarded. For tonight, Captain Fowler had taken Mr. Clemens to dinner with some local notables on Summit Avenue in St. Paul. That left me with the evening to myself. I decided to take the opportunity, which I knew might not come again, to look at the bustling city, of which I had seen only the train station and the steamboat landing. So I walked up to look at the city hall, which includes a public library. A few blocks north I found the fine state capitol building, although I decided to forgo the climb up into the dome for the view at sunset. Along the way, I saw several prosperous churches, and regretted not having been here the day before to visit one of them. The city supports two opera houses, and a number of newspapers, and is so obviously a thriving center of government and commerce that I found it difficult to believe that it had received its civic charter less than forty years before.

Finally, after I had spent several hours exploring the hilly streets, dusk began to fall. I found a restaurant in one of the hotels and dined on pork chops, boiled potatoes, and fresh spring peas, which I washed down with an excellent lager. I arose from the table satisfied, but not quite ready to return to the boat. Something I heard in the room off the restaurant aroused my curiosity. I followed the familiar muted clicking sound and soon found myself in the hotel's billiard room, with two tables and half a dozen men playing the game or lounging about smoking and conversing.

I had learned billiards at my club at Yale, and enjoyed watching others play as much as wielding the cue myself. So for a while I took a seat and watched the game. At one table, two stout middle-aged men were engaged in a leisurely game of "straight" pool; two old friends, from their manner and their talk. Neither was especially good, but they were evenly matched, and clearly enjoying themselves too much to care about an occasional miscue.

The action at the other table was hotter: a hawk-nosed fellow with slicked-back hair was evidently taking on all comers. His game was "eight-ball," or "stripes and solids," a fast-moving variation that had been popular at Yale. He kept up a stream of chatter while he played, commenting on each shot, deprecating his opponents' skill, joking with onlookers. Everyone ignored the prominently posted "NO GAMBLING" sign, betting twenty-five cents a game, and sometimes a nickel or dime side bet on a difficult shot. The hawk-nosed fellow—whose name appeared to be Dick Kenney—was winning steadily, although never by a large margin. He won four or five games while I watched; his last opponent then laid down the cue and said, "That's enough for me. Dick's got all the luck tonight, and all my money, too."

"Same here," said another. "The damned balls don't want to drop for me. I'm ready for a beer. Who's with me?"

The fellow who'd just lost was with him, and one other, and the three of them left for whatever watering spot they favored. Kenney watched them leave, the trace of a sneer on his lips, then turned his gaze on me. "What about you, stranger? Do you play this game or just watch?"

"I've played before," I said. There was something in Kenney's expression I didn't like; on the other hand, a game or two of billiards might be relaxing. At worst, I

might lose seventy-five cents or a dollar, a cheap price for an evening's light entertainment; I had spent that much on dinner. Besides, there was no reason to think I would lose—I had been a decent player in college.

"Pick a cue, if you're game," said Kenney. "We're playing eight-ball for quarters."

I found a cue I liked, and Kenney racked the balls. "You can have first break," he said. "After that, the winner breaks. No combinations off the eight ball. Break 'em."

I drove the cue ball into the rack and scattered the balls; a striped ball went into the corner pocket. I pocketed another "stripe" and then missed; Kenney made a tricky bank shot, then ran three more balls before missing an easy cut into the corner pocket. I tried a long shot on the fourteen and scratched, then Kenney made two more balls before missing—again a shot I'd have thought he'd make easily. I wondered why his play was so erratic. He had a smooth stroke, and usually left himself in good position for his next shot. I ran three balls before missing. Kenney pocketed the last "solid," then left the eight just hanging on the lip of the far corner. "Damn!" he said. "Didn't hit it hard enough."

"You didn't leave me much," I said. The two most tempting shots on the table were both into the pocket where the eight was hanging; an inaccurate shot could easily knock it in, which would forfeit the game. My only real opening was a bank shot the length of the table. I bent over to line up the shot, and Kenney threw a dime on the table directly in front of me. "Ten cents says you can't make it."

I straightened up and looked at him—he was definitely sneering now—then looked at the shot again. It wasn't really a difficult shot; a bigger problem would be leaving the cue ball in position for pocketing the remaining balls. And if I missed, I would leave him with an easy winning shot on the eight. "You're on," I said, and placed the dime on the rail, out of my way. I lined up the shot and stroked the cue firmly; the ball caromed off the far rail and returned, almost in a blur, into the pocket I'd aimed for. I smiled and picked up the dime.

"Good shot," said Kenney. "Too bad about the position." I looked at the table and saw the cue ball resting against the far rail. In my eagerness to win the side bet, I'd hit my shot too hard, and left myself almost no chance to pocket the remaining striped balls. I tried to play safe, leaving Kenney without a clean shot at the eight, but the rail kept me from getting enough English to stop the cue ball where I wanted it. It rolled to the middle of the table, and a moment later Kenney tapped the eight ball home and collected his quarter. "Good game," he said. "Want to try again?"

Silently, I began to rack the balls. While I couldn't point to outright cheating, I felt that my opponent had beaten me not by playing better, but by taunting me into an unwise shot. This time, I would be wary. I removed the wooden frame from the balls and we began another game.

I lost again, and then a third time—both times by slim margins. "Bad luck," said Kenney. "Tell you what—let's make it fifty cents a game, so you have a chance to win it back." I was about to decline the offer, recognizing that Kenney was a far better player than he pretended to be, but I was interrupted by a resonant voice from the spectators' bench, saying, "I have a better idea." I turned to see Major Demayne, the amateur poet, standing there. I'd been so preoccupied with the game that I hadn't seen him come in.

"And what's that, stranger?" said Kenney.

"As much as I enjoy watching the game, I'd enjoy playing even more," said the Major. "Now, I know you gentlemen are enjoying your match, and I don't want to evict you from the table. What say I team up with this young fellow, and you choose a partner, and we play two a side? For a dollar a game, just to keep it interesting."

"I don't know you from Adam," said Kenney. "How

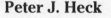

112 do I know you're not a pool shark, trying to steal an honest working fellow's money?''

"How do I know *you're* not a pool shark?" countered the Major. "I've only seen you play a few games, and you've won them all. You get to pick your own partner— you must know the local players—and I'll play with this young fellow you've been beating all night. And just to show you I'm not up to anything funny, I'll play every other shot left-handed.''

Kenney thought for a moment, then nodded. "Get yourself a stick, mister. Froggy, grab a cue. We've got ourselves a money game." A little fat fellow with a wide mouth and bulging eyes got up from the bench, where he'd been half dozing, and went to the cue rack. I looked at the Major with open curiosity, but he simply smiled and turned to select a cue. A moment later, Kenney was breaking open the racked balls, and the game was on.

Just over an hour later, walking back to the boat, the Major told me, "You should never play billiards for money with strangers, young man." We had ended the evening nineteen dollars richer, split evenly between the two of us.

"Shouldn't you be telling that to Dick Kenney?"

"Oh, he knows it perfectly well, now. But you, having won a few dollars this time, might be tempted to try it again. Believe me, there's no profit in it. Absolutely no profit.''

"How did you learn to play so well left-handed?" I had never seen such an exhibition of ambidexterity as the Major had put on, sinking every conceivable kind of shot with equal skill with either hand.

"It's the easiest thing in the world," said Major Demayne. "You see, I *am* left-handed.''

≈ 11

The next morning, I was awakened by the noise and bustle of the crew's bringing the luggage of the last few passengers on board the *Horace Greeley*. It was just after nine o'clock when I made my way down to the main deck for a late breakfast—paper-thin cornmeal pancakes with bacon, and excellent coffee.

I was just finishing up when Mr. Clemens walked in. He had come aboard after I turned out my light—I heard him and the captain laughing as they climbed the stair up to the texas. He took a seat opposite me, ordered breakfast, and then regaled me with an account of the previous night's dinner and conversation with the social and literary set of St. Paul.

I laughed at his description of the company, and then recounted my own adventures exploring the city, while he polished off a plate of eggs. His face lit up when I told of playing billiards with Dick Kenney, and even more when I told of Major Demayne's riding to the rescue. "Billiards, eh? Best game in the world," he said. "I didn't know you played, Wentworth—we'll have to find a table somewhere and shoot a few racks. And this Major Demayne may be worth paying attention to after all—he can't be all bad, if he shoots a good game. Have you looked at the fellow's poetry yet?"

"Not yet, sir. I haven't yet steeled myself to the task."

"No great rush. If he's anything like the rest of the poets

I've dealt with, he'll think we've slighted his epic if we read it too quickly and then tell him it's not the best thing since Homer. But try to get to it by the end of the week, so he doesn't think we're avoiding it. A fellow that's taken up your cause twice in twenty-four hours deserves at least that courtesy.''

The whistle sounded—the first time I'd heard it—and Mr. Clemens smiled. ''Now, that's music to my ears.'' He looked at his watch. ''If everything's on schedule, we should be casting off in fairly short order. Let's go up to the pilothouse and see who's going to be steering us downriver.''

There was unmistakable excitement in the air as we came out on deck. The sun was already bright, with harmless little white clouds dotted about the sky. Tiny Williams had his crew on the lower foredeck, ready to handle the ropes, and a haze above the twin smokestacks at the front of the boat gave evidence that Frenchy Devereaux had a fire going in the boilers. Many of the passengers had crowded onto the open decks for a good view of the proceedings. A number of them smiled and nodded to Mr. Clemens as they spotted him, and he stopped several times to exchange greetings with someone he knew. I began to see how this mode of travel might hold more charm than the usual businesslike railroad journey.

As we reached the hurricane deck, I saw Miss Patterson again, wearing a pretty lace shawl and carrying a parasol. She smiled and waved to us as we turned up the stairway to the texas. I waved back, then hurried to catch up with Mr. Clemens, who was climbing toward the pilothouse like a man half his age. At the foredeck of the texas, I spotted Captain Fowler with a megaphone in his hand, overseeing the colorful assembly of crew and passengers. And then Mr. Clemens opened the door to the pilothouse and we stepped into the calm center of all the *Horace Greeley*'s preparations for departure.

I don't know if it would describe the man standing by

the wheel more accurately to call him "thin" or "plump."
His arms and legs were as spindly as toothpicks, and his
chest and shoulders were in proportion; but underneath his
blue uniform jacket, his waistline showed a distinct bulge,
and his clean-shaven face was as round as a pumpkin. His
high, tight collar gave the first impression that he had no
neck at all. Combined with his short stature and rigid posture, his severe expression seemed to make his incongruous
appearance more, rather than less, comic. Next to him stood
a boy of perhaps sixteen, who could have been a miniature
version of him, right down to the tight collar and sour expression.

The pilot (as I assumed the man before us to be) gave
Mr. Clemens and me a disapproving look, but Mr. Clemens
slid onto the broad bench at the back of the pilothouse
without a word, and I followed his example. After impaling
us with his gaze for an uncomfortable span of time, the
pilot turned back to the wheel and continued his preparations for castoff. The young fellow next to him—his apprentice—continued to stare at us as if he had caught us
nipping on a flask of whisky during church services.

Presently, I heard the captain shout, "Cast off, you men!
All ashore that's going ashore! Mr. Parks, she's yours."

Mr. Parks nodded and pulled on one of the cords dan-
gling from the roof, sounding the whistle twice, then spoke
into the wooden tube I had noticed on my previous visit to
the pilothouse. "Give me dead-slow back speed, Frenchy,"
he said, and the sound of engines came from below. As if
by magic, the boat began to inch away from the dock. The
pilot made little adjustments to his wheel; then, after we'd
cleared the boats on either side, he swung it around hard,
turning the prow of the boat downriver. He sounded the
whistle again and spoke into the tube: "Half-speed ahead,"
and we were off on our expedition downriver.

"Nicely done," said Mr. Clemens, standing up and taking a couple of steps toward the pilot.

"Where do you think you're going?" said the pilot in a

loud voice. "Nobody asked you to come up here, and I'll be danged if I can see what business you have getting in my way when I've got a boat to run."

Mr. Clemens stopped as if someone had leveled a pistol at him. "Hold on now, son," he said. "My name's Sam Clemens, and I used to be a pilot."

"I don't care if you used to be General Grant," said Parks. "I've seen your kind before. Just because you used to steer some two-bit backwater boat, you think you know all about being a pilot. Well, I'll tell you something, mister. The river's changed, and the boats have changed, and you old-timers don't have a shade of a notion how things work these days. When's the last time you were behind the wheel, anyway?"

Mr. Clemens stood there dumbfounded for a moment, then said, "About twelve years ago, below St. Louis."

"So, it's been twelve years since you were a pilot, and below St. Louis, at that." The pilot snorted. "And then took retirement and an old-age pension, did you?"

"Why no, I quit piloting in '61, when the war broke out. You must have heard of—"

"I've heard a lot of foolish things in my time, but that tops 'em all. The pilot who let you steer should have lost his license," said Parks, with some vehemence. "It's not reg'lar to let passengers steer a boat, and a man who hasn't run the river in thirty years is no better than any other passenger. The insurance companies won't allow him to get behind the wheel, and the United States gov'ment won't allow it, and no pilot worth a brass penny *would* allow it. I suppose you think I'll give you a turn at the wheel. Tell the truth!"

"Well, I didn't think there'd be any harm in it. . . ." Mr. Clemens was shrinking back toward the bench, visibly intimidated by the pilot's tirade.

"You didn't think there'd be any harm in it! Did you think about what would happen if you ran this boat into the riverbank and drowned two hundred people? Did you think about how you'd pay the owners and the passengers after you sank it, larking about as if a steamboat were some sort of toy? Did you think about how I'd find a job after they took my license away for letting some old fool steer my boat?''

''No, but . . .''

''Look at you, anyhow!'' Parks continued, stepping away from the wheel and backing Mr. Clemens down. ''Look at that long hair! Against every regulation on the books. What if it got caught in the wheel? What then, eh? I bet you'd have a fine time, then.''

Mr. Clemens stiffened. Apparently he had had enough. ''Why, you young puppy, you wouldn't even have a *ride* on this boat if it weren't for me. I was one of the top pilots on the river before you were even born, and never once had anybody say a word about my hair. I'd bet twenty-five dollars I can outsteer you with one hand behind my back, hair or no hair.''

''It wouldn't be reg'lar,'' said Parks, returning to his wheel. ''I just *might* let you steer if you paid me fifty dollars and got all your hair cut off, and that filthy mustache, too, but not a minute sooner.''

Mr. Clemens turned visibly red. He opened his mouth to reply, and I shrank down in my seat, anticipating a retort of volcanic intensity, when the pilothouse door opened and Captain Fowler stepped in. ''Well, very smoothly done, Mr. Parks. Good morning, Sam,'' he said, smiling broadly. ''I assume you've met our pilot, Elmer Parks?''

Mr. Clemens's jaw dropped for an instant; then he cut loose with a string of invective so loud and sulfurous that I expected the pilothouse's windows to shatter and the river water to boil. He complained of the insults he'd been offered, and wished a host of calamities on the pilot and all his ancestors. Finally, he came to the crowning indignity. ''And this no good half-breed son of a deaf mule has the gall to tell me I can't steer the boat unless I get all my hair cut off, and my mustache, too!''

Captain Fowler listened patiently, an indulgent smile on his face. When my employer had finished, the captain said mildly, "Why, Sam, if I'd known you was so anxious to steer the boat, I'd have told you all this before. I thought you knew how things have changed on the river—these gol-durned government regulations are the devil's work, but there's no getting around them. Now, if you really want to take the wheel, I'm sure the barber can give you a clean shave and a nice short trim in no time flat."

For a moment, I was afraid that Mr. Clemens was about to have a stroke. His face turned red, his eyes grew wide, and he began to sputter. I was ready to come to his assistance, when he stood erect and gazed suspiciously at Mr. Parks and the captain for several seconds. Then Parks's apprentice giggled, and Captain Fowler grinned. At that, Mr. Clemens slapped his knee and broke into a great peal of laughter, in which he was joined by the captain and the pilot. He finally regained control of himself enough to say, "You got me, boys—Oh, you got me! Baited me like a catfish, and I swallowed it whole!" He laughed again, and tears ran down his cheeks.

The pilot smiled broadly—an expression that made his face a good bit more pleasant than before. "For a minute there, I was afraid you weren't going to go for it," he said, shaking Mr. Clemens's hand. "But Captain Mike played his part to perfection. Welcome aboard, Mr. Clemens. I've been hearing stories about you since I was a cub."

"I know I'm back on the river now," said Mr. Clemens, wiping his eyes. "Next thing I know, you'd have been shaving my head and painting it blue. I should have known Mike Fowler wouldn't have a rule-book man for a pilot, but you sure had me fooled. Captain, you're an unprincipled rascal, and I love it!"

"It didn't seem right not to have some sort of hoax ready to spring on you," said Captain Fowler, putting his arm around Mr. Clemens's shoulder. "The old days may be gone, but some of us remember them, Sam. Why, I'll never forget you telling me about alligator nets, and how the critters would crawl up and catch the passengers, back when I was a cub. I was too scared to sleep for most of a week.'' Something clicked into place in my mind as the captain said this, and I looked suspiciously at my employer, but for some reason he avoided my eye.

"A hell of a way to bring back memories," said Mr. Clemens. "Mr. Parks, I hope you won't mind if I come up here now and then to get away from the crowd. Just sitting in a pilothouse makes me feel young again."

"My pleasure, Mr. Clemens," said the pilot. "I'd feel bad if you didn't think you could come up here and relax. And once we get out on the open river, if you want to take the wheel for a spell, just say so."

"Call me Sam," said Mr. Clemens. "And I expect I'll take you up on that offer, Mr. Parks. I'm glad to know that pilots still know how to hoax a stranger. I was afraid that the riverboat life I used to know was dead and gone, but now I know there's some of it still alive and kicking."

The captain grinned. "Well, Sam, next time you need a kick in the pants, you'll know where to apply."

Mr. Clemens laughed. "It's good to be back on the river, boys," he said. Elmer Parks turned around and grinned, then reached up and pulled the whistle cord again, and we heard the muted sound of cheering from the passengers on the deck below. The *Horace Greeley* was on its way to New Orleans.

⁓ 12

"**D**o me a favor and read this," said Detective Berrigan. He handed me several sheets of paper.

I had spent most of that first morning watching Mr. Clemens talking happily (and ceaselessly) to the pilot. The majority of the talk was about people, places, and events I had never so much as imagined, let alone heard of, so I sat there restlessly until appetite got the better of me. A little after noon, I made my way down to the main cabin for a sandwich.

I was annoyed that Berrigan had chosen this time to interrupt me, but I looked at the top page. It was a neatly written list of names and cities; at the top of the first page I saw *Sam'l Clemens, Hartford, Connecticut.* The rest of the names on the page were completely strange to me. "What is this?" I asked.

"Mr. Snipes gave me the complete passenger list of the *Horace Greeley*," said Berrigan. "Take a look at it and see if you recognize any names."

I glanced over the document, taking a bite of my sandwich every now and then. A good number of the names were those of passengers I had met the previous day aboard the boat: Laura Cunningham, the Reverend Elijah Dutton and family, the reporter Andrew Dunbar, Martha Patterson, and Claude Dexter, the steamboat enthusiast. Toward the bottom of the third page, I saw *Ed McPhee, Cincinnati,* and then *Bill & Al Throckmorton, Cincinnati.* The latter two

names were struck out, with *KIKKED OFF BOAT & pas-
sige refunded* written in the margin in a different, coarser
hand. On the final page, I found my own name, followed
by *Paul Berrigan, New York City police*, and *Maj. Roy
Demayne, GAR, Trenton, New Jersey*. I told Berrigan which
names I recognized, and he nodded.

"About what I figured," the detective said. "Do you see
any names you know from before you took the job with
Mr. Twain?"

I scanned the list again. "No, I'm afraid not. Is this connected with the murder in New York?"

"Sure, and why else would I be asking?" said Berrigan.
"My chief sent me on this trip because the political boys
who give him his orders think the murderer might be following Mr. Twain. If that's so, our suspect's name—or the
name he's using now—is somewhere on this list. I want to
eliminate the people who couldn't possibly have done it. If
I can eliminate everybody on the list, I can go back home."

"Then why is Mr. Clemens's name still on the list?"

"I told you, this is the *complete* passenger list. If I
showed you a list with names crossed off, and my conclusions noted in the margin, it might keep you from saying
something I need to know about. Maybe someone's given
me an alibi, and you know something that contradicts it.
Maybe you saw people someplace they forgot to tell me
they'd been to."

"But surely you don't consider Mr. Clemens a suspect."

"Why, he was the first one I eliminated. I told my chief
about the note at Mr. Twain's hotel, and he decided to settle
that question before we went a step further. So he got *his*
boss to call somebody in the mayor's office, who called
Henry Rogers, and he vouched for Mr. Twain. They'd been
in a business meeting with two people from the steamboat
tour all morning, and Mr. Twain and Rogers had a long
lunch afterwards. He's not a suspect—that you can be sure
of."

"Well, I'm glad to hear I'm not working for a criminal,"

I said, in my best sarcastic tone. I flipped through the list to the final page. "My name's still on here, too."

Berrigan cleared his throat. "I've been meaning to talk to you about that. Can you tell me your whereabouts last Thursday afternoon?"

I thought a moment, somewhat taken aback by the question. "I arrived at my hotel a little before noon. Mr. Clemens was out at his business appointment, so I spent the afternoon in the art museum uptown."

"You did, now? And what did you see there?" I mentioned a few canvases, and Berrigan surprised me by showing a rather detailed familiarity with them, even asking about others that were hung near the ones I'd mentioned. I wouldn't have thought a policeman would have such a knowledge of art, and told him so.

"You won't find many," the detective said with a grin. "Last year, I had a case that sent me to shadow a suspected art thief, and guess where he spent his afternoons? I shadowed him through the museum about five times, all told, before we cleared him and arrested another man. I found myself missing the paintings, so I went back to the museum on my own about a month ago, and he was there again— so I struck up a conversation and we had a jolly time talking about art and artists. You never know, in this business. Anyhow, you've obviously been to the museum. That doesn't prove it was on Thursday, of course, but I have ways of verifying that if I need to."

"Surely you don't think I killed this fellow in New York! What reason could I possibly have?"

"Suppose you came in while he was still in the lobby, and the clerk pointed him out as the man who was asking for Mr. Twain. He talked you into going with him, and when he got you away from the hotel, the two of you got into an argument."

"This is preposterous," I said, somewhat heatedly. "Why would I have gone with the fellow?"

"He might have claimed that Mr. Twain had sent him

to find you, and persuaded you to follow him downtown,''
said Berrigan. His face was expressionless. ''Then, in the
alley away from the hotel, he tried to rob you and you killed
him in self-defense. Or maybe he threatened to blackmail
Mr. Twain, and you killed him to protect your employer—
and your job.''

''You dare accuse me—'' I began, rising from my seat,
but he stopped me with a raised hand. I realized that I must
have been speaking loud; people at nearby tables had
stopped talking, and some of them were looking at me out
of the corners of their eyes. I was uncomfortably aware of
Laura Cunningham among the onlookers.

''Calm down, Mr. Cabot,'' said the detective. He said it
quietly, but there was a firm, no-nonsense tone to his voice.
I sat down, acutely aware that I had been making a spec-
tacle of myself. ''Nobody's accused you of anything,'' Berrigan said. ''In fact, the sooner I can eliminate you for
certain, the happier I'll be. The main reason I'm here is that
somebody with a load of influence back in New York is
afraid that Mr. Twain is in danger from persons unknown.
Now, wouldn't it be a fine mess if it turns out the private
secretary of the man I'm supposed to be guarding is dangerous, and I haven't investigated him properly? And if I
eliminate you from my list of suspects and you go ahead
and kill him, where am I then?''

''I suppose it makes sense, if you look at it that way,''
I admitted.

''Nothing personal, of course; I just have to consider all
the angles in a case like this. You can't deny that you *were*
in the right town at the right time, and you're the only
person who admits to having seen the dead man in New
York, and you're employed by Mr. Twain, and so I can't
eliminate you entirely—even though you don't strike me
as a very likely murderer. You can be sure we'd be having
a much less friendly conversation today, if I thought you
were the man I'm after.''

''Not a very likely murderer, am I? Well, I guess it's a

compliment of sorts. What can I do to make myself even less likely in your eyes?'' I leaned back and crossed my arms across my chest. I was beginning to understand my employer's view of this interfering detective.

"Help me find the one who did it," said Berrigan. "You're the closest thing to a witness we have at this point. You saw our victim, and there's a chance you may have seen his killer without knowing it at the time. Keep an eye out on the passengers, and let me know right away if you see a face that you might have spotted in New York last Thursday, especially if they were at Mr. Twain's lecture or in his hotel.''

I thought a moment, trying to think whether I'd noticed anyone on board the boat I recognized from elsewhere. I mentioned having seen Miss Cunningham at the Chicago lecture, and Berrigan duly noted the fact, with a chuckle. "Hard to forget that face, isn't it? I'd be surprised if she's our killer, but I've been surprised before.'' I glanced at the spot where she had been sitting earlier, and realized that she was gone. I wondered whether my outburst had been part of her reason for leaving.

I had the feeling that I was omitting someone else. Perhaps, I thought, something would come to me when I'd met more of the passengers and had faces to attach to these names. Thinking about the list reminded me of something else: "What about the Throckmorton brothers? They've been thrown off the boat, but they were scheduled to be on the trip originally.''

"I doubt it was that pair, nasty as they are. They're trouble, for sure, and I'm just as glad to be rid of them, but unless something new pops up, they're not suspects in this case. I can imagine them knifing a man without batting an eye, but not leaving money in his pockets afterwards. Besides, their alibi looks good. Now, McPhee's another story, and a fishy one at that. If I could place him in New York on the day of the murder, I'd arrest him this minute. And I'm keeping an eye out for that Jack Hubbard as well—I'll wager he's still in the game, somehow. The question is whether we can spot him—if he's here, he didn't give his right name when he bought the ticket.''

"I'd be amazed if he had," I said. "He's probably changed disguises, too. But Mr. Clemens might recognize him, if he's on the boat.''

"Aye, that he might," said the detective, folding the list and standing. "I'll have to find Mr. Clemens and ask him. Meanwhile, keep your eyes open, and let me know if you spot anything funny.''

While I was vexed that Detective Berrigan had not been willing to remove me entirely from his list of suspects, I was not sorry that we had talked. He had reminded me that the criminal he was pursuing remained at large, and might very well be among the happy passengers surrounding me on the decks of the *Horace Greeley*. It was sobering to glance at the people in the main cabin and on the decks, wondering whether one of them might be a murderer—and, if Berrigan was right, a real and present danger to Mr. Clemens. I had allowed the simple pleasures of seeing new places and meeting new people to distract me. It was time to rededicate myself to my search for the killer.

The only problem was, where to begin? I scanned the faces of my fellow passengers, looking in vain for one I recognized from New York or anywhere else. There were depressingly few who seemed even vaguely familiar, and fewer still whom I could imagine in the role of a criminal.

Chief among these was Ed McPhee, who sat at a round table in a corner of the main cabin, already engaged in a lively game of poker with four other men. He was obviously wasting no time lamenting the absence of the Throckmorton boys, and was instead avidly pursuing his vocation, if one can dignify cardplaying with so lofty an appellation.

But while Berrigan claimed to have found discrepancies in McPhee's story, nobody had reported seeing him in New

York at the time of the murder, and he denied ever having visited that city. His expression of surprise on seeing the murder victim's photograph had seemed genuine. On the other hand, Mr. Clemens had characterized him as a liar, and a man not to turn one's back on. And it was quite possible that he suspected the truth about Mr. Clemens's story regarding the treasure in "Napoleon, Arkansas." McPhee would bear watching, I told myself.

Besides Mr. Clemens and myself, the only passenger I could remember seeing in New York before our departure was Detective Berrigan himself. But there seemed to be no profit in that line of speculation, despite Mr. Clemens's initial doubts as to Berrigan's bona fides. The detective had put himself too squarely in the middle of the affair to escape attention. Besides, there was no reason to believe that he knew anything at all of the hidden gold, which was the only motive I could imagine for his killing a man in New York, then manipulating events to allow himself to follow Mr. Clemens down the river.

The newspaper reporter, Andrew Dunbar, was another who had probably been in New York on the day of the crime. But given his obtrusive manner, and his apparent hostility to Mr. Clemens, I could hardly have missed noticing him had he been anywhere in our vicinity on the day of the murder. As for a possible motive, killing a man to get a newspaper story seemed too far-fetched to credit.

The passenger list had included several other people who'd given New York as their residence, although I knew far too little about any of them to support even the wildest theory. Could one of them, I wondered, be the elusive Farmer Jack Hubbard? I had to grant the possibility. Never having laid eyes on the fellow, I had only the vaguest of descriptions to go by—a tall man, who had been in the habit of posing as a rustic. I would have to make note of any unusually tall passengers—I realized, with a sense of irony, that I myself would be on that list if Berrigan were compiling it. Of course, if Hubbard were on board, even in a new disguise, Mr. Clemens would have the best chance of spotting him.

Considering all these uncertainties, I could understand why Berrigan had been reluctant to remove me from his list of suspects. I was perhaps the only person on the boat who was in New York at the right time and who had an undeniable connection (however innocent) to Mr. Clemens. The detective's speculations concerning me were obviously rubbish; even he admitted that they were unlikely. But who knew what he might do if he came under pressure to make an arrest, or what his superiors might be ready to believe? It was clearly in my best interests to help him find the real murderer. Unfortunately, I seemed to be no closer to doing that than I had been when I'd first learned of the crime.

I decided to take a stroll around the decks. After all, I had met only a small fraction of the passengers. There was a reasonable chance that I might spot someone who had been in the crowd at the first of Mr. Clemens's lectures I had attended, or even in the lobby back in the Union Square Hotel. As things stood, there was a shortage of credible suspects. It was time to see if I could make any additions to the number.

The sun was still shining brightly as I came out of the cabin. The river had widened out into a sort of lake, and it seemed we were now in a separate little world of our own, free for a brief while from the rules and customs of the rest of civilization. The thought that one of our group might be a cold-blooded killer struck home even more sharply at the realization that there was nowhere to escape him, should he turn his hand to slaughter once again.

What, I wondered, would a murderer look like? The faces of my fellow passengers, smiling at the simple pleasure of seeing the natural beauty of the river on a fine, clear day, gave no sign of darker passions. There was no hint of guilt about them, nothing I could interpret as evidence of criminal propensities. I had seen more anger and passion in

Mr. Clemens's face over the course of a few days than in those of my fellow passengers, yet I was quite certain he was no murderer.

The Throckmorton brothers came far closer to my notion of criminal physiognomy than any of the faces before me. I had vivid memories of Billy Throckmorton's smirk as he'd shoved me into the river at St. Paul. I could as easily imagine the same brutish expression on his face as he leveled a revolver or a knife at a defenseless victim. On the other hand, McPhee, whom Berrigan evidently believed to be capable of such a bloody deed even if he was not necessarily the murderer he sought, had sat at the card table with a calm, businesslike expression. He might as well have been an attorney greeting new clients. Would his face appear the same as he snuffed out a life?

I realized that I had spent much of my life in a state of comparative innocence. It seemed highly unlikely that there were habitual criminals among my playmates, or in my parents' circle of acquaintance—my father, as an attorney, may have had the occasional unsavory client, but if so, he never brought him home to meet the family. I had witnessed no murders, and few enough serious fights; the football field was as close as my life had come to violence. Until Detective Berrigan had pulled out the photograph of poor Lee Russell in the New York morgue, I had never laid eyes on a body dead of any cause other than age or disease. How could I judge what the visage of a killer would show?

Berrigan must have seen many hundreds of criminals in his time, some of them from the worst levels of society. Most likely he had had occasion to defend himself from deadly assault by some felon resisting arrest. Yet he somehow walked through the world with a placid expression, and showed no external sign of an acquaintance with death and corruption. Perhaps too great a familiarity with evil made a man comfortable with it, even a man who had to fight it every day. If so, what would a truly hardened criminal look like? Was there *no* external sign of that inner deficiency of soul?

By the time I had circled the boiler deck and the hurricane deck, I was convinced that nobody on board could be a killer—and a moment later, that every single person aboard the *Horace Greeley* was a potential assassin, waiting only for the opportune moment to drop the smiling mask and, like a mad dog, run through the crowd dealing death to all and sundry. Just as my thoughts reached this depth of despair, I turned the corner of the cabin and found myself face-to-face with Miss Patterson.

"Good afternoon, Mr. Cabot," she said. "Whatever causes you to frown so on such a beautiful day?"

13

I was taken aback, as much by Miss Patterson's sudden appearance as by her question. My face must have shown my confusion, for she twirled her parasol and gave a little laugh. "Of course, you needn't answer if I'm intruding. It just seemed strange to see you with such a dark expression. I do hope nothing's wrong!"

I shook my head. "Nothing really," I said. "Just a passing mood." Her eyes twinkled at me, and the afternoon sun sparkled brightly off the waters of the river. I could hear music from the lounge and the voices of other passengers laughing and chatting pleasantly as the boat glided smoothly down the broad expanse between the banks. It was hard to think unpleasant thoughts in such surroundings, and in such company.

"Well, I hope it won't pass my way," she said. "It would quite spoil this marvelous scenery. Do you think that mountain is Maiden Rock?"

"Maiden's Rock, I think it's called," I said. I had seen an engraving of it in my guidebook, but the reality was far more imposing. "There is some sort of Indian legend associated with it, but I can't recall the details."

"I remember the story now," said Miss Patterson. "An Indian maid named Winona had given her heart to one handsome brave, but her parents insisted that she wed another, a famous warrior of the tribe. On the eve of the wedding, they sent her with the other maidens of the tribe to gather flowers on the summit of the rock, as was their custom. But rather than marry against her will, she threw herself off the rock. They say that travelers on the river can sometimes hear her singing as they pass by the rock.''

''A melancholy tale for such a picturesque place,'' I said. ''Is it true?''

She thought for a moment, then said, ''I'm not sure whether it is true, but it is such a pretty story that I find myself wanting to believe it nonetheless. Sentiment can be as meaningful as what the history books tell us, don't you think?''

''I'm sure it can,'' I said. ''Although I must confess that if I heard someone singing from the top of the rock, I would be more likely to suspect a prank than an Indian ghost.''

''Mr. Cabot! Have you no imagination?''

''Mr. Clemens seems to think not,'' I told her. ''However, he appears to consider the lack of it something of an asset, though I'm not sure whether or not to take him seriously.''

''How remarkable!'' she said, with a little laugh. ''It must be very interesting to work for such a famous literary man. Does he always say peculiar things like that?''

''I suppose he must; at least I can't say I always understand him,'' I admitted. ''Have you read many of his books?'' We turned and began to walk along the deck.

''Not very many, I'm afraid. I like to read romantic things, things that make me wish I could meet the person in the book—things like *The Three Fates,* or *Sara Crewe.* It's not the same as really meeting somebody famous in real life, of course—I never *dreamed* I'd meet Mr. Twain the very first day aboard the ship. And there are so many other interesting people aboard, too.''

''Oh, which ones?''

''Captain Fowler, for one,'' she said. ''The captain looks just as I've always thought the captain of a ship ought to. Then there's the detective you mentioned when we first met. I still don't know which one he is, and I've been trying

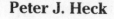

to guess who he is, and whom he's following, and whether he's going to arrest someone. And the men who play cards are so intent on their game, so feverishly concentrated—I don't think there's anything more fascinating than men wagering vast fortunes on a single turn of the cards, whether they win or lose.''

"I'm afraid that makes me hopelessly dull," I said. "I'm not much of a cardplayer, and I certainly don't have vast fortunes to wager, even if I were."

"Oh, I'm sure you're being modest," she said, smiling. "I can't imagine Mr. Twain having a dull person in his employment."

Before I could reply, I saw Major Demayne come around the bend in the deck. His face broke into a broad smile as he recognized me. "Hello, young fellow," he said. "Have you spent all your winnings yet?"

"My goodness," said Miss Patterson. "Mr. Cabot was just now telling me he doesn't play cards." She turned to me with a stern expression. "Have you been misleading me, sir?"

The Major laughed. "No, no, miss. Young Mr. Cabot and I were partners in a billiard match, in which he acquitted himself quite well, in my opinion. I don't know a thing about how he plays cards, except that he's almost certainly luckier than I am. I consider it a good game when I manage to break even."

"I'm always very lucky," said the young woman. "Perhaps I'll show you both how to play cards. My luck might be catching!" She smiled, twirled her parasol again, and ducked into the main cabin.

Seeing Major Demayne set off a twinge of conscience that I had not yet looked at his poetry. We chatted idly for a little while, then I excused myself and headed to my stateroom, still keeping an eye out for possible suspects in the New York murder case. As before, I saw nobody whom I could say with any confidence had crossed my path in New

York—or anywhere else, except on the boat. Nor could I concoct any reason to point a suspicious finger at any of my fellow passengers, who were as ordinary a group as ever I saw.

Slightly disappointed in the results of my detective work, I went into my cabin and picked up the Major's manuscript. It was every bit as thick as when he'd given it to me, and as I lifted it now it seemed to have gotten even heavier. The first page bore a title in a clear, bold hand: "The Sanguinary Clash of Two Great Armies at Antietam, as Describ'd in Verse by an Eye-Witness." Below that was the author's name, "Maj. Roy Demayne, 25th New Jersey."

The text began on the second page. It read:

> Somewhere I hear the cannon's fearsome roar—
> Antietam! Waves of blood roll on thy shore!
> My Comrades fall, their lives not spent in vain—
> I lov'd them, and remember still their pain.
>
> Napoleon's armies reach'd no greater heights;
> Engrave in Golden numbers, Muse! their fights.
> E'en I, unworthy wretch, am spar'd to tell
> Deeds of renown, in Sharpsburg's deadly dell.
>
> Ten thousand fell on that ensanguin'd field,
> O'er whelmed by fire, but not about to yield!
> Secession's minions cannot win the day;
> E'en Lee himself cannot the Vict'ry stay!
>
> Eagles of Triumph above our standards soar—
> Youth's slain and crippl'd, but the battle's o'er.
> Out of the blood the Union rises whole—
> Union Forever! I shout with all my soul.

I was not sure what to make of this. The sentiments were certainly just, and the language vigorous. But I could make neither head nor tails of what the fellow was trying to say.

134   The next page was even more obscure—and the verses did not even rhyme! I remembered a sorry, rather argumentative, fellow at Yale who fancied himself (among other things) a poet. That young nonconformist had maintained that rhyme was a vestige of a less refined era, but I had paid no more attention to him then than when he railed against private property, religion, marriage, and the like. On one occasion, these opinions got him dunked into a watering trough by two of the proctors. But the Major had little except obscurity in common with that campus iconoclast. As to the merit of his verses, I was as much in the dark as if they had been written in Chinese.

I leafed back to the first page; perhaps a second reading would make the verses more perspicuous. But beyond the theme of victory and sacrifice, and of the Union triumphant, I could make no more sense of it than on my first reading. At last, I resolved to put it aside for now and give it another try later before reporting to Mr. Clemens. After all, the Major had done me a good turn on at least two occasions, and I owed it to him to give his writing a fair chance before condemning it. I put the manuscript back on my bedside table and went out on deck.

Proposing to resume my observation of my fellow passengers, I climbed down to the hurricane deck, where the sightseers seemed to be gathered. But no sooner had I found an open space by the rail than the Reverend Dutton's wife spotted me. "Well, good day, Mr. Cabot," she chirped, sweeping forward with her daughters Gertrude and Berenice on either flank, in an enveloping maneuver that would have done credit to the Prussian General Staff. "I was just telling the girls how fortunate we are to be traveling in such distinguished company. Why, who would have expected to find a Cabot way out here, practically on the frontier?" Gertrude and Berenice giggled in a sort of unmelodic unison.

"I would hardly have expected it myself, before this summer," I said. "But this is a far cry from the wild frontier, Mrs. Dutton. With electric lights on board, and all the latest conveniences, we're hardly going to be camping out. Most of the towns we'll be stopping at even have telephone service.''

"Yes, but the people are so unrefined," said Mrs. Dutton. "They all speak with the most dreadful accents—why, I can barely understand them, half the time.''

I was somewhat surprised to hear myself responding, "I can't really agree with you, Mrs. Dutton. After all, the man I work for speaks in one of those 'dreadful accents,' and I have no trouble understanding him.'' It was true; a few short weeks ago, I might have felt much as she did, but Mr. Clemens's rich Missouri drawl had insinuated itself into my ear so thoroughly that I hardly noticed it nowadays. And at the moment, I could think of other western accents I found a good bit more listenable than Mrs. Dutton's dry New England speech. Deciding that I preferred to enjoy the scenery in privacy, I politely extricated myself from the conversation and climbed back up to the texas deck.

"How do you like the ride so far, Wentworth?'' I turned around with a bit of a start; Mr. Clemens had caught me daydreaming again. The views had been dramatic all afternoon, with stands of trees atop high banks and the sun shining brightly on the river. Somewhat to my surprise, after having heard all the old river hands lament the falling-off of traffic, I had seen several other boats on the river during the day. Most of them were freighters of some kind, or stubby towboats pulling barges. We saw one other passenger ship, the Diamond Jo St. Louis-St. Paul packet— going upriver. Mr. Parks blew his whistle at the pilot of the other boat, and everyone on both decks waved gaily as the other pilot signaled back. It was a grand way to travel.

Perhaps the hot sun and the leisurely pace at which we were rolling down the mighty river had mesmerized me, or perhaps I was just a bit tired. Whatever the reason, I had fallen into a deep state in which the Major's verses, the murder mystery, and the ten thousand dollars in gold hidden somewhere in Arkansas played a strange counterpoint against the half-seen landscape drifting by. I had felt myself on the verge of some profound revelation when Mr. Clemens brought me back to reality.

"Did the scenery put you to sleep already?" Mr. Clemens laughed. "I knew the river was tame these days, but I hadn't guessed it was soporific. Mind you, Wentworth, don't sleep leaning on the rail, unless you know how to swim. I'd hate to have to try finding another Yale man in Iowa."

I laughed. "I assure you I can swim. Of course, I can't guarantee that I can keep up with a steamboat."

"Usually they stop, if they know somebody's fallen over—unless he's jumped off the deck to escape a jealous husband, in which case letting the passenger swim ashore unimpeded is the best policy. As Slippery Ed could probably tell you, there've been shots fired from on deck at a man in the water more than once over the years. If you do fall in, make sure you clear the wheel, either by going wide or diving under. With a stern-wheeler like the *Greeley,* going wide is better."

"I'm not planning to fall in, but I'll remember your advice."

"Good. I'd hate to have such exemplary advice go to waste." Mr. Clemens took out a cigar. "I've had a wonderful day today, Wentworth. It takes me back to when I was your age."

"Yes, sir, I could see that you were enjoying yourself."

"I enjoyed myself even more when Parks let me steer the boat. It's a grand feeling, standing way up there and holding the wheel in your hands, looking out over the river like a king. No, it's better than a king. Kings have parliaments and ministers they must please. In the old days, a Mississippi river pilot was beholden to no one but himself, and today I felt like that again for a little while—until that damned detective came up and started waving papers in my face.''

"Ah, he said he was going to look for you," I said. "Did you learn anything useful from his passenger list?"

"Well, I managed to identify a couple of dozen names—people I felt I could vouch for. Most of them are ordinary folks with an interest in travel and literature, about as likely to fly to the moon as to stab somebody in an alley. He scratched them off his list pretty much on my say-so."

"He certainly didn't eliminate me so quickly," I said, somewhat put out.

"Oh, Berrigan has to act like a policeman sometimes, or nobody will take him seriously," said Mr. Clemens. "He has to bluster around and search for clues, and make most of the passengers uncomfortable, or he won't feel as if he's earning his salary. It doesn't occur to him that he's making enough commotion to scare away his suspect, if you swallow the notion that there's a suspect on board this boat to begin with."

"I take it you still have your doubts about that."

"I ask myself why a murderer would be following me, and I don't get any good answers. If somebody was looking to rob me, he's missed a dozen better opportunities than he's likely to get on board a boat—not that I carry around enough money to be worth bothering with, these days. And while I have my share of enemies, they're more likely to write a scurrilous article about me than to hire an assassin."

I glanced around to make certain there was nobody close to overhear us; then I asked, "Wouldn't the gold in Arkansas be reason enough? Men have been killed for a good bit less."

"That supposes someone who knows about it—not impossible, I grant you. But there can't be very many men alive who know about it, and what are the odds one of them's on this boat?"

"Couldn't McPhee be one of them? Detective Berrigan doesn't believe his alibi for New York," I said.

"Why, neither do I," said Mr. Clemens. "Slippery Ed would lie to a policeman just on principle; you're best off not believing anything he said in Berrigan's presence. But Ed wouldn't pull a knife on a bigger man—which is what we're assuming here—unless he was cornered and had to fight for his life. And in that case, he'd have shown some damage himself. No, Ed has an instinct for keeping his skin in one piece. In the old days, given a choice between standing and fighting or lighting out for the next town, Ed would always run. The Throckmorton boys probably handle Ed's dirty work these days, and Berrigan thinks their alibi is good."

"What if McPhee had an accomplice in New York?"

Mr. Clemens turned and gave me a sharp look. "Now, that's another question entirely," he said. "Of course, it doesn't change one thing—Slippery Ed's still not likely to pull a knife on me himself. So we're still looking for some other person, assuming he's on board at all. The trick is to find that person, or more likely to find proof that he doesn't exist, so we can relax and enjoy the rest of the trip without Berrigan's impositions."

"What about Farmer Jack Hubbard? Have you seen anyone on board who looks like him?"

"Nobody who looks the way he used to, at any rate. I'm sure I haven't talked to everyone on board, so I may yet spot him. But I don't think he's our man, either. I never knew Jack to harm a fly. He always managed to talk his way out of trouble—I once saw him persuade a fellow who'd been ready to throw a punch at him to buy the house a round of drinks instead. Of course, Jack wasn't likely to get caught with an extra ace in his pocket, so he had a lot less trouble than somebody like Slippery Ed to begin with."

"That may be so, but all the evidence points to him as being involved in this case somehow."

"Granted. And both he and Ed might know something about that Napoleon, Arkansas business," he said. "But to capitalize on that, they need to keep me alive. And unless everything I know about human nature is wrong—and human nature is a novelist's stock in trade, Wentworth—neither one of them's a killer.''

"If neither one of them is the killer, then who is?'' I asked nobody in particular.

"Nobody on board this ship, I hope,'' said Mr. Clemens. "Nothing would make me happier than a telegram at the next town telling me that the New York police have found their man, and are calling Berrigan home.''

"Then we should have a grand journey downriver,'' I said.

"Oh, I'm having a grand journey already,'' said Mr. Clemens. "It would be close to perfect if it weren't for this highly improbable notion that somebody on board might want to kill me.''

⤳ 14

Our journey down the river gradually fell into a pleasant routine, varied by the ever-changing scenery and the different towns in which we docked for the night. Except when we had an unusually long run between towns, we did most of our traveling during daylight—especially on the upper river, with its lofty banks and picturesque views. After Lake Pepin, the Chippewa River joined the stream; the outline of the bluffs along the shore became even more striking, and small islands dotted the waters. There were two bridges at Winona, and an island that towered some five hundred feet above the river's surface at Trempealeau, near the confluence of the Black River. At La Crosse, we passed under the railroad bridge we had gone over on our way to St. Paul.

The towns were closer together below La Crosse, but the landscape between them continued to present a picturesque wildness unlike anything I had seen back in Connecticut. We crossed from Minnesota into Iowa near Victory, where in 1832 Black Hawk and his army of renegade Indians were brought to their knees after a desperate fight. A few miles farther south, the Wisconsin River joined our course near Prairie du Chien. We passed into Illinois just opposite Eagle Rock, three hundred feet high, and the banks became lower, the scenery less romantic. Still, the weather continued fine, and I would spend much of the day looking over one of the rails at the river and its banks. The hours slipped by as easily as the miles of river.

My employer had continued to spend a good deal of every day with the pilot, reminiscing about the river and taking an occasional turn at the wheel. But after the first couple of days aboard the *Horace Greeley*, he began compiling notes for his new book about the river, making a special point of talking with any passenger old enough to remember the great era of steamboating, before the Civil War. Often he asked me to sit in on these interviews, and I would hastily jot down the subject's reminiscences; I began to regret that Yale had not included shorthand in its curriculum. I also began to despair for the health of our native tongue in the hinterlands—the convolutions of grammar and pronunciation I was forced to inscribe on my tablets would have given my old schoolmaster fits. At the end, Mr. Clemens would ask his interviewees to write out a paper giving him permission to quote them in his book—"the damned lawyers are always afraid people will sue me for stealing their stories," he said—which I dutifully filed, along with my notes on the interview.

Usually we would arrive at a town a little before suppertime, to allow passengers to go ashore while there was still daylight, for sightseeing or whatever other entertainment the town afforded. In the smaller towns, it was not uncommon for the mayor and a selection of local officials to meet us at the dock. As often as not, a local brass band (usually surprisingly good for such small towns) would be there to contribute a bit of joyful noise to the occasion. Mr. Clemens and Captain Fowler would shake hands with the local notables, and my employer would say a few words, mostly inviting the townspeople to see his lecture at eight o'clock that evening. Then the local band would play another piece or two, and the shipboard band would play a few pieces of its own. Finally the assembly would break up until "the trouble started," to use Mr. Clemens's term for the beginning of his talk.

After these brief ceremonies, I would usually head directly for the post office to dispatch Mr. Clemens's mail and pick up any letters being held for him. He was always eager for any letters from his wife and daughters; he kept up a steady correspondence with them, and often expressed his frustration at not being able to join them in Europe, due to his financial obligations. On the few occasions where there was no mail from them awaiting him, he fell into a dark mood that made me wish I could avoid his company—but alas, there was no way to do so and still perform my work.

The *Horace Greeley*'s lecture hall was larger than anything available in most of the smaller towns we visited. (On Sunday mornings, it doubled as a chapel—the Reverend Mr. Dutton conducted the services, with his wife leading the singing in a determined, if wobbly, contralto.) So, even in towns with a suitable hall, we arranged to give the lectures on board in order to avoid paying rent. Only in the largest cities did we bow to necessity and engage a local hall. There were even a couple of smaller towns where, at the last minute, Mr. Clemens scheduled a second performance at ten o'clock so as not to disappoint all those who'd come from miles away to spend an evening with "Mark Twain."

The lecture varied some from one night to the next. While the core of it was the same talk I had seen in New York and Chicago, there were impromptu interludes in which Mr. Clemens alluded to something of local interest or recalled previous visits to the town we were in. But while the event lost some of its novelty for those on board, crowds eager to hear it packed the boat almost every evening—sometimes there would be two or three rows of local youngsters lining the deck outside the cabin, trying to get close enough to a door or window to hear what everyone inside was laughing at. The smiling faces at the end of the lecture were all the proof anyone needed that Mr. Clemens had lost none of his energy and good humor, despite a schedule that would have broken many a younger man.

The success of the lecture tour, and the unhurried pace of daily life aboard the boat, did not distract me from the problem I had set myself: solving the New York murder case. But as we made our progress southward, I found myself no closer to the solution than before. I spoke occasionally to Detective Berrigan, who claimed to be narrowing down his list of suspects. On two or three occasions, I saw him ashore at the telegraph office, evidently communicating his latest findings to his superiors back in New York.

I also crossed paths with the reporter, Andrew Dunbar, in the post office in nearly every town where we touched shore, presumably dispatching his stories to his paper— although what he had to report, other than the changing landscape and the size of the crowd from one night to the next, I had no idea. Once or twice I saw him huddled with some of Tiny Williams's crewmen, although they surely had little enough to tell in the way of news. Mr. Clemens had steadfastly refused to give him an interview. Occasionally I saw the reporter among the ever-changing knot of cardplayers who congregated in the main cabin. From what I could tell, he was rarely a winner.

Slippery Ed McPhee, for his part, seemed regularly to arise from the table with more cash than he sat down with. He was always vocal and ebullient, bantering with his fellow players and cajoling them into betting higher amounts. He never seemed to have any shortage of opponents, either; if he was cheating, as Mr. Clemens had hinted he had done in the past, none of the others seemed to suspect it. Perhaps he was refraining from winning too much too soon, so as not to deplete the crop of potential victims before the end of the voyage—or perhaps not having the Throckmorton boys handy to protect him from angry losers made him careful. Once we arrived in port, he would leave the table until after Mr. Clemens's lecture. I assumed that he was merely taking a break for dinner and a rest before his usual late-night sessions. It wasn't until our second night in St.

Louis that I discovered how McPhee was spending his evenings.

At first, I had faithfully attended Mr. Clemens's lectures, not as a listener but to lend a hand before and after—rescuing him from local bores, making sure that a friend of his got a special seat. I eventually realized that as long as I delivered him to his dressing room and met him backstage after the talk, I could use the time while he was actually talking as I saw fit. So I began to avail myself of the opportunity to spend an hour or so reading, or conversing with passengers who had skipped the lecture—as many of them did, after they learned that it was essentially the same from night to night.

This particular day, a Saturday, Mr. Clemens had gone to dinner with old friends in St. Louis, and told me to take the whole day off. I took the guidebook's advice and walked across the Eads Bridge—the view of the river, with barges and riverboats crossing beneath you, is worth a good bit more than the nickel I paid to cross. I spent the rest of the afternoon walking about the city. The St. Louis Museum of Fine Arts had casts of the Elgin marbles, which were impressive enough, but the paintings were nothing special. After a while, the entire city began to strike me as a bit dull. I had an early dinner in a little beer garden, a pleasant enough place, but the lager was thin and too sweet for the sauerkraut and sausages I had ordered. When the relentlessly cheerful German band began to grate on my ears, I decided to go back to the boat while it was still light out. Perhaps there would be someone interesting to talk with, I thought idly—perhaps Miss Cunningham, or Miss Patterson.

The most direct route to the steamboat landing took me past the Olympic Theater, where Mr. Clemens was lecturing that evening. A good number of ticket-holders had already begun to gather, but it was not so crowded that I didn't see Miss Patterson, wearing a blue dress and standing at the fringe of a small group of people near the entrance. To my surprise, at the center of the group was Slippery Ed McPhee.

I came closer, curious to see what McPhee could be doing to draw such a crowd. He had an upended barrel in front of him, with three playing cards, creased lengthwise, on top. "I've got the mama, and the papa, and the baby," he said, turning the cards over to show a black queen, a black king, and a red jack. "Who wants to try to find the baby? I'm paying two to one." He picked the cards up between the fingers of both hands, and with a well-practiced flick, threw them back down and mixed them, chattering like an auctioneer the whole time. To my utter astonishment, Alligator Throckmorton stepped out of the crowd and said, "Ten bucks says I can find it."

"Ten dollars; will anyone bet fifteen?" said McPhee. "Find the baby and win two for one! No takers? Ten it is, then." Throckmorton put the money on the barrelhead and pointed at the center card with an evil grin. "You're a lucky man," said McPhee, flipping the card over to reveal the red jack. He peeled a twenty-dollar bill off a fat roll and gave it to the sneering lout. "Want to try again? I'm paying two to one."

"Sure," said Throckmorton. "Let's make it twenty this time." He threw the bill McPhee had just given him back onto the barrelhead. McPhee picked up the cards again, two in his right hand and one in his left, and again threw them down and mixed them. "Who'll bet twenty-five?" Just then, Miss Patterson tapped me on the shoulder.

"So, you are interested in gambling, after all!" she said, smiling.

"Not really," I whispered. "Besides, Mr. Clemens has told me that McPhee is a cheat. If I played against him, I would surely lose."

"Oh, but *that* man seems to be lucky," she said. Alligator Throckmorton had again found the "baby" card, the red jack, and McPhee had peeled two twenties off his roll.

"There's no luck involved. That fellow is in cahoots with him," I said. "McPhee is letting him win only so that he can draw in someone else who doesn't know the secret."

"Aha!" said Miss Patterson, staring at the cards. "I wonder how he knows which is the right card, then. There must be some signal that he knows to look for, and that we can't see."

"Really. I never thought of it, but you must be right." I peered closer at the cards, wondering by what means McPhee was signaling the right card to his confederate. It made sense that there was some secret signal, or perhaps a mark on the cards, but I didn't detect anything suspicious as McPhee threw the cards down again.

"Look," whispered Miss Patterson. "The corner of the middle card is bent. Do you think that could be it?"

"I don't know," I said. Throckmorton put down ten dollars this time and pointed to the bent card. McPhee picked it up and turned it over, and it was the "baby" card.

"That must be the secret mark," said Miss Patterson, barely holding back her excitement. "If you bet on the bent card, you can win!"

"But that wouldn't be fair," I protested. "Besides, he's a cheat. He'd find some way to keep me from winning."

"If you make the highest bet, he has to take it," she said. "If he's a cheat, wouldn't it serve him right to lose to someone who sees through his shabby tricks? Give him a taste of his own medicine!"

"Perhaps you're right," I said. The man was such a fraud that turning the tables on him would be a public service of sorts. Soliciting some of the spectators in the crowd to bet, McPhee threw the cards down once again, with a dramatic flourish. Throckmorton pointed to the bent one. "Ten dollars," he said.

"Bet twenty! You can beat him," urged Miss Patterson. I looked at the barrelhead; the corner of the right-hand card was clearly bent. "Fifteen," I said, reaching for my wallet.

"Twenty," said Throckmorton, throwing down another

ten. He glared at me, insolently.

"That's the kind of action I like to see! Bet more to win more, two to one if you find the baby," said McPhee, looking at me. I shook my head. McPhee shrugged his shoulders and turned to Alligator Throckmorton. "Twenty dollars it is. Turn it over and see if you're still lucky." Sure enough, the bent card was the jack again, the "baby." Throckmorton picked up his winnings and waved it at me, snickering. "I'd think a big fellow like you would have more guts," he said.

"You should have topped his bet," Miss Patterson whispered. "You would have won."

"Twenty dollars is a lot of money, miss," I said. "I can't risk being cheated out of it."

She whispered in my ear. "I've heard that cardsharps always let you win a little at first, so you'll keep playing for higher stakes. But if you're smart enough to quit while you're still winning, you can beat them. Try it!"

McPhee had picked up the cards again and was holding his hands at shoulder height, like the conductor of an orchestra. "The hand is quicker than the eye, but anybody can get lucky," he said, then threw the cards back down with a flourish. After he mixed them, the bent one lay on the barrelhead next to me. "Find the baby," said the gambler.

"Ten," said Throckmorton, pointing to the bent card.

"Fifteen," I said. I threw a ten and a five down.

"Twenty," said Throckmorton, throwing down another bill. McPhee reached for the cards.

"Wait a minute," I said. "Twenty-five." I put another ten on my pile.

"Twenty-five it is," said McPhee. "Where's the baby, son?"

I pointed to the bent card. McPhee reached for it, then stopped a moment and looked me in the eye. "Bet more to win more, if you're sure," he said, grinning.

"I'm sure," I said, firmly. "But I'm only betting twenty-five. Let's see the card."

He turned over the king of clubs, and scooped up my twenty-five dollars before I could say a word. I turned and looked for Miss Patterson, but she was nowhere to be seen.

"Damnation, Wentworth! I thought I told you not to play cards with that rattlesnake," said Mr. Clemens, shaking his head sadly from side to side. When I'd met him backstage after the lecture, he had taken one look at me and dismissed the local grandees and amateur writers in jig time, then dragged me back to his dressing room and poured two glasses of whisky. It hadn't taken me long to confess everything.

"I thought I had figured out the game," I said.

"That's exactly what that scheming son of a bitch *wants* you to think," said Mr. Clemens. "Nobody above the age of four believes it's an honest game—it's too transparently crooked. But there are plenty of people fool enough to believe that they can outswindle the swindler. To the likes of McPhee, that's as good as a gold mine."

"I thought that gamblers always let you win a little bit at first, so they can lure you into a bigger game," I said. The argument had been convincing enough a couple of hours ago, but it sounded hollow at the moment.

"You thought! What's the world coming to when a man can graduate from Yale and still believe such unalloyed hokum? Why should McPhee let you win anything? For all he knows, you'll walk away with the profits after the first game. Get it through your head, Wentworth—Slippery Ed McPhee is running a business, and the first rule of the three-card-monte business is that the customer always loses."

"If that's so, why isn't it against the law? Why don't the police come and arrest him?"

"It is against the law, in some places, but that doesn't mean much. Sometimes they bribe the police, but if they're careful, they won't even have to do that—every three-card

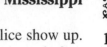
monte gang posts a lookout to signal if the police show up. The dealer can pick up the money and disappear before anybody can lift a finger. Sometimes the monte crew will stage a fake police raid—usually just after some poor sucker has lost big money—and disappear with the winnings before the sucker can start complaining.''

''What if someone complains to the police?''

''Usually they don't—it would mean admitting what a fool they've been. Even when someone does complain, the swindler has usually moved on to the next town down the road. Or in this case, down the river.''

''Why doesn't Captain Fowler throw him off the boat, the way he did the Throckmorton brothers?''

''McPhee hasn't been caught doing anything illegal on the boat, and the captain's authority doesn't extend to things his passengers do on shore. Mike Fowler's got the best heart in the world. But he can't run the world, and he knows it, and so he pretty much ignores things that don't affect his boat. If one of the other passengers catches McPhee cheating on board the *Greeley,* that'll be a different story. Mike would probably put Ed off at the next port, if the passenger hadn't already put him off somewhere in mid-river. But short of that, it's live and let live, as far as Mike's concerned.''

''Does the captain know that the Throckmorton brothers are following the boat?'' Billy Throckmorton had suddenly appeared at his brother's side, immediately after McPhee had pocketed my money. It was an effective way to discourage protest, had I been so inclined. But common sense had gotten the better of foolish valor: seeing the two ruffians, I had retreated to the lecture hall, somehow feeling cheated of far more than twenty-five dollars.

''He may. They've probably been meeting us at every town where McPhee intends to set up his monte stand, and Mike's been ashore enough times to have spotted them. But what do you want him to do? He's already thrown them off the boat, and he can't tell the railroad not to sell them tickets."

"I don't know," I admitted reluctantly. "I suppose I just want somebody to stop them from preying on innocent people."

"It would be about as easy as stopping a candle from burning a moth," said Mr. Clemens. "If the suckers stopped coming, McPhee would be out of business. The only person he can't cheat is the one who won't play to begin with. Everyone knows he's a swindler; that just makes some people think it's all right to try to swindle *him*. The fools think they can beat an expert at his own game, and they're wrong every time. Between pure unadorned greed and every man's conviction that he's too smart to get bit, McPhee has a lifetime job, if he wants it."

He paused and took a sip of whisky, then added, "Not that he's ever likely to see his full three score and ten. Mind you, Wentworth, I don't buy the notion that every evil in the world is somehow balanced out by something good. It's too facile, too sentimental. Still, I take some satisfaction in the belief that Slippery Ed isn't going to retire comfortably and die in his sleep at a respectable age, surrounded by adoring relatives and faithful friends." He paused again, looked me in the face, and grimaced. "Then again, neither may I."

15

The next morning found me still angry about losing money to McPhee. I attempted to reopen the subject with Mr. Clemens at breakfast, but he had no comfort for me. He had told me the night before that, by sleight of hand, a three-card monte dealer could make any of the three cards appear in any position, but that didn't explain why the bent corner could be on a winning card three times straight and on a losing one the next. "I still don't understand how McPhee changed the card," I said.

"Why the devil do you need to know how he did it? All you have to know is that he *will* do it. Playing cards with the likes of McPhee is just like sticking your hand in a wildcat's den—you're lucky if all it costs you is a finger or two. Learn the lesson, and be grateful it was so cheap." And that was all Mr. Clemens had to say on the topic before he climbed up to the pilothouse "to have a smoke and a look at the river."

I lingered over coffee, still not satisfied with how things had gone. It was one thing to learn not to gamble with cheats, another to see them go unpunished. I had seen McPhee come into the cabin just before Mr. Clemens's departure; he had taken his customary seat at the card table, bold as brass, and in short order was reeling out his usual line of cant and braggadocio. My coffee suddenly tasted stale, and I stalked out onto the foredeck for a breath of fresh air.

I saw Miss Patterson first, and then Detective Berrigan, leaning on the rail and smoking his pipe, in his rumpled brown suit. Miss Patterson sat on a bench holding her parasol and reading a book, which upon a closer look I recognized as Mr. Clemens's *Life on the Mississippi.* "I see I'm going to have to read that book," I said, sitting down beside her. "Everyone on board seems to be reading it except for me, and soon I won't be able to talk to anyone." I wasn't sure whether I ought to chide her for having encouraged me to bet against McPhee the previous evening, but I was not about to engage her in an argument with another person present.

She disarmed me with a musical laugh. "Oh, but surely you, who work with Mr. Twain every day, know his work better than I!"

"Not necessarily," I said, cautiously. "I've only worked for him for a short while, you know. But here's someone you've been asking about. Detective Berrigan! Miss Patterson has been wanting to meet you."

The detective turned, then doffed his hat and smiled. "My pleasure, miss."

"My goodness, Mr. Berrigan," she said. "May I ask what mysterious errand brings you onto a simple pleasure cruise? It must be something very unusual."

"Nothing really unusual, miss," said Berrigan. "Mr. Twain's backers in New York think he ought to have a bodyguard, and I'm the fellow they sent."

"But Mr. Cabot said you were a regular police detective, following a criminal from New York," she said. "Isn't that true?"

The detective looked at me through narrowed eyes. "He really shouldn't have told you that, miss. I'll ask you to promise not to repeat it; if the suspect were to learn that I'm this close to him, he might escape."

"Oh, I promise!" said Miss Patterson.

"Have you narrowed down your list of suspects?" I asked.

"There are still some passengers I haven't ruled out completely," said Berrigan. "But something on the passenger list jogged a memory, and I'm trying to follow that line of inquiry as well. I can't go into detail yet, of course. Wouldn't want to arouse suspicion about somebody who might be innocent."

"Well, this is fascinating," said Miss Patterson. "Do promise to tell us all about it when you've captured your man—it is a man you're after, isn't it?"

"Sure, miss, and are you studying to be a detective yourself?" Berrigan laughed; then his expression turned more serious. "I suppose I can tell you that much, but I'm afraid I really shouldn't talk any more about it. I've already told you more than I should have. Now that Mr. Cabot has tipped my hand, I'll just have to depend on your discretion. Please don't talk to anyone about it."

"Certainly not!" she said fervently. "I won't tell a soul!"

"Perhaps you can advise me," I said. "Last night I was fool enough to play cards with that McPhee fellow, and he cheated me. Do I have any recourse with the law?"

"Well, that would be up to the local authorities, of course. How do you know he cheated you?"

I began to tell him about the bent corner on the winning card, but he raised his hand. "Say no more. That's the oldest trick in the book. Most people are so embarrassed to fall for it that they never report it."

"But how does he do it?" I demanded.

"Any of about three ways, but the easiest one is to bend the corner on the wrong card to begin with, and then exchange it for the right one when he shows it. Did McPhee turn it over with a hand that was holding another card?"

I tried to remember. "I think so. But I didn't see him do anything!"

"You aren't supposed to. McPhee's probably been practicing that move for thirty years, and a dozen others just as hard to spot. If you're asking my opinion, I'd advise you

to forget about it, Mr. Cabot. The law can't help you.''

"Perhaps you're right," I said. I had gotten myself into the game by forgetting the advice of older, more experienced heads; it might be time to start paying greater attention to them. "Still, there he sits at the card table, and cheating everyone who plays with him, for all I know."

"If the captain won't stop him, it's not my job," said Berrigan. "You're talking to the wrong boy."

"And what about the case you're supposed to be investigating?" I demanded. "Have you eliminated McPhee as a suspect? Have you even questioned him?" I couldn't stand the thought of his getting off scot-free.

"Don't tell me how to do my job, Mr. Cabot. I'm following what I think is the most promising direction, and that's all you need to know. As for you, I hope you'll be more careful how many people you tell about this matter. If you'll excuse me." He turned and nodded. "Miss Patterson, my pleasure. . . . Could I possibly have seen you before—in New York, perhaps?"

"Oh, no," she said, laughing. "I've never been east of Ohio."

Berrigan smiled and said, "I suppose I must be mistaken, then. It would be hard to have seen a young lady as pretty as yourself and not remember her." He bowed and took his leave.

When he'd left, she turned to me with an excited whisper. "My goodness! Is it really a murder case? He wouldn't come this far from New York for anything less, would he?"

"I suppose I shouldn't tell you, if he didn't want to," I said. Berrigan's criticism stung; I felt that my interest in the case was legitimate, since it was my employer who was at risk. "But it is a very serious crime," I said, "and the detective thinks the person who did it might be on this boat."

"And that gambler, McPhee, is a suspect? I can't believe he'd be a murderer, could you?" She leaned forward as if eager to hear my opinion. Someone, at least, recognized the value of my contribution.

"I don't know if he did it or not," I said, "but I wish the detective would take this business more seriously. He's here on an important case, and he's got no notion how to go about solving it."

I turned to go to my cabin to get on with my duties, but Miss Patterson laid a soft hand on my arm and said, "I'll bet we could solve it, if we put our heads together." She smiled encouragingly. "Will you tell me what it's all about?"

Somewhat hesitantly, I told Miss Patterson—or Martha, as I had begun to think of her—most of what I knew. I held back Mr. Clemens's story of the treasure hidden in Arkansas, knowing that he had told it to me in the strictest confidence. Perhaps it was foolish not to reveal that, having revealed so much else. But the cache of gold was one detail about which Mr. Clemens had not told even the detective, and so I felt honor-bound to keep it back from Martha—at least for now. When I finished, she nodded her head gravely and said, "I can see why Mr. Twain's backers might be worried. But I doubt that Mr. McPhee is as dangerous as you think. Old animosities may have colored Mr. Twain's perceptions. You and I don't have to let that govern our conduct. What do you think of this—I'll eavesdrop on the gamblers, and listen to McPhee's conversation; he won't suspect me of being in league with you. He may let something slip, not knowing that anyone is listening who can put two and two together. We'll meet again this evening, and see what each of us has learned. The two of us can surely get to the bottom of things." She smiled brightly, and put her hand on my arm again for just a moment.

"Very well," I said. It felt good to have someone with whom I could discuss the case, since Berrigan had become so closemouthed. "But promise me you'll be careful. McPhee may seem colorful and exciting to you, but I have reason to think he's more dangerous than he appears. Not only is he a cheat at cards, but he continues to associate with those two Throckmorton brothers, a nasty pair if ever I saw one.''

"Don't worry," she said. "I'll keep my wits about me. Mr. McPhee may be an expert at the card table, but a clever woman always has an advantage over his sort.'' She winked at me and twirled her parasol.

"I certainly hope so," I said. Somewhere inside I was not entirely sure, but there was no point in letting her know. Martha was undoubtedly very bright—anyone could tell that from her conversation—yet at the same time her head seemed full of romantic ideas of adventure. McPhee might be a creature of bluster and bluff, but as I had learned to my own regret, he was no easy mark.

I spent another lazy afternoon watching the river. It continued to present a constantly changing panorama along its banks, sleepy little towns alternating with farmlands and woods. The shoreline was somewhat less dramatic than in the upper reaches of the river, although there was a good bit more traffic here. Claude Dexter stopped to talk, and within a few sentences managed to convince me there was nothing in the world quite so boring as the history of steamboats on the Mississippi. Eventually he left; a glance at my watch showed that we had been talking only ten minutes, although it had seemed like hours. I was struck with the fact that precisely the same topic became a matter of utter fascination when Mr. Clemens was the speaker. For that matter, the river itself provided far more entertainment than Dexter's pedantic dissertations, which were designed more to display his own learning than to illuminate the subject.

The day was hot, with little cottonlike clouds drifting across the sky and barely a hint of any breeze to mitigate the oppressive heat. So around four o'clock, when Mr. Clemens found me on the shady side of the boiler deck, fanning myself with my hat, it did not take him long to persuade me to join him and the captain for a cold drink up on the texas.

I blew the foam off a tall mug of beer, then settled back in expectation that my employer and Captain Fowler would begin another session of "swapping yarns," usually preposterous tales of their youthful high jinks in their early days on the river. While many of the incidents remained obscure to me, I never failed to find a certain quota of amusement in the stories, of which they had an ample fund. So I was frankly surprised when Mr. Clemens turned to me and said, "Cabot, why don't you tell the captain about what happened in front of the theater last night?"

Captain Fowler listened intently, nodding gravely, while I told of the incident involving McPhee and the bet I'd lost. "Well," he said at last. "Can't say I'd expected much else of Slippery Ed. He'd best watch himself, though. If I get any complaints of his cheating on my boat, he'll wish he'd learned to walk on water. There's nothing I can do about his antics on shore, mind you, but I'll not have my passengers cheated on board the *Greeley*."

"That's all well and good, Mike," said Mr. Clemens. "I know you can't police the whole length of the Mississippi. And you can't stop people from betting a few dollars on a turn of the cards. But I wonder if you couldn't do something to convince Slippery Ed that your boat isn't a convenient place to carry on his trade. After all, his two sidekicks are making their trip by train. It shouldn't be all that hard to get Ed to join them."

"And what do you have in mind, Sam?" The captain took off his hat and fanned himself with it.

"Suppose you got somebody from the crew to stand beside the table—right next to Ed—and watch the action. If anybody asks what he's doing, let him say he's just making sure the game is all according to Hoyle. That should be enough to make some of the players think maybe it *isn't* according to Hoyle, and that McPhee's the reason. That

158 might make some of them decide to sit out the game as long as he's at the table.''

''And if the game dries up, Ed leaves the boat,'' said the captain. ''Well, it might work. Charlie Snipes would be a good man for it; he's something of a cardplayer, when he's ashore. I'll think about it, Sam—but I can't promise anything. There are always a few passengers who like playing against a professional cardplayer, even if they lose most of the time. I could stand to see Ed go, but not if he takes the rest of the players with him.''

''You run an honest boat, but you don't want it so honest that nobody has any fun,'' Mr. Clemens suggested, leaning forward and raising his eyebrows.

''There you have it,'' said Captain Fowler, with a sigh. He stood up and spread his hands. ''I've got to offer my passengers more than just a ride from one town to another. If that's all they want, the railroad's quicker and cheaper. But if I give them a little bit of entertainment—''

A loud knock on the door interrupted him. ''Now, who could that be?'' said the captain. He went to the door and opened it, and in walked Slippery Ed McPhee.

''Howdy, gents,'' said McPhee. He rubbed his hands together, looking at Mr. Clemens, then at me. ''Just the party I was hoping to find. Hope I'm not intruding on anything.''

''Why, no, Ed,'' said Mr. Clemens. ''As it happens, we were just speaking about you.''

''Just like the devil, eh?'' said McPhee, with a chuckle. ''Well, I won't take up much of your time, Sam. I just wanted to come see if your boy here learnt his lesson from last night.''

''Excuse me?'' I said. ''Are you referring to the card game?''

''And what else would I be talking about, sonny?'' McPhee swelled out his chest and struck a pose as if he were about to deliver an oration. ''I seen you come up the street, and I seen you thinking you could outsmart an old fox at his own game, and I says to myself, *Ed McPhee, this boy's looking to learn a hard lesson, and better he learns it from a friend than from an enemy."*

"A friend!" said Mr. Clemens. "That's a considerable stretch of the term, don't you think?"

"There you go making your jokes again, Sam," said McPhee. "You know old Ed wouldn't hurt a bug, 'less it bit him. Fact is, I come up here to give Mr. Cabot his money back, and hope it learns him not to try to bet over his head. There's lots of men along the river would've taken every cent he has, and not shed a tear about it. But let it never be said that Ed McPhee's that kind of man." He pulled a wallet out of his breast pocket and proceeded to count off two tens and a five, which he put on the table next to my beer. "There you go, sonny."

I was frankly dumbfounded. I stared at the money as if it were a hot poker. Mr. Clemens seemed every bit as shocked as I, but he managed to blurt out, "Jesus, Ed, what have you been drinking?"

"You know I never drink during business hours, Sam. A fellow's got to keep his wits about him in my line of work; never know when somebody might take something amiss. That's why I wanted to make sure your boy understood that I took his money just to make a point. Never did mean to keep it. Don't forget to take that money, young feller—one of these two old buzzards is likely to snatch it if you don't." He laughed, then turned to me and reached out his hand, which I shook almost by reflex. "I hope this little hoax will teach you to steer clear of gambling with strangers, now, Mr. Cabot. Stick with folks you know, and you won't get burnt."

"I still don't believe what I'm seeing," said Mr. Clemens. "Is this the same Ed McPhee who got chased off the *Natchez* for dealing off the bottom of the deck? Are you sure you don't have an extra pair of aces up your sleeve?"

"I've changed my style, Sam," said McPhee, smiling like a man selling patent medicine. "I suppose it's seeing so many young folks ruined by bad judgment over the years. Given me a soft spot, it has. So every now and then, I see a boy needs to learn a lesson, and I teach it to him— then make sure he gets his money back, so he'll know it wasn't out of malice. Just a little hoax, like you used to pull all the time, Sam. Remember that business about Napoleon, Arkansas, when you rode downriver on the *Gold Dust* and fooled everybody into thinking you was after buried treasure? George Devol said you pulled their legs till they was a mile long before you let loose with the stinger. Well, Mr. Cabot just got hit with the stinger, and got his money back, to boot. Let it be a lesson to you, sonny.'' He clapped me on the back and took his departure, leaving all three of us with our mouths open.

He had barely left when another knock came on the door, and Mr. Snipes, the chief clerk, stuck his head into the cabin. ''Beg your pardon, Cap'n, but I just saw that McPhee fellow come out of here. Was he stirring up more trouble?''

''Damned if I know, Charlie,'' said the captain. ''I thought I'd seen everything there was to see along this river, but a gambler giving refunds is a brand-new one.''

''I second that,'' said Mr. Clemens. ''Slippery Ed's the last man I expected ever to change his stripes, not that I'm sorry to see it, if it's true. Next thing you know, he'll be preaching temperance sermons. Of course, if he starts that, I'll have to insist you throw him overboard. I don't mind a man reforming his ways, but I draw the line when he starts trying to reform mine.''

''I'll drink to that,'' said the captain, and we all three raised our glasses. Snipes nodded and withdrew. The captain and Mr. Clemens soon turned to old stories and began carrying on in their usual way, while I sat there sipping my beer and staring at the money on the table. I myself was not quite certain McPhee had changed his stripes, however it appeared. And I was not at all happy that he had mentioned the treasure—exactly the thing we were most anxious to keep anyone from thinking about. The more I thought about it, the less I liked it.

≈ 16

"I've had a busy day," said Martha Patterson. I was not surprised. It seemed as if our earlier conversation had taken place several days before, rather than just a few short hours ago. "The gamblers had no idea I was spying on them," she said. "It was all I could do not to laugh out loud. I didn't expect I'd be able to eavesdrop quite so easily!" She laughed, leaning toward me in a conspiratorial manner. A lock of her dark hair fell across her forehead, and her smile almost made me forget our mutual purpose. With an effort, I brought my mind back to the subject at hand.

"What did you learn?" I asked. We were docked in Cairo, Illinois, a fair-sized manufacturing town on a long, flat point of land near the mouth of the broad Ohio River. After the boat made port, the two of us had met at the rear of the hurricane deck, whence we could see across the river to the west bank. Many of our fellow passengers had taken the opportunity to go ashore, and (as usual) Captain Fowler and Mr. Clemens had been invited to dinner by some local person of importance, so we had all the privacy we needed.

"Oh, I learned a great deal," she said with an impish smile. "A lot of what they talk about is sheer nonsense, of course—men seem to think that inflating their own importance will make the others back down when they bluff. Why, to listen to them, you'd think that half a dozen of the richest and most powerful men in America are sitting at that table every day.''

"Perhaps they think it's true," I said. "McPhee certainly seems to have an exaggerated notion of his place in the world." I was still smarting at the fellow's arrogance in handing me back the money he had cheated me out of, representing it as a lesson for my own good.

"Ah, but listen to this," she said, touching my sleeve. "Today, one of the gamblers started to brag about the different places he'd played cards—England, Spain . . . half the world if one could believe him. Of course, the others chimed in with all the places *they'd* gambled. A few of them are from the East, so the talk eventually turned to clubs and private games in New York. *New York is where the real money is,* said one of them. *If you really want to see gambling, you have to come to New York. I've seen some of your Wall Street tycoons put five hundred dollars on the table at the turn of a card, and not bat an eye.* And the others all chimed in with stories of their own about the high stakes they'd played for in New York.''

"Including McPhee?''

"No," said Martha. "Mr. McPhee scoffed at them all, and came down squarely for western gambling. *We used to fleece the New York fellows regularly when they'd show up out here,* he said. *They'd come in claiming to know it all, and we'd teach them pretty quickly that they didn't know anything about cards. Every now and then, some boy who could barely cut the mustard on the river would go east and come back with his pockets full. But I never saw the point to it. There's more money to be made right here on the river than on the whole East Coast, from what I see. I wouldn't go to New York City if you gave me fifty dollars a day.*''

"That sounds like his sort of cant," I said. "A provincial to the bone.''

"But don't you see? McPhee had every chance to brag about going to New York and winning big money there, and he said exactly the opposite. That clears him of the murder in New York.'' She pressed her point rather vigorously, and I could see she was taking her role as ''detective'' very seriously.

''I suppose it looks that way,'' I admitted. ''Still, I would be careful of taking his word on anything. The fellow is a born liar, according to Mr. Clemens.''

''I think Mr. Clemens has some grudge against him, and I think you do, too,'' said Martha, putting her hands on her hips and looking up at me with a stern expression on her pretty face. ''How can you hope to solve the murder case if you won't look at things objectively? You're inventing reasons why Mr. McPhee must be guilty, instead of looking for the real criminal. If you're not serious about solving this mystery, I shan't waste my time trying to help you.''

''Oh, I am serious,'' I said. ''And I do appreciate your help. Perhaps I just need time to absorb all the new information.''

''Take all the time you need,'' she said. She gave me another little smile. ''I'll keep my eyes and ears open, and let you know anything else that comes up. Believe me, the two of us together can find out more than you're likely to alone. But you do have to trust me.''

''I do trust you, Martha,'' I said, trying to make it sound as sincere as I felt. She had no idea how pretty and appealing she was, and I was anxious not to lose her as an ally in this business.

She took my hand and gave a little curtsy, now smiling broadly. ''Then we shall solve this mystery together!'' she said. Then she released my hand and walked away, turning to look back at me and wink just before she rounded the corner of the cabin.

I leaned back against the rail, thinking. Martha appeared to have logic on her side. As much as I disliked McPhee, I would be foolish to continue suspecting him in the face of evidence that exonerated him. And yet his remarks about Napoleon, Arkansas, were grounds for treating him

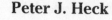

with suspicion. But there was no way I could tell Martha all this without telling her about our real mission, and something in the back of my head argued against revealing that last secret.

A loud voice roused me from my musings. "Well, Mr. Cabot! Still playing Sherlock Holmes?"

It was Detective Berrigan. Something in his voice and demeanor seemed unusual, and when he drew closer the reason became clear—I could smell liquor on his breath. "Mr. Berrigan," I said. "I didn't know you were a drinking man—or are you off-duty now?"

"I'll have a taste or two when there's something to celebrate," said the detective. He stuck his thumbs into his belt and struck a swaggering pose. "But tell me, Mr. Cabot, have you solved your murder? Have you and the young lady delved out all the deep secrets and found the guilty parties?"

"No, I'm afraid not," I said. "I didn't know we were so obvious."

"Maybe not to everybody, but you can't fool a professional," said Berrigan, smirking. "Let me give you a little hint, Mr. Cabot. When you want to have a private conversation out here on the deck, you can't just look to the left and right of you. Sound carries very nicely over the water. You might think you're all alone, but a man standing on the deck directly above you can hear every word you say— and if he's careful, you'll never know he's there."

"You've been eavesdropping!" I said.

"It's part of my job, thank you. And you don't seem to mind it when pretty Miss Patterson eavesdrops on Mr. McPhee and his cronies, do you now?"

"McPhee is a murder suspect," I protested.

"Aye, I forgot about that," said the detective. "McPhee's a murder suspect—have to note that down." He went through an exaggerated charade of looking for his notebook, finally finding it, then pulling it out. He flipped through the pages, with a show of peering intently at each one. "Oh, never mind. I have him down already, right after you. You did remember that you're on my little list, didn't you, Mr. Cabot?" He tucked the notebook back in his pocket and grinned at me.

"Damn your little list!" I was getting annoyed at his drunken shenanigans. "Surely you don't consider me a serious suspect. You've had plenty of opportunity to check my story, if you thought you needed to."

He shook his head in mock sadness. "You'll never make a detective, me boy. The first rule is to suspect everyone, don't you know? You've gotten all fascinated by Mc-Phee—who's a rotten enough apple, no denying—and clean forgot about everyone else. Meanwhile, your poor ignorant Irishman plods along and solves the case." He made a mocking bow in my direction.

It took a moment for his words to sink in. "You've solved it? But how? Who is the killer? Have you made an arrest?"

He held up his index finger and shook it at me. "You'll find out soon enough, Mr. Cabot. I told you, something on that passenger list tipped me off. At first it seemed a false lead, but now I know exactly who did it. I've one little bit of business to attend to before I can take him into custody, but that should be a matter of a day or two at most. And if I tell you everything I know, how can I be sure Miss Patterson and half the people on board won't have heard it by bedtime, and the other half by breakfast? And how long do you think the villain would wait around after finding out I'd spotted him?"

I stiffened. "I know how to hold my tongue when I need to," I said, although my conscience suggested otherwise. "Just be sure the fellow doesn't harm anyone else while you're letting him run around unhindered. Better safe than sorry, with a murderer on the loose."

"I'm not giving him that much free rein, believe me," said Berrigan. "If this were New York, I'd have him behind bars right now; but I'm out of my jurisdiction here, so I

166 have to step softly. Once I convince the local authorities he's the man, I can put the cuffs on him anytime I please.''

"Well, I hope you don't delay any more than necessary,'' I said, somewhat annoyed to learn that I had been preempted in my investigation. I turned and made my way to dinner, not at all happy with the day's events, even though I was twenty-five dollars better off than I had been upon arising in the morning.

I took my supper at Planter's, a respectable place in town. The food was plentiful and well-cooked—a thick slice of ham, with baked sweet potatoes and green peas and plenty of light buttermilk biscuits—and it somewhat restored my energy, if not my spirits. At first I thought to see what entertainment Cairo might offer, but I found little to entice me, unless I took a sudden fancy to smoke-filled workingmen's saloons. Perhaps my sour mood was to blame, but in any event I finally gave up and walked back to the *Horace Greeley* in time for the beginning of Mr. Clemens's lecture.

I was pleased to see that nearly all the seats were taken; not only did this guarantee us a good return for this stop on our tour, but it would put Mr. Clemens in a good mood—a full house always elevated his spirits. There is something contagious in the response of a large audience, whether one is sitting in it as a member or (to judge from Mr. Clemens's reactions) standing before it as a performer. Mr. Clemens was always energized after one of his lectures, but the level of excitement seemed to rise proportionately to the size of the crowd. On the other hand, so did the temperature, and many in the audience had converted their programs into paper fans.

Almost by habit, I scanned the audience for familiar faces. The passengers seemed to make up a larger fraction of the audience than usual tonight; perhaps they'd had no more luck than I in finding amusement on shore. Before the lights were lowered, I saw that Major Demayne was seated a few rows in front of me, with Miss Cunningham across the aisle from him, and Detective Berrigan not far behind them; Andrew Dunbar, the reporter, was in the front row, toward the side. Even a few of the crew members had put in appearances—I saw Chief Clerk Snipes, his apprentice Tommy, and Frenchy, the engineer, occupying seats near the middle of the audience.

Mr. Clemens made his typical unobtrusive entrance, and began, as usual, with some preliminary remarks tailored to the local audience. "Back in the good old Silurian period, when I was a river pilot, it always made my heart glad to see Cairo when we came downriver from St. Louis. The town wasn't nearly as big back then as it is now, and there weren't as many fine brick buildings in town then. Mr. Dickens"—several of the audience members made disapproving noises—"I say, Mr. Dickens gave Cairo a pretty thorough running-down in his book. Well, Mr. Dickens was a pretty good writer of novels, I'll give him that much credit. But I can't take his part, not when it comes to Cairo." (Cheers.)

"I have to admit that I never spent much time here in Cairo. The boats would tie up long enough to load any cargo that might be going our way, and take on passengers, and then we'd head back to the river. So I don't have a lot of memories of the town—none I can tell with the ladies present, anyhow." (A general round of laughter.) "No, the reason I liked to see Cairo when I came downriver was that the river between St. Louis and Cairo was a steamboat killer, and getting to Cairo meant we were in safe water at last, with the Ohio's waters swelling the stream.

"The captain tells me the whole river's safer, nowadays. There used to be nearly thirty wrecked steamboats in sight of Hat Island—but I couldn't even find that old landmark, last time I came through. There used to be a hidden rock just above Cairo that took out the bottom of more than one boat; no sign of it, now. Another stretch north of here was called the Graveyard, there were so many dead boats in it.

Old-timers could count two hundred wrecks, nearly one a mile, for the whole length of the river between St. Louis and Cairo. So when we got to Cairo, we knew we'd come out of the jaws of the nutcracker, and we were mighty glad.'' He paused and looked around. ''Of course, we purely *hated* the sight of Cairo coming upriver, but that's a story for another time. Tonight, I'm mighty glad to see the town again—and all of you.'' (More laughter, and applause.)

At this point, Mr. Clemens began a transition to his usual speech, and (given the familiarity of the matter) my attention began to wander. At first, I watched the audience's reactions to the stories I myself had heard some dozen times by now, fascinated by how skillfully my employer manipulated their emotions. (Despite my knowing the speech almost by heart, I was not entirely immune to its appeal.) Then the sight of Detective Berrigan a few seats ahead of me ignited a train of speculation about the New York murder. Assuming that he wasn't merely bragging, Berrigan had solved the case, which meant that the killer must be among us on the boat. But who could it possibly be?

The detective had indicated that McPhee was not the guilty party. My own instincts still argued for the gambler as the main suspect, but I had to assume that Berrigan knew his business—even though I might not like the way he went about it. Besides, McPhee was nowhere in sight—most likely he was somewhere ashore, fleecing the citizens of Cairo of their hard-earned gold. If Berrigan could be taken at his word, he was keeping a relatively close rein on the suspect. Therefore, his attendance at Mr. Clemens's lecture might mean that the murderer was sitting in the audience with me. The very thought gave me a chill.

Again I glanced around the darkened hall, but had little luck picking out faces more than a few seats away from me. I was forced to fall back on pure deduction. The detective had placed himself behind Major Demayne; could it be in order to keep him under watch? The Major listed his home as New Jersey, which was certainly close enough to New York for him to have been in the city on the fateful day. But what possible connection might he have to the dead man? Besides, he had gone out of his way to help me on two occasions. Why would he have done so if he had designs to harm Mr. Clemens?

Mr. Clemens had taken an instant antipathy to the New York newspaper reporter, Andrew Dunbar. And the reporter (or perhaps the paper he wrote for) certainly seemed to be seeking reasons to reflect discredit on Mr. Clemens. Moreover, it seemed probable that the reporter had been in the city when the crime took place. Those seemed remarkably thin threads on which to hang a murder charge, but perhaps the detective had discovered some clue that had escaped my notice. While it would certainly give me satisfaction to learn that someone so thoroughly dislikable was in fact the criminal, I had no real reason to suspect Dunbar.

Who else might there be? Two rows in front of me sat a balding fellow with glasses and a double chin, who looked more a gourmand than a criminal; I seemed to recall that he was from Chicago, but there my knowledge of him ran out. Claude Dexter, the riverboat enthusiast from Boston, was on the center aisle, but he seemed more interested in arguing about the authenticity of every minute detail of the boat than in anything else; hardly a strong candidate. Two seats to his right was a lean, long-nosed man with greasy blond hair, who'd been at the card table with McPhee almost every day. Did his association with the gambler make him a suspect, or was I letting my dislike of McPhee stain everyone who had dealings with him? What about the swarthy, ill-kempt fellow with drooping mustaches on the aisle to the left of me? If physiognomy were any clue to character, I would cast him as a knife-man in an instant. But I had overheard him talking to one of the crew earlier in the day, and his voice and manner were as mild as a minister's. Perhaps physiognomy was overrated.

When the lights came up and Mr. Clemens took his final

bow, I found myself with no firm conclusions. After watching the crowd drift out, I went backstage for my usual post-lecture meeting with my employer.

We exchanged the usual comments about the size of the audience and how well they reacted; then Mr. Clemens must have noticed something in my demeanor. "You look down in the mouth, Wentworth," he said. "What's wrong?"

"I know this shouldn't be anything to get annoyed at, but Berrigan tells me he's solved his case. He expects to make an arrest shortly."

He gave me a curious look. "You're right, Wentworth. If it's true, that's the best news I've heard in a week. What's the catch?"

"As far as I can tell—he won't tell me the entire story—he doesn't think McPhee is the murderer. And that means that McPhee will probably be with us all the way to the end of the river."

"Meaning that he's still here to interfere with our treasure hunt, assuming he knows about it," Mr. Clemens said gravely.

"But he almost certainly knows about it! He all but said so this morning when he gave back my money—surely you heard him?"

Mr. Clemens leaned back in his chair, propping his feet up on the makeshift dressing table. "Wentworth, that story's in a book that thousands of people have read, including half the passengers on this boat. Napoleon was pretty notorious in its time—the wickedest town between New Orleans and Cincinnati, they called it, and they were mostly right. Once they had more prisoners than the jail would hold, so they just threw the extras in the river. It was big news on the river when Napoleon finally washed away—it happened piecemeal over a period of years, but the last straw was the flood of '82. It'd be mighty surprising if Slippery Ed McPhee didn't know Napoleon—he probably got into his share of crooked card games there, and I wouldn't be surprised if he got run out of town once or twice. It doesn't mean anything that he remembers the place.'' He smiled.

''But what if Berrigan's wrong? It isn't unheard of for the police to arrest the wrong suspect.''

''It's always possible. I'll talk to him in the morning; maybe he'll tell me what's up his sleeve. I'd certainly like to know what's going on before we make Memphis, and that's all too soon. Damnation—now I wish we'd been able to schedule a night in one of the little towns between here and there. It'd give me one more day to poke around and find out what Berrigan knows, and figure out whether he's on the right track.''

''Lord help us if he isn't,'' I said.

''Let's hope we don't need that kind of help,'' said Mr. Clemens. ''Nothing against the Lord, but I'd just as soon take care of the problem myself.''

We finished our discussion, and Mr. Clemens retired to his cabin. I wandered out onto the main deck, where the crew was preparing to cast off. Having no lectures set up between Cairo and Memphis, we had scheduled a nonstop run between the two cities. This would be our first night-time run, and I was curious to see the river pass by under moonlight.

After a while the whistle sounded, and Mr. Parks backed the *Horace Greeley* away from the Cairo dock. The moon—a few days short of full—shone brightly over the eastern bank, and the broad Ohio was a shimmering expanse of silver as we slid by on our way downriver. I climbed the stair up to the hurricane deck for a better view. Several other passengers were there, taking advantage of the clear evening for a bit of conversation or sightseeing. I spotted Miss Cunningham standing alone by the aft rail, and went to join her.

''Good evening, Mr. Cabot,'' she said. ''The river is very picturesque tonight, is it not?''

''Yes, although it would be more to my taste if there

were a bit of a breeze. My New England blood isn't really used to this kind of weather.''

She nodded. ''Nor is mine, really. I suppose it is only natural, as it is the middle of summer, and we are headed south, after all. I doubt it will get any cooler.''

''I wish it would,'' I said, taking off my hat and fanning myself. ''I'm afraid the heat has put me rather out of sorts.''

A serious expression came to her face, as if she were searching for the right words. ''So I have heard,'' she said at last, lowering her voice. ''Perhaps it is not my business, but I am somewhat distressed to hear your behavior being discussed in very unflattering terms.''

''What do you mean?'' I was astonished. ''Who has been talking about me?''

''If what they say is true, does it really matter who they are?''

''Tell me what they say, and I'll tell you if it's true,'' I said. ''What have you heard about me?''

She looked at me with a grave expression. ''I suppose it is only fair to give you the opportunity to refute what is being said about you, considering that what I have heard really casts more doubt on your judgment than on your character. I have heard that you lost a good bit of money gambling with that McPhee person. I also heard that you spoke in profane language to Mr. Berrigan—who despite his origins, deserves some respect as a representative of the law. Neither accusation does you credit, Mr. Cabot.''

I was thunderstruck; I could deny neither accusation. But even more distressing was the fact that the incidents had apparently become public knowledge. All I could think of to say was, ''Who told you this?''

''Someone quite respectable, whose word I do not doubt,'' she said. ''I see that you do not choose to deny either accusation. I must say I am disappointed in you, Mr. Cabot. I hope you will take it upon yourself to examine your conduct very carefully. I do not think you are a bad person, but perhaps you should choose your company more carefully. And now, I think I should say good night.'' Before I could say another word, she turned and left.

As I was attempting to absorb the implications of what Miss Cunningham had said, Detective Berrigan came out on deck, swaying a bit, although the river was calm. He leaned against the rail, sipping from a little flask. After a moment, he turned and looked at me, and gave a mocking bow. Not anxious for any more of his company, I continued up to the texas deck. But behind me I could hear him, softly whistling a tune I recognized—it had been one of my father's new favorites the last time I was home from Yale, and he had sung it loudly and incessantly. I could still remember the words, even though Berrigan confined himself to the melody. ''I've got a little list; I've got a little list.''

I was not sure whether he intended it to annoy me, but it had that effect.

⇒17

I meant to go to bed early and get a good night's sleep, but it was not to be. The weather had been oppressively hot ever since St. Louis, and this was the hottest night so far. There was almost no breeze, except what the boat's motion stirred up, and little of that seemed to find the one small window of my stateroom. Besides, for some reason the steady sound of the engines and the movement of the boat kept me from dozing off. I had barely noticed our motion when traveling at daytime, but now trying to lie down somehow magnified every roll and lurch. I was in no danger of seasickness, but neither was I able to relax.

It didn't help that my mind was full of the events of the last few days. I thought again about McPhee's cheating me at cards, and his arrogantly returning my money; Berrigan's claiming to have solved the New York murder, and his refusal to confide his findings to me; McPhee's apparently casual mention of Napoleon, Arkansas, alluding to the treasure which Mr. Clemens and I hoped to recover; Miss Cunningham's admonition, which put my recent actions in an unsettling light; and always near the surface, Martha Patterson's face and voice, which had somehow cast a spell on me—not an unpleasant sensation, but not one conducive to rest.

I tried a few mental tricks that had served to conquer insomnia in the past, but counting sheep bored me without relaxing me, and recalling peaceful landscapes only reminded me that I was in a hot, airless cabin on a moving steamboat, with one of my fellow passengers a cunning murderer. I had nothing to read, unless I wanted to reread Major Demayne's verses—not an appealing prospect, although I realized it might indeed put me to sleep. Finally, sometime well after midnight, I decided to walk out on deck and seek whatever breeze and comfort might be there. Perhaps, I thought, a few turns around the deck would use up my excess energy.

A light gleamed in the pilothouse high above me, but I was in the mood for solitude, not company. Were I so minded, I knew, I could undoubtedly find McPhee and his gambling cronies burning the midnight oil in the main cabin, where their games went on until near dawn. But the river and the moonlight were company enough for me, and I strolled aimlessly around the promenade deck, enjoying the reflection of the moon on the surface of the water. Our wake shone brilliant white behind us, and the blades of the paddle wheel gave off silver images as they rose dripping from the river. The moonlight seemed to cloak the river and the boat in a romantic veil, removing everything ugly and modern from the view. Even as a no-nonsense modernist who expected to live the better part of my life in a new century, I could understand the nostalgia Mr. Clemens and the other old river hands felt for the era when steamboats had ruled the Mississippi.

While I was vaguely aware of a few other late-night prowlers on the decks, I was not anxious to converse with them. I have no idea what put me in this curious mood, unless it was the desire to avoid scrutiny, now that I had somehow become the object of gossip. At any rate, on two or three occasions when I heard footsteps coming up or down a stair from another deck, I drew back around the corner of the cabin to avoid meeting anyone face-to-face. While this little game of secrecy had no object other than to preserve my solitude, after a couple of "close escapes" I began to play it half in earnest, as if discovery would entail serious consequences. I would peek around each corner to make certain the next stretch of deck was empty before proceeding to the next corner, creeping along quietly to listen for voices or footsteps.

Thus, I was nearly frightened out of my skin when a hand fell on my arm and an unfamiliar voice from behind me said, "Young man, come with me."

I turned to see a small, elderly woman in an old-fashioned nightcap and robe, with a grim expression on her face. While I had no notion what she might want of me, the set of her mouth made it clear that she would brook no refusal. "Yes, ma'am," I said. "What seems to be the matter?"

"Come and I'll show you," she said, pulling my sleeve. Since she offered me no choice, I followed her up to the hurricane deck and into the dimly lit corridor, past a row of stateroom doors. About a third of the way down the corridor, she stopped and pointed to a door. "Someone in there is hurt, and they don't answer the door," she told me.

"How do you know they're hurt?" I asked.

"I was awakened a little while back by voices—my room is next door to this one," she said, pointing. "Two men were arguing loudly, and they sounded very angry."

"What were they arguing about, ma'am?"

"I couldn't make out what they said. I'm afraid I'm a little hard-of-hearing these days. But they were shouting, and the tone of voice was very angry—make no mistake about that, young man; I know an argument when I hear one. Then there were sounds of a struggle, and one of them gave a dreadful cry. I heard the door open and close, and someone walked past in the corridor—only one person, mind you. I went to look, but there was nobody in sight when I got to the door. I knocked, but there was no answer. I think there was a fight, and someone in there is badly hurt."

"Well, let me try," I said. I knocked loudly, calling out, "Is anyone here? Are you hurt?" but heard no reply from within. I tried the knob, but the door was locked. I turned back to the woman. "Are you certain this is the right door?"

"As certain as I'm standing here," she said adamantly. "Do you think we should call the captain?"

"I'm not sure we ought to disturb the captain," I began, but I was interrupted by the opening of an adjacent cabin door.

A stout man with squinting eyes looked out at us, obviously in a foul mood. "Well, isn't it enough for those two men to shout and wrestle at all hours to keep a man awake? Now you have to bang on the door and raise a ruckus to wake the dead! Don't you have anyplace else to go?"

"I beg your pardon, sir," I said. "Do I understand you to say you heard an argument and a struggle in this room just a short time ago?"

"Aye, and no thanks to you for keeping the racket going. Will you be quiet and let a fellow sleep?" And with that, he slammed the door.

That put a different face on matters. Without the neighbor's corroboration, I might have tried to persuade the woman to return to her cabin and sleep. But now I knew that at least one other person had heard an argument and apparently a fight in the room. "I'll find someone to open the door," I told her, keeping my voice low. "Go into your room and close the door; I'll be back shortly."

She nodded gravely and went into her stateroom, and I went to look for help. I hesitated for a moment when I came out on deck again, not entirely certain which way to turn—was this incident serious enough to warrant calling in the captain, who might well be sound asleep at this hour, or would some lesser authority suffice? If there was an injured passenger, we might need a doctor. Then I recalled that one of our number might well be a killer, and decided to take no chances. I turned my steps upward to the texas deck.

However, it was not the captain's door, but Mr. Clemens's, upon which I decided to knock. He answered the door almost at once, wearing a plaid bathrobe. He took one look at my face and asked, "What on earth is going on, Wentworth?"

I briefly told him what I knew.

"Yes, it sounds as if it could be serious," he said. "Do you have any idea whose cabin it is?"

"I forgot to ask," I admitted.

"Well, there's nothing to do but go see what's happened. I'll get dressed and try to wake up Mike. You go down to the engine room and see if you can get one of the stokers to come up; we may have to break that door in. And if you see Berrigan, bring him along, too. This may be out of his jurisdiction, but if there's been a murder on board, he's the only expert we have."

Sobered by Mr. Clemens's voicing of what I realized I had already feared, I made my way down to the lower decks.

Thinking that Detective Berrigan might be in the main lounge with the cardplayers, I looked in there on the way to the engine room. The detective was not in view, but McPhee was at the corner table with the usual noisy group: half a dozen habitual gamblers, along with a small group of spectators. Among the latter was Mr. Snipes, the chief clerk. I caught his eye and beckoned to him to come over to the door, not wanting to advertise my purpose to the group at large. "Have you by any chance seen Mr. Berrigan?" I asked him.

"No, not tonight," he said, pulling at his goatee. "What do you want with him at this hour?"

I briefly told him the situation, and he nodded. "I'm just the man you need. Come on down to my office, and I'll look up which cabin is Mr. Berrigan's—we can fetch him on our way up. There's a doctor aboard, too, if we need him, but we don't have to call him just yet. I'll bring the master key so we can get in without breaking the door in.

That'll keep the whole thing quiet—no point bothering the other passengers unless there's an emergency.''

In his office, Mr. Snipes fished a ledger from some papers atop his desk and flipped through the pages. ''Berrigan, let's see now—by God, what cabin did you say the trouble's in?''

''Number forty-one on the hurricane deck,'' I said.

''That's the very one Mr. Berrigan's staying in!'' he said, slamming down the ledger. ''Come on!''

He grabbed a ring of keys, locked the door behind him, and we went flying up to the hurricane deck. Mr. Clemens was waiting there, as was the captain, in his shirtsleeves. I quickly explained the situation while the chief clerk tried his master key in the door. ''It's double-locked,'' he said. ''Berrigan must have locked it after the other fellow left.'' After a moment's turning and pushing, it opened. In the light from the corridor, I saw a crumpled form on the floor.

We crowded into the cabin, Mr. Snipes leading the way. Even from a distance I could see that the body was lying in a pool of blood. And the rumpled suit it wore was all too familiar. Mr. Snipes bent and turned the body over. The face was ghastly, but there was no doubt of the identity. ''It's Berrigan all right,'' said the clerk. ''Nothing the doctor can do—he's dead as a doornail.''

Captain Fowler bent to look at the corpse. ''Knifed,'' he said in a sorrowful tone of voice.

''But why would someone want to kill him?'' I said, shaken by the presence of a corpse.

''That seems clear enough to me,'' said Mr. Clemens. ''It looks as if Berrigan was telling the truth when he told you he'd found the murderer he was after. Damn it all, why didn't the poor fool tell somebody the killer's name while he still had the chance?''

The captain made some sort of answer, but my head was full of noise, and I couldn't make out what he'd said. A moment later, the cabin began to whirl about me, and I found myself collapsing helplessly to the floor—fainting like a frightened girl, for the first time in my life.

≈ 18

I came to my senses to find an unfamiliar face examining me from close range. I was lying on a bed, and there was a cool, wet cloth on my forehead. "Feeling better, are we?" said the man. He had thinning, sandy hair and wire-rimmed spectacles over an aquiline nose.

"I think so," I said, in a weak voice. "Who . . . ?"

"Dr. Savin, at your service," he said. "Take a sip of this; it'll help restore your strength." I drank from the flask he held out toward me and got a draft of strong brandy, which made me sputter a bit.

"Back among the living, I see," said Mr. Clemens. I turned to see him sitting in a corner chair not far from where I was lying. "Better than we can say for poor Berrigan."

"I'm sorry," I said. "This has never happened to me before. . . ."

"No need to apologize," said the doctor, his hand on my pulse. "Do you hurt anywhere?"

"I don't think so," I said. "Where am I?" Without even looking at the floor, I could tell that this was not the cabin where the murder had taken place.

"Just down the hall from Berrigan's cabin," said Mr. Clemens. "There was an empty cabin nearby, so we brought you down here until Charlie Snipes could bring the doctor."

"I appreciate your coming, Dr. Savin," I said. Then the

terrible truth of the situation struck home. "My God, Berrigan's really dead, isn't he."

"I'm afraid so, son. I doubt he suffered very long, though. The wound was directly to the heart."

"No consolation to the victim," said Mr. Clemens. "He didn't deserve to die this way—hellfire, nobody deserves it. I blame myself for not going to see him earlier. If I'd persuaded him to tell me what he knew, he might still be alive. I could have talked Mike into putting the killer in irons straightaway, and to the devil with the legal niceties."

"There's no use making yourself responsible for the man's death," said Dr. Savin. "People die every day, and there's not a man alive who can stop it. You learn to accept that pretty early if you're a doctor. You never learn to like it, but if you take every death to heart, you'll drive yourself mad."

"Well, maybe I couldn't have prevented it, but I can damned well make sure it doesn't go unpunished," said Mr. Clemens fiercely. "The fellow who did this is going to pay, I promise you."

"Do we have any idea who it is?" I asked. I sat up on the edge of the bed.

"No, but we'd better do what we can to find out," said Mr. Clemens. "Unfortunately, the fellow nominally best qualified to play the role of homicide detective is playing victim instead."

"What about the police in Memphis?" I asked. "Won't they investigate the case?"

"Oh, I'm sure they'll take an interest. But there are problems of jurisdiction. I'm not even sure what state we're in at the moment—Kentucky? Kansas? Elmer Parks could probably tell us—that's the sort of thing a pilot has to keep track of. More to the point, the trail will be a whole day old by the time we land. For all we know, the murderer's already swum ashore."

"If he has, we're well rid of him," said Dr. Savin, looking up as he closed his medical bag.

"True enough, although I'd rather have the fellow in jail than running loose," said Mr. Clemens. "First thing in the morning, Captain Fowler's going to verify who's on board. If there's anybody missing, we'll know who our killer is."

"And if everyone's still here?" Dr. Savin asked, a worried look in his eye.

"We'll know he's still on the boat. Then we'll have to figure out who the devil he is."

"The devil? I'm afraid you're right," said the doctor. "What worries me is that he may decide to favor us with more of his deviltry before we reach shore. I don't mind telling you, one corpse per voyage is quite enough for me."

"It's one too many for me," I said with much feeling. "What will the other passengers think when they learn of this atrocity?"

"For now, we're going to do what we can to *keep* them from learning about it," said Mr. Clemens. "Can we trust you to keep it quiet, Dr. Savin?"

"I see no reason to cause a panic," said the doctor. "But I can't promise to be quiet if I think there's imminent danger to anyone."

"I'm glad you see it that way," said Mr. Clemens. "All I ask is that you keep the news from spreading until we reach Memphis tomorrow. So far, only the three of us, plus the captain and Mr. Snipes, know about the murder. That's five—plus the killer. The captain and Mr. Snipes have both agreed not to tell anyone else for the time being, except for those crew members who'd find out anyway—and they won't know any more than that there's a dead man aboard, not who it is or how he died. If we can keep the news of the murder from the rest of the passengers, maybe we can trick the killer into letting it slip that he knows about it."

"But won't the news come out in Memphis?" I asked. "Once the police start coming aboard and questioning people, everyone will know something's amiss."

Mr. Clemens nodded. "That's why I want to find the murderer before then. Do you think you're up to taking another look around Berrigan's cabin?''

I looked at Dr. Savin. ''Have you put that brandy away yet, or do you think I could have another small taste of it?'' He gave me a knowing look, nodded silently, and reopened his bag.

After the doctor took his leave of us, Mr. Clemens and I returned to the detective's cabin, a few doors away. ''The captain found Berrigan's key,'' said Mr. Clemens, pulling it out of his pocket. ''It was in Berrigan's vest pocket.'' He opened the door, and I saw (to my relief) that the body was gone.

Mr. Clemens must have read my expression. ''Mike searched the body, and then he and Charlie Snipes smuggled it down to one of the meat lockers to keep it on ice—and I'm glad I wasn't the one who had to do the job. There's the rest of what they found.'' He waved in the direction of a bedside table, where personal effects from the detective's pockets were piled next to a nearly empty whisky bottle. A battered valise sat on the floor next to the table.

I looked at the items on the table, wondering what it must have been like for the captain to search the body. Just thinking of the grisly task made me shudder—I remembered the pool of blood on the floor, and deliberately turned my mind to examining the objects on the table. There was a well-worn pigskin wallet, a briar pipe and a brown corduroy tobacco pouch, some loose papers, a medium-sized envelope, two pencil stubs, and a penknife. I picked up the wallet and looked inside. There was no money, but pinned to the inside was the badge the detective had shown me in New York. ''It looks as if he's been robbed,'' I said.

''No, Snipes took the money for safekeeping,'' said Mr. Clemens. ''There was forty-eight dollars in greenbacks and another five and change in coin—he had me count it. Good thinking, though, Wentworth. Do you see anything else out of the ordinary?''

I poked around in the pile of papers taken from the dead man's pockets. "This might be worth a closer look." It was the passenger list the detective had shown me.

Mr. Clemens glanced at it perfunctorily and said, "I saw that before, but didn't think much of it. What makes you think it means anything?"

"Something Berrigan said yesterday—he mentioned having seen something on this list that jogged his memory. It must have been a name he recognized, perhaps an alias some New York criminal has used before."

Mr. Clemens looked at the paper more carefully, then refolded it and put it in his breast pocket. "Well, then, I'd best give it a look-over. Let's see the other papers, too— maybe there'll be something useful among them."

We spent the next few minutes passing the papers back and forth, but found nothing of any obvious relevance to our case until we opened the envelope. That turned out to include the photograph of Lee Russell, the New York murder victim, and two notes: one the scrap of paper with the names of Mr. Clemens and the Union Square Hotel that the police had found in Russell's pocket, the other the message, supposedly from Farmer Jack Hubbard, that had been left for Mr. Clemens at the hotel desk. Mr. Clemens put those in his pocket, along with the passenger list. He also took the wallet and the badge to give the clerk for safekeeping. "Poor Berrigan may have had a wife and family," he said. "They ought to have these things, at least. I'll try to find out when we get to Memphis. Now, let's go over the rest of the cabin and see what clues we turn up. You take that side and I'll take this. Pick up anything you find, even a pin."

The stateroom was small enough that we completed our task in a short time. The results were, in a word, disappointing: a penny under the bed, a burnt match-end, a broken pencil—and, to Mr. Clemens's amusement, a bent pin. None of them suggested anything about the murder; for all we knew, they had been on the floor for weeks. That left only Berrigan's valise to search. We turned that out on the bed and pawed through his clothes, discovering a Smith & Wesson revolver. "Have you ever used one of these things?" asked Mr. Clemens, holding it as if he feared it might turn and nip him.

"I'm afraid not," I admitted. "Is it loaded?"

He looked at it, then nodded his head. "It's loaded, all right. A lot of good it did Berrigan, packed away where he couldn't get to it. I'm going to give this to the captain for safekeeping, then. I probably couldn't hit the floor if I pointed it straight down, and giving it to you is no protection for either of us if you don't know how to shoot it."

"Why wasn't Berrigan carrying it?" I wondered.

"Good question. Maybe he didn't expect to need it, or maybe he was too drunk to realize he needed it. A fatal mistake, either way." Mr. Clemens began to pace in his usual way, then was brought up short by the bloodstain in his path. He shook his head sadly and turned back toward me.

"If he were planning to arrest someone, he'd have been carrying it," I said. "I think we can assume that the person who did this is the one who killed Lee Russell in New York."

"No question about it, in my mind," said Mr. Clemens. "I can't think of any other reason for anyone to have done him in, other than his personality. What I wonder is whether Berrigan knew the killer was coming to visit. If he was caught by surprise, it would explain why he didn't have his gun ready."

"But that suggests that the killer knew Berrigan had spotted him," I said. "I was alone when he told it to me, and I haven't told anyone but you. Could he have told anyone else, do you think?"

Mr. Clemens pointed to the whisky bottle. "I can't say what Berrigan might have done with a few drinks under his belt—for all I know, the idiot went down to the saloon and shouted it at the top of his lungs. Or maybe he sought the fellow out and invited him to his cabin for a few hands of cribbage. More likely, somebody overheard him talking to you—or you talking to me, come to think of it.''

"I suppose that makes sense." An uncomfortable thought crossed my mind. "You were serious about giving me the gun, weren't you.''

"Yes, until I found out you haven't shot one before. I won't take the risk of giving it to you unless I know you can use it—and that you *will* use it, if you need to. We're up against a man who's killed twice, Wentworth. He won't be anybody you can bluff or scare off. And he must have some notion that we're wise to him. That's the other reason I want to solve this case before Memphis; it's simply too dangerous to travel any farther with a known murderer among us. If we haven't settled this, one way or another, before we leave Memphis, I'll have to call off the expedition to recover the gold. I'd be looking over my shoulder every foot of the way.''

"Yes, I suppose we don't have many alternatives. I wish he'd told me who his suspect was.''

We glanced over the room once more to make certain we hadn't missed anything, but found nothing more out of the ordinary—to the extent one can say that of a room where a man has just been stabbed to death. Finally, Mr. Clemens put his hand on my shoulder and said, "Better call it a night, Wentworth—this has been the devil's own work. I know it must have been hard for you to come back into this room—it wasn't easy for me either—and I appreciate the help. Try to get a few hours' sleep now. We'll both need all our wits about us.''

"Thank you, sir,'' I said. "I don't know how easy it'll be to sleep after this, but if I can't sleep, it won't be because I'm not tired.''

We locked the door behind us and made our way slowly up to the texas deck, where we parted company; it was after three o'clock, by my watch. I took off my jacket and lay down on my bed, and was almost asleep when I realized what else had been missing from the room: Berrigan's little notebook. I'd seen it in his hand that very afternoon, when he'd teased me about his "little list." Could the captain have missed it in his search? It didn't seem likely, although I supposed the only way to check would be to search the body again—a task I wasn't eager to perform myself. There, if anywhere, was where Berrigan might have written down the name of his main suspect—and its absence seemed to confirm our guess that Berrigan had been killed to prevent his bringing the New York killer to justice.

Assuming, for the moment, that the notebook really was missing, I wondered where it could be. The most likely answer was that the killer had taken it; perhaps Berrigan had brought it out and waved it in the killer's face before he was stabbed. In all probability, the killer had thrown it overboard under cover of darkness. At least, that's what I should have done in his place, knowing its importance. If that were the case, I knew, we might never learn the killer's identity.

Or, worse yet, I found myself imagining, we might learn it only when he revealed himself to us in some lonely place, with a dagger in his hand and no help in sight. On that disturbing image, I finally managed to drift off to sleep. Mercifully, for once I did not dream.

19

I awoke at first light, not really rested. But my mind was seething so furiously that, after a futile attempt, I gave up trying to go back to sleep. The odd thought struck me that this must be how soldiers felt on the morn of an impending battle. And almost inevitably, the notion of a battle made me think of Major Demayne's poem on Antietam, which I had promised to read over for Mr. Clemens and had all but forgotten.

It was too early to go looking for breakfast, so I turned on the light and dug out the Major's manuscript from my suitcase. The verses seemed no better than before:

> Somewhere I hear the cannon's fearsome roar—
> Antietam! Waves of blood roll on thy shore!
> My comrades fall, their lives not spent in vain—
> I lov'd them, and remember still their pain.
>
> Napoleon's armies reach'd no greater heights;
> Engrave in Golden numbers, Muse! their fights.
> E'en I, unworthy wretch, am spar'd to tell
> Deeds of renown, in Sharpsburg's deadly dell.
>
> Ten thousand fell on that ensanguin'd field,
> O'er whelmed by fire, but not about to yield!
> Secessions's minions cannot win the day;
> E'en Lee himself cannot the Vict'ry stay!

Eagles of Triumph above our standards soar—
Youth's slain and crippl'd, but the battle's o'er.
Out of the blood the Union rises whole—
Union Forever! I shout with all my soul.

I searched the page for any evidence of poetic merit.
Something in these lines had made me want to look at them
again, but I was at a loss to discover anything to set their
author apart from dozens of amateur poets in the newspapers. The verses scanned, and the rhymes did not clash in
my ear, but I discerned no flash of genius, no feeling that
the poet was describing scenes that had any great meaning
for him. The veterans of Antietam would have to await
some other Homer to sing their deeds. Surely there was
nothing here worth Mr. Clemens's time, with two murders
hanging over our heads. . . .

Suddenly, I realized what I had missed on my first reading: there in front of my eyes were the words "Napoleon,"
"Golden," and "Ten thousand." I was thunderstruck; how
could I have overlooked so many obvious references to the
treasure Mr. Clemens and I were seeking—ten thousand
dollars in gold that he had described as hidden in the van-
ished town of Napoleon, Arkansas? Even "Eagles" seemed
to fit, now that I was thinking in terms of gold pieces.
Major Demayne had given me the broadest hint imaginable,
and it had gone right over my head. No wonder he was so
anxious for Mr. Clemens to see his "poetry"!

Clearly, I would have to give Mr. Clemens the manuscript immediately. But what could Major Demayne know
of our treasure hunt, and what sort of message could he be
trying to pass to my employer in such a mysterious way?
Why didn't he simply approach Mr. Clemens and ask to
speak with him privately? Did the message mean that he
was involved in the murders, or that he was also in danger
and afraid to reveal himself directly?

I found it difficult to believe that the kindly old soldier
(who, after all, had twice come to my rescue) was in league

with a murderer. But I had to admit that such a connection could explain the "secret message" inserted into the manuscript of his rather pompous epic. I scanned the verses eagerly, looking for other clues, but saw nothing more of obvious significance. Whatever else lay on the pages, it was somehow concealed behind the Major's antiquated rhetorical flourishes and self-consciously "poetic" diction.

I glanced at my watch and realized that it was now after seven, so I set the manuscript aside, put on my jacket and shoes, and headed below in search of breakfast. The events of the previous night still seemed unreal to me, although the image of Berrigan's body lying in a pool of blood remained fixed in my mind like a luridly colored photograph. The doctor had told me and Mr. Clemens that Berrigan must have died almost instantly, but I found it impossible to recall the slumped body without thinking of incredible pain. It wasn't until I was halfway through my second cup of coffee that the discrepancy struck me: how had the mortally wounded detective managed to lock the door behind his assailant without leaving a trail of blood across the floor of his cabin?

The captain had found Berrigan's key in his pocket, but the door had been locked. Either the detective had been alive long enough to lock the door from the inside, somehow managing to avoid bleeding, or the killer had taken Berrigan's notebook and key from his body, left the cabin, locked the door from the outside, and then magically conveyed the key back into the dead man's pocket through the closed door. Neither solution made sense to me. Why even bother to lock the door on a dead body, unless to create pointless mystification?

This new mystery made me especially anxious to speak to Mr. Clemens. As he had not appeared for breakfast yet, I took my half-finished cup of coffee and climbed back up to the texas to see if he was awake. I was in luck; he was at my stateroom door, tapping softly. "There you are, you rascal," he said gruffly. "A shabby trick, to get up early

and leave an old man knocking at your door trying to wake
you up when you're already gone. After last night, a locked
door with no answer to my knock makes me nervous.''

I laughed. ''Believe me, it wasn't done on purpose to
fool you,'' I said. ''I hope the fact that I've been thinking
about our murder last night will compensate. I've found a
couple of things that puzzle me—perhaps you can make
sense of them.''

''Good man, Wentworth. Only don't speak so loudly
about that business last night—remember, we want to keep
it quiet as long as possible. Come on in the captain's cabin.
He's had a pot of coffee brought up from the galley, and
we can go over what you've found out without the whole
boat being able to overhear us.''

Captain Fowler admitted us to his cabin with a somber
expression. After topping up my cup of coffee, I told the
captain and Mr. Clemens my speculations about the missing
notebook and the locked cabin.

''Well, I'll be dagnabbed,'' said the captain. ''Here I was
so bothered about that fellow being killed on my boat that
I never did notice there was anything else funny about it.
How the hell does somebody get a key into a dead man's
pocket through a locked door? Or lock it from outside without the key?''

''I spotted that problem, too,'' said Mr. Clemens. ''I
think Wentworth's right about the notebook; most likely,
it's at the bottom of the river, eighty miles behind us. As
far as the locked door, I can think of a few possible answers—too damned many answers, in fact. How many sets
of master keys are there?''

''Tarnation! The master keys!'' said the captain, setting
his coffee cup down with a thump. ''Of course—all the
cleaning women will have a set, as well as the clerk's office. I've even got a set, not that I ever use 'em. You don't
think one of the crew killed poor Berrigan, do you, Sam?''

''I'm pretty sure *you* didn't kill him, Mike, but so far I
can't *prove* you didn't—or that anybody else did or didn't,

for that matter. The cleaning crew, the clerk's office . . . Who else has keys?''

"I couldn't rightly say, Sam—it's Charlie Snipes's job to hand 'em out, not mine. He's pretty careful with 'em. But I reckon there's more'n half a dozen keys somewhere or another on board that can open that stateroom door.''

"That's what I thought. So somebody could bribe one of the cleaners, or sneak into Snipes's office and lay hands on a master key. And if the fellow we're looking for is somebody who's spent time on a riverboat before, he probably knew that. This isn't going to be an easy job, Mike. Almost anybody could have gotten hold of a key to that room.''

"I'm not sure how easy it would be to sneak into Charlie's office without him noticing," said the captain, although without much conviction in his voice. "He usually knows just what's going on: who's in every cabin, what port they got on the boat at and where they're getting off, whether they have checked baggage. You'd have to get up mighty early in the morning to put one over on him, Sam.''

"But he was out of his office when I found him," I pointed out. "He was in the main cabin, watching the poker game. Couldn't someone have gotten into his office then?''

Captain Fowler shook his head. "It ain't like Charlie to leave his office unlocked—there's a good bit of cash, not to mention the passengers' valuables and all, in the safe there. It don't make sense he'd leave it sitting open for any jaybird to waltz in and help himself. More likely they'd try to bribe a cleaner, although I don't know how we'd find out if they did.''

"Which leaves us no further along than when we began," said Mr. Clemens. "Unless . . .'' He put his hand to his chin and stared off at the window.

After a few moments of silence, the captain cleared his throat loudly. "Unless what, Sam?''

"What do you know about that assistant clerk of Snipes's?''

"That young fellow? Tommy something, I think. This is his first trip with us. Charlie hired him, and I don't see much of him except when Charlie has him run a message up to me. What about him?"

"I don't know; it just occurred to me that he's the one looking after the office when Snipes is out. Maybe somebody slipped him a few dollars to look the other way while they borrowed the keys, or maybe they just reached over the counter and snagged a set of keys while he was daydreaming. Hell, maybe he killed Berrigan himself, although I can't imagine why. I suppose I'm just fishing for answers, Mike. Any decent answer will do about now."

"Amen to that, Sam," said the captain. He took out his watch and looked at it, then polished it with a handkerchief before returning it to his vest pocket. "Speaking of Charlie Snipes, he should be coming up in about an hour to report on exactly who's on board this morning. Once we know that, we'll have a better idea which tree to start barking up. I've got a couple little chores to attend to before then; why don't we meet back here about nine o'clock and see what we know?"

As we left the captain's cabin, I remembered the other half of my news for Mr. Clemens. "Do you remember that manuscript you asked me to look at for you—Major Demaync's poetry?" I said.

Mr. Clemens gave me a weary look. "I'm afraid so," he said. "Don't we have enough calamities for one morning without taking on a load of godforsaken amateur poetry?"

"Normally, I'd agree," I said. "But I think you'll want to make an exception for this one. In fact, I think it's directly relevant to our case."

"You're baiting me, Wentworth," said Mr. Clemens, no trace of humor in his voice. "Are you going to tell me about it, or am I going to have to read the fellow's verses for myself?"

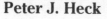

We were standing right next to my cabin door. "I think you'd better take a look at the manuscript," I said. "Step inside, and I'll show you what I mean."

He came in, grumbling a bit—more or less pro forma, I thought. But when I gave him the manuscript, and pointed out the key words on the first page—Napoleon, Golden, Ten thousand, and Eagles—his demeanor changed. "I see what you mean, Wentworth. If the fellow wanted to grab my attention, he chose a pretty sure way. It's a shame he's turned all this good blank paper into puerile nonsense you wouldn't light your cigars with on account of the stench. But I think he's accomplished his main purpose. Did you notice how these lines begin?"

I looked again at the verses. *"Somewhere I hear the cannon's fearsome roar . . .* I don't know, it seems perfectly commonplace to me. Is there some allusion I'm missing?"

"No, man, look at the first letter of each line. Read them straight downward as if they were a sentence."

Suddenly the letters jumped out at me, as if written in a different color: *S-A-M I N-E-E-D T-O S-E-E Y-O-U.* "Good Lord, it's a hidden message!" Now that I saw it, all in bold capitals, I wondered how I'd missed it first time through. It was as obvious as a turkey in a flock of geese.

"Yes, an acrostic—an old schoolboy game. Most people never notice that the first letter of each line spells out a message of some kind. What do you think it means?"

"Clearly, it's from someone who knows about the gold we're searching for—I don't think the reference to Napoleon could be accidental. And since he calls you Sam, I suppose it's someone who knows you. But if that's the case, why didn't he just ask for a chance to speak in private?"

"Exactly what I was wondering," said Mr. Clemens. "I'm not all that hard to talk to. In fact, if he'd chosen almost any other way to approach me, he would have bettered his chances. So he must be worried about a direct approach—which means that he thinks there's danger in it.''

''Or that he has some sort of mischief in mind,'' I said. ''What if the fellow wants to get you off somewhere and torture the location of the gold out of you? I'd advise against seeing him unless I'm present.''

''And if he pulled out a pistol to argue his position, what could you for me do that I couldn't do by myself?'' Mr. Clemens looked me straight in the eye, and all I could do was shrug and grin. ''Exactly what I thought,'' he said. ''But frankly, I don't think the person who wrote this is our killer.''

''Why not? He appears to know about the treasure, and he's trying to arrange a meeting without telling anyone else about it. And as you yourself point out, he might very well be armed and desperate. I'd approach this fellow with the greatest caution.''

Mr. Clemens clapped me on the back and said, ''You're a good man, Wentworth. You've got the right instincts, and I appreciate it. Major Demayne is certainly something other than he appears to be, and I have a suspicion about what— or rather, who—he really is. If I'm right, I'd be very surprised to learn that he's the killer, either of that man in New York or of Berrigan.''

He pointed to the manuscript. ''For one thing, this message is the work of a man of some education: the handwriting alone would tell you that, let alone the fact that it's written in competent verse—execrably bad verse, but competent nonetheless. If you'll remember the two notes we saw from the killer, they were both barely legible scrawls. I don't think the man who wrote those notes could have written this.''

''You almost convince me,'' I said. I didn't want to believe that a man who'd helped me could be the murderer we feared. Still, I had to follow my reasoning to its logical conclusion. ''Couldn't the killer have disguised his handwriting? For that matter, why assume that the killer wrote them? Perhaps they were written by the victim, Lee Russell.''

"Ed McPhee told us that Russell could barely write his own name. Granted, Ed doesn't have a fine regard for the truth, but this time I think we can take him at his word. For one thing, he doesn't stand to gain anything by it, as far as I can see.''

"Russell could have learned his letters after he moved to New York,'' I argued. "But that's a side issue. The real point is that we don't know who wrote those notes, and until we do, there's no reason to assume the killer did it.''

"I suppose you're right about that,'' said Mr. Clemens, seating himself on my bed. "You did tell me that Berrigan claimed he'd solved the case, and I think we can take his being killed as corroboration. He couldn't have done it without some sort of tangible evidence, and those two notes are just about the only solid clues he had. I wish his notebook hadn't disappeared, although I can't say it surprises me.

"But remember, he told you that something on the passenger list had given him a lead. Perhaps we ought to look at that again. The two of us may notice something neither of us has spotted independently.''

"As good an idea as any,'' I agreed.

Mr. Clemens stood and walked to the cabin door. "I left it in my stateroom; there's a bit more room to sit over there, and a table to spread things out on. Why don't we adjourn next door and see what we can learn.''

I gave my assent, and we went out on deck. I brought along Major Demayne's "poem'' to see if it contained any further clues. We had barely stepped out on the deck when I heard a loud commotion from the deck below—voices raised in anger, and the unmistakable sounds of a fight in progress.

"What the devil?'' said Mr. Clemens. Before he could say anything more, I thrust the Major's manuscript into his hands and dashed headlong down the nearest stairway in the direction of the disturbance. It occurred to me briefly that the fight might be none of my business, but I thought I had recognized one of the voices in the uproar. From behind me, I heard my employer shout my name, but I paid him no attention.

The sounds of the altercation came from the main corridor of the hurricane deck. I plunged in. Ahead, I saw a group of men struggling by the door of a cabin, although it was too dim for me to make out who they were. I thought I recognized Chief Clerk Snipes's voice, and that of Tiny Williams, the mate; and one other sounded familiar to me, one I was not pleased to hear.

"Stand back, you double-crossing son of a bitch! Give a man room—"

"Watch it, Billy, he's got a shiv!"

"I told you worthless ****** skunks to stay the **** off my ****ing boat . . ."

"What the *hell* is going on here? Belay that, Mr. Snipes!" The last voice signaled the arrival of Captain Fowler, who pushed his way past me and put his hand on the chief clerk's shoulder. Mr. Snipes half turned, his clothing disheveled and a feral look in his eye, and I thought for a moment he would strike out at the captain. I was startled to see a foot-long blade in his hand. But when he recognized the captain, he was instantly calm.

"I'm sure glad to see you, Captain," said Snipes. "I was down here checking the passengers, like you said. Well, this cabin was supposed to be empty, but I thought I heard somebody inside. So I opened the door, and lo and behold, there they sit, cozy as a pair of bedbugs!" He waved in the direction of the cabin door, where, craning my neck, I could make out the porcine features of Billy Throckmorton, firmly in the grasp of Tiny Williams. It didn't take a great leap of imagination to realize that the other occupant of the cabin, whose voice I had heard from on deck, must be Billy's brother, Alligator Throckmorton.

"I think you can put away the knives, boys," said Captain Fowler. To my surprise, he was holding a pistol—was it Berrigan's or his own? "Easy now. I don't want any more nonsense. Mr. Williams, would you take that other blade? Thank you. Now, if both you fellows will sit on the bed—and keep your hands in sight, if you please—we can try to sort this out."

Captain Fowler stepped forward, and I moved aside to let him through. On both sides, I was vaguely aware of other passengers peering out of their cabin doors with worried and frightened expressions. The captain must have noticed them at about the same time, for he turned and said, "The show's over, folks. Nothing more to see." Then, noticing me, he nodded. "Right in the middle of things again, eh, Mr. Cabot? You might as well come in and help me keep these rascals in order. You too, Sam—I should have known you'd be along in good time."

Mr. Clemens, who had come up behind me—puffing as if he'd run down the stairs—followed me into the little cabin, which seemed barely big enough to hold the Throckmortons, let alone the rest of us: Captain Fowler, Chief Clerk Snipes, First Mate Williams, Mr. Clemens, and myself. The captain kept his gun trained on the stowaways, while Williams was holding a wicked-looking knife, which I assumed he'd taken from Alligator Throckmorton; Mr. Snipes, who was sporting a black eye in addition to a torn jacket, had already returned his blade to wherever he kept it concealed.

"So," said Captain Fowler after the cabin door was closed. "How long have you two been aboard?"

"I ain't sayin' nothin'," said Billy Throckmorton. He glared from face to face, and I had the firm impression that he was considering jumping up and resuming the fight, whatever the odds against him.

"You can say as much or as little as you like," said the captain. "Riding a boat without paying is the same as stealing, and I'd just as soon call the sheriff on you the minute we dock in Memphis. Maybe a few days in the lockup will change your attitude.''

''I doubt it, Mike,'' said Mr. Clemens. ''These fellows look to me as if they've seen the wrong side of the bars before now. We aren't going to scare them all that easily.''

''You're right about that, Mister,'' said Billy Throckmorton, a half-beat ahead of his brother's ''Shut up, Billy.''

''*You* shut up, Al,'' said the larger of the two brothers. ''We ain't got nothin' to worry about. Soon as Ed finds out we're in the can, he'll be down to go bail for us. We'll be struttin' down Beale Street 'fore you can say 'boo.' ''

''If he knew you were on board, he'll be in the can himself,'' said Snipes. ''And for a lot worse than just snitching a ride without paying. They'll be measuring the three of you for hemp neckties, if I know the law in Memphis.''

''Have you gone plumb crazy, Charlie Snipes?'' said Alligator Throckmorton. ''They don't hang a man for anything we've done.'' But his brother Billy was in no mood for words. He leapt up from the bed, and with one pawlike hand knocked the pistol from the captain's hand on his way to the door. He felled Snipes with the other hand before the clerk could make a move, knocking him into Tiny Williams before yanking open the door and bursting out.

I was the only one in a position to pursue him. I ran after him, out the door and down the corridor. He paused as he came onto the afterdeck, and I overtook him and hit him shoulder-high with as good a flying tackle as ever I'd made on the football field at Yale. We both went down. I struck my head on the railing, and the next thing I knew he was on top of me with his hands around my throat and his knee jabbing into my groin.

I tried to break his choke hold, but his hands were like iron. I landed a punch on his nose, another just below his ribs, but could get no leverage behind them. I could feel myself losing strength, and tried to gather what little I had left to defend myself; I lay with my head through the railing, and below me I was vaguely aware of the river and the paddle wheel. I threw a feeble punch at his Adam's apple, but he tucked his chin under and absorbed it without effect. "Good try, city boy," he growled. 'Now it's lights out. . . .''

I threw another ineffectual punch at his face. He laughed, and then I saw a huge hand descending on him and pulling him upward by the hair before I lost consciousness—for the second time in as many days.

20

I opened my eyes to see Mr. Clemens and Captain Fowler standing over me with concerned expressions on their faces. Behind them several passengers peered at me, undoubtedly drawn to the scene by the noise and the fight. I must not have been unconscious for long, because not far away I could see Tiny Williams holding Billy Throckmorton against the cabin wall. I sat up and shook my head, trying to clear it.

"Are you all right, son?" asked the captain.

"I think so," I said. I was still a bit groggy—my head hurt where I had hit it—and I suspected that I would have a few bruises when I next looked in a mirror. But, in view of the fact that two men had already been killed in the short time I had been working for Mr. Clemens, I was content to find myself still among the living.

"I didn't know you could move that fast," said Mr. Clemens. "I might have tried to stop you, if I'd known it. I can't really blame you for chasing that rascal when he ran away; it's the most natural thing in the world. But did you ever stop to think what you'd do with him if you caught him?"

"Leave him alone, Sam," said Captain Fowler. "He did a brave thing, and he's lucky Mr. Williams got back on his feet in time to help. Now, we'll lock up these blasted Throckmortons until we make Memphis, and that'll be the end of it."

"Go ahead and lock them up, but don't expect it to be the end of anything," said Mr. Clemens.

"What do you mean, Sam?"

"I'll tell you shortly, Mike—this whole crowd doesn't need to know all the details. For now, let's just get these two rascals locked away where they can't cause any more trouble."

We took the Throckmorton brothers down to the main deck, to a storage room near the clerk's office. It had not previously occurred to me that a riverboat might require a place to confine violent passengers, but the reinforced door was proof that someone had anticipated the need. Mr. Williams held Billy Throckmorton in an apparently effortless armlock, while Mr. Snipes brought along the smaller brother Al with a firm grip on one arm. Captain Fowler followed with his pistol drawn, and Mr. Clemens and I brought up the rear, with a few curious passengers staring after us—among them, to my discomfort, Miss Cunningham. The prisoners scowled out at us as Mr. Snipes swung the door shut, but made no further effort to escape. The chief clerk shot the bolt and brushed his hands off with a satisfied expression.

"That ought to hold 'em," said the captain, thrusting the pistol into his trouser pocket. "Good work, Charlie, Tiny—and Mr. Cabot, too! I thought sure that villain would be over the side and halfway to shore."

"At least he'd have been off the boat," said Mr. Snipes. "I'd have led three cheers if he'd drownded himself, but I'll be just as glad to hand the pair of them over to the Memphis police and wash our hands of the whole mess. Damn shame we didn't catch McPhee in there with them. It'd be a good excuse to get rid of the master along with his dogs."

"We haven't gotten to Ed McPhee yet," said the captain. "And he ain't home free yet, either. I guarantee you he'll have some questions to answer as soon as I lay eyes on him—I'm going to make the deck hot under his feet, believe you me. Unless he has the right answers, I'll put him off at Memphis and not shed a tear about it.''

"I'd like to be there when you ask those questions, Mike,'' said Mr. Clemens. "They don't call him Slippery Ed for nothing. But maybe the two of us can smoke him out.''

"Aye, two pairs of hands are better than one, when you're trying to catch a snake,'' said the captain. "What cabin is McPhee in, Charlie? We'll go haul him out of bed, if we have to.''

"Let me come show you,'' said Snipes.

"Oh, we can manage,'' said Mr. Clemens. "We'll bring Cabot along, in case Ed tries anything foolish, not that I expect him to. But I think it's more important for you to finish checking whether all the passengers are still on board. You didn't find anyone missing yet, did you?''

"No,'' said the clerk, frowning. "But there's your killers, right in there,'' he said, gesturing toward the bolted door. "Why keep looking for what you've already found?''

"Because if you don't, we'll never know what else you might have found out,'' said Mr. Clemens. "If we're going to convince a judge to put the Throckmortons on trial for murder, we've got to have an airtight case. I can imagine some slick lawyer finding out we didn't know whether all the other passengers were still on board—even a Tennessee hanging judge would have a hard time ignoring that big a loophole. We've got to account for everybody on the boat, passengers and crew. And since you're the one who started the search, you should finish it.''

"Sam's right, Charlie,'' said Captain Fowler. "Them doggone Throckmortons might be guilty as sin, but we ain't proved it yet. Just being on board when a man gets stabbed doesn't prove they're the ones who did it. We've got to do this right. Go wash your face and fix up your uniform, and then go finish up that count, and let me know as soon as you're done. I'll bring you up to date on anything we find out from McPhee.''

Snipes consented—somewhat grudgingly, it seemed to me—and the captain, Mr. Clemens, and I went to find Slippery Ed McPhee and learn what we could about his role, if any, in the events of last night and this morning.

We stopped first at the main cabin, to check whether McPhee might already be at his usual spot at the poker table. Knowing the gamblers' preference for late hours, we were not surprised to find the table empty, except for a pair of white-haired ladies with birdlike features who had in front of them not cards but tea and biscuits. They smiled and tittered when the captain went over to them, but their expressions changed when he asked whether they had seen any of the cardplayers. ''Oh, no,'' said one of them, pursing her lips in evident disapproval. ''They never come here before noon.'' We thanked the ladies and made our way up to McPhee's stateroom, on the aft end of the texas deck.

Captain Fowler knocked firmly on the door; then, after a few moments without a response, again more loudly. ''Who the hell is it? Go away!'' came a muffled voice from within.

''It's the captain. Open up!''

This information was greeted with a curse and some stumbling about; footsteps came toward the door. ''Hang on, Mike,'' said the voice, now recognizable as McPhee. ''Let me at least get my pants on.'' More stumbling sounds came from within, and then at last the door opened a crack. ''Damnation, Mike, you ought to know better than rouse a man up this early,'' said McPhee. ''What do you want that won't wait till a decent hour?''

''We need to ask you some questions,'' said the captain. ''Open up and let us in, Ed.''

''Wait a minute, Mike. Give me another minute, and we'll go down to the main deck. If you mean to quiz a man first thing in the morning, it's only civilized to let him have a cup of coffee so's his memory don't play tricks.'' He disappeared again, and there were more sounds of stumbling about, after which McPhee emerged, fully dressed but looking distinctly unhappy about the bright sun. He closed the door quickly behind him. "Hello, Sam," he said sourly, shading his eyes with an unsteady hand. "When did you join the early-bird society?"

"Morning, Ed," said Mr. Clemens. "I've got an idea, if nobody objects. Just so we can have some privacy, why don't we go to the captain's cabin? We can have fresh coffee sent up, and I've got a bottle of whisky handy. Ed might like a drop or two of that to sweeten up his morning coffee, and I could use a taste myself."

"Now you're talking more my style," said McPhee. "But what's the matter? Don't tell me somebody's complaining I beat 'em playing cards. I'm barely breaking even, the last few nights."

"Nothing about the cards, Ed," said the captain, leading the way up the stairs. "We'll get to it in a moment, when we're more private." He unlocked his stateroom door, waved us in, and we took seats. Mr. Clemens arrived a minute later, bringing the whisky bottle from his cabin. The captain produced glasses, and Mr. Clemens poured generous amounts for McPhee and himself; Captain Fowler and I decided to wait for the coffee.

"Ah, that's the way to start the morning," said McPhee after a sip. "Now, what's the inquisition about? You'd think somebody was dead, from the way the three of you look."

"Funny you should mention that—" began the captain, but Mr. Clemens cut him off. "Do you know where Billy and Al Throckmorton are?"

"With any luck, they're in Memphis," McPhee said. "If they got to drinking and fooling around, they might still be in Cairo, sleeping it off. It ain't that long a train ride, and I don't much care when they get in, as long as they're ready for business when we dock tonight." He looked around at our faces and frowned. "Something's wrong, ain't it. What's going on, Sam?"

"They aren't in Cairo or Memphis, either one," said Mr. Clemens. "We found them holed up in an empty cabin right here on the boat. You say you didn't know they were on board?"

"Hell, no—I gave 'em money to ride the train!" McPhee stood up, still holding his whisky glass. "Those crazy hoot owls! They must have drunk up their ticket money and snuck on board before we cast off. I'll tar and feather the both of 'em!"

"You could probably get some help doing that," said Mr. Clemens. "Charlie Snipes and Cabot here will be glad to lend a hand. But sit down and relax, Ed. We still aren't quite done yet. Were you playing cards all last night, after we left Cairo?"

"Sure, sat there all night long and sweated like a hound dog for maybe thirty dollars profit. Might as well have gone to bed early, like a regular citizen—I *would* have, if I knew you was going to wake me up to answer questions first thing in the morning. Where's that boy with the coffee?"

"Shortly, Ed. Here, let me top up your glass while we're waiting." Mr. Clemens poured two more fingers of whisky for McPhee, then did the same for himself. "Did you leave the table for any length of time?"

McPhee took another sip, then snorted. "I can hold my water as well as the next man, Sam. You can't just get up from the table every few minutes in a serious game; never know what might happen while you're gone. There must be six or eight people who can tell you I was there all night, except maybe one or two hands. Ask that Charlie Snipes—he was looking over my shoulder most of the time."

There was a knock on the door, which turned out to be the boy with the coffeepot. All of us helped ourselves to the steaming brew, then McPhee settled back down in his chair and Mr. Clemens resumed his questioning. "So, if you were playing cards all night, you wouldn't know when the Throckmorton boys came on board."

"Hell, I done told you I didn't even know they *were* on

board, Sam. I can promise you those damn fools will get an earful when I catch up with 'em.''

"They'll be lucky if that's *all* they get," muttered Captain Fowler, but Mr. Clemens gave him a look and McPhee continued.

"Look here, Mike, I can understand you gettin' upset when they sneak on board after you throwed 'em off the boat; sometimes I think those boys ain't got good sense. But no real harm done, is there? They ain't bad boys, just a little wild. Tell you what I'm gonna do. Why don't you have Charlie Snipes calculate how much a cabin from Cairo to Memphis ought to cost, and I'll cover their fare. And add on a few dollars extra if you need to cover any busted furniture. That should square things away, right?''

"We'll think about it, Ed," said Mr. Clemens. "For now, we've got them cooling their heels down below—they got a bit rowdy when we caught them. I'd appreciate it if you didn't try to see them before we land in Memphis, just to let them stew a little more. Got to teach 'em a lesson, you know?''

McPhee sipped his coffee and nodded. "I can see your point, Sam. Sure, let 'em pickle for a while, teach 'em a lesson. And Mike, you just tell me how much I owe for their passage, and I'll ante up." He took another sip, draining the cup, and grinned. "And then I'll take it out of their hides!''

Mr. Clemens laughed. "I'll bet you will, Ed! Well, thanks for coming up to talk, and I'm sure Mike will let you know how much you owe.''

McPhee stood up and took his leave, smiling and joking as if it were the pleasantest morning of his life. After the door closed behind him, Captain Fowler walked over and peered out, perhaps to make certain McPhee hadn't lingered to eavesdrop on us. Then he returned to his chair and shook his head. "Smoothest durn liar I ever *did* see," he said. "Why, you'd think McPhee didn't have a notion them scoundrels was even on the boat.''

"It makes you wonder, doesn't it?" said Mr. Clemens. He fished a cigar out of his breast pocket, clipped the end, and lit it, then continued. "What if he's telling the truth? I know, it's a preposterous notion, but suppose, just this once, that he is. What then, Mike?"

The captain looked at Mr. Clemens as if he'd left his senses, but he thought a moment and then admitted, "I suppose those boys *could* have snuck on board without McPhee writing out invitations for 'em. But I still think he's behind it somehow."

"Forget whether he knew about the Throckmortons being on board," said Mr. Clemens. "Maybe he did and maybe he didn't, but if he knows anything about the murder, I'll eat my hat. He seems to think that stowing away and busted furniture is all we're worried about, and he still believes a couple of dollars will straighten that out."

"Well, that may be true, Sam. But that doesn't mean the Throckmortons didn't kill that Berrigan fellow—they could have done it on their own, easy enough."

"It still doesn't make sense, Mike. Think for a minute— why would they sneak onto a boat they've been thrown off of, kill a man, and then go lie down to sleep in a cabin on the same deck? Why didn't they just swim ashore after they'd done it? Even a fool should know we'd search the boat after we found Berrigan dead. Why stay around to get caught?"

"I don't know, Sam. Maybe they were drunk, or maybe they're just a whole lot stupider than you give 'em credit for. I'll tell you one thing: they're staying locked up good and tight until we make Memphis, or I'm not the captain of the *Horace Greeley*."

"Oh, keep them locked up, for sure," said Mr. Clemens. "I'd be the last one to tell you to turn that kind of walking trouble loose on board. Though I just can't figure out why they would kill Berrigan—if they're the ones who did it."

"Seems easy enough to me. Berrigan probably caught 'em on board and threatened to turn 'em in," said the captain with the air of a man settling accounts.

"I doubt Berrigan would even have noticed," said Mr. Clemens. "You and Charlie Snipes got all stirred up when you found them stowing away, because it's your boat and your business. But Berrigan didn't care a rap about that. The only thing he was interested in was catching the man that killed Lee Russell in New York. And he'd scratched the Throckmorton boys off his list—that murder was on Thursday, and they were in Chicago the next evening. They couldn't have gotten there unless they sprouted wings and flew."

The captain rubbed his chin. "So. Maybe you're right. But if they didn't do it, what are they doing on my boat? And who the dickens *did* kill Berrigan?"

"I don't know yet," said Mr. Clemens. "But I'm going to find out. And I'll start with the easy part. Do you think those two wildcats have cooled off enough to answer a few questions?"

⁓21

Down on the main deck, we found Mr. Snipes's young assistant clerk leaning back in a chair against the door of the storeroom where the Throckmorton brothers were being held. He was reading a western novel with a lurid cover, his stringy blond hair nearly hiding his face. He leapt to his feet when he noticed the captain, dropping his book and nearly knocking over the chair in the process. "Hello, Cap'n Fowler . . . Mr. Twain. Can I help you?"

"You sure can, son—it's Tommy, isn't it?" Captain Fowler smiled paternally, towering over the slightly built apprentice.

"Yessir. Tommy Hazelwood." He smiled, nervously.

"Well, Tommy, we're going to talk to the prisoners. But I figure we ought to have a little help, just in case they decide to get rough. Could you go find Mr. Williams, the mate, and bring him here? And ask him to bring along one of his men, somebody he can trust in a pinch."

"You want Tiny? Sure, I'll be right back." The boy dashed off in the direction of the engine room.

Mr. Clemens stared at the book lying on the floor; it purported to be the true adventures of some western hero, in his own words. The cover showed him on horseback, firing a rifle at what looked like an entire tribe of Indians. "Fine taste in literature," he said at last, shaking his head. "Remind me, Wentworth, I want to talk to this boy after we're done with the Throckmortons. He might have answers to a couple of questions that are puzzling me.''

I nodded in the affirmative, and then young Tommy Hazelwood reappeared, leading Mr. Williams and another muscular crewman. ''Good work, Tommy,'' said the captain. ''Now, Mr. Williams, and you, Coleman, stand at either side of the door and make sure neither of them Throckmorton boys tries anything hasty. Mr. Cabot, I'll ask you to be ready to help as well, if you feel up to it.''

''I'm ready,'' I said, and the two crew members took up their positions. The captain took his pistol out of his coat pocket and stood to the side. ''Open the door, Tommy,'' he ordered, and I moved in to back up the boy. He slid the bolt aside and jumped out of the way as the heavy door swung wide.

The Throckmortons were sitting on the floor, and Alligator rose to his feet as the door opened. ''Easy there, boys,'' said Captain Fowler. ''Nobody here wants any more excitement today, and I hope you two are in the same mood.''

''What's going on?'' said Alligator Throckmorton, a puzzled expression on his face. ''We can't hardly be in Memphis yet. You goin' to let us go?''

''Afraid not,'' said the captain. ''Mr. Clemens here thinks you might be able to come up with some useful information. You fellows want to answer a few questions for him, and promise not to make any more trouble than you already have?''

''Will you let us go if we answer you?'' said Billy Throckmorton, standing up.

''I can't guarantee that,'' said Mr. Clemens. ''But you aren't much worse off in here than if we hadn't caught you, are you? If you weren't doing anything worse than catching a ride without a ticket, maybe we can persuade the captain to turn you loose when we get to Memphis. But you've got to give us straight answers.''

''We have nothing to hide from you, Mister Sam. Be a

lot easier to talk if we didn't have a gun pointed at us, though,'' said Alligator Throckmorton, glancing toward the captain. ''Something like that could make a man sort of nervous, make him forget things you asked him about 'cause he's worried 'bout getting shot.''

''Or maybe remember things that didn't happen,'' Mr. Clemens said. ''What do you say to this—I come inside with you, and they shut the door behind me, and we talk. No guns, no threats, just the three of us talking.''

''Hold your horses, Sam—I can't let you do that,'' said Captain Fowler. ''If anything happened to you, I'd never forgive myself—and neither would anybody else on the river. 'There goes the man that killed Sam Clemens,' they'd say, and they'd be right, and I'd know it. The only way I lock you in that cabin with them two is if I'm in there with the pistol, too.''

''Now, Mike, you know I've been in rough spots before. I can handle myself,'' said Mr. Clemens.

''That was when you was a lot younger, Sam. And you weren't no John L. Sullivan even then. I won't do it.''

''We ain't talking to nobody with a gun,'' said Alligator Throckmorton, seizing his advantage. ''You want us to talk straight, the gun stays outside.''

Mr. Clemens thought a moment, then looked at me. ''What about Cabot here? Assuming he's game, of course. That would mean I've got somebody with me to even the odds, but we can leave the gun outside. What about it, Mike?''

''I'm up to it,'' I said, not waiting for the captain's answer. Just let Billy Throckmorton try something again! I told myself.

The captain scowled, but after a pause he nodded. ''I guess I have to take the chance on it,'' he said. ''But I guarantee you, I'm going to have Tiny Williams out here guarding the door, and if he hears one yelp he doesn't like, he's going to tear that door down and beat the tar out of the first two Throckmortons he sees. And Sam, you better

make sure you don't fall down and scrape yourself anywhere, because I'm holding young Mr. Cabot personally
responsible for your safety. Does everybody understand
that?'' He glowered at me, at Mr. Clemens, and finally at
the Throckmorton brothers.

''I understand it perfectly,'' said Mr. Clemens. ''If we're
all agreed, then let's not waste any more time jabbering
about it.'' He strolled calmly into the little storeroom, with
me right behind him. The door closed, and I heard the bolt
being shoved home. For a moment I looked back longingly
at the thick wooden door, wondering what kind of trouble
I had gotten myself into. Then Mr. Clemens began talking,
quietly but forcefully, and I focused my attention on the
subjects of his questioning.

The Throckmorton brothers sat on the floor in a room
not much larger than five feet square. There was a lightbulb
on the ceiling, and a bank of shelves bolted to one wall
held paper and other supplies for the clerk's office. Al—
was that *really* short for Alligator, or did it stand for some
more civilized name such as Alan?—leaned forward, his
arms wrapped around his drawn-up knees. His expression
was unreadable, but his posture betrayed pent-up energy,
undoubtedly hostile.

His brother Billy, the larger and rougher-looking of the
two, lounged back in a deceptively peaceful pose; he
showed a few scrapes from this morning's fight, and one
of his shirtsleeves was nearly torn off. His eyes bored into
me as if he was remembering the two times he had bested
me and was thinking of doing it again. He would be the
greater danger, in these close quarters—not that I dis-
counted Al's ability to inflict damage if it came to fighting.
For Mr. Clemens's sake more than my own, I hoped that
neither of the prisoners was so inclined.

''Let's start from the beginning,'' said Mr. Clemens.
''You two have been following us downriver ever since St.
Paul. Nobody's laid eyes on you aboard the boat until this
morning, so I figure you've been riding the trains.'' Billy

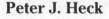
Throckmorton nodded, but said nothing. "So why, all of a sudden, did you get back on the boat? You must have known there'd be trouble if Charlie Snipes caught you."

Al Throckmorton cursed. "That backstabbin' snake," he said. "Snipes better hope me and Billy don't catch him on shore. If it hadn't been for him, we could have rid the boat the whole way, 'stead of sneaking on in Cairo."

"If it hadn't been for you two pushing my secretary into the river, you mean," said Mr. Clemens. "Maybe it's just a little rough fun to you fellows, but Charlie sees it as his bread and butter you're messing with, and you shouldn't be surprised if he takes it seriously. Besides, it may be a little less convenient to ride the trains than to be on board with McPhee, but you're ending up in the same places, after all. Why change the routine in Cairo? There are plenty of trains from Cairo to Memphis."

"Yeah, but they every one of 'em go through Kentucky," said Billy Throckmorton.

"Kentucky? I'd think so; it's more or less in the way." Mr. Clemens stopped and looked at the Throckmorton brothers. "I take it you boys have some reason to avoid Kentucky."

"You could put it that way," said Al Throckmorton. "A little mix-up a couple of years back. Ed was dealing monte on the Illinois Central, headed for New Orleans, and there was this conductor that took it all wrong."

"I see. By any chance did you try to change the conductor's mind?"

Billy Throckmorton grinned. "Ed tried. He always tries—I got to give him credit. But some folks just won't listen to sense, even when you want to give 'em good money for keeping their nose out of other folks' business. This fellow kept on making a stink until we pulled into Clinton, and me and Al decided to bushwhack him. He got off'n the train and went to the toilet, you know? So the two of us made sure he didn't get back on the train. Nothin' too rough, just putting him on ice for a while so's Ed could run his game without no interference. We didn't even steal nothing from him.''

His brother nodded. ''You'd a'thunk a mail train would have better things to do than wait around for some monkey in a blue suit, but they just set there and *set* there waiting for him, until somebody thought to go look in the toilet and find Mr. Conductor tied up with his own belt. So he sent out the hue and cry, and me and Billy and Ed had to skedaddle. We got out so fast I lost a carpetbag and a nearly full jug of good corn liquor.''

''I see,'' said Mr. Clemens. ''It must have been pretty serious to abandon good whisky.''

''Well, we hadn't done all that big a thing, but some folks just don't understand a fellow trying to make some room for himself to make a living,'' said Billy Throck-morton. ''That conductor didn't have no call to sic the yard bulls on us, let alone the deputy sheriff, all of 'em waving guns. But me and Al can take a hint. We jumped right off that train, and got out of town double fast, you better believe it. We've been sort of touchy about Kentucky ever since. That's how it goes—one little town doesn't treat you right, sometimes you just get a bad feeling about the whole state, you know?''

Mr. Clemens nodded gravely. ''I know just what you mean; I once ended up leaving Nevada in a hurry, on account of some shooting, and the law just didn't want to hear my side of it—but don't let me interrupt you, Billy.''

Billy Throckmorton gave Mr. Clemens a surprised look, then picked up his narrative with something like respect in his voice. ''Well, to make a long story short, last night we were in Cairo station with our tickets and everything, all ready to get on the train to Memphis, and damn if Al don't look down the track and see that same stiff-necked conductor standing there, twice as mean as ever. And he's looking straight at me and Al, or I'm a skinned muskrat.''

''So we naturally didn't wait around to see what he had on his mind,'' said Al, picking up the story. ''We'd have

been damn fools to try to get on that train with him right
there giving us the eye. We didn't have no choice, when
you get right down to it. So I says to Billy, 'Let's sneak
on the boat and just stay hid until we hit Memphis, and
nobody has to be the wiser,' and he says, 'That's just what
we'll do.' Lucky for us, I'd kept the key to the cabin we
were in before that no-good Charlie Snipes kicked us off,
and there still wasn't nobody in it. So we bought a jug and
a couple of sandwiches and waited for dark, and then we
come aboard while everybody was down at the lecture.''

"And you stayed in your cabin," said Mr. Clemens.
"You didn't see or hear anything unusual late last night,
did you? No kind of noise or commotion?''

Al managed to look thoughtful, but after a moment he
shrugged and shook his head. "Well, not really. We was
pretty tired by the time we snuck on board, and it was sort
of hot and close in the cabin, so we had a couple of drinks
and just lay down and dozed off early. There's always some
kind of noise on a boat, so we didn't pay it much mind.
What were we supposed to do—run out and tell folks to
be quiet?''

Mr. Clemens laughed and slapped his knee. "I reckon
not! So you didn't tell Ed McPhee you were on board,
then?''

"Hell, no! Ed would have walloped the two of us, after
he went and gave us money to ride the train. We figured
if he don't know about it, everybody's better off. You
won't tell him we was on board, will you?'' Billy Throckmorton's face took on a worried expression, and his brother
gave Mr. Clemens a nervous look.

"I'm afraid he knows already," said Mr. Clemens. "In
fact, the whole boat must have known about it by the time
the captain got you boys hidden away down here. If you'd
just taken your medicine quietly when they caught you, we
might have been able to keep it under wraps. After all, it
wasn't to anybody's advantage to let out that you two were
on board, was it now? But once some of the passengers

knew it, there wasn't much the captain could do to hide it.
There's nothing travels faster than a secret, once it's out of
the bag.''

''Guess you got that one right,'' said Al Throckmorton
with a resigned expression. ''Well, we'll just have to grin
and bear it once we get on shore. You don't think the captain's really going to give us to the sheriff, do you? It's
going to be bad enough having Ed mad at us. Besides, that
old cabin was going to be empty whether or not we slept
in it, no matter what Mr. Charlie Snipes thinks.''

''Well, it wasn't going to be empty while you boys slept
in it,'' said Mr. Clemens, grinning, and (to my surprise)
the Throckmorton brothers laughed. ''But if all you did was
take up a cabin nobody else was using and sleep the night
in it, and didn't break up any furniture, maybe Ed can
smooth things over with a couple of bucks in the right
place. There's not much the captain can hold against you.
I can't speak for my man Cabot here, though. He might not
take it so lightly, being knocked down and choked, and I
can't say I blame him.''

''I guess Billy's got to speak for himself about that,''
said Al Throckmorton, looking significantly at his brother.
''You can't rightly hold it against a man if he tries to defend himself when somebody runs him down, but maybe
he didn't have to push it quite so far. I suspect he's sorry
for it now, ain't you, Billy?''

To my astonishment, Billy Throckmorton stood up and
extended a hamlike paw in my direction. ''I guess maybe
I am sorry,'' he said. ''It weren't nothing personal, you
know. I heard that no-good clerk talk about jail, and hanging, and I just decided to skip out. If I'd kept my wits about
me, I'd have known it was nothing but wind he was
blowing. I'm not the man to hold a grudge, if you ain't.
No hard feelings?''

Sensing that I had gotten as much apology I was ever
going to get from the likes of Billy Throckmorton, I managed to take his hand and shake it; he tried a bone-crusher

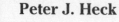 grip, but I was ready for it, and gave him back as good as he gave. After a moment, he grinned at me and disengaged his hand. I gave him a perfunctory smile in return, although I had the distinct feeling that the handshake was far from the end of things between us. Mr. Clemens watched the encounter closely, and when Billy and I had stepped back from one another, he nodded.

"Good, good," he said. "You've played square with me, and I'll tell Captain Mike just that. If there's anything else you think of about last night, tell Tommy outside to send for me, and I'll come down directly and listen to what you have to say. I'll put in the best word I can for you, don't worry."

"We sure appreciate it, Mister Sam," said Alligator Throckmorton.

"I appreciate your help, boys," said Mr. Clemens. "I won't forget it." He knocked on the door, and after a moment it opened; Tiny Williams glowered at the Throckmortons as Mr. Clemens and I walked out, and then the mate shot the bar home again. "Well, that's done with," said Mr. Clemens. "Thanks for keeping watch, Tiny—it was a relief to know you were just within earshot if anything had happened."

Williams looked relieved to see us safely out of the room. "They didn't try anything, did they?"

"No," I said. "I'm just as glad they didn't—that Billy is a rough customer, as I've found out already."

"Let me give you one piece of advice," said the mate. "You get in a fight with a fellow with a great big beer belly like that, don't never try to rassle him. He'll just fall down on top of you, and then it's his game and your pain. And don't go trying to punch him in the face, neither—you got to reach up to hit him, you don't get no force behind it, and he'll just grab you and laugh. But you hit him solid in the belly a few times, he'll get tired of it right fast." He gave me a light tap with his fist just above the navel, by way of illustration.

"I'll remember that," I promised, glad that he hadn't felt the need for more vigorous demonstration of what he meant. We shook hands, and this time he left me with a bit more feeling in my fingers than the last time we'd compared grips. For some reason, all these westerners seemed to consider handshaking a contest of strength.

"I'll hope he won't need that advice," said Mr. Clemens, shaking hands with the mate with no visible sign of discomfort. "But I suspect you know what you're talking about, Tiny, if anybody does. Now, Wentworth, we should go find the captain and tell him what we've learned." He turned and headed for the passageway to the upper decks, and I followed, trying to decide exactly what it was we'd learned from the Throckmortons.

22

Mr. Clemens and I came up the stairway to discover a small crowd of passengers milling about and talking excitedly; we stood for a moment trying to assess the situation, before they noticed our presence. "There's Mark Twain," said one man, pointing at my employer. "He'll tell us what's going on."

We were quickly surrounded, several of the crowd shouting out questions at once, so that it was impossible to understand them. "Wait a minute," said Mr. Clemens. "One at a time—I can't make heads or tails of what you're saying. Now, what's the matter here?"

One portly man with a top hat and full beard took it upon himself to speak for the group. He struck a belligerent pose, pointing a finger at Mr. Clemens's chest, and said, "We demand to know the truth about what happened last night. The captain flatly refuses to talk to us, and the crew is obviously under orders not to answer questions. I've paid good money for this vacation, and I won't be lied to. If my wife and I aren't safe aboard the ship, I will insist on a complete and total refund of my passage."

"Safe? Of course you're safe," said Mr. Clemens. "This boat is in perfect running order, and Elmer Parks is as good a pilot as you'll find on the river. Why would you think it's not safe?"

"That's not what I'm talking about, and you know it," the man bellowed. "I hear there were two men murdered in cold blood last night, and a knife fight on deck this morning—your secretary was cut nearly to pieces. Everybody saw it.''

''Why, here's my secretary right here. Step forward, Cabot, and let them see you.'' Mr. Clemens gestured to me, and I did as he said. ''Does this look like a man who's been cut to pieces in a knife fight?'' The crowd was quiet for a moment, then began a buzzing conversation as they took in my presence.

''Who saw this knife fight? Did you see it?'' said Mr. Clemens, staring at the bearded man. The fellow removed his hat and wiped his bald head with a large white handkerchief, looking around for someone to corroborate his statement. ''I thought as much,'' Mr. Clemens said, glaring at the crowd. A few voices murmured, but nobody spoke up. For a moment I thought the disturbance was over.

Then a little white-haired lady in a plain black dress and an old-fashioned bonnet stepped forward. ''I saw this young man last night,'' she said, and I recognized her as the woman from the cabin next to Berrigan's. She came up to me and looked in my face, then turned back to address the crowd.

''It was very late, and there was a loud argument in the cabin next to mine,'' she said. ''It woke me up, and I came out on deck to look for help. I was afraid someone was hurt. This young man knocked on the door, and when there was no answer, he went to find the captain. When the captain came, he told me to stay in my cabin. But I could hear them talking—the captain and some other men. There's something wrong, and I want to know the truth.'' She raised her chin and fixed her eye on me. ''You tell me the truth, young man. What really happened in that cabin?''

''I don't really know,'' I said, looking to Mr. Clemens for help.

''You *do* know,'' she said, shaking a finger at me. ''You know, too,'' she said, turning to Mr. Clemens. ''I heard your voice in there last night. I don't like being lied to. I expected better of you, Mr. Twain.'' The crowd rumbled in chorus, adding its assent to her indignation.

"Everything's under control,'' said Mr. Clemens, raising his hands to silence the crowd. "There was some trouble, but the men who caused it are safely locked up, and there's no reason to worry about them.''

"Are they the killers?'' said the bearded man, stepping forward again. "I don't want some sort of whitewash, Mr. Twain. You say there's no danger, but do you really know?''

"Yes, what do you really know?'' said a familiar voice. Andrew Dunbar, the New York reporter, stepped forward, his pencil and notebook poised. "Why are you and the captain covering up the murders? There were more than one, weren't there. And your man *was* in a fight this morning—I've spoken to witnesses.''

"Yes, there was a fight,'' said Mr. Clemens with the air of a man willing to tell the whole story. "Two stowaways got on board last night—a couple of rough customers. They'd had a few drinks, and they got into a fight with a passenger, and I'm afraid it turned ugly. Thanks to the lady in the next cabin, it was reported very quickly. Mr. Cabot happened to be on deck, and he informed the captain—but the disturbance was over by then. The crew searched the boat, and they found the stowaways first thing this morning; Mr. Cabot helped catch one of them who tried to escape. I tell you there's no further danger, and I know what I'm talking about.''

But Dunbar wasn't to be put off so easily. He swayed back and forth on his heels, and said, pointing to me, "If there's no danger, why are you traveling with a bodyguard? This fellow's obviously not any kind of secretary—I've talked to a few people, and I happen to know that he spent more time on the football field than in the classrooms at Yale.'' I bristled at the calumny on my education, and was about to respond, but Mr. Clemens laid a hand on my arm. The reporter continued his harangue.

"And where's good old Paul Berrigan this morning? The New York police wouldn't send a detective all the way out here unless there's something important at stake. Don't try to tell me he's here on vacation. Everybody on board has seen him skulking around, asking questions and taking notes. Will you confirm or deny that he's here to investigate a murder?"

"I'm not authorized to speak for the police. Why don't you ask Berrigan?" said Mr. Clemens.

"I think I'll do just that," said Dunbar. He scribbled a few lines in his notebook, flipped it closed, and put it in his pocket as he strode away.

With the reporter gone, Mr. Clemens turned back to the crowd. "Well, that's the whole story, folks," he said. "A brawl on board, started by a couple of drunken stowaways! We wouldn't have thought much of it in the old days— why, I remember trips when there were knife fights and gunfire just about every night, and nobody even bothered to turn around to watch a mere fistfight. It just goes to show you how the river has changed, and I guess it's for the better, even if it's not colorful enough for some folks. But the excitement's over. The captain and crew did their jobs, and the troublemakers are locked up where they can't bother anyone. We'll be turning them over to the police when we dock in Memphis, and then it'll be up to the law to decide what becomes of them.

"There's plenty to see today, if you'll settle for some diversion short of bloodshed. This is one of the most historic sections of the river. We'll be passing Chickasaw Bluff before long—some of you may remember that's the site of the terrible Fort Pillow massacre during the war. Off to the east is Reelfoot Lake, created eighty years ago, when the New Madrid earthquake made the river run backwards. Pull out your guidebooks and enjoy the scenery—it's a mighty fine day for it."

He stepped forward, and the crowd parted to let him through. With me close behind him, we made our way up

Peter J. Heck

the stairway to the next deck. The passengers murmured uneasily behind us; among them I made out Claude Dexter's voice lamenting that there *hadn't* been an authentic bowie knife fight on deck. But I sensed that while Mr. Clemens had allayed the crowd's fears for the moment, they weren't entirely satisfied. I felt especially bad about not having been honest with the woman who'd confronted me. Perhaps, with the Throckmortons in custody, the danger was now behind us. But somehow, I wasn't convinced of that.

We pushed through another small group of passengers outside Captain Fowler's cabin. They fell silent, looking expectantly at Mr. Clemens, but he simply smiled at them and knocked firmly at the door. The door opened to a narrow crack and the captain peered out; then, recognizing Mr. Clemens and me, he opened it wider to admit us. "Sam," he said as he closed the door behind us, an anxious expression on his face. "Somebody's gone and spilled the beans. The whole durn boat's talking about murder and I don't know what all."

"I know," said Mr. Clemens, plopping himself into a chair. "That damned reporter is wandering around asking questions, too. I've got him sidetracked for the moment, but I'm afraid he'll sniff out the truth soon enough. Now we'll have to come up with a new plan to keep the passengers from panicking. It'd be a calamity if we lost half the paying fares in Memphis, and it could easily come to that unless we show them that we've solved the problem."

"But how do we do that, Sam? We've got a dead body down in the meat locker. It's just a matter of time before one of the crew shoots off their mouth, and then the passengers will be after us like a swarm of hornets."

"I'm afraid you're right," said Mr. Clemens. "For the time being, we can stall the passengers with the story that we've got the guilty parties in irons; enough people saw Wentworth tackle Billy Throckmorton that they'll believe that those two roughnecks are the killers. I'm not at all sure of that, myself. Still, we could march them off the boat for everybody to see when we get to Memphis, and quiet down the passengers. But that would only solve half the problem.''

"What's the other half?'' Puzzlement replaced despondence on the captain's expressive face.

Mr. Clemens leaned forward. "Finding the real murderer—and finding him before he does something else. At this point, I have to believe that he's following *me*.''

"You! What the devil for?'' exclaimed the captain.

"It's a long story, Mike, but I guess you need to know it,'' said Mr. Clemens. "Reach me that whisky bottle and a clean glass and I'll give you the particulars.''

For the next half hour, my employer repeated the story of the dying German man, the renegade soldiers, the bloody thumbprint, and the hidden ten thousand dollars in gold. The captain interrupted him with the occasional question, but for the most part, he listened attentively.

Mr. Clemens paced the small cabin as he spoke, stopping every now and then to take a sip of whisky or to light his pipe. "On my last trip downriver, back in '82,'' he said at last, "I had plans to recover the gold, but George Devol was on board the boat with some of his cronies, and I was afraid they were going to rob me of the money when I retrieved it. So I concocted a story that the treasure was hidden in Napoleon, Arkansas, and that it washed away in the floods that year. I hoped everybody would decide that the whole story was a hoax, and I thought it had worked. But I think somebody's decided the original story was gospel truth—at least two people on board have mentioned it in one form or another. And there are two men dead because of it.''

"Ten thousand is a good piece of money,'' said the captain. "It might tempt a lot of people. But who do you think the killer is? Ed McPhee was one of Devol's cronies, so he could have heard the story from him. But do you think he

226 has the stomach for knifing a man? Or did he put the Throckmortons up to it?''

Mr. Clemens shook his head. ''I can't see Slippery Ed getting close enough to a younger and stronger man for knife work—not as long as he could order somebody else to do it. Alligator Throckmorton could be that somebody else—especially since he and his brother were on board last night, and he did have a knife. If we don't come up with any better explanation, the Memphis police ought to believe that one. But I'm not comfortable with it. For one thing, Berrigan found a witness who saw the Throckmorton brothers in Chicago within twenty-four hours of the New York murder. That doesn't calculate—unless you think the New York murder and the one last night are completely unconnected.''

''Do they have to be connected?'' I asked. ''After all, there's no proof that the New York murder was inspired by the treasure. The story of the stolen gold is, as you say, in a book that anybody could buy, or take out of the library—half the passengers on the boat seem to be reading it. Even Berrigan read it.''

''Yes, that's right,'' said Mr. Clemens. He paused for a moment, a surprised look on his face, then said, ''Of course—it makes perfect sense, now that you mention it. Berrigan must have made the connection between the murder and that old story about the gold. Why else would he have been talking to the murderer, instead of just arresting him without warning?''

''I don't follow you,'' I said. ''Why does Berrigan's guessing the truth about the gold have anything to do with his questioning the suspect before arresting him?''

''At midnight, the two of them alone in his cabin, and without his gun at hand? I can allow a certain amount of slack for Berrigan's being drunk, but he didn't strike me as a man intent on suicide. He must have had some reason to believe he was safe from the fellow—even though he knew he was dealing with a murderer.''

"Maybe there was a third party there, somebody he trusted," suggested Captain Fowler.

"That's possible," said Mr. Clemens. "But if so, it must have been somebody both of them trusted; why else would the killer have been willing to talk in front of him? And why didn't this third party try to stop the murder—or come forward as a witness, afterwards? That theory poses more questions than it answers, Mike. I'd rather start off with a simple theory, and not add complications unless they're the only way to explain the facts we already know."

Captain Fowler frowned. "And what's your simple theory, Sam? You say it ain't the Throckmorton boys, and that's about as simple a theory as I've got handy."

"I think the ten thousand dollars turned our policeman's head," said Mr. Clemens. "He wouldn't be the first cop to offer a suspect a deal—a chance to escape in return for a share of the money. But something went wrong—either Berrigan wanted it all, or the killer didn't want to go shares. Or maybe Berrigan wanted money right now, and the killer couldn't come up with it. And so the killer let his knife do the talking, and Berrigan wasn't ready for it."

"Who was the killer, then?" demanded the captain.

"That's the one part I don't know," admitted Mr. Clemens.

"That's what I was afraid of," said Captain Fowler, shaking his head. "Unless we solve this murder before we dock in Memphis, it'll be the devil to pay, with police all over the boat and half the passengers screaming for refunds. There's a pack of people waiting outside for me to tell 'em there's no danger to anybody, and I doubt I can do it with a straight face. Then again, who's to stop the killer from just stepping overboard and swimming to safety before we even dock?"

"Well, I can manage the public relations part for you," said Mr. Clemens. "Lying to crowds and making them like it has been my business for nigh on thirty years. I'll go on out and talk to them—I ought to be able to figure out something to keep their attention. When I've got them distracted, Wentworth will give you the word that all's clear, and you can sneak up to the pilothouse, or anywhere else you think you can get your work done without interruption.''

"That's all well and good, Sam, but it's *my* business to see to the welfare of my passengers, and I can't rest easy knowing there's a killer loose on my boat. I've got to make it my first job to find whoever killed Mr. Berrigan before we reach Memphis, and if I can't, the *Horace Greeley* ain't going another mile downriver until the Memphis police have put somebody in jail. And I don't see how hiding out in the pilothouse is going to make that any easier.''

"I should have known you'd see it that way, Mike," said Mr. Clemens. He stood up and shook the captain's hand. "That leaves us just one choice: we're going to find the killer, and make sure everybody on board knows we've found him. That way, I can go get that treasure without having to worry who's behind my back every step of the way, and you can take the boat downriver knowing your passengers are safe.''

"You've got yourself a deal, Sam. But how the dickens are we going to do all that? We can't be more than fifty miles out of Memphis, and we don't even have a start on finding our killer, unless it's the Throckmortons and Slippery Ed that done it, but you think it ain't. I know you're a mighty smart man, but I'm afraid we're going to need a miracle worker for this one.''

Mr. Clemens put his hands on the captain's shoulders and looked him in the eye. "For now, the main thing is to keep the passengers from panicking. We've got to act as if we have everything under control, as if it's all over and solved. We can admit that Berrigan's dead, but at the same time spread the word that we've got the Throckmortons locked up, and that we'll turn them over to the Memphis police. People will talk, but they'd do that no matter what we told them. The important thing is that they won't worry—and that neither will the real murderer.''

"I get it," said the captain. "We use those two wildcats as a blind, and the man we're after thinks he's home free."

"And while the killer's off his guard, we have time to contrive a way to smoke him out before we reach Memphis. But promise me you'll keep everything under your hat until I give the word. I don't want anybody except the three of us to know that the Throckmortons aren't our main suspects—not even your own officers. Agreed?"

The captain seemed puzzled by the request, but after a moment's consideration, he acquiesced. "Good," said Mr. Clemens. "Now, why don't we go talk to the passengers. I'll let you give them the basic story first, and then I'll take over. Here's how we'll play it. . . ."

23

Directly outside the captain's cabin, we encountered Mr. Snipes and a small group of agitated passengers surrounding him. Almost immediately, one of them spotted the captain, and before we could move the group was around us, jabbering questions faster than I could understand them. "Wait a minute! Slow down!" shouted the captain. "We'll answer your questions, but we have to be able to hear them. One at a time, now—what's the problem?"

Snipes answered for them. "I'm mighty glad to see you, Cap'n. The passengers have been hearing rumors of a murder on board, and they're worried there's a killer loose. Now, I've told 'em not to believe every story they hear, but they won't listen to me. They want to hear it from you."

Captain Fowler nodded slowly, a serious expression on his face. "Folks, I can tell you there's nothing to worry about. It's true we had a little bit of an occurrence last night, but it's all over and done with. There's two fellows already locked up—a couple of good-for-nothing stowaways. And we'll be giving them over to the police soon as we dock in Memphis. So you all can rest easy and enjoy the trip now."

"Sir, we'll not be put off so easily," shouted one of the passengers. It was Mr. Dutton, the minister from Boston. He stepped forward. "I want to know, was there a murder last night or not? I insist on the whole truth!'' The crowd muttered in agreement.

''You're not in any danger, and that's all you need to know,'' said Snipes angrily. ''Show some respect—''

''That's all right, Charlie,'' said the captain. ''I don't reckon it makes much difference whether the reverend knows or not, so I don't mind telling him and these other folks. Yes, there was someone killed last night.''

''I knew it!'' said Mr. Dutton. ''What with strong drink and gambling, and swearing, too, something like this was bound to happen. I brought my wife and two young daughters with me, and I'm ashamed of what they've had to see and hear on this boat.''

''Yes, it's scandalous,'' said another familiar voice; I looked to the back of the group and recognized a stern-faced Miss Cunningham. The other passengers began talking excitedly, all together.

''Do you want to know the whole truth, or just enough of it to flavor your sermons and gossip?'' said Mr. Clemens vehemently. The crowd fell quiet again; a few of the passengers had guilty expressions. ''Captain Fowler is bending over backwards to let you know what's happened. I've known captains who would tell you to go to blazes if you questioned how they ran their boats. But I think I know a way to settle this. Captain, may I suggest something?''

Captain Fowler looked puzzled at Mr. Clemens's outburst, but he nodded and said, ''Sure, Sam. I'll consider anything.''

''Thank you, Captain Fowler,'' said Mr. Clemens. ''Now, as the captain said, there has been a killing on board, and we have two men in custody. We've questioned the suspects, and we're pretty sure we know the whole truth of it. But rather than tell you all a few at a time, and repeat the story until we're blue in the face, I'm going to ask the captain to call a meeting of everyone aboard at three o'clock this afternoon, in the lecture hall.''

The captain nodded. ''I think we can do that,'' he said.

"Good!" Mr. Clemens said, then turned back to the crowd. "I want everybody on the boat to be there—no exceptions! I promise you you'll hear the whole story then—but not one more syllable of it before then! Now, get along and tell everybody to be there. Three o'clock sharp!"

The passengers dispersed, still muttering, leaving just the captain, Mr. Clemens, Chief Clerk Snipes, and me. "Well, Sam, I guess that'll start the tongues a-wagging," said the captain. "Are you sure you want to face the lot of them all in a gang?"

"We'd be facing them in gangs of three or four for the rest of the trip if we didn't promise to face them all at once," said Mr. Clemens. "A crowd of a couple hundred's no harder to handle than one of ten or twelve, if you're used to doing it—and I am. We've got to prove to them we have things under control, and the easiest way is to let them all see it together. Better to give them something solid to speculate on than a mess of hearsay to badger us about all the way to the end of the river."

"That's all well and good, Sam, but what if this meeting gets out of hand?"

"I'll take responsibility for that, Mike. You can help me by making sure we've got enough of the crew present to keep order—of course, you'll need the pilot, and a few men to stoke the boilers and keep watch, but I'd like everybody else to be there."

"Easy enough, Sam," said the captain. "Mr. Snipes, will you pass word to the crew? Let Elmer Parks handle the wheel, and Tiny and Frenchy can assign their men as they see fit. But make sure everybody knows about the meeting. I don't want anybody to miss it who isn't working."

"I doubt that'll be a problem, Mike," said Mr. Clemens, grinning, as the clerk went to convey the captain's orders to the crew. "You may have trouble finding people willing to work, if it means missing this meeting."

"I don't know, Sam," said the captain. "I'm not looking forward to it one bit."

"Now, don't worry, Mike. Just stay with me and follow my lead. I'll make a showman of you in no time." Mr. Clemens threw his arm around the captain's shoulder, but the captain still looked worried. I myself was not entirely sure what Mr. Clemens meant to do—let alone whether he would be able to do it as easily as he seemed to think.

Mr. Clemens and I followed Snipes down to the main deck, since my employer wanted to ask a few questions of the apprentice clerk, Tommy Hazelwood. The boy was back in his chair outside the storeroom where the Throckmortons were being kept. He looked up eagerly as we came in; I had noticed him as a frequent and enthusiastic hanger-on in the crowd when Mr. Clemens started "spinning yarns" for the passengers, and he was perhaps the most faithful of all the crew in attending Mr. Clemens's lectures. At the news that my employer wanted to interview him, Tommy's eyes lit up. "Sure," he said. Then, he asked Mr. Snipes hesitantly, "Is it okay?"

"I don't see why not, as long as you come straight back to work afterwards," said the chief clerk. "You lollygag around, though, and you'll get a piece of my mind. Go ahead now!"

"Yes, *sir!*" said Tommy, and he followed us out to the open deck. Mr. Clemens leaned back against the rail and looked out at the river for a moment. "We're coming up on Centennial Island," he said. "What's that make it, about three hours to Memphis?"

"A little bit less, sir," said Tommy. "We should be there by mid-afternoon, if there's no problems."

"Oh, there are problems all right," said Mr. Clemens. "Just not the kind to slow down the boat. If anything, I'm worried about the boat getting there too soon."

"What do you mean, Mr. Twain?" The young boy

234 leaned forward; he looked worried, and at the same time
eager to help.

"I guess Mr. Snipes hasn't told you the whole story yet.
There's been a murder on board."

"Je—jeepers! Is that right? Is that why those men are
locked up? Did they do it? Will they hang them?"

"One question at a time will get you better answers,
Tommy," said Mr. Clemens, chuckling. "I'm not sure
those two men did it, and I'll tell you why. But you have
to promise not to tell anyone. The passengers and crew
must think that we've got the killers safely locked up. Can
you keep this a secret between us?"

The boy straightened up, and a proud look came over
his face. "Yes, sir, Mr. Twain!" he said. "You can count
on me."

"Good," said Mr. Clemens. "Now, I think this murder
is connected to another one in New York City, almost a
month ago. Mr. Berrigan, the detective, was investigating
that case, and he told Mr. Cabot that he'd solved it. He said
the answer was on the passenger list Mr. Snipes gave him,
and those two men are stowaways—they weren't on the
list."

"Oh, but they were," said Tommy. "They were crossed
off in St. Paul, after Mr. Snipes threw them off the boat."

"That's right," I said. "Their names were on the original list, then crossed off."

"Hmm—I'd better take a closer look at that list, then,"
said Mr. Clemens. "Berrigan did say that his clue came
from the passenger list, didn't he?"

"Yes," I said. "Although he phrased it oddly—*Something on the passenger list tipped me off* was how he put
it. But it was just a list of names and addresses. What could
he have meant, I wonder."

"I don't know. It may not be important. Right now, I'm
interested in a couple of things that may be easier to figure
out, especially with Tommy's help." Mr. Clemens stared
out at the riverbank again, then down at Tommy Hazel-

wood. "The murder last night was on the hurricane deck. The cabin door was locked when we got there, and at first we just assumed it was locked from the inside. But after thinking about it, I'm pretty sure the dead man didn't get up and lock the door after the killer left. Do you have any idea how the killer might have gotten a key to that cabin?"

Tommy's face was a study in concentration. Finally he said, "No, sir. Mr. Snipes is mighty partic'lar about the keys—when he gives one out for some reason, he wants it right back in his hand, as soon as you're done with it, and if you don't bring it back fast enough, he'll chase you down, and give you the dickens too."

"Could somebody have 'borrowed' a key out of the office while nobody was looking? Is the office ever left open or unguarded late at night?"

Tommy shook his head. "You don't know Mr. Snipes. He locks the door behind him every time he leaves the office empty, and I do the same if I'm working there alone. That's his first rule—*always lock up behind you*. The only way anybody could get in to steal a key is if they already had one. And then they wouldn't need one, if you see what I mean."

I had a sudden inspiration. "I wonder . . . if one of the cleaning crew lost a key, or had it stolen, would they be afraid to report it to Mr. Snipes?"

"Sure, but he'd find out in the end. They'd need the key to clean the rooms, and if the rooms weren't clean, they'd get in trouble. The passengers would gripe when their beds weren't made, and Mr. Snipes wouldn't let that slide."

"There's something we ought to look into," I said. "If any of the other passengers on Berrigan's level complained about their cabins not being cleaned, that would tell us right away if there's a stolen key."

"Good point, Wentworth," said Mr. Clemens. "Why don't you look around that deck and ask the passengers, and let me know before the meeting. Meanwhile, I want to grab an hour or so to look over that passenger list, and maybe find the time to talk with Major Demayne about his poetry, too. Maybe he has some of the answers I need.'' He looked down at the apprentice clerk and smiled. ''Thanks for talking to us, Tommy—you've been a big help. We'll see you this afternoon; the captain's called a meeting for three o'clock, and I want you to be there. I think we can catch the murderer before we dock in Memphis. Don't be surprised if I ask you to come on stage and answer a few questions for the people.''

''Me? A witness in a murder case?'' The boy was obviously thrilled. ''Why, I wouldn't miss it for anything!'' He skipped off in the direction of the clerk's office, excited as only a young boy can be. Mr. Clemens watched him with a wistful expression.

''I wish I was still that young and full of fire,'' he said when the boy was gone. ''It's a shame how soon we lose our enthusiasm for the world. Why, even old sourpuss Charlie Snipes used to be like that, back when he was mud clerk on the *Gold Dust*. I remember how he used to follow me, listening to me tell stories, same as Tommy here, and like to got himself fired. I wonder if he ever looks at Tommy and remembers how he used to be.''

I spent nearly an hour on the hurricane deck asking passengers if their beds had been made, but came up empty; in fact, the cleaning crew was going about its business even as I asked, as if to quiet my speculation by its very presence. Unfortunately, my attempts to get the maids to talk about missing keys were even less fruitful—too many people knew about the trouble with the stowaways, and the maids unanimously refused to talk about anything that might connect them to the incident. At length, I gave up and wandered down to the main deck for a bite of luncheon before the meeting.

I had just finished eating when Martha Patterson came through the doors, wearing the pink dress I had seen her in when first we met. She looked around, and her face broke into a smile as her eyes lit on me. Tired as I was, it gave me a welcome lift to see her stride purposefully over to my table. "May I join you?" she asked. I returned her smile and waved her to the chair opposite me.

"Make yourself at home," I told her. "I was up till past midnight searching a dead man's belongings, and spent the first part of the day wrestling a man who tried to strangle me. After that, it's good to see a friendly face."

Her mouth fell open in surprise. "My goodness! What on earth have you been doing?"

I gave her an account of all that had happened since we had last spoken, omitting only the more grisly details of the murder. "But we'll soon know all the answers. Mr. Clemens asked the captain to call a special meeting at three o'clock today, at which he'll unmask the killer," I said in conclusion.

"I heard about the meeting, but not the reason for its being called. Isn't it exciting? Has Mr. Clemens told you who the culprit is?"

"No, but the prime suspect has to be McPhee. When we woke him up this morning for questioning, he claimed he'd been at the card table all night. But I don't trust the scoundrel one bit—his alibi looks good for now, but while he sat there cheating the other players, the Throckmortons could have been doing the dirty business under his orders. What else were those two doing on board?"

She looked puzzled. "But what motive would he have? Mr. McPhee is a gambler, not a criminal—he'd have no reason to kill anyone."

"I don't know; isn't it enough that he's of poor character?" I tried to think of some reason for McPhee to kill Berrigan; his general iniquity was so obvious that it annoyed me to have to deal with a distraction like motive.

"That may be, and yet it's no reason to convict him of murder," said Miss Patterson. "Surely if Mr. Clemens means to accuse him, he has some better explanation than poor character."

"I suppose he does," I admitted. "The fellow is a gambler, with no real occupation; perhaps there's money involved."

"What about the other players—he doesn't play alone, you know. Why isn't everyone who gambles a suspect, as well as Mr. McPhee? Or is it merely the lack of conventional employment that makes him suspect?" Her eyes flashed, and I felt ashamed of my shoddy logic.

"Mr. Clemens hasn't told me his conclusions, but I'm confident he'll tell us everything at the meeting," I said.

"I certainly hope so," said Miss Patterson. "I'll be very curious to learn what has happened. And until then, I shall look at every passenger and wonder if perhaps I'm seeing a murderer!"

"We'll know soon enough," I agreed. "Perhaps we can get together afterwards and compare notes."

"We'll see," she said, smiling. "Who knows—Mr. Clemens may identify you or me as the murderer."

"I am quite confident that you are no murderer," I told her, returning her smile.

"Why, Mr. Cabot," she said, with a pretty little laugh and a toss of her head. "I do appreciate your confidence— after all, we hardly know each other. I could be almost anything—and so could you!"

"Well, we'll find out at three o'clock, won't we." I was pleased that her annoyance at my accusing McPhee had passed so easily.

"Indeed we shall," she agreed. "I think there'll be quite a few surprises in store for us."

24

The *Horace Greeley*'s auditorium was full, almost as if for one of Mr. Clemens's lectures. But this audience was made up entirely of the passengers and crew, with no townspeople in their Sunday best crowding aboard, and the atmosphere was a good bit more somber. There was nonetheless an air of expectation, thanks to the stories that had circulated among the passengers all day. Likewise, everyone's interest was piqued by the unusual convocation, which Captain Fowler had made it clear was mandatory—although Elmer Parks was conspicuously absent, presumably up in the pilothouse, tending his wheel; and I supposed that Frenchy Devereaux and his stokers were down below feeding the boilers.

Mr. Clemens and Captain Fowler stood quietly together on the stage while the passengers took their seats. Mr. Clemens was puffing on one of his corncob pipes, the first time I had seen him smoke on stage. And he had on his white summer suit instead of the formal evening dress he wore for lectures. But, as he told me before we let the audience in, this was no routine performance. ''Anything can happen here, Wentworth—there's no predicting how our man will react when I name him as the killer. Let's hope he doesn't do anything too foolish.''

Mr. Clemens had stationed me at the right front corner of the stage and Tiny Williams at the other corner, where we each had a good view of the crowd. Several of Mr.

Williams's roustabouts were unostentatiously placed around the audience, in seats near the exits. The captain had made it clear to us that our primary duty was to protect the passengers; the person whom we hoped to unmask had already murdered Berrigan, and might not hesitate to use his knife again if cornered. I hoped the captain was wrong about that, but held myself ready to do whatever might be necessary.

When everyone was seated, the captain stepped to the front of the stage. "Ladies and gentlemen, Mark Twain has asked me to call you here for some important business, and I hope we can get it done without much trouble. Some of you saw the little skirmish on deck this morning, and I guess you've heard a bunch of rumors since then. Well, I've brought you all here to get to the bottom of things, not to gloss anything over. The long and short of it, I'm sorry to say, is there's been a murder on board. . . ."

For the first time in my life, I understood the meaning of the word "pandemonium." Half the crowd began talking and gesturing wildly, and many of them rose to their feet and tried to call out questions to the stage; the reporter, Andrew Dunbar, pulled out his notebook and began shuffling toward the front of the room, scribbling wildly. The rest of the audience, passengers and crew alike, seemed stunned. The captain let the hubbub go on for a few moments, then raised his hands to quiet it. "We'll answer all your questions soon enough, I hope—but let us do it in the right order and it'll all go smoother."

"Is it true there were two murders?" shouted Dunbar.

"Yes, and the two were connected," said Mr. Clemens, somewhat to my surprise; I myself had abandoned that line of speculation. The noise began to build again, but Mr. Clemens cut it off. "You won't learn anything from your neighbors, and you'll be more comfortable if you all sit down," he said, raising his voice slightly. "Let the captain finish what he has to say, and you'll learn the truth that much sooner," he said. The crowd fell quiet.

Captain Fowler looked at the audience, then back at Mr. Clemens. "Why don't you just go ahead and tell 'em, Sam? I was never much of a speechifier, anyways."

"Thank you, Mike," said Mr. Clemens, tamping out his pipe and moving to the front of the stage. "If you'll indulge me, I'll begin a few weeks ago, in New York City, although the story's roots go deeper than that. I was making final arrangements for this trip when a New York police detective, Paul Berrigan, came to my hotel. There'd been a murder nearby, and the victim had my name and address in his pocket. Naturally, the police suspected some connection. So did the people who are financing this lecture tour. They had Berrigan detailed to come on this cruise, to act as a guard for me as well as to sniff around for clues to the murder.

"Berrigan had the theory that the murderer might be following me, not just because of the note, but because at first we thought the victim was a gambler named Farmer Jack Hubbard, whom I'd met thirty years ago—although later we learned it was a different man entirely, another gambler named Lee Russell. But as it happened, Hubbard had sent me a note that same day, trying to arrange a meeting. So there was a speck of logic in the idea that something in my past might be the key to the New York murder case. That got me to thinking about what the connection might be, and it took me back to the last time I'd taken a steamboat trip down the Mississippi."

Mr. Clemens shook his head. "That was a dozen years ago," he said. "I could spin the yarn out right through suppertime, but I've told it once already today, and don't feel like going over it all again. Those of you who have copies of my book *Life on the Mississippi* can read the story there, in chapter thirty-one. It's a story of murder, hidden treasure, and revenge, ending when the treasure is washed away in a flood. Most people assume that the story is pure fiction, with a long buildup to a deliberate anticlimax, and that's the way I wanted people to read it. But I'll tell you

now—it really happened, just the way I tell it in the book!''

There was a stir in the audience, presumably among those who had read the story. From my vantage point to the right of the stage, I saw Slippery Ed McPhee sit up straight in his seat, a look of wonder on his face. ''Sam, you old fox!'' he said, shaking his head.

Mr Clemens continued. ''My trip down the river, back in '82, was partly for research on *Life on the Mississippi*, but I also meant to recover the hidden gold and forward it to its rightful owner. I made the mistake of talking about my errand, and the wrong people overheard me. Someone on board that boat made plans to follow me to the treasure, and steal it. When I learned of this, I changed my story, claimed the treasure had been washed away, and told it in such a way that most people would take it as a fabrication. The ruse seemed to work, but I had to put off recovering the gold. I meant to return and do it, but time got away from me—as it has a habit of doing.'' There was muted laughter from the audience at this. ''Finally, when I set up this cruise, I thought I could return and complete my long-postponed mission.

''But the New York murder threw me off stride, although for a while I wasn't sure whether it had anything to do with my treasure hunt. In one sense I was annoyed that the New York detective was snooping around, and in another I was glad that he was here. He was following his clues, trying to put two and two together, and mostly staying out of my way, although he had a run-in or two with Cabot, my secretary. Finally, just yesterday, Berrigan told Cabot he'd identified the murderer, although he didn't say who it was. And then—well, why don't we ask Mr. Cabot to tell you what happened next.''

I was not at all prepared to talk, but somehow I found my way to center stage. There, with a little gentle coaching from Mr. Clemens, I recounted my late-night walk on deck and my meeting the lady who complained of a disturbance in the cabin next to hers. I had just gotten to the point of knocking on the cabin door when a white-haired woman stood up in the audience; I recognized her as the very one who'd accosted me on deck the night before.

"I knew there was something wrong!" she said, shaking her finger at me with an air of accusation. "You tried to put me off, and told me to stay in my cabin, but I knew there was something fishy going on! That man was dead, wasn't he."

"Yes, he was, ma'am," said Mr. Clemens. "Would you like to come up front and tell everybody what you heard? It could help us get to the bottom of these terrible murders. You're the closest we have to an eyewitness—or an ear-witness, to be precise."

The woman walked briskly to the stage, with an assurance that reminded me of my mother's Sunday morning progress down the aisle of our church toward her seat in the family pew. Mr. Clemens, on his most courtly behavior, gave her a hand up the stairs, then asked, "Now, if you'd be so kind as to tell everyone what you heard last night—and perhaps it would help if we knew your name, Miss . . . ?"

"I am Caroline Fairbanks, of Albany, New York, traveling in cabin thirty-nine on the third deck. Last night, after midnight, I woke up to hear two men arguing in the cabin next door."

"Number forty-one, that would be?" Mr. Clemens prompted.

"Yes. The argument was loud enough to keep me from getting back to sleep. I tapped on the wall to let them know they were disturbing me, but they must not have heard. They were shouting at one another, and they sounded very angry."

"Do you remember what they were arguing about?"

"I didn't hear enough to make it out. One of them did say something about gold, and the other said it was too much, and I'm afraid there was a lot of bad language used between them."

"German, no doubt," said Mr. Clemens, surprisingly calm despite the mention of gold.

"Excuse me?" said Miss Fairbanks, giving him a puzzled look, but he merely gestured for her to go on, and she continued. "There was a sound as of a struggle, very loud, as if someone had crashed into the wall, and then someone cried out. That was when I decided to get help. I got out of bed, threw on my robe, and went out on deck, where I found that young man and asked him to help me."

"This is very important now. Did you recognize either of the voices? Could you identify either of the men who were in that cabin?"

"No, I'm afraid not. My hearing isn't what it used to be, and there was a wall between us, after all. Putting two and two together, I assume one of them must have been that poor Mr. Berrigan. But I have no idea who the other person was."

"A shame," said Mr. Clemens. "It would have made things so much easier." He paused briefly, as if thinking about what the woman had said. "But that's not going to stop me. Before this meeting's over, I intend to be able to tell you all just who the killer is."

25

Once again, the crowd noise rose to a hubbub of excited speculation, and Captain Fowler had to call for quiet. Andrew Dunbar was on his feet again, trying to call out a question over the noise, but Mr. Clemens waved him off. "There'll be time enough for questions later. First let's establish the facts; then you can all misinterpret them however you please." The reporter turned red and sat back down. Mr. Clemens looked out at the audience again, and said, "While we're calling up possible witnesses, would the passenger who was in cabin number forty-three last night please come up front?"

There was a stir in the back of the auditorium, and the same stout man who'd complained of the noise the night before waddled up to the stage, a smug expression on his face. "Well, it's about time," he said, climbing up to the stage. He gave a little bow. "Augustus Knepper, of St. Paul, Minnesota, at your service, sir. You could have solved this whole thing in an instant if you'd just asked me earlier."

"Why, this is splendid," said Mr. Clemens. "I'm sorry I didn't think of calling you before, Mr. Knepper. By all means, tell us what you know."

Knepper looked out at the audience, squinting into the lights. "Well, I heard the argument, just the same as the lady did, but maybe my ears are a little sharper. Those two fellows were shouting and wrestling around, and I knew

246 there was dirty business of some sort even before your Mr.
Cabot came knocking on the door. I came to the door and
gave him a piece of my mind, and it seemed to me he went
away right quick. And that got me to thinking—wouldn't
an honest man have stood his ground? And just what was
he doing out on deck at exactly the same time as this murder took place, at an hour when decent folks are in their
beds asleep, or trying to sleep?''

"Sir, I resent your implication!'' I said, somewhat angrily, but Mr. Clemens gave me a little smile and lifted his
hand. "Let the gentleman have his say, Cabot. I'll make
sure you have a fair chance to defend yourself, if it seems
necessary. Please go on, Mr. Knepper.''

"Well, that got me thinking about something I'd seen
just that afternoon. I was out on deck, enjoying the scenery
and the breeze, and I overheard two people arguing on the
rear deck. I peeked around the corner, and saw it was Mr.
Berrigan and that fellow there, Mr. Cabot. My ears perked
up a little bit, because I had heard that Berrigan was a
detective and that he was on the trail of a dangerous criminal from back east. And that Mr. Berrigan as good as said
that Mr. Cabot was his suspect: *You're on my little list,* he
said, and Mr. Cabot cursed him. I didn't hear everything,
because I was afraid to show myself. The detective was
playing it very cagey, but I could see he was telling Cabot
that he was onto him.

"Well, it wasn't until this morning that I started to wonder why a detective would warn a criminal that he had the
goods on him. But when I remembered that those two men
next door had been arguing about money, things fell into
place. That detective was looking for a bribe to let his man
go, and Cabot must have balked at the price. When the
Irishman wouldn't back down, Cabot went for his knife,
and that was the end of it for Berrigan. When the lady came
and found him on deck, he had to play along, of course,
and pretend he'd come out for some air. But it's plain as
the nose on your face—there's your murderer right there!''

And he pointed straight at me.

There was a stunned silence from the audience, then several audible gasps. I saw Miss Cunningham, toward the front of the audience, looking at me with a shocked expression on her face; then she saw me looking back at her, and quickly turned her face away. I could see heads turning toward one another as people began to pass comments on my presumed guilt back and forth.

"This is sheer fabrication!" I said indignantly. "I never killed anyone! I admit that I argued with Berrigan yesterday, but it's absurd to think I could have killed him."

"Let the gentleman have a little more rope, Cabot," said Mr. Clemens. "Mr. Knepper, are you quite certain it was Mr. Cabot's voice you heard last night in Berrigan's cabin?"

"Absolutely," said Knepper, thrusting his chin forward and narrowing his eyes. "One more thing. After the ruckus died down, everything was quiet, and then I heard him walk to the cabin door and shut it. After a few moments, he walked past my cabin. I went to the door and peeked out, but he was already gone."

"Interesting," said Mr. Clemens. "Your cabin door can't be more than a few feet from the one next door. Why would he delay before coming past?"

"At the time, I didn't think much of it. I suppose he was locking the door behind him," said Knepper, thrusting his thumbs through his suspenders.

Mr. Clemens rubbed his chin. "There's an odd detail. Locking the door behind him? What kind of person stabs a man to death, then takes the time to lock the door behind him?"

"I couldn't say—a depraved criminal, for certain. I have no desire to know him any better."

"Nor do I," said Mr. Clemens. "Let me go back to something. When you saw my secretary at the door, did he show any signs of having been in a struggle—disarranged clothing, bloodstains, or anything of the like?"

"No, but by then he'd had enough time to go to his room and repair his clothing. It must have been twenty minutes or more between when he left and when he came back knocking."

"But if he'd gone back to his cabin, why do you think he would come back out on deck again? Wouldn't that attract attention when he least wanted it?"

"The criminal always returns to the scene of his crime," said Knepper, stubbornly. "Besides, what should I know of how a criminal's mind works? Perhaps he came back to gloat, like a ghoul, over his victim's lifeless corpse." He crossed his arms on his chest.

"That's about as likely as a boar hog sprouting wings," said a voice from the audience. It was Dr. Savin, who'd stood up next to the side aisle. "That boy fainted dead away at the sight of the victim."

"He must have been shamming," said Knepper, scowling. "What better way to deflect suspicion?"

"I say nonsense," said the doctor, moving forward up the aisle. "That sort of act might fool a layman, but not a physician. His face was pale, he was breathing shallowly, and there was cold sweat on his forehead. You can't concoct those symptoms on the spur of the moment. I'd bet my reputation he'd never seen a corpse before in his life, let alone stabbed the man to death twenty minutes before."

"Well, that's your opinion," said Knepper, fidgeting with his watch chain.

"Yes, sir," said the doctor. "That is my *professional* opinion." He stared straight at Knepper, and climbed the steps up to the stage.

"Mr. Knepper, unless you have anything to add, we'll let you sit back down," said Mr. Clemens. The man shook his head in the negative. "Thanks for giving us your time and your information. We'll put off the question of Mr. Cabot's possible involvement—he's going to stay right here where everybody can keep an eye on him, and I trust you all to make sure he doesn't sneak out while my back is turned. But for now, I'd like to get the doctor's opinion on one other matter. Dr. Savin, would you be so kind as to tell us what you saw last night?''

Mr. Knepper stalked off the stage, still scowling, and the doctor took his place. Mr. Clemens turned to question him. ''Dr. Savin, you had a chance to examine Mr. Berrigan's body last night. In your opinion, what was the cause of death? I'm sure you don't need me to remind you that there are ladies in the audience, and also that none of us are medical specialists.''

The doctor grimaced. ''The cause of death was nothing more nor less than a stab wound to the heart, causing massive loss of blood. Death must have been nearly instantaneous.''

''I see. Can you venture an opinion on the nature of the weapon?''

''My guess, based on the size of the wound, would be a bowie knife, or perhaps a large butcher knife.''

''Not a pocketknife, a letter opener, or anything of that sort?''

''I doubt it,'' said Dr. Savin. ''The wound indicates a very broad blade, at least an inch across, and probably eight inches long or more.''

''Was there any indication that the victim had attempted to escape, or to defend himself?''

''There were slash marks on the right hand and left forearm, which are consistent with the victim's attempting to fend off a right-handed attacker. But the main wound was just below the victim's sternum, and to me that rules out his trying to escape. It's almost impossible to stab someone frontally after he's turned to run away.''

''One last question. You say that the victim died almost instantaneously. How quickly do you mean? Could he have walked across the room to lock the door after his assailant fled?''

''Absolutely not,'' said the doctor. ''I can say that with no fear of contradiction; the victim bled profusely. He would have left a clear trail of blood anywhere he had gone, and there was nothing of the sort. I would be surprised if he took even two steps between being stabbed and falling to the floor.''

''I see,'' said Mr. Clemens thoughtfully. ''Well, I can't think of anything else I need to know, unless you observed something I haven't asked about that you consider relevant. No? Does anyone else have a question for the doctor?'' He peered around the audience. ''Thank you then, Dr. Savin. You can sit back down, and I'll ask Mr. Snipes to come up next.''

Mr. Clemens waited while Dr. Savin stepped off the stage and resumed his seat and Chief Clerk Snipes walked up from his place near the front of the auditorium. ''Mr. Snipes, you saw as much of what went on last night as anybody, and maybe the easiest thing is for you just to tell the people everything that happened from the time Mr. Cabot came looking for you.''

Mr. Snipes pulled on his goatee, gathering his thoughts, and then began. ''I was keeping an eye on things down in the card room when young Cabot come in the door, and I could see he was a bit flustered.''

''Excuse me, I have one question,'' said Mr. Clemens. ''How long had you been there when he came in?''

''Practically the whole evening, I'd say. The cap'n wanted somebody to make sure all the card games was on the up-and-up, and I'd taken that chore on myself, being that I know a little about what kind of tricks to look for. I reckon I'd been there since nine o'clock, except for a couple of turns around the deck to get the cigar smoke out of my eyes.''

''Fine, fine. So Cabot came in approximately when?''

''About quarter to one; I remember looking at the clock when we went down to the office shortly after. Anyhow, he comes in and looks around sort of anxious, and then he spotted me and called me over. I said to myself, *Something ain't right—that boy don't keep these late hours.* Then he told me he thought there might be trouble, maybe somebody hurt pretty bad, in one of the staterooms, and he asked me which cabin Mr. Berrigan was in. Well, I didn't remember exactly, so we went down to my office to check the passenger list.''

Mr. Clemens interrupted him again. ''I'm sorry, I'm confused about one thing. I thought you gave the passenger list to Mr. Berrigan—in fact, we found it in his cabin.'' He held up the papers we'd recovered.

''Oh, that's just a copy. When the detective asked me for a list, I had my mud clerk write one out for him. We had to keep the original list in the office, of course.''

''Of course; that explains everything. Please go ahead.''

''Well, the minute I seen the list, I knew that Mr. Berrigan was in the same stateroom the complaint was about. I said to myself right then, *Something smells funny*. Berrigan wasn't the sort to cause trouble, although maybe some folks might have got annoyed at him snooping around asking questions. We double-timed it up to the hurricane deck. You and the cap'n was waiting there, and so you know the rest.''

''Yes, I suppose I do. Of course, these other folks weren't there, so why don't you just tell them quickly what happened next.''

''Not much else to tell. We opened up the door, and there was Berrigan laying on the floor. Right away I figured he was dead, but I went over to make sure. Next thing I know, that Cabot fellow is falling over on his face. We put Mr. Cabot in an empty cabin I knew about across the hall, and I went and fetched the doctor to look at him. Then the cap'n and I went through Mr. Berrigan's pockets together. We wanted to see if there was anything that would tell us who might have done him in, but we come up empty. I took the dead man's money for safekeeping—it came to fifty-three dollars and eighty-five cents—and the cap'n sent me to bed, since he wanted me to search the boat first thing next morning.''

"You have an excellent memory," said Mr. Clemens. "I'm sure I could never keep track of so many things."

Snipes smiled broadly. "Well, thank you, Mr. Twain. I do my best. I figure it's my job to keep an eye on all the little details, and the best way to do that is to have 'em in my head."

"Well, it's much appreciated," said Mr. Clemens. "Just one more thing, and we'll let you sit down. You said the captain put you in charge of searching the boat the next morning. Did you turn up anything unexpected?"

Snipes laughed. "Oh my, did we ever! We were going along right smooth, everybody present and accounted for, when we got to a cabin on the hurricane deck that was supposed to be vacant. Now, some folks might have passed it by, but I thought I heard something inside. I says to Tiny Williams, *We'll look in this one, too.* I pull out my keys and open up the door, and who should be in there but them two good-for-nothing Throckmorton brothers, acting like they owned the place! That little one jumped up and pulled a big ugly knife, and we like to had us a real Arkansas standoff going until the cap'n came in and trumped everybody with a pistol."

"Yes, there was a good bit of excitement this morning," said Mr. Clemens. "I suspect a few people here saw the tail end of it. Not to jump to conclusions, but do you have any reason to believe that the Throckmorton brothers were involved in the events in Mr. Berrigan's cabin?"

"I can't say for sure, but I wouldn't be surprised," said Snipes. "The little one, Alligator, pulled out his blade at the first sign of trouble, and they're as mean a pair of rowdies as ever I saw. I didn't want those two on board the *Horace Greeley* to begin with; everybody knows that. Odds are they know more about the killing than they're letting on. Best thing to do is turn 'em over to the police when we hit Memphis, and good riddance to bad rubbage, says I."

Mr. Clemens nodded. "Well, I think we'll all breathe

easier once we know the killer's in the proper hands.
Thanks very much for your time and help, Mr. Snipes.''
The chief clerk left the stage and returned to his seat near
the front, and Mr. Clemens moved to the center of the stage
again.

"Now, ladies and gentlemen, we've all heard about what
happened last night, and we have a few suggestions as to
who might have done it. I don't beat around the bush, so
let's go to the heart of the matter. Captain Fowler, if it's
not too much trouble, could you have the Throckmorton
boys brought in?''

At this, a rising murmur went through the audience. I
noticed a few of the ladies looking about as if to scout out
the nearest exit. The captain nodded his head to Tiny Williams, who took two of his roustabouts and went to get the
Throckmortons. Mr. Clemens raised his arms and said,
"Now, I want all of you to stay right where you are. It'll
be a few minutes until the Throckmortons are here. While
we're waiting, you all can think about what you've just
heard, and maybe somebody will remember something the
rest of us have missed—something that'll help us find the
real killer. Maybe something that didn't make sense before
fits into a pattern now. Put your minds to work, and let's
see if we can solve these two murders.''

The audience began to buzz with speculation. Meanwhile, I found myself thinking about how best to refute
Knepper's statement that I was the probable murderer,
should he reiterate the allegation. I was still trying to decide
how I would defend myself from the false accusation when
the back doors opened and in came Billy and Alligator
Throckmorton, led by Tiny Williams and three of his crewmen.

⫷26

The audience fell quiet as Tiny Williams led the Throckmorton brothers up the aisle. Alligator Throckmorton strode along with a sullen expression on his face, looking neither right nor left; but Billy gawked frankly back at the spectators, grinning like the end man in a minstrel show. They climbed the three steps at the corner of the stage right next to me, and Billy winked at me as they went by.

Williams brought them to center stage, and Captain Fowler nodded. "That'll be fine, Mr. Williams. You Throckmortons, now, listen to me. I don't want any trouble from the two of you. You're up here to answer questions, not clown around. Somebody's life could be at stake, so you'd best take this seriously. Do you understand me?"

Billy Throckmorton shrugged and said, "Sure, Cap'n," still grinning. His brother looked up and nodded, not changing his expression. But the captain was evidently satisfied, and he motioned to Mr. Clemens to begin.

"This won't take long, boys," said Mr. Clemens. "Do you remember when we first met back in Chicago, that New York detective, Mr. Berrigan, showed you a picture?"

Billy Throckmorton's grin disappeared. "Sure, I remember. It was Lee Russell. The copper said he got killed in New York. Is that what this is about? You don't think we killed him, do you? Ain't neither one of us ever been to New York."

"If you weren't in New York, you couldn't have killed him," said Mr. Clemens. "But maybe you boys can help us find the no-good dog who did. Are you willing to help us?"

"I don't know," said Billy. "It ain't right to go telling tales on people. My old pap said it was in the Bible, not to be a witness against your neighbor. And like I explained, we ain't ever been to New York. How would we know about a killing there?"

Mr. Clemens gave Billy Throckmorton a penetrating look. "I think Lee Russell knew the man who killed him before he went to New York, and that means you two might have known the killer, too. Who did Lee use to pal around with? What do you remember about him?"

It was Alligator Throckmorton who answered. "We played poker a few times when Lee first showed up, but after a while, he acted like we weren't rich enough for his blood. He was always trying to get us to throw more money in the pot, and me and Billy didn't want no part of that. Not that we couldn't hold our own, but you got to have the money before you can bet it."

"Was Lee Russell a good player, then?"

Alligator frowned. "Like I said, we pretty much held our own with him when he did play with us. But Lee fancied himself a high-stakes player, and he usually ended up with Ed and his bunch. You'd have to ask Ed how he did in that company."

"Thanks, I think maybe I will," said Mr. Clemens. "Can you remember who some of the people he played with were, besides Ed?"

"Well, different folks in every town," said Alligator. "Mostly just suckers, if you know what I mean—I don't think Lee had any partic'lar friends. He'd have a drink or two with most anybody, but that was mainly drumming up business. Lee was always trying to smell out a high-stakes game, and if you couldn't help him with that, he didn't have the time for you. He didn't even chase after the girls, that I ever saw.''

"Well, I guess that's that,'' said Mr. Clemens. "You don't have any idea who might have killed him, do you?''

"Nope,'' said Billy Throckmorton. "Most likely somebody he owed money, or somebody thought he cheated 'em at cards. Had to be money in it somehow—that was all Lee Russell ever much cared about.''

"That's how I'd figure it,'' said Alligator, nodding his head. "He was a cold fish, except when he was buttering up somebody to get 'em in a game.''

"Now, think for a moment,'' said Mr. Clemens. "Can you boys tell me where you were the two days before you came to Chicago?''

"Sure,'' said Billy. "We come up on the morning train from Cincinnati; got there Friday afternoon. Ed met us there the next day, and we all went to the baseball game.'' He smiled, proud of having remembered events of almost a month ago.

"That's very interesting,'' said Mr. Clemens. "Ed told me you'd all arrived together. Do you know where Ed was while you were waiting?''

"Jesus, Billy!'' said Alligator. "You've gone and spilled it, now. Can't you keep your mouth shut?''

"I don't see where we're in any trouble, and Ed can look after hisself,'' said Billy, pouting. "I ain't telling nothing else.''

"That's fine with me,'' said Mr. Clemens. He looked out over the audience and beckoned to McPhee. "Ed, now's your chance to clear yourself. Why don't you come on up here and tell people where you were and what you were doing when Lee Russell was murdered in New York?''

"Wait a minute, Sam, I ain't killed nobody,'' protested McPhee, rising to his feet. "I never went to New York! I told you and that detective both, and you had plenty of time to check on my story, if you was going to arrest me.''

"You know I'm no policeman, Ed. I couldn't arrest you

if I wanted to," said Mr. Clemens. "Not that I haven't wished I could, every so often, just to get you out of my way. But all I want now is your answer to a few questions. Do me a favor and come up front where people can see you without craning their necks."

Somewhat reluctantly, McPhee made his way up to the platform. Tiny Williams herded the Throckmorton brothers to the back of the stage and signaled me to be wary of any trouble from them. The captain had barred the back doors to the stage, so the only direction the Throckmortons could move was forward, toward the audience. I nodded to acknowledge the mate's signal, and moved into position to act quickly should I need to.

McPhee stuck his thumbs in his trouser pockets and looked at Mr. Clemens with a suspicious expression. "Well, Sam, what's your game? I hope you didn't bring me up here just to look like a fool in front of all these folks."

"You're the only one who can make yourself look like a fool, Ed," said Mr. Clemens. "Lie and get caught out at it, and you've only yourself to blame. Give me straight answers, and you'll walk away from here as free as you ever were."

"Well, fire away. But it ain't right to quiz a man without giving him a chance to see a lawyer. I thought better of you than this, Sam."

Mr. Clemens shrugged. "Think whatever you want, Ed—that's one of the blessings of a free country. But if you're innocent, you can prove it by helping us catch the guilty party. Now, would you like to tell us where you were the Thursday and Friday before you arrived in Chicago?"

McPhee shook his head. "Sam, you may not like this, but I ain't going to tell you. I got my reasons, and I think they're mighty good reasons, and that's all I'm saying."

"Well, let's try a different angle," said Mr. Clemens. "You heard me tell the boys that I think whoever killed Lee Russell was somebody who knew him before he went to New York, and I'm pretty sure it's the same man who killed Berrigan last night. You've got an alibi for last night, and the Throckmorton boys seem to have one for New York. But that doesn't mean much if you're working as a team.''

"What the hell do you mean by that?'' said McPhee.

"Exactly what I said,'' said Mr. Clemens. "The three of you *are* a team—don't deny it. I know how you work together to pluck the pigeons at three-card monte, and you were mighty put out when Charlie Snipes wouldn't let you travel together. Why did those boys sneak on board last night, of all nights? The very night when somebody was killed? Maybe you stabbed Lee Russell in New York while they were in Cincinnati. And maybe they took care of Berrigan last night while you were at the card table. Can you give me one good reason why I shouldn't turn the three of you over to the police in Memphis, and let you all stand trial for murder?''

A roar came from Billy Throckmorton at the back of the stage. "Why, you double-crossing skunk! You didn't say nothing about no murder last night!'' He lumbered forward in the direction of Mr. Clemens, his fists raised menacingly. But I had been on guard for just that sort of move. I leapt to the stage and met him halfway; he took a roundhouse swing at me, but this time I was prepared for him. I ducked underneath his wild punch and planted a solid blow to his solar plexus. Billy swung a grazing right hand at the back of my head, but I answered it with a clean uppercut to the jaw, then leaned into him and threw three short punches in rapid succession to his midsection. He tried to grapple with me, then suddenly sat down, his face colorless. Somewhere behind me, I heard the roar of the excited crowd. By then, Tiny Williams was by my side, and the two of us stood over Billy Throckmorton, daring him to rise again. But the fight was all gone out of him. He raised his hand toward me pleadingly, gasping for air.

I turned to see that half the audience was on its feet,

shouting as if at a sporting match. Captain Fowler had stepped in between the fight and Mr. Clemens. I was very relieved to see that the pistol in his hand was pointed at the floor, rather than in my direction. At the back of the stage, Alligator Throckmorton stood quite still, his hands raised above his head. Meanwhile, Mr. Clemens and Slippery Ed McPhee stood almost together, both looking on as if nothing out of the ordinary had occurred.

The captain was the first of those on stage to speak. "That settles it!" he roared. "Lock them boys back up, and put Ed McPhee in with 'em for good measure. They're the killers, or I'll swim the rest of the way to New Orleans!"

Mr. Clemens had gone to the front of the stage to try to quiet down the crowd. Now he turned around and said, "Better take your boots off then, Mike—it's a mighty long swim. Those boys are innocent."

"Innocent! That's too durn many for me," said the captain. "How the devil do you come up with that? Why, that half-shaved bear was no more'n two steps away from knocking you down just now—that looks mighty guilty to me. And we still ain't heard why Slippery Ed was late coming into Chicago. I say we give 'em to the police and let a judge decide whether or not to hang the bunch of 'em. If I weren't a peaceful man, I've half a mind to do it myself."

"And if you did, you'd be a murderer yourself," said an unexpected voice from the audience. I turned around astonished, to see that Martha Patterson had come to the front of the theater and was standing with her hands on her hips, looking angrily at the captain. Even Mr. Clemens seemed surprised by her vehemence.

"Martha, don't get yourself in trouble," said Ed McPhee, raising his hands imploringly. "I can take care of this situation."

"A fine job you've done of it so far, Edward McPhee! It's time to tell the truth, and it looks as if I'm the only one here capable of telling it.''

"I beg your pardon, Miss Patterson," said Mr. Clemens. "What do you know about the case?"

"I know that Mr. McPhee could not have been in New York on the day of the murder. He was in Chicago, and I was with him." She paused and looked at me with a pained expression, then turned back to Mr. Clemens and lifted her chin defiantly. "And I will ask you to call me by my right name, Mr. Clemens. I am not Miss Patterson, as I have led you to believe; I am Mrs. Edward McPhee."

⮑ 27

"**M**rs. Edward McPhee!" said Mr. Clemens. He turned to Mr. McPhee and smiled. "Congratulations, Ed! This *is* a surprise. And congratulations to you, as well, Mrs. McPhee—I must say you had me entirely deceived." He gave a little bow in her direction.

For my part, I stared at the young woman at the front of the stage. Martha Patterson? McPhee's wife? My head spun; for a moment I feared I might faint again, but I recalled where I was and summoned up my strength. I might have been a fool, but there was no reason to let that distract me from the business at hand. I would have plenty of time to lament my folly after the murderer was revealed. Tiny Williams nudged me, and I helped him pick up Billy Throckmorton, who had recovered some of his color, but still seemed reluctant to rise. We carried him to the rear of the stage and plopped him in a chair against the wall. "You'll stay right where you are, if you know what's good for your arse," growled the mate in a low voice, and Throckmorton nodded weakly. Then I turned my attention back to the front of the stage, where Mr. Clemens had taken over the proceedings again.

"Mrs. McPhee, I'm pleased to have you confirm what I'd already guessed," he said. "Ed may have done some shady things in his time, but I don't think he's a murderer. The most I can prove against him is running that larcenous

262   three-card monte game, and even that's been on shore, so
it's not rightly my business or the captain's.''

"You're right. It's nobody's business but his," said Martha—Mrs. McPhee—with a hint of defiance in her voice.

"His and the Throckmortons', since they're his partners
in the swindle," said Mr. Clemens. "And your business
too, Mrs. McPhee. Cabot has told me how you persuaded
him to bet, back in St. Louis.''

"And Edward returned his money, so there was no harm
done," she said, still holding herself proudly erect.

"None to him, perhaps, but what about to all the other
losers? Does Ed return their money? And did you decide
to return Cabot's money to him simply because you were
afraid that Cabot would persuade the captain to have Ed
thrown off the boat?''

"Yes, I suppose so," she said. "I knew Edward had
tipped someone aboard to let us work the boat without
interference. Then Mr. Snipes threw the Throckmortons off
the boat, and I was afraid to give him any pretext to throw
Edward off, too. Because then I would have had to leave
with him, and I was enjoying the journey, and your lectures,
far too much to give them up so easily.''

"I appreciate the compliment," said Mr. Clemens. "And
I appreciate your willingness to come forward in this matter. I'm convinced that Ed and the Throckmorton boys had
nothing to do with that business in New York, or with the
murder last night. Billy Throckmorton, just now, acted as
if he had no idea Berrigan was dead, and I don't think he's
a good enough actor to carry off an imposture like that.
Even so, I fear I have to press you on what business you
and Ed had in Chicago. Convincing me is one thing; convincing the law is another. If I let you go without a good
explanation, I may regret it before long.''

"I have nothing to hide. Mr. McPhee and I were in Chicago for our wedding. I stayed with my mother, and my
older brother stayed with Ed in the hotel Friday and Saturday, before we all got on the train to St. Paul.''

I was thunderstruck by this revelation, but Mr. Clemens plowed ahead as though she had said nothing at all unusual. "Why, that's remarkable. But why didn't Ed just tell us that, when we asked him what he'd been doing in Chicago? I'd think he'd be proud of having such a lovely wife!"

Martha looked toward McPhee with an exasperated expression that nonetheless conveyed a genuine affection. It pained me to see it. "Poor silly Edward," she said. "He doesn't like to reveal anything he thinks might put him at a disadvantage, but this is one place where we have to tell the truth and face the consequences. If it were public knowledge that we are man and wife, I would have no chance of drawing bettors into the monte game. I have told you the complete truth; if you doubt me, I can give you names and addresses of people who'll corroborate my story."

"I'll ask you for them if we find the need," said Mr. Clemens. "For now, I'm inclined to take you at your word, unless something turns up to change my train of logic. I'm afraid we'll still have to put the Throckmorton boys off the boat in Memphis, but if Ed will come up with their passage from Cairo, maybe the captain will overlook the trouble they've caused. And it might be a good idea if you and your husband decided to end your journey in Memphis, as well. I'm sure we can arrange a refund of the unused portion of the ticket, seeing that it's your honeymoon."

Ed McPhee was about to open his mouth in protest, but Martha cut him off. "Very well," she said. "You've been more than fair, Mr. Clemens, and I don't wish you any trouble. Ed and I will manage."

"I'm sure you will," said Mr. Clemens, bowing to her again. Ed McPhee climbed down from the stage and joined Martha—it gave me a twinge to see her take his hand and give him a kiss on the cheek—and they went back into the audience and took seats next to each other. The passengers on either side of them gave them distasteful looks, and Miss Cunningham turned up her nose as they passed in front of her, but Mr. and Mrs. McPhee ignored them.

"Now," said Mr. Clemens, "it's time to take a good hard look at the New York murder. I think there's a connection between that murder and the treasure I was looking for on my last trip down the river." Mr. Clemens paused and looked around the auditorium, until his gaze settled on a spot about halfway back in the audience.

"I'm going to call a man who knows as much as anybody about that part of the story," said Mr. Clemens. He pointed to the middle of the auditorium. "Jack Hubbard, will you come up front? You've always wanted to be an actor, anyway—here's a chance for you to get on stage in front of an audience."

There was a flurry of talk as all heads turned to see the object of his invitation, and a tall, familiar figure stood up next to the center aisle. To my astonishment, it was none other than Major Demayne! "I guess you've spotted me, Sam," he said, laughing, and began to walk briskly toward the stage.

"By God, is that Farmer Jack Hubbard?" McPhee had stood up to stare at the man I had known as Major Demayne. "I'd hardly know him without his big red beard."

"That's the beauty of wearing a disguise all those years, Ed," said Major Demayne, whom I supposed I'd now have to learn to call "Hubbard." "None of the old gang knew me without it, so I figured I could take it off and be a new man," he explained as he continued walking forward. Then he climbed energetically onto the stage and shook hands with Mr. Clemens. "I've been wanting to tell you my story, Sam, but I never thought that when I did it'd be like this. How did you ever spot me?"

"After I realized there was a hidden message in that dreadful poem of yours, I remembered Cabot's telling me how you beat the pool sharks in St. Paul at their own game, and then it all fit together. You were the best billiard player I ever knew, Jack. But we can talk about that later. For now, there are two murders to solve, and I suspect you know something about them.''

"Well, all I know about the one last night is what we've heard from on stage just now,'' said Hubbard. "But I'll tell you what I know about the rest of it. Where do you want me to start?''

"Let's go back to New York, Jack. How did you meet Lee Russell, and how did he get hold of your disguise?''

"Well, I moved to the city a few years back. I always wanted to go on the stage, and finally decided to give it a shot. I was living down in a cheap part of town—the actor's life is not the royal road to riches—going to auditions and casting calls. I'd kept my old disguise, because it was a way to pick up a few dollars now and then—most people see a man dressed like a farmer and they don't expect him to play billiards well. One day I'd run a little low on funds, so I put on my outfit and went looking for a game. I was standing on the corner of Canal Street, and somebody sang out, *Jack Hubbard, is that you?* And it turned out to be a young cardplayer I'd met a few times on the river, before I came east.''

"That was Lee Russell?'' Mr. Clemens prompted him. Mr. Clemens had moved to one side of the stage, and was loading up his pipe again, but his manner left no doubt that he was directing the show, even though another man had taken the spotlight, as it were.

"The very same,'' said Hubbard. "He was new in town, he said, and looking for a place to stay. I offered to put him up for a couple of days until he got his bearings. If I'd known what kind of trouble it would lead to, I might have been less friendly. It bothers me to think that my befriending poor Lee may indirectly have gotten him killed.'' He shook his head, gravely, and I sensed that his remorse was genuine—although I forced myself to remember that I was listening to an accomplished impostor. He had, after all, carried off the role of Major Demayne well enough to deceive men who had known him as Farmer Jack for thirty years.

266   After a moment he continued his story. "Well, Lee got
settled soon enough, and found his own place a few blocks
away from mine. We'd see each other on the street every
now and then, but we didn't travel in the same circles—he
was running with the gambling crowd, and I'd given up
that life except as I needed to earn some rent money every
now and then. Then, one evening just over a month ago,
Lee showed up at my door, wanting to talk about the old
days on the river, he said. That was fine with me, and I
poured us a couple of drinks and pretty soon I was telling
all the old yarns I could remember, with Lee prompting me
every now and then.

"He started asking about old George Devol, who used
to deal three-card monte on all the riverboats—George
taught me most of what I know about gambling for a living.
And then, after a while, he turned the conversation around
to you, Sam," Farmer Jack said, pointing to Mr. Clemens.
"He said he'd heard about your lectures in New York—
there was one that same night—and he started asking about
that trip you'd taken on the *Gold Dust* back in '82, when
George Devol was on the boat, and about the money you'd
claimed was hidden in Napoleon, Arkansas. Of course, I
couldn't tell him much besides what George told me—I
wasn't on that trip, and I hadn't even read your book then,
although I have since."

"What was George's version of that story?" asked Mr.
Clemens. "I've always wondered what he thought of my
little hoax, especially since it was concocted on purpose to
mislead him."

Hubbard thought for a moment before continuing.
"George told that story two or three times that I heard.
He'd get all excited about you going after all that money,
and talk about how he meant to swindle you out of it, until
he found out it was all washed away. Then he'd start mop-
ing about how close he'd been to being rich—until he realized you'd been selling him a bill of goods. And then
he'd laugh, and slap his knees, and say it was the best joke

in the world. *Serve me right to think I could count Sam's chickens before I looked in the henhouse,* he used to say. So I suspect you had him pretty well fooled.''

Mr. Clemens nodded. ''Well, that's gratifying,'' he said. ''It'd be a shame to invent such a splendid imposition and not fool the person you aimed it at. But I've interrupted you, Jack. Go ahead with your story.''

''Well, Lee told me he'd met someone who'd been there—on the same trip down the river, I mean—and this fellow thought the story was suspicious. Said you'd pulled that business about the gold being in Napoleon out of your hat—*after* the *Gold Dust* docked in Memphis, and everybody learned about Napoleon being flooded away. *He* heard about it the same time you did, he said. So when you claimed the treasure was in Napoleon, he smelled a rat, but he wasn't in a spot to do anything about it at the time, or so he told Lee. But when he learned you were planning a trip back to the river, he figured that you might be planning to go get the money this time.''

''Very astute of him; that's close to the truth. Did Lee Russell say who this other fellow was?''

Hubbard shook his head gravely. ''No, he didn't, Sam, and I wish he had. Because I'm pretty sure this other fellow was the one that killed him.''

A ripple of excitement went through the audience, as passengers turned to their neighbors to comment on this new revelation. Mr. Clemens waited a moment for the hubbub to die down, then turned back to Hubbard. ''I expect you have a reason for saying that, Jack. But if you don't know who this person is, why are you so sure he killed Lee Russell?''

''Yes, that's a very convenient accusation,'' shouted Andrew Dunbar from the front of the audience, waving his reporter's notebook. ''How do we know you didn't do it, Hubbard? Why are you here under an assumed name if you don't have anything to hide?''

''I figured somebody would get to that question sooner

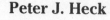

or later,'' said Hubbard, fixing the reporter with an icy stare. ''It's one of the reasons I haven't been in any hurry to drop the masquerade. But there's a good answer, if you'll be civil enough to hear me out.''

''Yes, by all means let Jack have his say,'' said Captain Fowler. ''If he can't satisfy our questions, he can explain himself to the police in Memphis. This isn't a courtroom, you know.'' Dunbar looked unhappy, but he sat back down, and Mr. Clemens gestured to Hubbard to continue.

''Lee Russell and I talked a little more, about this and that, although he kept coming back to that treasure, and I could see he was leading up to something. At last, he told me that this other fellow had an idea that he could trick you into telling him where the gold was. By then, I already suspected that tricks was the least of it. So I told him to count me out; I didn't think there was any gold, just a long story with a surprise ending, and I thought I had him convinced. We talked a little longer, and called it a night.

''Then, a couple of days later, I got a note telling me about an audition at the Standard Theater on Thirty-third Street, and I went up there the next morning eager to try out. But when I got there, nobody in the theater knew anything about auditions. Well, I was pretty hot at being called uptown for nothing, but once I realized nobody knew what I was talking about, I knew I'd been tricked. All I could think of was to turn around and go home. And when I got home, I found out somebody had broken into my place.''

''It sounds as if somebody wanted you out of the way,'' said Mr. Clemens. ''Did you manage to figure out why?''

''I sure did, and it didn't take me long, either. They'd only taken one thing, which was my farmer outfit—the false beard and the straw hat I used to wear when I went looking for a game of billiards. Nothing else was touched, and most of it was a lot more valuable, if somebody was looking to pawn it. I didn't have anything in the way of jewelry or money around the place, but there were things a man who knew where to take them could trade for a few drinks, or a dose of opium in Chinatown.''

''Why do you imagine anyone would go to all that trouble just to get something of no particular value except to you?''

''Well, I figured out pretty fast that the only reason anybody would want my old disguise was to impersonate *me*. And the only person in New York they might want to fool like that was you, Sam. I remembered that Lee Russell talked about tricking you into telling him and his partner where the gold was, and thought, *This doesn't mean any good for Sam.* I was mad enough that they'd broken into my place, and madder that they would use my name to trick you. We were friends, Sam—I'd never forgive myself if somebody hurt you when I could have stopped it. So I went to warn you that something was going on.''

''Ah,'' said Mr. Clemens. ''That must be when you sent me the note I got at my hotel.''

Hubbard looked puzzled. ''I never sent you any note, Sam. What note do you mean?''

''Why, this note right here,'' said Mr. Clemens, pulling a scrap of paper out of his pocket. ''I suppose Lee Russell must have written it, then.''

''Not likely,'' said Hubbard, reaching out his hand for the paper. ''Lee was the next thing to illiterate—he could read the pips on a deck of cards, but not much more. When he was looking for a room, I brought home a newspaper for him to look at the advertisements, and he hemmed and hawed and finally asked me to read them to him. I don't think he could write at all.'' He looked down at the paper in his hand and looked back at Mr. Clemens with a surprised expression. ''But here's something—this is Lee Russell's address on the note. Whoever sent it must have been working with Lee. I'd bet that handwriting is the same as on the note I got inviting me to the bogus audition.''

''So—Lee Russell's mysterious partner must have written this,'' said Mr. Clemens. ''And quite likely that's the man who murdered him, and murdered Berrigan as well.''

"Yes, that makes sense," said Hubbard. "It looks like they wanted to lure you down to Lee's place, under the pretext that it was for a meeting with me—God only knows what would have happened if you'd gone down there to meet them. That has to be why they stole my disguise, so when the hotel clerk described the man who delivered the note, you'd think I was the one. Lee Russell couldn't have fooled you very long, beard or no beard."

"They took a big chance," said Mr. Clemens. "What if I had been at the hotel when the note arrived, instead of at a business meeting?"

"Maybe Lee waited until he saw you leave," said Hubbard, handing back the note.

"I suppose so," said Mr. Clemens. "But let's get back to your story. What happened next?"

"Well, first of all, I had to do a good bit of sleuthing before I learned you were staying at the Union Square Hotel. I fast-stepped it up to the hotel, and got there just as you came in the door. I thought I was home safe. But before I could say anything, young Mr. Cabot called you, and you started talking to that detective, Berrigan. Then Mr. Cabot said something about murder, and I knew I better figure out what was going on before I stuck my neck into a noose.

"The three of you went upstairs, so I slipped fifty cents to the bellboy to find out what room you were in, and went up to see what I could hear through the transom. Well, I knew I was in trouble when I found out that somebody with a false red beard and Mr. Mark Twain's address in his pocket had been murdered. Of course, you figured it was me that was murdered—you couldn't have known I was standing right outside your door, listening to you. But I didn't dare come in—I knew I'd be the main suspect the minute I heard you say my name. I didn't know whether Lee Russell or his partner was the dead man, but I figured it had to be one or the other. And I thought there was a good chance that the killer had left that beard there to make it look like I was the murderer.

"Then a room maid came along the hallway and I couldn't just stand there without drawing attention. I walked down the hall as if I were headed for the stairway, meaning to turn back and eavesdrop some more. And then that detective came out of the room, and I was afraid to look him in the eye. So I just kept going right down to the street, and when I got there I didn't know what to do next."

Hubbard shifted his cane from hand to hand, staring off into the distance, then resumed his story. "I decided that my best chance to clear myself was to follow you and try to talk to you, Sam. From what I'd learned, somebody had decided that your story about the gold was true and meant to get his hands on it. He couldn't trap you in New York, so he would probably follow you down the river and try to steal the gold after you recovered it. He'd already killed one person, and likely wouldn't balk at killing again. I couldn't just walk away and leave you in that kind of danger. To tell the truth, I didn't know if Lee Russell was the killer or the corpse. It wasn't until we got on the boat and Lee didn't show up that I felt sure that Lee had to be the dead man."

"I can understand why you were confused," said Mr. Clemens. "For a while, I thought *you* were the dead man, Jack. But why didn't you tell me your story as soon as we were out of New York? You had plenty of chances to come up and start talking; instead, you went through the charade of Major Demayne and that awful poem with messages hidden in it. Why, Jack?"

"Well, Sam, that was my plan at first, just to come up to you and tell you the whole story." Hubbard shuffled his feet and looked at the floor. "Then I saw you on the train talking with the detective, and I began to worry. I was afraid he'd think I was the murderer. If he'd convinced you of that, I might not get a chance to talk to you. And I knew the police wouldn't give me a fair chance to tell my story. So I lay low, trying to figure out a way to get your attention without tipping my hand, and I came up with the idea of the poem. Now I wish I'd just come forward, because I might have saved that Berrigan fellow if I'd said the right thing right away.''

''I wouldn't blame myself if I were you, Jack,'' said Mr. Clemens. ''Maybe Berrigan would be alive if I'd looked at your poem earlier, but that's as much my doing as yours. Now, the best we can do is to try to catch the killer before he has a chance to hurt anyone else.''

''And how do we know this fellow here isn't the killer?'' said a stern-looking man from the back of the auditorium. Half the audience swiveled around in their seats to look back at him, while the rest seemed to be staring at Hubbard. ''His story is as phony as anything I've heard in years. Why should we believe in some mystery man, when Hubbard fits the picture so well? I say we hand him to the Memphis police and be done with it.''

''Yes, give him to the police,'' shouted Knepper, and the audience rumbled its approval.

Mr. Clemens raised his hands and waited for silence. ''I've never seen a crowd so generous in accusing people of murder,'' he said. ''If this goes on much longer, the Memphis police will have to hang everyone aboard the boat. First you were all convinced that Cabot was the killer, then you were ready to convict Ed McPhee and the Throckmortons, and now you want to put Jack Hubbard's neck in the noose. And once again, I have to tell you that you're wrong.''

''Who is it, then?'' shouted Andrew Dunbar. ''Or are you just distracting everyone until we get to port by pretending that you know?''

''Up until now, I wasn't really sure,'' Mr. Clemens admitted. ''I had a pretty good idea who *wasn't* the killer, but it wasn't until a few minutes ago that all the pieces of the puzzle finally fit together and I figured out who it *was*. And of course, it was the man I should have suspected all along.''

28

Mr. Clemens's announcement that he knew who killed Berrigan brought the audience to an expectant hush. The ladies even stopped fanning themselves, lest they miss the next word. While the audience absorbed his statement, Mr. Clemens stuck his hands in his pockets, as he often did during his lectures, and let his gaze wander about the auditorium while Jack Hubbard returned to his seat. The passengers looked nervously at their neighbors, as if they had finally realized that one of their number was a murderer. I tried to read the expressions on their faces, but without success—perhaps the killer believed that Mr. Clemens would accuse someone else, or possibly he intended to bluff his way out of the accusation if it came his way.

Finally Mr. Clemens broke the silence. "It's funny how getting on a boat and traveling makes people act differently than they do at home," he said. "There's something magical about boats—I felt it when I was a boy dreaming about being a pilot, and I've seen it a thousand times since. I'm sure all of you have felt some of it. Travel's very seductive. It makes people look back at their everyday life and wonder why they put up with it, and sometimes they decide they *won't* put up with it anymore. I've seen it happen to the most respectable folks, businessmen and judges and even ministers. And I think something like that happened to Paul Berrigan.

"Berrigan was a police detective, a man with ten or fifteen years on a dangerous job, grubbing through the dirt of other people's lives. He must have seen some dreadful tragedies, and even worse miscarriages of justice—innocent people irrevocably harmed, and men he knew to be guilty as the devil walk away free because of some idiotic loophole in the law, or because a witness wouldn't tell the truth. A policeman gets mighty disillusioned after seeing this kind of thing year in and year out, and knowing he can't do anything about it. It's no wonder so many of them become cynics—or go bad.''

Mr. Clemens shook his head. ''And suddenly, after all that, Berrigan got an assignment that must have looked like a dream. It started out looking like a run-of-the-mill stabbing in a New York alley—the kind of murder a policeman sees dozens of in a career, and never has much chance of solving. The only thing at all different about this one was that the victim had a famous man's name and address in his pocket—*my* name. Naturally enough, Berrigan came to visit me, to see if I knew anything that might help him. He probably didn't expect much to come of it—there are dozens of clues in any case, and most of them aren't worth a wooden nickel. But without knowing it, he'd stumbled on the mother lode—a lost treasure! And I was the only man who knew where it was hidden. Of course, I didn't tell him that. I was already worried that somebody might be on my trail, planning to take it away from me.

"As it turned out, I was right. You've heard Jack Hubbard tell about Lee Russell and his mysterious partner hatching a plot to lure me to an out-of-the-way place and force me to tell them where the gold was hidden. The two of them fell out, and Lee Russell ended up dead. Cabot, my secretary, saw Russell at one of my lectures a few days before the killing. My guess is that Russell heard me spin a few tall tales and decided the story about the gold was a hoax—just as I meant everyone to believe. So Russell decided to back out of the plot, while his partner wanted to

follow it through, and it ended up with Russell being murdered.''

''That makes a certain amount of sense,'' said the captain. ''What I can't figure out is why Lee Russell would
have your name and address in his pocket. Jack told us Lee
couldn't read, so it couldn't have done him any good.''

Mr. Clemens nodded. ''It had me puzzled for a while,
too,'' he said. ''I knew Lee Russell was illiterate—Ed
McPhee mentioned it when Berrigan showed him a picture
of Russell's corpse. It wasn't until just now, when Jack was
talking, that I realized that Russell must have been embarrassed to let anyone know about it—remember how Jack
said he 'hemmed and hawed' before admitting he couldn't
read the newspaper ads? So when his partner handed Lee
my address, he never admitted that he couldn't read it—he
was afraid his partner would think he was stupid, and make
fun of him, if he found out. He just took the paper and
pretended he could understand it. He probably got some
stranger, a shopkeeper or somebody else he didn't mind
knowing that he couldn't read, to tell him what it said.

''I do know one thing: it's a good thing he kept that
address. Without it, the police wouldn't have thought to tell
me about the murder. And if Berrigan hadn't shown it to
me, and if I hadn't noticed that the handwriting was the
same as on the note asking me to meet Farmer Jack downtown, there's a good chance I would have gone downtown
to that apartment, expecting to meet Jack—and that might
have been the last anyone ever saw of me. By keeping that
little slip of paper, Lee Russell probably saved my life. If
for no other reason, I feel I ought to bring the man who
killed him to justice.''

''But how do you know it's the same man who killed
Berrigan?'' asked Captain Fowler.

''I'm getting to that, Mike,'' said Mr. Clemens. ''Once
Berrigan told his chief that he thought one of my old friends
might be the victim in a murder case, his superiors decided
they had to consider the possibility that I was a target, and

my backers in New York agreed with them. They ordered Berrigan to follow me, and act as an unofficial bodyguard for me as well as investigating the murder of Lee Russell. This was heaven to an old city cop—a chance to travel, to mingle with a better class of people, to concentrate on one single case. It was practically a paid vacation. The surprising thing is that Berrigan decided to take the assignment seriously, not just as a chance to get away from the job. You all saw him. He questioned all the passengers, looked at all the evidence, and kept the telegraph wires burning between the river and New York. And yesterday afternoon, he told Cabot he'd solved the case.''

''Aye, but he never told him what he'd discovered,'' said the captain. ''Now he's where he can't tell anyone. And with his little notebook missing, who knows what he'd figured out?''

''What Berrigan could figure out, I can figure out,'' said Mr. Clemens. ''One thing seems pretty clear: the killer somehow found out what Berrigan said to Cabot. Mr. Knepper told us he heard Berrigan and Cabot arguing on deck. It's not hard to guess that someone else overheard Berrigan bragging that he'd found the murderer. You know how sound carries on the water. It was Berrigan's bad luck that one of the people who heard him bragging was the killer. Later that night, our killer went to see Berrigan. And Berrigan made the fatal mistake of letting him in.''

''That's the one thing I just can't understand,'' said Captain Fowler. ''Why did Berrigan let a cold-blooded killer into his cabin late at night? He didn't even have his gun out where it would be any use to him.''

''Neither did he have his wits about him,'' said Mr. Clemens. ''To judge by the empty bottle we found in his room, he'd washed away whatever good sense he usually had by the time the murderer came calling. Also, the murderer came to his room planning to try to bribe him—and maybe Berrigan was ready to consider the offer. The people in the neighboring cabins heard them arguing about money.

Maybe Berrigan's price was too high, or maybe he was honest all along, and was just pretending to consider the offer as a way to draw his man into a confession; who knows? All we can say is that in the end our man let his knife do the talking, and that was the end of Berrigan.''

"That's a very entertaining theory,'' shouted Andrew Dunbar. "Maybe even true. But you still haven't told us who the killer is.'' People turned in their seats to see who was talking. And I could see a few heads nodding in agreement with the reporter. Dunbar smiled, sensing that he'd scored a hit.

Mr. Clemens stared at the reporter for a moment. "You're in an awful hurry for the answer, Mr. Dunbar. You should never rush a man who's telling a story. What if he gets to his point and you don't like it?''

"What do you mean by that?'' said Dunbar.

"Why, nothing particular. Just that, without any more evidence on the table, I could as easily point at you and say 'There's the killer!' as at anybody else in the room.''

"Who would believe you?'' said Dunbar, looking very uncomfortable. Now the whole audience was staring at him. "There's nothing to link me to the killings.''

"Don't be so sure,'' said Mr. Clemens. "You won't deny that you were in New York, will you? Or that you were on the boat last night?''

"That's a thin thread to hang your case on,'' said Dunbar. "Your Cabot was in both places, too. So was Hubbard. Either one of them is a more likely suspect than I am. Hubbard even admits that he knew the first victim, Russell, which is more than you can allege of me.''

"What does that prove? Suppose your paper sent you to snoop out any damaging stories about me; lots of papers like to print gossip about famous people, the more scandalous the better, and truth's got nothing to do with it. Your paper has taken quite a few potshots at me over the years. Suppose you were skulking around my hotel lobby, and overheard Lee Russell leaving a message for me at the desk. You sized him up as a shady character, and decided to follow him to see if he had any dirt on me. But you're no Indian scout, not even of the Fenimore Cooper class, so he spotted you and challenged you. One thing led to another, and you stabbed him—maybe it was even self-defense. But you panicked, and ran away. It wasn't until later that you learned that the police had connected the killing to me, and that Berrigan was on your trail. Of course, once he identified you as the killer, you had to eliminate him.''

Dunbar's face had turned red, and he was visibly quivering with suppressed emotion. ''This is a pack of lies,'' he shouted. ''What possible motive would I have? Why would I lie in wait at your hotel, then follow some tramp who leaves a message for you? No judge would believe that.''

Mr. Clemens put his hands into his pockets. ''Your paper recently invested a good deal of money in a Mergenthaler linotype system, did it not?''

''Yes. What of it?''

''You must have known that I was one of the main backers of the Paige typesetting machine—the major competing system.''

''I suppose so; it's not really my business. That kind of thing is the publisher's concern, not mine.''

''But your orders come from the publisher. What if your publisher was afraid that the Paige system would prove more successful? That would leave your paper behind the eight ball, with a huge investment in obsolete equipment. By discrediting me, you undercut the Paige system, both by damaging my ability to earn money to invest in it, and by making my testimony on its merits less credible to other investors. Suppose your orders were to make Mark Twain look bad, whatever the cost. The rest falls into place pretty neatly, I think.''

''You're inventing this out of thin air,'' Dunbar shouted. ''I know—you're trying to shield Cabot! Knepper heard him arguing with Berrigan just yesterday, and he swore that it was Cabot's voice he heard. You've been ignoring that evidence all along. You can't prove anything against me!''

"Well, I might mention your selling cocaine to the crew," said Mr. Clemens. "Now maybe the stuff is even legal in some of the states we've been going through. But until we dock, Captain Fowler is the law on board this boat, and I doubt that he and Tiny Williams much appreciate your turning their men into dope fiends.''

Dunbar turned pale. "What? How did you know about that?" he blurted out—then jerked back and glared guiltily around as he realized what he'd let slip.

"I thought there was something wrong with you the first night you came on board," said Mr. Clemens. "You were acting jumpy—seemed as if you were mad at the world. It wasn't until later that I realized there might be something more to it than just plain ordinary nastiness. But a few days later, I saw you talking to a couple of roustabouts, and looking over your shoulder like a schoolboy sneaking off for a smoke and afraid the principal was after him. And when I saw those same two roughnecks mouthing back at Tiny Williams later that same day, I *knew* something was fishy. The most likely explanation was that you had been selling them drugs of some kind. The cocaine was just an educated guess, based on what I've heard of its effects. Thanks for confirming my suspicions.''

A ripple of laughter went through the audience at seeing the reporter caught out; Dunbar had not made himself popular. As I watched him stand there, fuming, I heard the *Horace Greeley*'s whistle blow twice, the notes muffled by the closed doors. *We must be nearing Memphis*, I thought. *Mr. Clemens isn't going to have much longer to prove his case against Dunbar.* But Mr. Clemens was forging ahead, quieting down the audience and calling up one more witness.

"Berrigan told Cabot he'd learned the murderer's identity by looking at the passenger list Mr. Snipes gave him.

And for a while, I wondered what he could have seen in a simple list of names. Now I think I know—but just to confirm my guess, let me call up the one who wrote the list.'' Chief Clerk Snipes stood up, but Mr. Clemens waved him off. ''Not you, Charlie, I want the boy who actually wrote it out. Tommy Hazelwood, will you please come up front?''

The young mud clerk stood up in the back of the auditorium and raced up to the stage. I wondered if he ever simply walked anywhere. ''Yes, sir, Mr. Twain, what do you want?'' he said as he climbed the stairs, two at a time.

Mr. Clemens reached in his breast pocket and pulled out a folded sheaf of papers. ''Take a look at this, Tommy, and tell me if you recognize it.''

The boy took the papers and unfolded them. After glancing over them he nodded and looked at Mr. Clemens. ''Yes, sir, it's the passenger list Mr. Snipes asked me to copy out for Mr. Berrigan.''

''Why did he ask you to copy the list instead of doing it himself?''

''He always has me copy over things for other people to read. I guess my writing's a little clearer, and I have more time than he does. He always has a lot of things to do.''

Mr. Clemens reached over and pointed to one page. ''This is Mr. Dunbar's name, is it not?''

''Yes,'' said Tommy.

''And it's your handwriting, am I right?''

''Yes, it is,'' said the boy again. I wondered what possible significance there could be in who had written Dunbar's name on the list. From the puzzled look on Tommy's face, I could see that he was having trouble following the logic as well.

Unperturbed, Mr. Clemens turned to another page. ''But here, there's a note in different handwriting, about the Throckmorton boys having been kicked off the boat. That's not your handwriting, is it?''

The boy squinted at the paper where Mr. Clemens's finger pointed, then said, ''Oh, no, that's Mr. Snipes's writing.

I just copied the whole list and gave it to him, and he about threw a fit when he saw those two fellows were still on it. *This is supposed to be a list of who's* on *the boat, not who used to be on it,* he said, and he grabbed a pen and scratched out their names. He was still awful mad about having to give back their money when he threw them off the boat.'' Tommy smiled and looked eagerly up at Mr. Clemens, as if fishing for a compliment.

Mr. Clemens chuckled. ''I guess so—the chief clerk's *supposed* to worry about money. I wasn't happy to lose two paid-up customers, either—I've got a mighty big debt to work off before I can go home to Hartford. But we're about to lose some more fares. Mr. and Mrs. McPhee will be getting off in Memphis, I think. I suspect the captain and first mate might want Mr. Dunbar to leave, as well. And of course we'll be leaving the murderer with the police in Memphis.''

''Hold your horses, Sam,'' said the captain, stepping forward from the rear of the stage, where he'd been guarding the Throckmortons. ''I thought that drug-peddling skunk Dunbar was the killer. Now you're talking like it's somebody else again.'' Captain Fowler looked puzzled at the long story.

''Oh, I was just giving Dunbar a dose of his own medicine. He seems to think it's perfectly fine for him to fling around wild accusations, slander folks' good names, and create a general stink. I figured it was time to knock him off his high horse. He didn't do it—he doesn't have the guts to stab a man anywhere but in the back.''

''Then who in the world did it?'' said the captain. He seemed near the end of his patience.

''Why, I already told you, it's the man whose handwriting is on these two notes from New York—the one in poor Lee Russell's pocket, and the one he left at my hotel desk. It was also on the one Jack Hubbard saw, the one that sent him uptown on a wild-goose chase while the murderer stole his disguise.'' He reached in his pocket and pulled out two pieces of paper. "Tommy, do you recognize the writing on these?"

The boy looked at the papers, then nodded. "Sure, that's Mr. Snipes's writing. I'd know it anywhere," he said eagerly. Then his face changed as he realized what he'd just said. He looked at Mr. Clemens and stammered, "But—but—that means . . ."

"Yes," said Mr. Clemens, and then all hell broke loose. Snipes leapt out of his seat and made a dash for the nearest door, only to find two of the roustabouts blocking his way. I jumped off the stage and began to run toward him; out of the corner of my eye I saw the captain draw his gun again, but his target was surrounded by a crowd of innocent bystanders, and he held his fire. Seeing his escape shut off, Snipes whirled about, suddenly brandishing an improbably large knife, and with the other hand he grabbed a young woman seated on the aisle near him—the Reverend Elijah Dutton's daughter Gertrude. The other passengers drew back in terror, and someone screamed.

"Everybody stay right where you are, and won't nobody get hurt," said Snipes. He held one arm around the young woman's throat and held the knife up for everyone to see. I froze in my tracks. "You're smarter than I thought, Clemens, but you ain't got me yet. Now, tell the boys to ease out of the way and give me a clear path out, and I'll let the young lady go soon as I'm clear. All I ask is a fair head start."

"That's more than you ever gave Lee Russell or Paul Berrigan," said Mr. Clemens. "It's over, Charlie; put away the knife. I arranged with the pilot to let me know when we'd tied up to the dock in Memphis, and that whistle you heard a few minutes ago was the signal we agreed on. The police are on their way. You don't have a chance."

"Don't be so damned sure—I'll take a few more with me if I'm going to swing," said Snipes, brandishing the knife again, a wild look on his face. Gertrude Dutton writhed in terror, her mouth open and her eyes wide. Then from behind Snipes a tall figure rose from the audience, his left hand swinging a cane down onto Snipes's knife with the accuracy of a billiard cue shot. The blade went flying, and then Jack Hubbard brought his cane up backhanded into Snipes's jaw. Snipes's head recoiled from the blow, and he staggered to the side; before he could recover, two strong men were on him, bearing him to the floor. His recent captive slumped into her mother's arms, sobbing.

I waded forward through the crowd; from the stage behind me, I could hear the captain yelling to his crew, trying to get some semblance of order. It was futile—people close to Snipes scattered to avoid the struggle, while those farther away climbed on their chairs to get a better view or pressed forward in their eagerness to see. For a few moments chaos reigned in the small auditorium. Then the doors burst open, and two uniformed policemen strode in. At Captain Fowler's signal, they moved in on Snipes as he struggled against his captors. With rough efficiency, they shackled him and hustled him away, kicking and cursing.

Somehow, despite the tumult in the audience, my employer had managed to remain standing unruffled on the stage. When the murderer was finally safely in police custody, Mr. Clemens took a cigar out of his pocket and snipped off the end. ''That's all for this afternoon, ladies and gentlemen,'' he said. ''Tell your friends if you enjoyed the show, but I'm afraid I can't promise to repeat it for them tomorrow. Now, if you all will pardon me, I'm going to have a drink. Come along, Cabot.''

29

"The police found Berrigan's little notebook in Snipes's cabin," said Captain Fowler. He'd gone ashore to testify to the magistrate who booked Snipes on murder charges, then joined us in Mr. Clemens's stateroom. "And just as you figured, the detective had written him down as the killer—along with his own guesses as to where your treasure might really be. That must be why Charlie kept it. Anyhow, I guess that clinches it. But tell me, Sam, did you know all along it was Charlie Snipes that did it, or was it by guess and by golly at the last minute?"

Mr. Clemens took a sip of his whisky and soda, and smiled. "I'd like to claim I knew it all along, but it ain't so. I was on the wrong track for a long while, thinking it had to be another passenger—especially after Berrigan said that something on the passenger list gave him the answer. Of course, it was Snipes's handwriting he meant."

"How did you figure that out?" I was stretched out at full length on Mr. Clemens's bed, resting muscles I hadn't known I'd pulled until the whole affair was over. I'd felt this way before, after a hard-fought football game—exhausted and exhilarated at the same time.

"Once I looked at the list, I realized that the same man who wrote those two notes had marked the passenger list," said Mr. Clemens. "And Tommy Hazelwood told me that he had copied out the passenger list, and that Snipes added the note about the Throckmortons being kicked off the boat. Of course, Tommy could have been lying. But I'd gotten a sample of Snipes's handwriting weeks ago—remember when I interviewed all the old river rats for my new book, and had them write out notes giving me permission to quote them? I compared them today, and the writing on Snipes's note matched the ones from New York.

''When I spotted that, everything else made sense. Snipes had been in New York, and he knew my address because he stayed in the same hotel. He knew about the gold, because he'd been the mud clerk on the *Gold Dust* back in '82, when I first went looking for it. He knew Lee Russell, because he'd gambled with him. And of course, as chief clerk, he had keys to all the staterooms—and he was a stickler for locking doors behind him.''

Mr. Clemens took a long sip of his drink. ''What should have tipped me off even sooner was his acting as if he didn't know which stateroom Berrigan was in, when he prided himself on having every detail of the boat right at his fingertips. He must have been playing for time, trying to figure out what to say when he finally opened the door and everybody saw the dead man.

''So I was pretty sure it was Snipes before I went on stage. What made it a dead certainty was when he confirmed that Tommy was the one who wrote the passenger list. But I didn't want to finger him until we were safe in port, where we'd have the police for help. So I stalled for a while, letting some of the passengers spout off, even though I knew they were full of hot air. And it's why I took so long raking that Dunbar fellow over the coals—not that he didn't deserve a little grief, after all his self-important posturing. Once we'd docked and could get the police in to help out, I knew it was time to clinch the case. My only miscalculation was not realizing he'd react by pulling a knife on that poor girl. If I ever have to deal with a killer again—and I hope to heaven I won't—I won't be quite so cavalier with the safety of bystanders.''

"Well, Charlie Snipes sure had me fooled," said the captain. He twirled the ice in his glass—it was the first time I'd seen him drink whisky, but there was no denying that the occasion called for it. "I knew he had an appetite for gambling. Not that I hold that against anybody, as long as the crew doesn't get in games with the passengers—that looks bad, even if it don't cause trouble, and I've seen *that* more than once, too. But I didn't care about his playing a game or two on shore, as long as he stuck to business when he was on the boat. What I didn't know was how deep in the hole he'd got himself, and how desperate for money it made him."

"Desperate enough to kill two men he thought stood in the way of his getting hold of hidden treasure," said Mr. Clemens. He shook his head. "I know how money can look to a man over his head in debt, and there've been times I've been tempted to claim that hidden gold for myself— except it's just a drop in the bucket compared with what I owe. If I've still got to get ninety-nine percent of it honestly, I might as well get it all honestly."

"And you aren't the kind of man to knife anybody to get it," said the captain.

"No . . . slow poison's always been more my style," said Mr. Clemens, laughing.

I had a sobering thought. "Let's just hope that, after all this time, the money really is there. It would be a terrible comedown to find that it was all a hoax, or that somebody else found it years ago, considering how much effort you've put into finding it."

"My effort is the least of it, Wentworth. The renegade soldiers who hid the gold thirty years ago probably killed a few men to get it before Ritter caught up with them. Snipes killed two more, and he's likely enough to end his own life at the end of a rope. It would indeed be a cruel irony if they'd all died for nothing. But we'll know soon enough."

"Aye, that we will," said Captain Fowler. "And you'll

have a few stout friends with you when you go to find it, to make sure it doesn't claim one more victim. Can you tell us now where it was really hidden? Or was it somewhere near Napoleon after all?''

''Not in Napoleon, no,'' said Mr. Clemens. ''It was in Helena, Arkansas. High ground, above the flood lines—if the money's not there, it won't be the river's fault.''

''An easy day's run downriver,'' the captain said. ''We'll know the answer soon enough, then, when our business in Memphis is over.''

''This is the place,'' said Mr. Clemens. We had stopped at an abandoned building on the west side of Helena, Arkansas. Captain Fowler and Tiny Williams were with us, and we had hired a colored porter with a wheelbarrow down at the dock where the *Horace Greeley* was tied. But the ''secret'' of our treasure hunt was out, and our little group was swelled by some thirty spectators, not counting the local sheriff's deputies, who had been tipped off by the Memphis police. We had managed to lose most of the newspapermen, who had swarmed over the boat while we were docked in Memphis. But quite a few of the more astute passengers (including Miss Cunningham, who seemed to have forgiven me my scandalous behavior now that my motives had become clear) had seen through the ruse of a luncheon date with a local businessman, and had followed our exploration party up the hill. At first I was annoyed at the large numbers, but Mr. Clemens just laughed. ''The cat's out of the bag, however you figure it,'' he said. ''At least we can be sure nobody's going to rob us, with so many spectators.''

It was another blazing-hot day, and the late-afternoon sun had beaten down hard upon our heads as we climbed the steep hill to the old livery stable where Mr. Clemens said the gold was hidden.

''Are you sure this is it?'' said the captain, mopping his forehead with an oversized handkerchief. ''I don't see anything to mark this place out from any of a hundred other buildings in the state of Arkansas.''

"It's just as Ritter described it," said Mr. Clemens. "I put the exact description of the place in my book, except for moving it to a different town and changing the street names. Let's go around to the north side of the building." We clambered over a decaying rail fence into a weed-filled yard and stood facing the stone foundation. The crowd filed in behind us.

"At least there's a little shade here," said the captain.

"We shouldn't be long in any event," said Mr. Clemens. He walked to the northwest corner of the building and pointed to the foundation. "We'll either find the money or an empty hole where it used to be. Wentworth, see if you can move that stone. Fourth row from the top, third from the corner."

I knelt down and peered at the foundation. The stones were large and thinly covered with moss; the one Mr. Clemens had indicated was about the size of my head. I tried to get a grip on the stone, but the moss made it slippery, and the chinks between stones had filled with dirt over the years. I took out my pocketknife and scraped the stone to get a better grip. It seemed loose, but I couldn't quite get my fingers between it and its neighbors. "The foundation must have settled," I said. "Did we bring along some sort of pry-bar?"

"Got it right here," said Tiny Williams. "Let me give 'er a try." He knelt beside me, and I slid over to make room for him. He used the end of the bar to scrape away more moss, then put its point between the stone and its left-hand neighbor and pushed. The stone came slightly forward, and a little pile of dirt tumbled out of the crack. "There, she's moving," said Williams. "Stand back, everybody—we don't want to bring this whole wall down on you."

Williams and I put our hands to the stone, and now it moved more freely. Another little avalanche of dirt and pebbles came down, and then the stone was out. Despite Williams's warning, Mr. Clemens and the captain pressed close behind us, peering into the cavity behind the stone. "Can you see anything in there?" said Captain Fowler.

"I could if you all weren't blocking the light," said Mr. Clemens. "Here, boys, let me see what's in there. I've been waiting over twelve years for this." We stepped back, and he knelt down and reached into the cavity. "This is the place!" he crowed. He pulled out a fistful of gold pieces. The spectators cheered at the sight, and pressed in to see the treasure up close.

"Lordy, mister, I sure wish I knowed that was here," said the porter. "Walked past this old stable every mornin' and every evenin' since I was a little boy, and never once thought I was goin' past a gold mine. What you gone do with all that money?"

"I've owned my share of gold mines, and couldn't afford to keep 'em," said Mr. Clemens. "This is the first time I've ever pulled real money out of a hole in the ground. But it's not mine to keep—I promised to give it to a young man in Germany, and that's what I'm going to do with it."

"That's mighty big of you, Sam," said the captain. Tiny Williams was now kneeling by the hole, passing out big handfuls of gold pieces to the porter, who piled them in his wheelbarrow with a stunned expression on his face. "How much money is it supposed to be?"

"Ten thousand dollars is what the German claimed," said Mr. Clemens. He'd pulled out his corncob pipe and was filling the bowl. "We'll count it when we get it all back to the boat. But I wouldn't even want to *think* about keeping it. Too many men have already been killed over it, and Charlie Snipes will be one more, when they finally hang him. I want nothing more than to get it out of my hands and to its rightful owner as quickly as possible."

"That doesn't seem much reward for all the trouble and danger you've been through to find it," I said. "What do *you* get out of it?"

"What do I get out of it?" Mr. Clemens thought for a moment, then smiled. "I get the satisfaction of helping a man who needs the money more than I do, of bringing a long and difficult task to a successful conclusion . . . and best of all, of having a story that'll have the audiences on the edges of their seats all the way from here to New Orleans!"

About the Author

Peter J. Heck was born and raised in Chestertown, on the Eastern Shore of Maryland. After earning a degree in English at Harvard, he taught college-level English, managed an air freight office in New York, and sold musical instruments in a store on Long Island before becoming a full-time freelance writer and editor in 1983. His book reviews have appeared in numerous publications, and from 1990 to 1992 he was a science fiction editor at Ace books.

In addition to Mark Twain, whose books he has read ever since he can remember, Heck's interests include music (he plays blues and country guitar), chess, baseball, travel, and computer bulletin boarding. He has one son, Dan, from a previous marriage. He currently lives in Brooklyn, with his wife, Jane Jewell, two cats, several guitars, and a constantly growing library.